Praise for the Mercenary Librarians series

"A full-throttle read! Action-packed, edgy, and engrossing, I can't wait to see what happens next!"

—Jeaniene Frost, *New York Times* and *USA Today* bestselling author, on *Deal with the Devil*

"The stakes are high, the danger is imminent, and the sexiness is through the roof."

—*BookPage* on *The Devil You Know*

"This sequel has all of the action, smolder, snark, and surprising warmth of the first, with more development of a postapocalyptic Atlanta that is slowly finding its feet again—with the help of the mercenary librarians."

—*Booklist* on *The Devil You Know*

"This series entry begins to peel back the layers of the characters that make up the mercenary librarians and the Silver Devils, while giving hints to deeper secrets and conspiracies of the corrupt TechCorps and its plans for control."

—*Library Journal* on *The Devil You Know*

"A risky and frisky adventure."

—*Kirkus Reviews* on *Deal with the Devil*

"This postapocalyptic tale of espionage and romance will have readers eager to know what happens next."

—*Publishers Weekly* on *Deal with the Devil*

"My advice? Cancel all your plans so you can read it in one delicious gulp."

—Thea Harrison, *New York Times* and *USA Today* bestselling author, on *Deal with the Devil*

"Nina is everything I love in a heroine—smart and badass, but with a core of hope and kindness. And Knox is jaded, honorable, and so very conflicted. I loved it!"

—Jessie Mihalik, author of *Polaris Rising*, on *Deal with the Devil*

TOR BOOKS BY KIT ROCHA

Deal with the Devil
The Devil You Know
Dance with the Devil

DANCE
WITH THE
DEVIL

A MERCENARY LIBRARIANS NOVEL

KIT ROCHA

TOR

A TOM DOHERTY ASSOCIATES BOOK
NEW YORK

This is a work of fiction. All of the characters, organizations, and events portrayed in this novel are either products of the authors' imaginations or are used fictitiously.

DANCE WITH THE DEVIL

Maps by Jon Lansberg

A Tor Book
Published by Tom Doherty Associates
120 Broadway
New York, NY 10271

www.tor-forge.com

Tor® is a registered trademark of Macmillan Publishing Group, LLC.

Library of Congress Cataloging-in-Publication Data

Names: Rocha, Kit, author.
Title: Dance with the devil / Kit Rocha.
Description: First edition. | New York : TOR/Tom Doherty Associates, 2022. |
Series: Mercenary librarians ; 3
Identifiers: LCCN 2022008282 (print) | LCCN 2022008283 (ebook) |
ISBN 9781250209405 (trade paperback) | ISBN 9781250781499 (hardcover) |
ISBN 9781250209399 (ebook)
Subjects: LCGFT: Apocalyptic fiction. | Action and adventure fiction. |
Romance fiction. | Novels.
Classification: LCC PS3618.O33895 D36 2022 (print) |
LCC PS3618.O33895 (ebook) | DDC 813/.6—dc23/eng/20220304
LC record available at https://lccn.loc.gov/2022008282
LC ebook record available at https://lccn.loc.gov/2022008283

Our books may be purchased in bulk for promotional, educational, or business use.
Please contact your local bookseller or the Macmillan Corporate and Premium
Sales Department at 1-800-221-7945, extension 5442, or by email at
MacmillanSpecialMarkets@macmillan.com.

First Edition: 2022

Printed in the United States of America

0 9 8 7 6 5 4 3 2 1

To Matt, Alex, Kat, and Mike

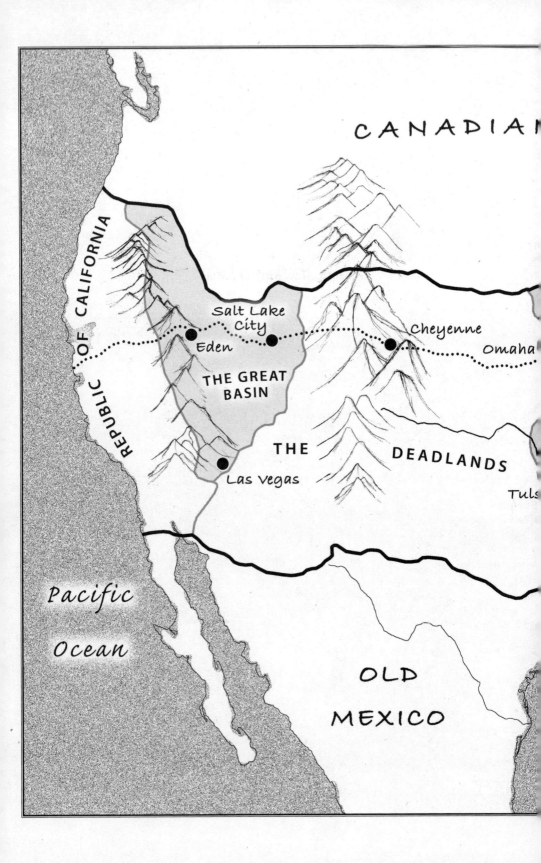

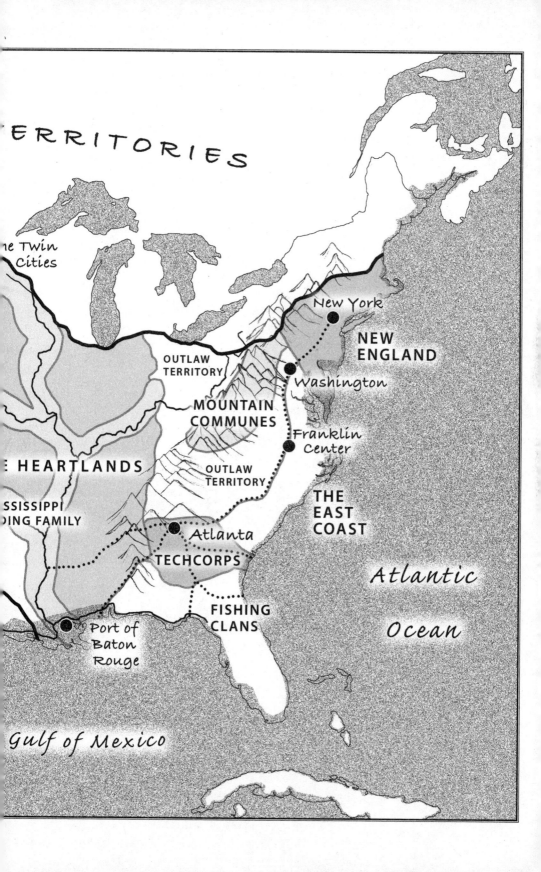

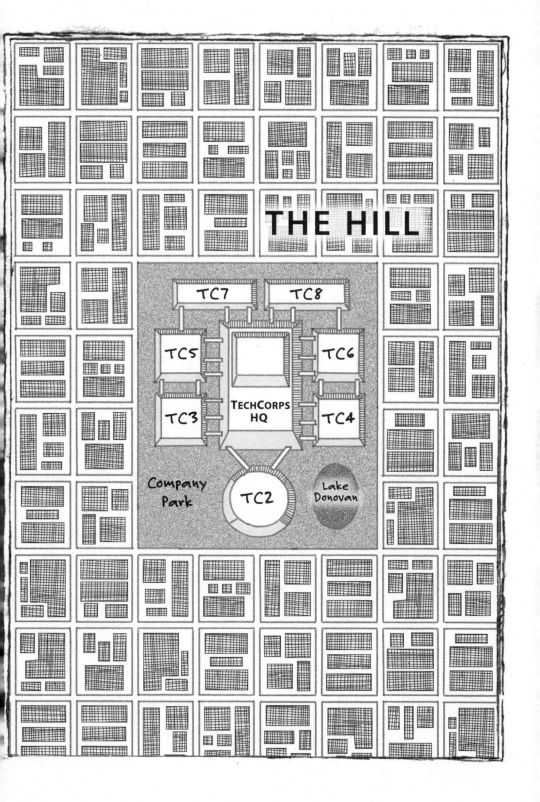

DANCE
WITH THE
DEVIL

TECHCORPS PROPRIETARY DATA, L1 SECURITY CLEARANCE

One week post 55–312's procedure, and the unexpected results persist. As far as we can ascertain, 55–312 is either indifferent or insensitive to pain. More interestingly, she fails to exhibit the detrimental complications typically seen in congenital sufferers, such as chewing injuries and corneal infections secondary to abrasion.

The department has requisitioned regeneration equipment in order to test the nature (indifference vs. insensitivity) as well as the limits, if any, of her condition. We anticipate prompt approval.

Recruit Analysis, February 2077

ONE

Hubris. It got 'em every time.

Dani cast a sidelong look at the man walking next to her. Though he looked about a decade younger, Christopher Bianco was forty-six years old, which meant he'd been born just before the Flares, when the world went dark. He was too young to remember the solar storms that had damaged power grids beyond repair, toppled entire governments, and left the survivors scrambling to regain some semblance of order. But growing up in the chaotic aftermath of those events—freezing, starving, struggling just to stay alive—must have shaped the man he'd become.

And Dani knew *a lot* about that man. Bianco had never been married, bore seventeen separate identifying tattoos and scars, and liked whiskey and redheads. His brown hair was burnished with hints of gold, and his wide, easy grin was more suited to a twentieth-century movie star than a murderer. But a murderer he was, nonetheless—commanding officer of the Golden Lions, an up-and-coming Protectorate squad that had been thriving under Captain Bianco's leadership.

She smiled back at him.

"So where *are* we going?" he asked, the grin lingering in his voice.

"Wherever the night takes us, of course."

He laughed. "I should demand details. You could be dangerous."

"I could be," she agreed solemnly. "Would it change your mind?"

His hand slid across her lower back to lightly grip her hip. "Not a chance."

Dani tossed her newly auburn hair over her shoulder and barely managed not to roll her eyes. She was as fond of a good game of cat-and-mouse as the next person—more, if she was being perfectly honest—but it wasn't as much fun when it was *work*.

And work was all she had lately. It turned out that mounting a guerrilla campaign against an all-powerful corporate dictatorship like the TechCorps monopolized your life hardcore, even with the workload split between an even dozen people. You had to monitor digital transmissions, gather intel from the streets, conduct a little creative spycraft, support the community in case of retaliation, and somehow manage to fund the whole damn op.

And then there was Dani's specialty: quick, bloody strikes against strategic targets.

Tonight's strategic target let his hand drift down until he was practically groping her ass. Dani gritted her teeth and lovingly imagined throwing an elbow at his face.

Patience.

He was steering her toward an alley just off of Forsyth. She'd checked it out during her reconnaissance earlier—it was a narrow dead end, no more than two and a half, maybe three meters wide, littered with garbage and broken glass. It was secluded, grimy, and disgusting.

It was perfect.

"Nice place," Dani murmured dryly.

The hand on her hip tensed, and he whirled her around a split second later. Her back hit the pitted brick, and he loomed over her, a tiny smile on his lips. "Only the best for you, darling."

Oh, he was smooth. She had to grant him that, from one practiced honeypot to another. It was part of what made Captain Bianco a strategic target, after all. He had a knack for covert work, was adaptable and quick on his feet, and his instincts were top-notch.

Still, as much as she admired his dedication to the fine art of seductive deception, it was getting late. And she had a job to do.

Almost there.

His smile only grew as Dani slowly wound one hand in the front of his shirt, his lips curving as genuine amusement sparkled in his eyes.

So she asked the question she was supposed to ask. "What's so funny?"

"Oh, nothing," he practically purred. "It's just . . . you have *no idea* you've been made, do you?"

Finally.

"Made?" She tightened her hand in his shirt.

He didn't answer, but he didn't have to. The near-silent shuffle of boots tickled Dani's ears, and she turned her head just far enough to see four shadowy figures file across the narrow mouth of the alley, effectively forming a human blockade.

"You brought your whole crew," she murmured. "I'm flattered."

"I don't know if you're brave or crazy, lady, and I don't care." Bianco's silky voice hardened. "You've been taking out Protectorate squads, and now it's your turn."

"So . . . what? You haul me in like a good little boy?"

"Not exactly," he countered. "Terminate on sight."

So much for negotiation. She watched as Captain Bianco drew his arm back, his fingers already curling into a wicked fist.

Dani considered the situation.

A few things were immediately obvious. First: they knew what she'd been up to, that she'd been targeting Protectorate squads for elimination, but almost certainly not who she really was. If they had, Captain Bianco's orders would have been very, very different.

A random, murderous rebel who'd gotten lucky a few times while facing off against their men? The TechCorps no doubt considered that woman dangerous—and expendable. But Danijela Volkova, former Executive Security operative turned legendary assassin? One of only two survivors of an experimental nerve-rewiring procedure that had left her with superhuman speed and reflexes, not to mention impervious to pain?

No way would they let *her* slip through their fingers. Not when they could haul her back to one of their labs and dissect her like a fucking frog.

Second: the Golden Lions had turned the alley into an efficient killbox by deploying across the mouth of it like a firing squad, but they couldn't use it as one. They wouldn't risk their CO's life. No, they'd try to take her down via nonlethal means, *then* finish her off.

Finally, third: she had to be at the top of her game. All of her previous targets had been varying degrees of oblivious or overconfident. The Golden Lions would be neither.

She dodged Bianco's fist as it flew toward her face. It crashed into the wall instead, shattering brick and bone. He grunted in pain, but he wasn't about to let a crushed hand interfere with his mission. He reached for her with his other hand, already calling out an order to fire.

His second mistake. Dani grabbed his lapels and spun him around, putting him between her and his men. They fired their Tasers, long-range models that used wireless signals instead of cords and took forever to reload. They were designed to deploy an electrical current as soon as they burrowed into flesh—in this case, Captain Bianco's back.

They worked like a charm. The good captain went down, and Dani turned her attention to his men.

Two of them started reloading their Tasers. A third charged at Dani, while the fourth went straight for his gun.

Smart.

An old fire escape hung off the wall overhead, with only a few rusty bolts still securing it to the building. Dani took a running leap, grabbed the lower edge, and swung out, kicking the advancing Golden Lion in the face. His neck snapped with a sharp crack just as the metal frame pulled loose, and she reached for her knives as she fell. She hit the ground rolling and came up with her blades in her hands.

This was her sweet spot, the part of the hunt that made all the makeup and simpering worth it. Direct, decisive action to address a specific, discrete issue.

See a problem, stab a problem.

The armed soldier fired high, aiming for her head with the kind of confidence that spoke of excellent marksmanship. Dani ducked the shot and went in low, slicing across the front of his thigh. The blade bit deep, tearing through reinforced cloth, skin, and muscle.

She let her momentum spin her around, away from the hot spray of blood, and buried her knife in his back, right between the fourth and fifth ribs, angled to avoid the shoulder blade and penetrate the left ventricle of the heart.

The other two attacked in tandem, having abandoned the Tasers in favor of the close-quarters benefits of their own knives. Dani ducked slashes and stabs and *watched,* waiting for an opening.

The one on the left dropped his guard, and she grabbed his hair and dragged her blade across the side of his throat, opening his jugular vein. She dropped him, trusting the blood loss to quickly render him unconscious, and headed for his buddy.

Instead, a rough hand wrapped around her ankle, almost dragging her off her feet. Captain Bianco had recovered from being Tased by his own men—and he was *pissed*.

Dani stomped on his forearm with her free foot, sacrificing her balance for the blow. His radius and ulna snapped under her boot, and she fell to the pavement with a jarring thud.

Bianco scrambled to grab her, even with a busted hand and a broken arm. Dani dropped an elbow to his temple and pushed him onto his back, pinning him there with one knee on his chest. Then she looked him dead in the eye as she finished him off with a blade to the heart.

It was probably more consideration than he'd ever offered any of his victims.

There was no time to linger over the thought. By Dani's count, there was one more left. She pushed up onto her feet, then used her momentum to swing around, blade first.

Straight toward Rafe, who had just dropped the last Protectorate soldier.

Even she didn't have time to pull the attack. She released the knife instead, letting it fly across the alley as she stumbled against his chest. He caught her deftly, big hands locking around her arms. He hoisted her without apparent effort, swinging her around so his body formed a wall between her and the alley.

The gesture was one of protective instinct, but his expression was *furious*. "What the hell are you doing?"

How dare he? "What the hell am I doing? What the hell are *you* doing, Morales? I almost stabbed you in the fucking face!"

He took one shuddering breath, then another, like he was fighting for control of his temper. The moonlight slanted across his features, highlighting his impossible cheekbones and silvering his dark skin. He looked like a statue of a beautiful, angry god, and he ground out each word between clenched teeth. "You came out here to take on a full Protectorate squad. *Alone.*"

Of course she had. If you were going to bait a trap, you didn't do it with a pack of wolves. You did it with a single helpless lamb. Dani opened her mouth to tell him so—firmly and obscenely—but caught the telltale glimmer of a laser sight.

A sniper. She almost sighed. Why couldn't Captain Bianco have been a *little* less competent?

She shoved Rafe hard, pushing him back against the wall as the shot rang out. It pinballed off the wall, scattering razor-sharp shards of brick. Dani went for Rafe's pistol, but he already had it in his hand.

He fired, and the sniper's body plummeted from the roof. Rafe was already turning back toward her to resume his argument by the time it hit the cracked asphalt. "Alone," he repeated. "I thought we discussed having backup on *all* missions."

"When possible and necessary." She waved a hand at the grungy alley. "This was neither."

"Dani—" He bit off whatever he was going to say and threw up his hands. "Do you think I would have tried to stop you? I know you can handle yourself. But it's dangerous out here, woman. We all need some-one to watch our back."

Normally, she would have agreed. In this case, however, the situa-tion was . . . delicate. Her plan had hinged on Bianco knowing that she was luring him into a trap, but not realizing that she was on to both his awareness *and* his intention to turn it around on her. With so many variables at play, the best way to keep it all straight—and minimize ca-sualties in case of disaster—was to fly solo.

She retrieved her knife from the spot where it had landed, blessedly *not* in any puddles of mystery fluid. "I know you worry, and I get it. But some things, I just have to do on my own. It's my *job*."

Rafe's soft sigh echoed through the alley behind her. "It's my job, too. You don't always have to go it alone."

He said it like she didn't *know*, like she hadn't considered asking Nina to join her undercover or getting Conall to surveil her encounter with the Golden Lions. But that was Rafe—given the choice between solitude and surrounding himself with others, he'd always pick people. Anything else was just unthinkable.

The thought made Dani's skin itch. She loved Nina and Maya with all her shriveled black heart, and she was even learning to like the Silver Devils—most of them, anyway. They were her *family*, for fuck's sake. If they needed her, she'd be there—anytime, anyplace. No questions asked.

And they were always there for her. It wasn't their fault her brain didn't work that way. Dani's history—personal *and* professional—had instilled in her an almost pathological self-reliance. She knew it, and she'd tried to overcome the knee-jerk panic that gripped her when she thought about asking for help . . .

But things weren't pathological if you could just *stop* doing them, were they?

She covered her discomfort with an irritated grumble. "Can we have this conversation elsewhere? Like, someplace with fewer dead bodies?"

"Just a second." Rafe knelt beside Captain Bianco and methodically checked the corpse's clothes. When he rose, he held a small but sturdy tablet in his hand. "Conall would kick my ass if I didn't bring this back."

He pulled a small roll of shielding wrap from one of the many pockets on his tactical pants and began rolling it around the purloined tablet. Back at Protectorate headquarters, the analysts monitoring the Golden Lions' mission status would be watching the signal blink out of existence, taking with it any hope of tracking the device.

At least, that was how it was supposed to work. In Dani's estimation, it was worth the risk, but barely. "You think Con'll be able to get anything useful from it?"

"Probably not directly." With the device secured, Rafe stowed it in another pocket. "But he'll pull anything he can get for Maya, and maybe something will spark for her."

Maya would probably want the man's grocery receipts, if they could manage to dig them up. "Intel is intel, I suppose."

Rafe fell into step beside Dani as she squared her shoulders and walked as casually as possible out of the alley and turned toward home. After half a block in silence, he sighed softly. "I'm sorry I snapped at you. I know you can handle your shit."

"You're not sorry. You'd do it again in a heartbeat."

"Probably. Doesn't mean I'm not sorry." He shot her a sidelong look. "It just means you're really good at riling me up."

Oh, there were *layers* of meaning in that statement—layers Dani chose to ignore. "Whatever. It's who you are. Don't apologize for it. I don't plan to."

"Fair enough." He fell silent again.

Dani stifled a sigh of her own. She looked around for a distraction, but the streets were strangely quiet. There were no revelers headed home from a night at the bar, no spirited conversations happening on front stoops—even though there should have been.

Winter had crept over the South, but the night was warm, almost balmy. Normally, folks would be taking advantage of the break in the cold to get out and enjoy some fresh air. But the people of Southside—and Five Points, particularly—had damn good instincts for danger. They didn't know a handful of their own were waging war against the TechCorps, but they knew *something* was up. They felt the tension, like a taut rubber band about to snap.

So they stayed inside, and she and Rafe might as well have been alone in the world.

As they crossed under a flickering streetlight, Rafe reached out, his fingers barely grazing her hip. "Can I at least check to make sure you're not bleeding?"

She almost shuddered. She was too wound up for this right now, and he was too impulsive. If he started running his hands over her skin, searching for wounds she couldn't feel, they'd wind up stumbling into another dark alley. Their first time would unfold against the filthy brick, her wrists pinned above her head, his coffee-rich voice low and demanding in her ear.

Dani was no stranger to bad decisions, but this one? Could destroy *everything.*

Part of her wanted to do it anyway.

Instead, she brushed him away. "Captain Bianco and his Golden Lions meant business, Morales. If they'd managed to hit me hard enough to count, we wouldn't be having this conversation."

A muscle in his cheek jumped. He was clenching his jaw, hard—no doubt biting back another argument. Finally, he blew out a breath. "Fine, but you're letting me check when we get home, or I'm waking up Nina to do it."

"I can take care of my—" A low noise pricked at Dani's ears, a strange mix of whir and whine. Instantly recognizable.

She ended up dragging Rafe into an alley anyway, pressing one finger to his lips before he could speak. His gaze clashed with hers for a tense moment before he looked up, tracking the approaching drone.

It wasn't strange to see TechCorps surveillance drones canvassing Southside. They'd send a few out every now and then, and they'd get them back in pieces. The people in this part of Atlanta liked their privacy, and they'd gladly bring down any drones that crossed their paths.

But she could tell by the sound that this wasn't one of the older drones the TechCorps usually deployed, the ones they didn't care if they lost because they were a mere step shy of being decommissioned anyway. This was top of the line, new, with five different types of cameras, heat-seeking capabilities, and even small armaments.

This one was looking for *them*.

Dani held out her hand, one eyebrow raised expectantly. Rafe hesitated, then drew his pistol and handed it over without bothering to disengage the biometric lock. Out of habit, she swiped her thumb over the small scanner plate, and she felt a small jolt in her midsection as the trigger mechanism unlocked.

It was strangely intimate, like having the key to someone's apartment or the passcode for their computer system. Of course, he could have given the entire team access to his firearms. But somehow, Dani didn't think so.

She leaned past him, curling one hand around his upper arm as the drone came into view. The weakest spots were the three articulation points where the propellers attached to the main body, and Dani took aim. She shot out the first two, and the drone pitched and rolled before crashing to the street in a shower of sparks.

Rafe was on it in a heartbeat, disabling its broadcast capabilities with a flick of the knife he'd pulled from his pocket. Dani stood there, useless, as he dug out the memory and programming module next. She could shoot one of these things down, but she didn't know how to harvest any valuable intelligence from it.

Dani was a walking weapon, only capable of destroying things.

Rafe wrapped the modules with more of the signal dampening tape, then finished off the drone by yanking out the main control board. Wires and screws both snapped like gossamer threads in his grip. He probably could have torn the thing in half without strain.

But he didn't. He tossed the whole mess aside for the scavengers and rose effortlessly.

"Here." She shoved his pistol at him. It was all she meant to do, but with the painful reminder of her own shortcomings ringing in her brain, she found herself trying to justify her decisions. "I don't do it to fuck with you, you know. Come out by myself. It's just . . ."

His brow furrowed. "Dani, you don't have to explain."

"You're a unit," she told him haltingly. "You and the rest of the Silver Devils. You were trained that way. You *lived* that way. But that's not how it was in Executive Security. We were . . ."

She didn't even know how to describe the sense of isolation that had been drilled into her during her training as a TechCorps bodyguard. It was rigorous and thorough, with the latest technology and the highest quality—and most brutal—instructors, but Ex-Sec recruits were never meant to function as teams. They would guard their assigned executives. And they all understood that, eventually, they would die doing it. But they didn't work together.

"We worked alone," she said finally. "We always worked alone, and that's a hard habit to break. That's all."

Rafe holstered his gun, his eyes not meeting hers, his voice gentle. "Well, you're not alone anymore. You can be annoyed by us if you want. I'm annoyed by Conall daily."

He was changing the subject to a nonthreatening topic, awkward in his eagerness to coddle her the way he would a feral stray. And Dani let him, because she wasn't sure what else she could do or say.

"Conall is all right," she declared. "Except when he starts making fun of my paper files like I'm some thousand-year-old fossil. It's rude."

"Maybe, but is he wrong?"

"Look—"

She fell into the flirtatious banter. It wasn't comfortable—nothing about dealing with Rafael Morales was—but it was familiar, a dance whose customs and steps she knew intricately, because she practiced them all the damn time, for work and for play. The dance was easy, mindless. She could lose herself in it.

In another world, Dani didn't have to think about this. Their lives weren't so intertwined, and she and Rafe could simply enjoy one another. They weren't worried about implosions and awkwardness and the potential fallout if things went bad and they suffered a nasty breakup. They knew they could part ways easily, and never look back.

In another world, they had already become lovers.

Too bad Dani lived in this one.

TECHCORPS PROPRIETARY DATA, L2 SECURITY CLEARANCE

Recruit 66–942 has an unusual combination of aptitudes. Charisma is frequently noted in his file, and he tests well above average in all areas of STEM, as well, even without additional cognitive enhancement. My advice is to consider shifting him onto the military intelligence track.

Recruit Analysis, May 2076

TWO

Rafe was used to being underestimated.

Not physically, of course. Even before he'd signed up for a biochemical implant that gave him the strength to lift a car and the stamina to bench press it for hours, he'd been physically imposing. At seventeen, he'd been close to two meters tall and athletic, and more than a decade of strict military discipline had only enhanced his youthful muscle.

But his genetic gifts hadn't stopped there. He'd been graced with his mother's perfect cheekbones and perfect brown skin, along with his father's sultry dark eyes and seductive smile. His face was almost as potent a weapon as his body. Even the people who didn't assume he was a meathead tended to write him off as a vacant pretty boy. Sometimes, he helped them along to that conclusion with the flirtation that came naturally to him. Charm? He'd inherited that from *both* parents.

Few people credited him with the wits to see what was directly in front of him, much less the keen intellect required of a military intelligence officer. That was what had made him such a *good* military intelligence officer.

Even now, six months after his squad had broken ties with their mad-scientist creators at the TechCorps, Rafe couldn't entirely turn it off. He slouched in a chair in their recently constructed war room, his gaze analyzing and categorizing by habit.

War room was a glamorous name for what had been, until recently, part of the unfinished basement in Dani, Nina, and Maya's building. The shabby rugs had been replaced with thick, warm carpets that protected their feet from the cold cement floor. The walls were still naked wood, but they'd been completed with an eccentric mishmash of salvaged lumber from abandoned buildings, the color and grain so varied the effect almost looked deliberately artistic.

Almost.

The real investment was in the tech that lined the smooth surfaces of several folding tables, as well as the massive touchscreen affixed to the far wall. Maya stood in front of it, scrolling through a dizzying array of data that she'd exported into seven different columns. Her fingers danced across the screen, sorting and organizing, her body swaying gently as she reached toward its edges.

Now *there* was a kindred spirit—someone who understood what it was like to be underestimated. As good as he was with people, even Rafe had misjudged her at their first meeting. She was short and curvy, with no combat enhancements. Not strength or stamina or healing, not even speed, like Dani. A month ago, she'd abandoned her elbow-length braids for natural black curls that framed a sweet, heart-shaped face and an easy smile. Her brown skin glowed and her eye shadow *glittered,* the vibrant color matching her electric blue nail polish as well as the aquamarines that dangled from her earlobes on delicate chains.

She looked harmless. Not at all like a person who could shoot the wings off a fly in a pitch-black room, and *definitely* not like someone who held the darkest secrets of the TechCorps behind her guileless brown eyes. But thanks to her enhancements, Maya remembered *everything* she heard—and she'd grown up in the heart of the TechCorps, raised by a corporate vice president who'd planned to dismantle the monster from the inside. Birgitte Skovgaard had died for her internal revolution, and Maya was determined to see it through.

Easy to say. Harder to pull off. But Maya had taken up the challenge and run with it, and her growing information network and subtle corporate sabotage had the Board bleeding from a hundred wounds they couldn't find. She was the smartest person Rafe had ever met, and a stand-in for the little sisters he couldn't visit for their own safety.

The wall to Maya's left had been given over to Nina's community organizing. Instead of a chaotic and terrifying flow of data, Nina's domain was precise, organized, and efficient—much like Nina herself. A smart board held her to-do list, broken down into daily, weekly, and monthly goals. Next to it, a map of Southside had been affixed to the wall, with color-coded notations. The corkboard beneath it held a variety of neatly organized papers and index cards, tracking their efforts to feed, heal, educate, and arm the surrounding neighborhoods.

Nina, he had *never* underestimated. One look at her, and Rafe had known she was trouble. It wasn't even the fact that she'd been genetically engineered in some crackpot cloning facility, designed to be the perfect warrior. Supersoldiers were thick on the ground in Atlanta, and while he wasn't *quite* on Nina's level physically, he could hold his own with her.

No, the scary thing about Nina was her passion. Rafe's greatest asset as an intelligence officer had always been knowing who could be bought and who had to be won over. Most people had a price, and for too many in this world it was a bit of kindness, or a few credits to make life a little softer. Supersoldiers might be thick on the ground, but compassion wasn't. Rafe had plied it to excellent effect over the years, building himself a network of informants and favors owed.

One day with Nina, and he'd known her price: absolute honesty and complete integrity. Nothing less would sway her. An awkward truth when they'd entered into a relationship with her under false pretenses.

Shame writhed in his gut as Rafe sank deeper in the chair and watched Nina cross to her wall and attack her to-do list. She was dressed casually, her leather jacket abandoned over a chair, revealing a plain black T-shirt and comfortably worn jeans. Her long brown hair was caught up in a neat ponytail, and even in winter her skin had a golden sheen. Concentration creased her brow as she tapped on tasks, crossing them off or adding new notes.

It was Rafe's fault they'd been trapped into betraying Nina in the first place. Knox had meticulously planned their exit from the Tech-Corps, but all of his dozens of contingencies had possessed the same fragile link: the one person they needed to survive once they cut out their trackers and officially went rogue.

A biochem hacker. Someone who could stop the kill switch built into their implants from going off and taking them down. Rafe had cultivated that precious asset for *years,* knowing that someday their lives might depend on his ability to forge a relationship.

And it had. Too bad Rafe had led a kidnapper straight to the hacker's door.

Maybe he wasn't *always* a good military intelligence officer.

Forcing his gaze away from Nina left him staring at the third wall.

Dani's wall. Shame faded under wry amusement, as his lips twitched upward in spite of himself.

Dani's wall was so . . . *Dani.*

Maya had clearly had a vision for Dani's area of their war room. She'd hung corkboard on the wood and printed out pictures of their first high value targets to tack up, probably in acknowledgment of Dani's insistence that hard copy trumped mutable, erasable digital files anytime.

The targets—a senior Protectorate trainer, an Executive Security handler, even an entire elite strike squad—were long dead. Dani hadn't bothered to add information on her new targets. Her only contributions to the operation were a few dozen stab marks—from when she'd used the dossier photos for target practice—as well as one throwing knife that still protruded from the Protectorate squad commander's left eye.

Dani did her strategizing in her head.

She came whooping through the door, carrying a giggling Rainbow on her back. The child's laughter grew in volume as they ran a circuit around the room, with Dani making generic engine noises as she swooped and turned.

"All right, bug." She stopped and released Rainbow's legs, letting the girl down slowly and carefully. "Go see what Nina's got for you, okay?"

Rainbow bounced across the room, and Rafe's chest actually *hurt.* Especially when she stopped next to him and beamed up at him from beneath her shaggy pixie cut. "Hey, Rafe."

"Hey, Bo." He ruffled her short hair and laughed at her put-upon expression. "Nina's waiting."

She skipped off, almost childlike in her enthusiasm.

They still hadn't figured out exactly how old she was. The psychos who'd cloned her were too dead to talk, and they'd taken their records with them. Rainbow probably wasn't much older than six or seven, even if her dark green eyes seemed ancient sometimes. She was already well-versed in military strategy, and she talked about it using words no child should ever have even heard—*infiltration* and *decapitation strike* and *force multiplication.* But after a few months with them, she'd begun to relax into doing normal kid stuff. Watching vids, skipping her math homework, eating way too much ice cream . . .

"Dani," Maya said, her voice distracted. "Come here a second, would you?"

. . . hanging out while her new aunts and uncles committed some light sedition.

Dani prowled across the room, and Rafe's gaze swung to follow her. Poor dead Captain Bianco of the Golden Lions probably wouldn't have recognized the sleek, seductive assassin who'd lured him into a killbox with nothing but high heels, high fashion, and his enormously overinflated ego.

She was blond again—her natural color. Her hair was swept up in a neat, precise ponytail, a sharp contrast to the threadbare sweatshirt she'd donned over simple black leggings. The sweatshirt listed dangerously off one smooth, pale shoulder, a flash of skin all the more tantalizing because it didn't seem to be intentional.

When Dani was hunting, her clothes became weapons. As a fellow hunter, Rafe could appreciate the game. Sex could be a potent tool in any arsenal, and Dani's closet full of chic, skin-baring dresses and impossibly short skirts had led plenty of fools to their deaths.

If Rafe died, it would probably be because of the sweatshirt and the one tempting shoulder he couldn't stop thinking about kissing.

Dani glanced over at him from her spot in front of Maya's board, and their gazes locked. Slowly, she arched one eyebrow and licked the corner of her mouth.

Okay, so maybe if he died, it would be from thwarted sexual tension. But there were worse ways to go, and he didn't have to go alone. Leaning back in his chair, he stretched his arms, knowing exactly how well his T-shirt hugged his muscles.

Dani's eyes narrowed, then somehow managed to roll in pointed accusation.

Rafe raised his eyebrows suggestively and flexed.

"Excuse me, y'all." Maya didn't even turn away from her board, her fingers flicking across the surface. "Please flirt on your own time."

Rafe let his arms drop with a grin. "Sorry, Maya. Sometimes I just can't turn off the smolder."

Dani muttered something that sounded suspiciously like "conceited asshole," then turned to Nina with a bland expression. "Sitrep time?"

Nina lifted Rainbow onto a stool and nodded. "It's just us today. The rest of the guys are helping Clem with some renovations."

"They didn't have much to report anyway." Rafe straightened in his chair and dragged his tablet over. "Biggest news is we're just about ready to pull the trigger on the clinic. Mace has had me running down some of the harder to source materials this week, but they'll be ready to see patients in a few days."

"Good. Dr. Wells has been eager to work out of a proper space for once." Nina turned back to her board. "We finished the heating in the basement, and we've managed to source another freeze dryer. But the biggest news is that we finally secured the space over on Poplar."

Dani straightened. "We did?"

"We did. We're going ahead with the community kitchen, but there's also plenty of space for aquaponics. We'll raise fish and heirloom crops—that way, people can use the seeds at home."

Rainbow spoke up from her spot on the stool, her small face lit with anticipation. "I'm going to help in the kitchen. Tia Ivonne promised to teach me how to cook."

Her barely contained excitement was so adorable that looking at it almost hurt. Rafe channeled the pain into a glowing compliment. "I'm sure you'll be a big help to her, kiddo. You kicked ass at scanning books for Maya."

She beamed and kicked her feet, her blue shoes with their glitter laces bouncing cheerfully, and his heart tried to ache its way right out of his chest.

Rainbow didn't look much like his younger sister—not physically, anyway. Tessa's dark curly hair had tumbled around a face with their mother's brown skin and their father's dark eyes. But unlike Rafe's open, disarming charm, she'd always been serious. She watched the world with solemn, observant eyes. Her smiles were rare and hard-won, but they were like Rainbow's—brilliant and joyous.

God, he missed her. He missed *all* of them.

Maya finally turned from her smart board, a smaller tablet clutched in one hand. "I'm in the *no news is good news* camp this week. Conall and I have been collating all the data from drones and Protectorate sweeps, but I still can't find a damn pattern. There's definitely been more activity lately, but it's all over the place. They're looking for us, but I think it's safe to say they don't know exactly *where* to look."

"That *is* good news," Nina agreed. "What about you, Dani?"

"Got it done," she answered shortly. "The Golden Lions are no more. Shot down a drone, too. We gave all the relevant tech to Maya."

"We?"

"Yeah, we." Dani pinned Rafe with a withering glare. "Morales crashed my party last night."

If he'd been a less secure man, that death glare might have actually done him physical damage. Perversely, Rafe was starting to enjoy it— and he definitely didn't want to examine that awkward fact too closely. "I was providing backup," he drawled in his most charming *aww, shucks* voice. "You know, that thing we all agreed was important?"

Dani transferred her gaze to Nina, where it transformed into a look that screamed *do you believe this guy?*

Nina didn't even hesitate. "I'm with Rafe on this one."

"What?"

"You heard me. It doesn't take someone better to get the drop on you, not when you're alone." Nina's words and voice brooked no argument. "This is about your safety, Dani. Maybe even your life."

She propped her hands on her hips. "And if having someone else around blows my cover and I get made?"

"Then you abort the mission and we move on. All of your targets are important, but they're not worth dying over."

Dani made a noise of sheer disgust, then dropped her hands. "Fine. You're the boss."

It should have made Rafe feel better. But he *hated* seeing Dani defeated, even by her friends. Even by the truth. He had to bite down hard on the urge to point out she'd murdered most of the Protectorate squad before he'd even managed to make it down the alley. Dani wouldn't appreciate it.

Besides, Nina was the only one who could keep her from going out and risking her damn neck again. Lord knew she wouldn't listen to him.

Maya hummed as she scrolled through her tablet. "I think that was the last on our list for you, Dani. I'm still waiting for confirmation on another target, so give me a few days."

"Sure." Dani turned to her board and snatched the picture of the Ex-Sec handler from it. "Just point me where and when you want me to go."

"Will do." Maya tossed her tablet onto the table and grinned. "Y'all need anything else from me? Because if not, I'm gonna go watch Gray do hot sexy building things."

Rainbow wrinkled her nose, prompting a laugh from Nina as she swung the girl up in her arms. "We'll go with you. We're taking some lunch over."

"I'll catch up later," Rafe told them, dragging Maya's tablet toward him. "You mind if I look over that location data?"

"Knock yourself out."

"See you guys tonight," Dani told them. "Clem's. Don't forget."

Maya followed Nina and Rainbow out the door, leaving only Dani, who was methodically removing the remaining pictures from her corkboard.

The silence lay between them, heavy and fraught. Rafe could think of about ten ways to break it if he wanted to provoke an explosion . . . but *should* he? He'd had some pretty wild relationships in his day, including one or two that had been straight up cheerfully kinky, but there was nothing particularly healthy about the way he and Dani swiped at one another.

He just wasn't sure either of them wanted to stop.

Instead of poking at Dani, he glanced over the location data, hoping to see something Maya might have missed. But she was right. The Protectorate was *everywhere*. Literally everywhere.

"Do you need any help?"

Rafe looked up. Dani was standing beside the table, watching him expectantly.

The death glare was gone. Now he was looking at Dani the professional—cool, collected. Brilliant and deadly.

His fatal weakness.

He slid the tablet over to her. "I was hoping I'd notice a pattern Maya missed, but I should have known better. If it was there to see, she would have spotted it."

"Maya doesn't miss much." She didn't even look at the tablet, but her situational awareness was so precise she managed to turn it off and toss it on top of the other two Maya had been working with. "So. Do you want to tell me how this is going to work?"

He tore himself away from pondering the hotness of her casual competence. "How is what going to work?"

"Backup. Do I coordinate with whoever's available, or should it be you?"

An odd warmth spread through his chest, along with something sharper. He refused to call it jealousy. "It can be me. It *should* be me."

"Okay." She nodded decisively. "I'll be ready when Maya gets together the intel on our next target, then."

"Do you know who she's looking for?"

"You know." She lifted that damned bare shoulder in a careless shrug. "Your former coworkers."

Rafe flexed his fingers, mostly to keep from lifting them to the back of his neck. It had been more than six months since he and the rest of his squad had cut out their trackers and left the Protectorate.

Left was far too passive to describe those frantic weeks. The preparation, the fear, the knowledge that one wrong move could result in a fate worse than death. All of the planning and praying, all of the impossible odds that had somehow broken in their favor . . .

And they'd gained freedom only to discover the one person they needed to survive was missing.

Rafe supposed that had worked out the way it was meant to. Recovering their biochem hacker had brought Nina, Maya, and Dani into their lives, after all. Knox certainly wouldn't go back and change it, not when he was currently playing house and raising an adopted daughter with Nina. Gray wouldn't, either. He'd found the center of his universe in Maya.

Funny, that. On the first night they'd met the three women, Rafe had been the one starry-eyed and softhearted, to the point where he'd received multiple lectures on how he wasn't allowed to fall in love with Dani. But here they all were, smitten and domesticated, and Rafe . . .

Rafe was still waiting.

Something about his gaze must have gone a little too soft and yearning, because Dani took an abrupt step back. "I'll keep you posted," she mumbled, then took off for the stairs like her ass was on fire.

If his heart wasn't on the line, Rafe might have laughed. Hell, he laughed anyway, a hoarse, rueful chuckle as he rubbed his hand over his face and reminded himself of the harsh truth.

If he planned to wait for Dani, he might be waiting forever.

CLASSIFIED BEHAVIOR EVALUATION

Franklin Center for Genetic Research

HS-Gen16 remains our most frustrating failure. The potential of this genetic strain outstrips any comparable generation. They exceed expectations across the board.

Unfortunately, their failures are proportionately dramatic. So is the danger they represent without careful handling. Our hubris will be our downfall if we don't proceed with caution.

Dr. Reed, July 2080

THREE

Saturday nights at Clementine's were starting to get crowded.

The regulars had arrived long ago, shuffling off to their usual tables and booths to talk and laugh and drink the night away. Music and smoke hung in the air, but the place was quieter—and brighter—than usual.

Probably because there were far fewer troublemakers around these days. Most of the small-time criminals had taken one look at Knox and his men and had chosen to ply their trades elsewhere. The Silver Devils may have left the Protectorate in grand, spectacular fashion, but they still scared the shit out of the common thieves and con artists in Five Points.

Dani slapped a hand on the bar to get Clem's attention. The aging proprietor and namesake of the establishment had finally hired some help in the form of a burly young barback, but she still handled the drinks herself.

The silver in Clem's ginger hair caught the light as she paused in pulling a beer and tipped her head in Dani's direction. "Another round?"

"You're busy." Dani stepped up on the steel rail that ringed the lower part of the bar, leaned over, and grabbed two bottles. "I've got it."

Clem grinned. "I'll put 'em on your tab."

"I'd be disappointed if you didn't, Clem." Dani loaded a tray with shot glasses and the bottles. Balancing it was tricky, and she almost dropped it once or twice, but her enhanced reflexes saved the booze.

Dani made her way to Nina's corner booth first. She and Knox were deep in conversation with Syd, a guest from out of town. Syd was a bit mysterious, a slightly older lady who wore her years effortlessly. Her auburn hair framed her lightly tanned face, and she carried herself like a soldier. Like Nina, she was a product of genetic modification, created by a paramilitary program tasked with engineering perfect mercenaries.

Syd had never said so explicitly, but Dani assumed that her second-in-command, Max, had been part of the same program. He was younger than Syd but looked about the same age, with his salt-and-pepper hair and beard, a contradiction that spoke of a hard, hard life. His eyes were bright, clear blue, but he had a somber, guarded air, as if the mere thought of smiling hurt.

Dani slid the tray onto the booth's scratched and gouged table and smiled. "Pick your poison—whiskey or tequila."

"Tequila," Syd replied. "How's life treating you, Dani?"

"Cannot complain." She poured two shots and slid them over to Syd, then raised an eyebrow at Max, who shook his head. "Work is going smoothly, and the weather's been beautiful. What more could a woman ask for?"

"According to the kids on the farm? Snow." Syd tossed back one of her shots and nudged Max with an elbow. "Last year, Max built a snow machine so they could have a snowball fight on Christmas. Might have to do it again this year."

Dani clucked her tongue, poured a couple of shots of whiskey, and set them in front of Nina and Knox. "That's painfully adorable."

"Painfully," Nina agreed.

Knox looked thoughtful. "How hard is it to build a snow machine?"

Dani had zero doubt that, whether through natural cold fronts or Knox's mechanical aptitude, Rainbow would have her first white Christmas. She saluted lightly and retrieved the tray. "The liquor fairy must be off to bless other tables. But I'll be back."

When she turned, Gray waved her over. He and Maya had claimed a table with Jaden Montgomery, the seed smuggler who maintained a farm within the city—and dozens, if not hundreds, of contacts outside of it. He was a huge man, broad and muscled, with dark hair and dark skin.

And he'd brought one of his best drivers, who also happened to be one of Dani's favorite people. She'd gotten to know Dakota when the younger woman had dated Nina for a while. The relationship had ended, but they'd remained friendly.

Dani set down the tray, then leaned over to kiss the woman's cheek. Dakota also had dark hair, ironed flat at the moment, and her skin was a rich brown, though lighter than Jaden's. "When did you sneak in?"

"Just a few minutes ago. Have I missed anything exciting?"

"Hell, no."

"And we like it that way," Gray said as he claimed the bottles and began to pour shots.

"Dakota was telling us about her last run." Maya propped her chin on one hand. "She found a scientist in Alabama who's developed a strain of high-yield tomatoes that are awesome for rooftop gardens."

Jaden grunted. "I spent the last year getting the door slammed in my face when I tried to contact him. She goes over there once and convinces him to pull up his whole operation and move to Atlanta."

"Charm, Montgomery." Dani winked at Dakota. "Don't underestimate your lovely driver's smile."

"I can be charming," he grumbled. "I'm perfectly charming when I want to be."

"Oh?" Maya raised both eyebrows. "Have you ever wanted to be?"

He glared at her. "Not really."

"That's the Jaden we love." Maya accepted a shot from Gray. "Are you staying for the rest of the story, Dani?"

"Can't." She gathered the tray with an apologetic look. "Drink delivery waits for no man. But I'll catch you later?"

Dakota grinned. "Of course."

The last booth she had to hit was across the room, a broad semicircle set against the middle of the wall. Conall waved at her, and she focused on him to keep from looking at Rafe's too-welcoming smile.

It didn't stop her skin from prickling under his intense gaze as she placed the tray on the tabletop with a flourish. "Savitri, you look *ravishing* tonight."

It wasn't an exaggeration. The woman was dressed in head-to-toe black, with numerous jeweled accents that set off her gold-kissed skin. Not many people would have dared to walk around Southside wearing that much jewelry, but nothing about Savitri was typical.

For starters, she was a brilliant researcher and neurosurgeon who'd fled from the TechCorps to found her own cyberpunk empire. She ruled it from her underground club, Convergence, where she kept tabs on everything that went on in Atlanta. People with the kind of power Savitri had didn't walk around in fear.

Then again, maybe her bodyguard was the reason she saw no danger in wearing whatever the fuck she wanted on a night out in Southside. Adam was a hulk of a man, not as muscled as Rafe or even Jaden, but taller, and *trained*. He also, thanks to Savitri's former life as the smartest neurosurgeon in existence, basically had a computer for a brain.

Anyone who started shit with him would barely have time to ponder their life choices before said life ended.

He sat between Savitri and the rest of the room like a living wall. But Savitri only beamed past him at Dani, her dark eyes bright with pleasure. "Thank you, love. I was just talking to your handsome friend here, asking why the two of you haven't come to visit me at the club."

She gestured casually at Rafe, who flashed her a teasing smile. "I told her we've been busy. All the spying and recreational sedition, you know."

"Unfortunately, it's true." Dani poured a shot of tequila and claimed it for herself. "All work and no play, I know, but sometimes it can't be helped."

"Notice how she doesn't mention the fact that *I* visited," Conall grumbled as he snagged the whiskey bottle and a glass. "Everyone wants the Amazing Smoldering Duo."

"Don't take it too personally," Dani soothed. "I'm a *really* good dancer."

And so was Rafe. He was looking at her like he *remembered,* damn him, every grind and sway of their eye-catching dance at Convergence. The heat of his body pressed against hers, the careful, leashed glide of fingers over bare skin. His lips at the small of her back.

Dani flushed. No wonder the dance had succeeded in grabbing Savitri's attention. In hindsight, she realized that she and Rafe had been about thirty seconds from fucking on the dance floor.

They seemed to be about thirty seconds from fucking at any given moment.

Rafe's full lips twitched, as if he could *hear* the thought. Without looking away, he lifted the shot Conall had poured for him. He lingered with the glass at his lips before tilting the shot back. His strong throat worked as he swallowed, and his gaze never left hers.

Fuck.

He set down the shot glass and raised an eyebrow at her. A new song spilled out of the speakers tucked into the corners of the room, one with a strong, thudding bass line. "Care to show off some of those really good dance moves?" he asked with an innocent smile.

"Oh, you're on." Dani drank her tequila in one swallow, enjoying the flavor but missing the burn everyone seemed to love so much. "Let's go, Morales."

She took his hand and pulled him out to the middle of the room, where the jumble of tables had been pushed back to clear some space. He immediately slid a hand to the small of her back and tugged her against him, and Dani bit back a groan.

When had being close to him started to feel this good?

Rafe fell into an easy rhythm, close enough that their bodies were touching but just barely. He moved slowly, guiding her to match his leisurely sway with a light hand on her hip.

It was more affecting than if he'd grabbed her. Something about Dani's inability to feel pain made her especially sensitive to pressure. It didn't hurt, not in a traditional sense, but the firmer the touch, the more her brain associated it with potential injury.

But the way Rafe was touching her, featherlight and so, *so* careful? That was pure, unadulterated pleasure.

His voice rasped close to her ear. "So how'd Clem rope you into waiting tables?"

Dani edged closer, erasing the slight distance between them. "She was busy, and I don't like to wait."

His body tensed against hers, reminding her of just how much of him was solid muscle. His eyes were dark liquid fire. "Is that so?"

"Which part confuses you? That Clem's busy on a Saturday night, or that I tend to get impatient when I want something?"

Rafe's fingers spread wide on her lower back, and several of the patrons in the bar whooped as he dipped her back so far her ponytail almost touched the floor. He held her there for what felt like forever before hauling her back up and into a spin that left her back pressed to his chest. "What do you want, Dani?" he murmured against her ear.

She touched his hand where it lay on her hip. Wordlessly, she tugged, pulling it up, just under the hem of her shirt. His fingertips teased across her skin, gentle and taunting at the same time.

His voice dropped, the sound rumbling through her. "What do you want?" he asked again.

The moment felt surreal, almost dreamlike. Like a fantasy playing out under the dim lights. "There's a room in the back," she whispered.

His breath shuddered against the back of her neck. Every muscle in his chest and arms felt like steel. For a heartbeat, she thought he really would do it this time. He'd say *yes*.

Instead, he sighed, low and wistful. "What if I want more?"

What did that even mean? More of what? Of *her*? She'd offered him everything, in word and in deed, and he kept holding out. For what—assurances? Promises she wasn't sure yet that she could even make?

Frowning, she turned in his arms. "How do we get there if we can't even—?"

Warning prickled at the back of her neck as the normal rhythms of the bar halted abruptly. The music played on, but the *sounds* of the room—the chatter of voices, the clink of glasses, the crack of pool balls on the tables—were gone. Rafe froze, too, his sleepy gaze vanishing into a soldier's alertness as he pivoted smoothly so they could protect each other's blind sides from an attack.

She saw immediately what had everyone staring in silence. A perfect copy of Nina stood in the doorway—her sister, Ava, flanked by two women Dani didn't recognize.

"Well," she murmured. "Let's hope everyone buys that they're twins."

The people of Five Points trusted Nina.

Rafe had known that in his bones—it was the reason they were safe here, in this close-knit community that had a charming habit of shooting down drones, and where even the criminals would choose death before they snitched to the TechCorps.

But *seeing* it sometimes still threw him for a loop. The denizens of Clem's bar watched the three clearly dangerous women enter the bar. Their gazes swung between Nina and Ava, assessing their identical features. They watched Nina rise with a smile and rush to hug her sister.

And they shrugged and got back to drinking. Twin or clone or alien, they didn't care. Nina trusted the newcomers, so they were safe.

Clone was the correct answer, though Rafe supposed that *sister* worked, too. Ava was a copy of Nina down to her toes. Or maybe Nina was a copy of Ava. Rafe wasn't sure exactly how it worked with clones. They were probably *both* copies of someone who'd lived decades ago. Nina and her two sisters had represented the sixteenth generation of their particular genetic strain, and with each iteration the Franklin Center had tinkered and tweaked, struggling in their efforts to create . . .

What? That was the eternal question. Rafe had done his best to research the Franklin Center after he and the other Silver Devils had settled in next door to Nina. Not because he didn't trust her—Nina would cut off her own arm before she'd hurt an innocent, and she went pretty far to protect the reluctantly guilty sometimes, too. No, he'd done the research because Nina was like them, a genetic experiment on the run. As the squad's intelligence officer, Rafe had wanted to know what they might encounter if the Franklin Center decided it wanted Nina back.

Unfortunately, gathering intelligence on a distant private facility that only deigned to communicate with their extremely exclusive clientele had proven challenging. Most of what he knew had come from Nina herself. The Franklin Center produced their clones in trios called clusters, with each member of the trio designated for a specific role. Nina had been A-designation, making her a warrior and leader. Knox had been the TechCorps' most accomplished fighter, his strength and speed legendary, and Nina could put him on his back nine times out of ten.

Her sister, Ava, was the B-designation of their cluster. Nina always breezily described Ava's role as *tactician,* but her skill set was clearly diverse and a little terrifying. She was a hacker so proficient Rafe had once watched her encode malware into strands of DNA, and she seemed qualified as a combat medic. She'd also made an offhand comment or two that made him think her unfathomable wealth had come from high-tech money laundering with a hint of corporate espionage.

They'd had a third sister, too—the C-designation, Zoey. Her skill set was even more of a mystery, though she'd apparently been genetically engineered for a level of empathy that bordered on psychic ability. Why an evil corporation churning out designer mercenaries would want a softhearted empath with superpowers was beyond Rafe, though.

Then again, Zoey hadn't survived training. So maybe they hadn't.

Perhaps the two newcomers could solve some of his remaining mysteries. Rafe turned to ask Dani if she recognized them, only to catch a flash of blond hair. She didn't *quite* use her superspeed to book it away from him, but she moved pretty damn fast.

Figured. With his blood heated and her body flush against his, he'd broken his self-imposed rule. He'd asked her for more than just sex.

And she'd bolted.

Deprived of the distraction of pleasure, Rafe sighed and turned his mind toward business. He drifted over to where Nina stood with her sister and the two mystery ladies, providing introductions to Knox.

"This is Phoenix," she was saying. "We . . . grew up together. And this is—"

"Beth." The shorter woman stepped forward with a beaming smile and grabbed Knox's hand in a hearty shake. "I'm so happy to finally meet you. I've heard so much."

No doubt she had, but Rafe doubted it was anything good. Ava tolerated Knox with appreciable hostility, her jealousy over Nina's affections nakedly obvious. Even now, Ava's brown eyes were narrowed, her mouth set in a firmly disapproving line, her body stiff. She could mimic Nina's warmth and openness if she really tried, but Ava's resting state tended to be . . . angry.

It made Beth's eager excitement all the more endearing. Knox returned her smile and her handshake. "It's good to meet you, too. Did you just get into town? It's late, but Clem can throw something on the grill, if you're hungry."

Beth sighed gratefully. "That would be fabulous. We came straight here, Ava was so eager to see Nina again."

Knox slid out of the booth and gestured to his abandoned spot. "Sit. I'll see what we can come up with."

Phoenix slid silently into the booth. Ava slashed a look at Knox before turning her back on him, her focus completely on her sister as she looped an arm through Nina's and drew her away for a low-voiced conversation.

That left Beth. Rafe held out his hand. "I'm Rafe. I'm sure Ava told you all about how charming and wonderful I am."

"Something like that." She shook his hand while blinking up at him. "You certainly are very pretty. Would you like to join us?"

Well, that was damn adorable. Rafe grinned and slid into the spot Syd and Max had vacated. "I would love to. I've tried to convince Ava to tell me more about both of you, but she can be very . . ."

"Bitchy?" Phoenix spoke for the first time. She was tall and slender, her skin deeply tanned, even in winter, and her dark hair held back in a sleek, no-nonsense braid. Her gaze raked over him with zero sexual curiosity, just precise, professional assessment. She offered him a cool smile. "It's part of her charm. You never have to wonder where you stand with Ava."

"She's protective," Beth corrected as she slid into the booth across from him, her warm tone edged with icy reproof. "Of us, and of Nina. Surely Rafe has noticed that last part."

That was an understatement. Rafe was pretty sure Ava would strike the match that burned Atlanta to the ground and not think twice about it, if that was what it took to protect her sister. *Protective* didn't even begin to cover it.

But it did present an interesting picture. Ava's sparse commentary on both women had allowed Rafe to sketch a mental picture of them. Phoenix, with her sleek danger and wary eyes, was about what he'd expected. Tough, assessing, bristling with knives—Rafe had clocked two in her boots, a belt knife, and a slight bulge under her jacket that made him think she wore quick-release forearm sheaths, too.

Beth, on the other hand . . .

From the way Ava had spoken of her, Rafe had expected someone closer to Syd's age. A mentor figure, someone with the years and gravitas to influence Ava's decisions. Someone she respected enough to want to impress.

But Beth couldn't be that much older than Maya. Thirty, at most, with big brown eyes and a sweet, open smile. Her pale golden skin was framed by straight black hair that fell loose and free around her shoulders. Unlike Ava and Phoenix, who'd arrived in black leather that looked like armor, she was wearing a stylish yellow bomber jacket over a black dress with white polka dots. Combat boots finished off her look.

Definitely an intriguing mystery.

And one he'd only figure out if he made friends. "I understand being protective," he admitted, tilting his head to indicate the booth where Conall had joined Gray and Maya. "I'd do anything to protect them."

Beth rewarded his admission with a grateful smile. She looked around, then leaned closer. "Okay. Give me all the good intel."

Rafe mirrored her, lowering his voice to a conspiratorial whisper. "Tactical or juicy gossip?"

"Um, hello. The gossip, *of course.*"

The delight in her eyes was irresistible. Rafe had no idea how this cheerful ball of glee had become Ava's most trusted confidant, but maybe it was just the sheer cute factor. He couldn't say no, either. "Well, I'm sure you know all about Nina and Knox. They're *adorable.* Knox found out Nina really likes Italian food, so he's currently working his way through a cookbook Maya found, making an exhaustive list of her favorites."

Beth sighed happily and propped her chin on her hand. "Go on."

"Have you heard about Maya?" At Beth's nod, he continued, "Gray has been helping her digitize and organize some of the books we recovered. Half the time when I go into the warehouse, he's in there reading her favorite books to her while she works. It's *painfully* sweet."

"I love it," she declared.

Of course she did. It was delightful, especially when Rainbow joined them, and Gray read from Maya's childhood favorite series about Marjorie Starborn and her friends fighting an evil corporation on the moon. Sometimes, Rafe just stood in the doorway, watching Rainbow stare up at Gray in rapt anticipation as he lowered his voice during a tense action scene or adopted a sinister tone for the evil villain.

Beth was staring at Rafe with the same sort of captive fascination, waiting for his next story. Rafe's gaze scanned the bar and snagged on Dani, who had joined Jaden's table and was undergoing what looked like an animated interrogation from Max. It was irrational to feel like she was pointedly ignoring him, but rationality never had much to do with Rafe's interactions with Dani. How could he even describe their situation to Beth?

Well, she stabbed me a little, then I betrayed her, and she still saved my life. And now, every time we touch, we burn hot enough to set the room on fire, but . . .

But he was an infatuated fool, and she was as skittish as a wild creature. Fight or fuck, those seemed to be the options on the table.

Rafe was the one who wanted friendship first.

The silence had dragged on too long. Phoenix was studying him with renewed interest, and he remembered the other tidbit Ava had dropped about her. Phoenix was also a C-designation, trained in empathy and observation. Best not to give *too* much away by gawking at Dani.

So Rafe smiled and cheerfully threw Conall under the bus. "You see that guy Dani is talking to?"

"The silver fox?"

"Mm-hmm. Conall has the biggest crush in the world on him."

Rafe silently apologized to Conall as Beth beamed with delight. But Phoenix just kept staring at him, her lips quirked in the tiniest smile, and he had the sinking feeling he hadn't fooled her at all.

Please join us in congratulating Andrew Ross on his promotion to vice president of Security. He has more than proven his worth during his tenure as acting vice president, guiding the company through troubled times into a period of renewed security and vision.

December 2086

FOUR

Breakfast had started getting fancy.

Ever since Knox had taken over the lion's share of the cooking duties, breakfast had gone from scrambled eggs and soy bacon to frittatas and chia muffins and roasted potatoes cooked in the drippings from pork sausages. The offerings were varied and, without fail, delicious.

And now, Rainbow was experimenting with the pancakes. Dani didn't know what the hell was in them, but she was *in*.

"Hit me," she told Knox.

"Good move." Knox tossed her a grin over his shoulder. "My sous-chef has invented several promising combinations."

Rainbow was currently dropping chocolate bits onto pancakes already swirled with mashed banana. "They *do* look particularly yummy," Dani complimented, and the girl beamed with pride. "I'll take mine with extra everything, please."

"You heard her, Bo. Loaded pancakes for Aunt Dani."

Dani took her plate to her customary seat near the end of the table and watched as Conall shoved three slices of bacon into his mouth without looking away from his tablet. "Hey. Leave some protein for the rest of us, asshole."

Conall waved his middle finger at her, swallowed, and finally looked up. "Good morning to you, too, Dani."

She rolled her eyes at him. "It's your ass if Maya and Gray come down late and there's no pig left."

He tilted his head. "I think I could take Gray, but there are a *lot* of forks on this table, and Maya fights dirty."

"Exactly."

Mace dropped into the chair across from hers. Conall was young, pretty, and personable, if a bit too nerdy for Dani's liking. Mace was just the opposite—older, a bit battered, and rude as fuck.

It was a weird combination for a doctor, and Dani liked him all the more for it. For one thing, he didn't always want to talk at the dining table. He didn't even greet her, and he just grunted into his steaming coffee mug when Conall spoke to him.

Infinitely preferable.

The door to the warehouse beeped open, then slammed shut, and slow, steady footfalls began to cross the room. Dani didn't have to look to recognize the rhythm of Rafe's stride.

She didn't *want* to know what it sounded like when he walked across a room. It just seemed to happen, the way everything else did regarding Rafe. Because she couldn't seem to help herself.

"Rafe!"

Rainbow's excited greeting was swiftly drowned out by Rafe's laughing growl. He swept her up, perched her easily on his hip, and examined the stove. "What do you call this masterpiece?"

"Banana Chocolate Swirl," she answered seriously.

"Looks delicious." He smacked a kiss to her cheek before setting her back next to Knox and grabbing an empty plate and the one Knox indicated, that was already listing under an impressive stack of pancakes. Rafe carried both to the table and slid into the chair next to Dani's. "Morning, y'all."

Mace grunted again, and Dani focused as much of her attention as possible on pouring syrup over her pancakes.

"Lord, you're a sorry bunch of grumps." Rafe stabbed two pancakes full of blueberries and dragged them onto his plate. "Where's Maya? At least she likes to talk."

"Maya and Gray haven't come down yet." Conall looked up from his tablet again and made dramatic air quotes with his hands. "He's *reading to her.*"

"Aw, don't be jealous, Con," Mace drawled. "Surely we can find someone to read to you, too."

Dani choked on her coffee, mostly at Conall's affronted look. But her amusement vanished in a flash of heat as she and Rafe both shifted at the same time, and their legs bumped together.

She froze. It was the only way to suppress her automatic shudder of reaction. As soon as the urge passed, she cast a sharp look at Rafe. But he only grinned, as if the warm pressure of her thigh against his was completely unaffecting, no big deal at all.

By the time he slowly, carefully moved away, Dani was livid. Not at him—that would have been easier, but childish. *She* was the problem here. Particularly the parts of her brain and libido that made terrible decisions.

Rafe, seemingly utterly oblivious to her conflict, was still teasing Conall. "So when *is* Max coming back for a visit?"

The techie blushed. "Fuck off, Rafe," he muttered as he reached for another handful of bacon.

That managed to draw Dani's attention away from Rafe's deep brown eyes. And the hard line of his jaw. And his hands. "Wait, Max as in Syd's right-hand man, Max? The one who was interrogating me like a pro at Clem's last night? Conall's got a thing for *that* guy?"

"Of course he does," Rafe retorted. He held up a hand and ticked off a list of attributes on his fingers. "He's growly, he scowls all the time, he could probably kill half of us in a fight, and he likes teaching weird physics to kids."

Conall threw a muffin across the table, aimed directly at Rafe's face. Dani reached out and caught it absently, still mulling over this revelation as she tossed it back.

The muffin hit Conall directly in the forehead and bounced onto the table. He blinked, then swore. "Fuck, sometimes I forget how *fast* you are."

She tilted her head. "Yeah. Maybe think about that before you tease Maya any more."

Conall held up both hands in surrender. "Never again," he promised. Then he swept up the battered muffin, broke it in half, and popped a piece into his mouth. "Plus, I can hear them on the stairs."

Maya came down from the landing, her hand folded tightly in Gray's. She still looked a little sleepy, but her smooth, dark face bore no signs of distress. There was no indication that she'd spent a sleepless night battling racing thoughts or a brain that wouldn't shut off. She seemed relaxed, which was new, and Dani made a mental note to do something nice for Gray.

It was the least she owed him for making Maya's nights more bearable.

Maya's face lit up when she saw the table. "Are those pancakes? With *chocolate*?"

"And banana." Dani slid the plate closer to Maya's end of the table. "Our Rainbow is a budding culinary genius."

Rainbow beamed from the stove. Maya shot her a thumbs-up before grabbing a plate and heaping it with food. Her fork hovered over the plate of bacon, and her eyes widened. "Wait, is this the real shit?"

"One hundred percent," Nina confirmed as she came in through the back entrance. She paused to kiss Knox's cheek and hug Rainbow before grabbing an empty mug. "Jaden Montgomery has started importing it. He has a new arrangement with a farmer west of town."

Dani marveled at the man's lack of fear as much as his resourcefulness. Most people wouldn't dare flout the TechCorps' rules, written *and* unwritten, about breaking their stranglehold on the local food economy. Nina was, of course, with the new community kitchen venture, but that was different. It was a quieter sort of rebellion, a way to stay under the radar while helping Five Points to become more self-sufficient.

Montgomery just said fuck that, raised his middle finger to the TechCorps, and started his own chains of supply. It was hard not to admire his courage.

"Amazing." Maya shuffled a few pieces of bacon over to her plate, claimed a seat, and took her first bite. Her eyes closed, and she made a blissful sound. "I could get used to this."

"We all could." Dani grabbed a couple of slices for herself before Conall attacked the platter again.

Nina brought her mug into the dining area, but stood at the head of the table instead of sitting. "What's on everyone's agenda for the morning?"

"Training." Dani's answer came in unison with Rafe's. She pinned him with a glare, but he looked equally surprised. "Nina and I are going to spar."

"I'm hitting the weight machines," he explained.

"Fine." It *was* fine. If they could stay out of each other's way.

"I'll be in the clinic," Mace offered. "Wells is coming by so we can hash out some of the logistics of working together."

"I have a meeting with a contact," Maya said, reaching for another piece of bacon. "It shouldn't be any trouble, but Gray's coming as backup."

"Arm candy," he corrected, deadpan.

"That, too," Maya agreed with a grin. "I'm thinking of getting him a cape so he can really dial the Gothic brooding up to fifteen. People will swoon wherever we go."

They were adorable—and also kind of gross. Dani met Conall's *see?* look with a mildly apologetic grimace, then finished off her pancakes.

"What about you two?" Nina asked Knox and Rainbow.

Knox flipped another pancake onto the plate Rainbow was holding for him and grinned. "We're taking Tia Ivonne over to the new place on Poplar so she can make up her dream wish list for the kitchen."

"And I'm going with them," Conall mumbled around a mouthful of bacon. His attention was riveted to his tablet again. "Gotta get a jump-start on measuring and wiring for the security system."

"All right, then." Nina sipped her coffee. "If anything goes wrong, raise the alert. That goes for everyone."

Dani drained the rest of her coffee, rinsed her empty plate, and left her dishes in the sink. She had just enough time to do her meditations. Maybe if she got herself centered enough, she'd be able to ignore Rafe's flexing muscles mere meters away while she and Nina were sparring.

Maybe.

GRAY

Having a nemesis was turning out to be really exhausting.

Up until a few months ago, Gray hadn't even known Cara Kennedy existed. If pressed, he would have certainly acknowledged that a Tech-Corps executive as important as Tobias Richter, VP of Security, must have had a data courier. But he'd never really *thought* about it.

He thought about it now—all the time, in fact. Ever since he'd killed Richter, he and Maya had been in a race to find Cara before she could find them. Literally *and* metaphorically.

The hell of it was, Gray understood the woman's ire. Richter had been more than Cara's boss. He'd raised her, had been the closest thing she'd had to a father. That was a keen loss, a sharply personal one that called for some old-fashioned, almost biblical vengeance. Still, it didn't seem quite fair, since Richter had been the one to come after them, not the other way around.

And it wasn't like Gray had killed him for no reason. The man *had* been torturing him.

He rubbed his arm, which still bore scars no amount of med-gel had been able to heal, and scanned their surroundings again. The cramped, loud alley behind a laundry was uncomfortable—but it was the perfect place for the hushed conversation currently taking place.

"It came down officially two days ago," Asha said, retying the scarf that covered her dark hair. "They gave Andrew Ross the VP of Security spot."

"No surprise there," Maya murmured. "He's bland and unimaginative, but Cara always had him wrapped around her little finger. If she was going to help anyone . . ."

"That's the odd part," Asha said. "She definitely *was* helping him—at first. But no one's seen her on his floor in weeks. I tried to get something more concrete for you, but no dice. She's moving in circles I can't access."

Maya's easy expression didn't falter, but Gray could feel the sudden tension where her body brushed against his. "Higher than VP?"

"Chief officers," the other woman confirmed. "I could try to feel someone out . . ."

"No." Maya clasped Asha's hand. "Don't take any risks, especially with high-level executive staff. Have you heard anything else?"

"Just rumblings. Something *big* is happening." Asha shrugged uneasily. "There are always rumors, you know that. Everyone wants to seem important, so they pretend they have a big secret. But this time feels different. People who don't usually talk big are acting like they know stuff, but no one will spill."

"I'll put out some feelers." Maya dipped into her pocket and pulled out a credit stick, silencing Asha with a stern look when she tried to protest. "Take it," she said, folding the woman's fingers over the credits. "If you don't need it, share it with someone who does. And be careful, okay?"

"I always am." The woman squeezed Maya's hand, gave Gray a distracted nod, then hurried away.

Gray was suddenly glad for the reassuring weight of the pistol in the holster beneath his jacket. "What do you think?"

"That I hope Asha is wrong." Maya shivered and wrapped an arm around Gray's waist, leaning into him. "Cara egging on the VP of Security was bad enough. But if she's worked her way into a chief officer's confidence . . ."

Gray felt a spike of irritation—not at Maya, bless her, who was only trying to correct injustices, or even Cara Kennedy and her vengeance quest.

No, he was pissed at a dead woman. Birgitte Skovgaard, former vice president of Behavior and Analysis, had drawn a helpless child into her revolution. She'd used Maya to store all the information and intelligence too dangerous to commit to paper or digital record. She'd made her an accessory to treason, put Maya's very life in danger.

And she'd done it all *knowing it was wrong*. Worse, she'd left her journal to Maya, a book that documented all her tortured feelings over the things she'd done.

So yeah, he was pissed. For Birgitte, the ends had justified the means. And no matter how awful she'd felt about using Maya the way she had, *endangering* her, she'd still done it.

Hell, she was *still* doing it. Cara's enmity for Maya had as much to do with their cancerous shared history as it did Richter's recent death. Birgitte had planted these seeds, and they were still bearing their blighted fruit.

Gray refused to let the legacy of Birgitte's choices harm Maya any further. It didn't matter if he had to stand between her and a freight train, he'd do it. But only a fool failed to do proper threat assessment. If Cara Kennedy was running with the highest executives in the Tech-Corps, that meant she had access to power. Power made protecting Maya harder.

He'd just have to step up his game.

"Come on." He tugged her closer as they reached the end of the alley, his gaze scanning the street for possible threats. "Let's go home."

Ross, Andrew: Consider this my official request that a data
courier's services be made available to me.

Shaw, Jennifer: We were under the impression that you had
inherited your predecessor's data courier.

Ross, Andrew: The chief operating officer has requisitioned the
services of DC-025. I'll need my own.

Executive Internal Network

FIVE

When the Silver Devils had originally secured the building next to Nina's, Rafe had planned on carving out space to install a workout room. Those plans had swiftly fallen by the wayside, partly because of triage—functional bathrooms and getting the clinic up and running had been the priorities—but also because it just seemed pointless.

Nothing he could build would come close to the state-of-the-art training paradise Nina had constructed for her team and shared so willingly.

Rafe lifted his feet to the plate in front of him and checked the digital display. Nina had been the last to use it, and her light toning workout of 1200 kg would do for a warm-up.

Finding workout equipment that could accommodate the demands of the biochemically enhanced was a struggle. Resistance equipment that went up to 5000 kg wasn't exactly available on the open market, and inquiring about it was about as subtle as setting off fireworks that read *Genetic Experiment Right Here, TechCorps*.

Somehow, Nina had done it. Rafe pushed his feet forward and felt the gentle stretch of muscles warming up. An easy start to his morning, just casually leg-pressing the weight of a small car.

Being a genetically enhanced rogue supersoldier had its perks.

As he got into a rhythm, he shifted his attention to the other side of the room. Nina and Dani had come in, both dressed in leggings and sports bras, and headed straight for the treadmills that folded down out of the opposite wall. While Nina was starting her warm-up with an effortless jog, Dani had gone straight for it, quickly building up to a near-sprint. He couldn't see the display indicating her speed, but if he had to guess, he'd clock it near twenty-five kilometers per hour.

And she wasn't even pushing herself yet.

Of course, Dani *couldn't* push herself much on this equipment. Even the superpowered treadmills topped out at fifty kilometers per hour, a punishing speed that skated the edges of his endurance. He'd reached it more than once on a mission, only to see Dani shoot by him in a blur. She might not be able to hold top speed for long, but when she engaged the full power of her heightened speed, she moved like gravity had given up its grip on her.

A peal of Nina's laughter dragged his attention away from his brooding. She and Dani had abandoned the treadmills in favor of kicking off their shoes by the sparring mat. Dani dropped to the mat and bent over the length of one leg until her nose was touching her thigh. Nina eased down into a backbend, then slowly lifted her legs up and over her head. She kept going only to land in perfect splits.

Dani muttered something that sounded like "save it for Knox," and Nina blushed *hard*.

Rafe bit his tongue and bumped the weight up to 1500 kg. The weight of a decent off-road vehicle.

"So what's it going to be?" Dani lifted her arm behind her head and tugged at it with her other hand, loosening her muscles. "Blades? Boxing? Grappling?"

"Just a few friendly punches," Nina replied. "Try not to fuck up my face, okay?"

"I would *never*," Dani swore, then launched herself at Nina.

The speed of it stole Rafe's breath. One moment, the two of them were standing there, stretching. Before his next heartbeat, they turned into a blur—pale and tan skin, blond and brunette.

He was faster than an average human. In battle, he could never tell if time slowed down or if he sped up. But it was more than adrenaline, more than just the heat of the fight—he knew what that felt like from the few times he'd tangled with other kids in his neighborhood before his implant.

His biochemically enhanced reflexes were fast. Nina's were faster. And Dani . . .

His heart thumped once. Dani and Nina rolled across the room in the time it took to shudder through a second beat, a whirlwind of grappling arms and judicious kicks. Nina was stronger than Dani by orders of magnitude, but Rafe knew from his own sparring bouts with Dani that strength did shit-all if you couldn't lay hands on someone.

It was really fucking hard to catch Dani if she didn't want to be caught.

But she'd already put herself in Nina's reach. Her speed didn't help her as much as her sheer grit and determination as they fought. When they finally broke apart, Dani held a knife—though where the hell she'd been hiding it was a damn mystery.

She grinned as she tossed it from one hand to the other. "Ready to practice evading a knife-wielding attacker?"

The blade glinted in the harsh overhead lights as they began to spar again. This knife was new, a high-tech departure from the simple carbon steel Dani usually preferred. Rafe had heard her discussing its merits with Gray—it was a powder metal alloy with high levels of vanadium and molybdenum, with excellent edge retention. Hard enough to make sharpening difficult, but easier to care for on a daily basis.

How she'd gotten hold of it was another mystery. Rafe had tried to source one after he'd overheard the discussion. For purely practical reasons, he'd told himself at the time. Not because he got a thrill when he managed to track down some impossible-to-find weapon that Dani coveted. Not because he held his breath in anticipation of the way her eyes would light up in naked, uncomplicated joy.

Bullshit, a mocking voice whispered inside him, and he silenced it by bumping the weight up to 1750. A decent-sized truck.

It didn't help. Rafe always knew when he was lying to himself, and lying about Dani was pointless. He'd been fascinated and frustrated by her from the first night they'd met—the night she'd showed off those impossible reflexes in a dangerous game of knives that left him with a tiny cut on the back of his hand and a deep respect for her deadly skills.

They sparked. God*damn,* they sparked. He'd known from minute one that she'd be the hottest fuck of his life. She would wreck his world and ruin him for all the people who'd come before. For all the people yet to come.

And then she'd discard him, because Dani didn't do long-term. Not with her fuck buddies. She saved all her unguarded affection and soft, misty-eyed gazes for Maya and Nina—and for her weapons, which was why he'd wasted a damn month trying to find that precious high-tech steel, and was still pouting over his failure.

Gritting his teeth, he bumped the machine to 2000 kg.

On the training mat, Nina ducked a swing and jumped out of the way of a quick stab. "Someone's feeling vicious today."

"Got to keep you on your toes. Isn't that the point of this?"

They clashed again, so fast Rafe could barely track the movement. Their long familiarity with each other's styles evened out the difference in abilities, turning the fight into something graceful and chillingly beautiful. Grace and power, deadly precision—violence stripped of its cruelty, distilled into liquid art.

Fuck, competence was hot.

Nina was panting by the time she held up both hands and shook her head. "That's it. I'm done."

Dani dropped her hands and drew back. *"Already?"*

"I have a million things to do today." Nina grabbed a towel and looped it around her neck. "If I keep pushing, all I'm going to want to do is take a nap. Moderation, Dani." She grabbed her shoes and slipped out of the room.

Slowly, Dani turned toward the weight machines, her cheeks flushed, her eyes sparkling with appraisal. "What about you?"

Danger. *Danger.*

Rafe bumped up the weight again and maintained his smooth rhythm. "I'm still warming up."

She stepped closer, peered down at the machine's display, and arched one perfect eyebrow. "Twenty-five hundred kilograms. Would you really rather leg-press four grizzly bears than spar with me?"

"A rhino," Rafe corrected, then grinned. "According to Conall. Or half a million of those pre-Flare quarters. Or a huge cargo van."

Dani shrugged. "You can just tell me no. You don't have to blame leg day."

Her voice held just a hint of delicious challenge, and Rafe let his gaze drift over her in spite of himself. Over the black leggings that fit like a second skin, revealing lithe, firm legs. The bare skin of her toned abdomen. Strong arms with incredible muscle definition. He'd seen Dani dangle from the edge of a building by one hand, using a grip he would have deemed insufficient to support the weight of a human.

She'd turned her body into a weapon and a trap, and Rafe could barely remember why he'd spent so long fighting temptation. He was personable and charming. He knew he was hot. His body was a weapon and a trap, too. He'd been so sure that if he strung out the game long enough, those impossible walls she put up between herself and the world would fracture and fall.

Fucking would be fun, but he wanted her to *like* him, dammit.

Maybe it was hopeless. Maybe the only way this game ended was with the best sex of his life and his heart in pieces at her feet. It might still be worth it.

But not like this. If he sparred with her with that glint in her eyes and flush of excitement in her cheeks, he knew exactly how it would end—half-clothed against a wall or naked on the damn floor. And he couldn't give in. Not until he figured out how to navigate the fallout without hurting the people they both loved.

"Tomorrow," he offered, his voice rougher than he'd intended. He increased the weight on the machine again. 3000 kilograms—about as much as a killer whale, according to Conall. "I need to get through my whole workout."

"Suit yourself, Morales." The singsong words lingered in the air—along with the scent of her shampoo—even after she collected her shoes and vanished.

His leg muscles strained. He held the weight there, letting it burn for a moment before slowly releasing it. The discomfort faded almost immediately, and he almost regretted it. It was hard to push his body to a state of wrung-out exhaustion these days, and as for burning through thwarted sexual tension . . .

With a growl, Rafe bumped the weight up to maximum.

Doing leg presses with the weight of a large elephant was a challenge, even for him. It took all his focus and strength to move smoothly, to truly test his limits. Discipline met resistance and overcame it—the story of his life.

Until Dani.

He could bend metal with his bare hands, flip a car without breaking a sweat, or lift a pre-Flare menagerie's worth of animals with his legs . . . and none of it got him one step closer to scaling the walls around Dani's heart.

Violette: Got a hot lead on a new contract, D. 12k in clean credits. Got time for it?

D: Local?

Violette: Athens.

D: Sure, why not. Send me the details.

Violette: White male, 1.8 m, 82 kg. Scar on front of left shoulder. Name's Paul Edgewood.

Violette: Make it look like an accident.

SIX

Everyone loved Montgomery Farms' Market Day, but for a host of different reasons.

The community at large enjoyed the selections of produce the Montgomery clan grew or smuggled into the city, as well as the meats and small-batch goods they sourced, like honey and butter. Those sorts of things were pricey, but they were fresh and they were *real*—a grand improvement, in Dani's estimation, over the processed foodstuffs sold at lower prices by the TechCorps.

But Market Day held other enticements. Maya and Conall liked to browse the vendors who dealt in secondhand tech. Their wares ranged from gently used but functional tablets and vid screens to busted machinery only good for harvesting parts. Gray was fond of the crafts, homespun fabrics and carved wooden utensils and hand-dipped candles. For Nina and Knox, the day offered a chance for them to socialize—and strategize—with Jaden Montgomery himself.

But Dani? Dani always came for the *food*.

She'd wander through the stalls, enjoying the scents of open flame and roasting vegetables. It was so foreign it almost seemed magical, how the proprietors of the stalls managed to take a scant handful of ingredients and spices and turn them into something delicious.

It wasn't like she didn't eat well at home. In addition to their fancy breakfasts, Nina was a decent cook, and Knox was straight-up *good*. But meals at home didn't have this sort of instant variety. She could walk down one aisle of the market and find boiled eggs with spiced salt or fruit ices, apple hand pies or smoked trout sandwiches on fresh sourdough rolls.

The child at Dani's side was equally impressed. Rainbow clutched at her hand, bouncing slightly as she gazed around the bustling food court.

Dani grinned down at her. "What should we try first? A fish sandwich? Some grilled vegetable skewers?"

"Chocolate!" Rainbow replied instantly. "Maya said there's a lady who makes *all kinds,* and when it's wintertime, like now, she has a *hot chocolate drink.*"

So much for balanced nutrition. "All right, bug. Let's get you sugared up."

They'd just accepted their insulated paper cups of steaming, chocolatey goodness from the teenager manning the till when Dani heard her name. She froze even before she recognized the speaker, red-hot fury searing through her veins.

She smiled down at Rainbow, passing her the second cup of hot chocolate. "Here, why don't you take this over to Rafe? I'll get another one."

The girl stared up at her with ancient green eyes, clearly not buying Dani's bullshit for even a nanosecond. But she complied without argument, crossing the busy flow of foot traffic to where Rafe stood, chatting with one of the crafters.

Only then did Dani turn around.

Lucas Taylor was tall and broad. He was attractive in a very conventional sense, if a little rough around the edges. His light brown hair glinted almost red in the bright winter sunlight, as did his beard, but his eyes, which usually sparkled with humor, were flat and worried.

As they fucking had a right to be, because Lucas Taylor had landed himself firmly on Dani's stab-on-sight shit list. Though he'd served as Jaden Montgomery's second-in-command for as long as she'd known either of them, his true identity and purpose had come to light: he had been a plant, working for the TechCorps all along, reporting directly to Tobias Richter.

And he'd sold them out, getting Maya and Gray tortured, and everyone else almost killed.

He started toward her. "Dani, I—"

"We are not having this conversation," she told him flatly, sidestepping his advance.

"I'm so sorry. You have no idea—"

"Don't." It had never been his place to tell her what she knew or didn't know, but now was an *especially* bad time to try. "God, I can't believe Jaden didn't shoot you in the gut and let you bleed out slow."

He tried again, his gaze pleading. "I did it to protect my family. But just enough. I could always scrape by, you know? If I fed Richter a little serious intel, I could keep him off Jaden's back. Off *all* of our backs."

He sounded sincere, and Dani believed him. After all, she'd seen it before. If a TechCorps exec wanted something, they never asked for it outright. No, first they secured your cooperation with *collateral*— usually by kidnapping or threatening someone you cared about. Standard operating procedure.

So yes, she believed him. But she still hated him. She hated his hypocrisy and his duplicity and his lies. But mostly? She hated that she'd ever been stupid enough to sleep with this asshole. To let him into even the tiniest fraction of her life.

Thank Christ she'd never told him the truth about who she was. She'd probably be on a cold steel table right now, deep in the bowels of TechCorps HQ, being systematically vivisected.

He was waiting, so she tilted her head. "Got it all off your chest now?"

Lucas dropped his hands and sighed. "I'm not asking for forgiveness. I know I don't deserve that. But I owe you, and I swear I'll make good on it."

"You owe Jaden," she shot back. "You owe him your entire worthless life. Leave me out of it."

"I do," Lucas said immediately. "But you, I didn't think you'd get caught up in it. Richter said—"

Oh, no. *No.* "If you tell me you trusted him to keep his word for even a millisecond, I really will kill you," she snapped. "And it'll be for your own good."

He had the sense to look away, shamed. "No, of course not. But you have to know that I had *no idea* he'd give a shit. It was just supposed to be about bringing in the Silver Devils."

Something about the way he said it—as if it didn't just excuse his actions, it made them right and proper—scraped at Dani. If things had worked out the way Lucas had planned, he wouldn't be sorry at all. If Richter had killed Knox and his men—

If he had killed *Rafe*—

She took a step toward Lucas that somehow turned into her hand locked on the front of his throat. Her muscles trembled as she fought the urge to squeeze, but she did curl her fingers in so that her nails pricked his flesh. "Stop talking," she snarled.

"What the fuck?" He stared down at her, bewildered.

"Saying that only the Silver Devils were supposed to die doesn't make it better."

"You're upset over a *Protectorate squad*? Since when do you—"

The roaring in her ears intensified, and she tightened her grip, cutting off his words along with his airflow.

A heartbeat later, a familiar hand covered hers. Brown skin, strong, elegant fingers, and a tightly restrained strength evident in the body almost touching hers all along her back. Rafe's voice was a gentle whisper against her ear. "Dani."

She shook her head. Lucas had earned this. He *deserved* it.

Rafe's fingers tightened around her wrist. Still gentle. Still coaxing, just like his voice. "Not here. Not like this."

Slowly, Dani became aware of their surroundings—and the people who had stopped to watch the scene unfold. Their expressions ranged from entertained curiosity to outright horror.

And some of them were *kids*.

She released Lucas immediately, flexing her fingers in Rafe's loose grip. "It's fine. I'm fine."

Rafe exhaled softly and straightened, his fingers ghosting up her arm before falling away. After a moment, he stepped up beside her, his easygoing mask firmly in place. "I don't know what you said to her, man, but maybe you should start apologizing your ass off for it."

"*No*," Dani said firmly. The last thing she wanted to hear was one more word out of Lucas Taylor's face. "He was just leaving."

"Right," Lucas said slowly. His voice was a little hoarse, but filled with the same dawning realization she saw in his eyes. "I was just leaving."

"Seems smart." Rafe's smile was dangerous. "Just a heads-up—most of us are willing to let bygones be bygones, but no power on this earth is gonna save you if Maya lays eyes on you."

"I was just leaving," Lucas repeated. But he stopped long enough to frown at Dani, his brow furrowed in misplaced concern. "I hope you know what you're doing."

He disappeared into the crowd before she had a chance to strangle him, after all, leaving her to vent her ire on Rafe. "*Most of us are willing to let bygones be bygones*? What kind of bullshit lie was that?"

Rafe sighed and rubbed a hand over his head. "It's not a lie," he replied. "Would I like to punch his face a few times? Sure. Would I stop Maya if she went after him? Maybe not. But *fuck*, Dani. We were Protectorate. You know what that means."

It meant he'd spent years acting as the far-reaching—and brutally effective—right arm of the TechCorps. Protectorate squads kept order as defined by their corporate directives, and meted out punishments disguised as justice. They helped their bosses maintain a stranglehold on Atlanta, making problems and people disappear with the same flat-eyed ease and efficiency.

It was terrible. Maybe even unforgivable. But it was still nowhere near as bad as what Lucas had done.

"You wore a uniform," she said finally. "And that's not an excuse. It's a statement. When people saw you coming, they knew what they were getting. So it's *not* the same thing, Rafe. Not at all."

"It's not the same," he agreed. "But nine times out of ten, selling out a Protectorate squad is the right move." He flexed his fingers, and the friendly mask cracked. Not his face, which remained politely pleasant, but his eyes—deep brown and endlessly angry. "Doesn't mean I like the bastard. He got Conall shot, got Gray tortured, and damn near broke Maya's heart. But when the TechCorps have their hooks in you, there's no right move. Just the least terrible one."

"You're a more forgiving person than I am."

"Maybe I've just done too much shit that needs forgiveness." He hesitated, then looked away. "I lied to you, too, Dani."

Her stomach flipped. "When?"

"When we met. Fuck, we lured you into a damn trap, same as Taylor did."

She couldn't help it—she laughed. "Is that what you think? Really?"

Rafe looked back at her, perplexed. "That's exactly what happened."

"No fucking way." She faced him squarely and crossed her arms over her chest. "We didn't know what you were up to—*never* would have seen that whole Ava thing coming, honestly—but we knew you were up to something. We *chose* to go along with it."

He didn't argue or automatically refute her words. Instead, he seemed to actually consider what she'd said, turning it over and over. Processing this new piece of information. "Okay," he said finally. "The betrayal isn't the same. You never trusted us, so it wasn't personal. But that doesn't make me better than Lucas, it just makes me lucky."

"Fair enough," she allowed. "But you have something else going for you, too."

"My roguish good looks?"

"I like you." It was a dangerous admission. It was also the truth. "A lot more than I ever liked Lucas, anyway."

Rafe's entire expression softened. His gorgeous brown eyes damn near sparkled. "Keep that in mind next time I show up to guard your back."

She would not smile. She *would not*. It would only encourage him. "You like to tempt fate, don't you?"

"Cupcake, it's my favorite damn thing." He tilted his head toward the vendor selling the hot drinks. "Rainbow gave your hot chocolate to Maya. Can I buy you a cup?"

He was *flirting* with her. Honestly flirting, not the performative, over-the-top bullshit that he seemed to wear like armor sometimes. Warmth suffused her chest, and she found herself on the verge of agreeing.

Then she turned and locked eyes with the kid working the counter. He stared back at her in naked fear for the span of a heartbeat before bending to occupy himself with hauling a fresh stack of cups from beneath the counter.

Of course he was frightened. She'd attacked a man right in front of him. In front of *everyone*. The kind of casual violence she'd exhibited wasn't normal, even for Southside.

Stupid, Dani.

"Actually, I have some things to do," she lied. "I should probably take care of that."

Rafe's easy smile didn't falter. "I'll keep you company."

"Some other time."

He stared at her for several long moments, like he was getting ready to call her bluff, then simply inclined his head and turned away. There was something almost sad about it, as if he knew what kinds of thoughts he'd be leaving her to wrestle with alone.

But, in the end, wasn't that how it had to be? Especially for someone like Dani. She'd signed away her right to be just like everyone else when she'd volunteered for TechCorps experimentation. And the necessity of that loss had been proven over and over—when the surgeries had broken her ability to fully feel, when her parents had abandoned her, even when her trainers in Executive Security had chosen to focus her training on assassination techniques.

Maybe that was the key to finally getting him to let go of all his dreamy-eyed ideas about loving Dani. She could tell him the truth, all of it—who she'd been, the monstrous things she'd done.

If Rafe judged himself so harshly for his past misdeeds, surely he'd despise her for hers.

SECURITY MEMO

Franklin Center for Genetic Research

Sending someone to Atlanta is always a risk, but TechCon is the only place where we can find buyers for discarded genetic strains in sufficient quantities. Given HS-Gen16-B's heavy interruption of our funding sources, certain risks have become acceptable. Dr. Long possesses the necessary skills to navigate the political landscape.

Dr. Reed, December 2086

SEVEN

Rafe loved the quiet moments after dinner.

Nina's loft was one open room on the ground floor, with an island separating the kitchen from the dining area. A scattering of worn but immensely comfortable chairs and love seats comprised the loose borders of an informal sitting room. Most evenings, their odd little family sprawled throughout the open space, and tonight was no exception.

Mace had retreated back to the Silver Devils' warehouse to inventory the new supplies Rafe had obtained. Gray and Knox were washing the dishes from the evening meal, their quiet conversation a low background murmur. The remains of dessert still sat on the table—two flavors of almond cookies along with a stack of peanut butter, because they were Rainbow's favorite.

Sometimes, Rafe liked to imagine how Knox's Protectorate trainers would rage if they could see their much-decorated star soldier ruling over a kitchen, developing contingency strategies for meal planning and obsessively perfecting a cookie recipe to a tiny child's exacting standards. That had always been their mistake with Knox. They'd seen his drive, his dedication, his ruthless commitment to achievement, but they'd never understood what motivated it.

Knox was a protector. Sometimes that meant covert operations in high-stakes battle situations. And sometimes it meant learning how to make your own peanut butter because a little girl who'd seen too much disappointment in her short life really wanted a cookie.

At one end of the table, Nina and Tia Ivonne had spread out a stack of note cards and were rearranging them as they prioritized crops for the community garden. Rafe struggled with the urge to leap to his feet and help when Ivonne rose to pick up the teapot and bring it back to her chair.

The older woman was looking healthier than he'd ever seen her. Her thick black braid was still laced with silver, but her golden skin had a healthy glow again, and her eyes danced with a light he hadn't seen in years.

Miracle heart surgery with a custom-grown biosynthetic organ was, apparently, one hell of an energy boost.

Rafe supposed he would have to forgive Nina's sister eventually. Ava had been the one to kidnap their biochem hacker, Luna, and hold her hostage. The terms had been simple: if they wanted to survive, they had to deliver Nina to a set of coordinates, alive and unharmed. Rafe had been willing to do anything to get Luna back, and not just because she was the only one trained to maintain the delicate chemical balance on their implants. Rafe had cared about her, and her Aunt Ivonne. Probably more than he should have, all things considered. But that was what Rafe did. He cared about people.

Ava did not care about people. Unlike Nina, who was deeply compassionate and loved easily, Ava had all the emotional warmth of an iceberg. But he supposed she also possessed an iceberg's hidden depths. While she had never explicitly apologized to Luna for kidnapping her, she *had* arranged to grow a synthetic heart from her aunt's DNA, then had paid a doctor for the transplant that had quite likely saved Ivonne's life.

Rafe didn't want to give her credit for it, but watching Ivonne laugh as she poured tea, her brown eyes warm and excited . . .

Well, even weird and creepy apologetic gestures counted, he supposed.

"Can you pass the blue?" Rainbow asked at his elbow, and Rafe swung his attention back to the colored pencils spread out in front of him. He plucked up four different shades and obediently held them out. Rainbow tilted her head in serious consideration before she chose a deep teal. "Thank you."

"You're welcome. What are you working on?"

"The coloring sheet Aunt Dani got for me," came the absent answer. Rainbow was already bent over her work, her expression set and serious as she checked a tablet for reference.

Rainbow's foray into art was a new interest, and she approached it the way a child immersed in tactical training from the cradle approached everything: with precision, attention to detail, and a great deal of recon.

The coloring sheet in front of her displayed a rainbow arching over a storm-swept ocean, with a tiny oasis and a single slanted palm tree on one side. She'd colored in her namesake rainbow first, bright and vivid, but had taken time to research the correct colors for stormy waters. She carefully colored inside each line, her lower lip caught between her teeth in concentration, and the pang of memory was so intense, Rafe had to look away.

Tessa had only been eight when he'd left to join the Protectorate, probably the same age as Rainbow. But his younger sister had been an artist bred in the bone already, obsessed with color from the time she managed to wrap her fingers around a paintbrush. Painting supplies had been so expensive, but that hadn't stopped her. She'd mixed her own colors from flowers or clay or berries, anything she could get her hands on.

He hadn't been able to spoil her with fancy colored pencils or oil paints, not until far later, when he snuck home to steal an afternoon with his family, leaving behind credits and art supplies and a hollowed-out place in his heart filled with snapshots of a family swiftly growing up without him.

It had been almost six months since they'd escaped the Protectorate. Maybe there was time to sneak away and see them. Maybe—

The whisk of a blade against a whetstone brought him back to reality. Cookies and coloring sheets made for an idyllic scene, but Dani dominated the far end of the table with her knives spread out before her.

There was nothing domestic or safe about watching her hone her knives. Every graceful movement was dangerously erotic, and *not* something he needed to be looking at straight on with Rainbow tugging at his sleeve to pick her next color.

He held out a selection of greens for her and let Conall and Maya's voices cover the seductive *whisk* of Dani's knives. Listening to them exchange data on some esoteric TechCorps issue was the opposite of hot. They had six different tablets spread out around them in an uneven arc, and a holographic display between them, over which they exchanged cryptic half sentences that made sense to no one but them.

"But they're probably—"

"No, I thought of that."

"L2s?"

"Same issue. We could try—"

"Nah, geolocked. I actually had an idea about that, though. A—"

"Drone? It could work. Because it's still just—"

"Right, right. Exactly. Wait, let me look something up."

They fell silent for a moment, then Maya breathed a curse. "Ugh." She threw her tablet down with a clatter. "This is the third time I've received an urgent message from a contact saying *something* big is in the works, but no one knows what it is."

The gentle rasping of metal over stone ceased as Dani paused in her sharpening. "You think we should contact the Professor? He *did* say we'd need someone on the inside."

Maya looked to Nina for guidance. "What do you think?"

Nina hesitated, tapping a note card against her chin. "Not yet. We're still not sure we can trust him, but even if we can . . ."

"It's best to save him for a rainy day," Dani finished for her. "He might be a single-use asset."

"Fair enough." Maya returned to glaring at her tablet.

If Rafe had his way, they'd make the Professor a *never*-use asset. There was something about him that set Rafe's instincts to screaming, and it wasn't just the fact that he dressed like a spy from another century and thought *John Smith* was a great alias. And it wasn't that he'd come out of the same wacky genetic experiment that had created Nina, either. *She* never bothered Rafe.

Maybe it was the fact that he was an earlier model. Before the Franklin Center had realized that splitting their genetic tinkering into three main areas of focus might be the best way to optimize a human, they'd put all their eggs in one basket—so to speak. John was one of their original attempts, a genetic creation with all of Nina's warrior skills, Ava's icy intellect, and, supposedly, all of the warm and cuddly C-designation empathy.

If John was capable of warm and cuddly, Rafe hadn't seen it. But the bastard was clearly playing a long game none of them entirely understood, never mind that he'd dropped them all on the game board spread out in his imagination. The only thing Rafe trusted the Professor to do was whatever was in the Professor's best interests.

If only they could figure out what the fuck that was.

Maya sighed. "I didn't want to pull the trigger on this yet, but I might have to. I need to figure out a way to get in touch with Birgitte's mentor."

Rafe sat forward, every instinct abruptly alert. "Birgitte's mentor?"

"Helen Anderson," Maya confirmed. "Vice president of Research and Development. I didn't know the whole story until I got hold of Birgitte's journals, but apparently one of Richter's pet Protectorate monsters flipped out, murdered his entire squad, and took out Anderson's grandson, too. She might not be a full-on revolutionary, but she's definitely sympathetic."

"So . . . ?" Conall raised both eyebrows. "How do we get in touch with her?"

"Fuck if I know." Maya propped her elbow on the table and dropped her chin to rest on her hand. "If it were easy, I already would have done it. Birgitte left verbal passcodes, but Anderson never comes off the Hill. She's usually hip deep in Ex-Sec, and TechCon starts in . . ." Maya checked her watch. "Five days. So it'll be at least two weeks before I even have a shot at contacting her."

TechCon was a yearly gathering of the richest, most ethically dubious innovators on the Eastern Seaboard. Eight straight days of the TechCorps' power players mingling with the worst and brightest postcollapse America had to offer. No doubt the criminals who'd turned Washington, DC, into their debauched playground would be out in force. So would the geneticists from places like the one that had created Nina and her sisters. Every petty warlord and city-state despot who ruled the lawless territory that bordered the Appalachians would be looking for weapons, and so would the captains of every private mercenary company that had formed when the faltering US government had privatized all military bases east of the Mississippi. And *all* of those violent assholes would be selling their murderous, morality-free services to anyone who wanted a private army.

Even the reclusive trading clans who ruled the Mississippi River supposedly showed up, bringing exotic trade from the distant Republic of California and the odd cultlike cities that had sprung up in the Great

Basin. There were endless opportunities for mischief and crime for anyone with dangerous technology to sell or the credits to buy it.

Rafe couldn't decide if it sounded amazing or horrifying.

"I've been to TechCon before." Dani set her knife aside and wiped her hands. "Security's not as tight as you think it'd be. Rich people don't like too much electronic surveillance, not when it's pointed at them. If you could get in . . ."

Okay, so *attending* didn't sound all that appealing. But *infiltrating*? Excitement sparked inside him. "There's no facial recognition?"

She shook her head. "It's mostly Executive Security, personal bodyguards, that sort of thing. The whole event is a party for them—a little work, followed by a *lot* of play. And they don't want anything getting in the way of their fun. Or recording too much of it."

The idea formed as easy as breathing. Dani had been out of Ex-Sec a long time—long enough to be a stranger to most of them, given their short life expectancies. But even if she needed to be disguised, Rafe had witnessed firsthand her ability to disappear into a new persona. She could stroll into an executive party on the Hill and make them believe she was one of them.

So could he. It wasn't like a Protectorate soldier spent much time rubbing elbows with the rich and powerful. Most of the Silver Devils' missions had taken them far beyond the boundaries of Atlanta. And Dani wasn't the only chameleon in the room. "We could totally do it."

A hint of a smile curved the corner of her mouth. "We'd need supplies, and quick."

"Five days?" He waved a hand with a wicked grin. "I could do it in forty-eight hours. Supplies, I can get. But to really sell it, we'll need a penthouse."

"Good thing I keep one in my pocket for emergencies," Dani deadpanned. "Seriously, where the hell are we going to get a penthouse in less than a week?"

"From the kind of asshole who already has one," Rafe retorted. "You know, about one-point-eight meters, looks like your best friend. You dream of peeling off her face."

Conall choked on a laugh. "Ava?"

Behind Rafe, the soft beep of the front door's keypad sounded.

Maya's laughter joined Conall's. "Speak the name of the devil, and she appears."

Frowning, Rafe twisted in his chair and watched Ava stalk into the dining room. She had left a few hours ago when her apparent tolerance for sharing a roof with Knox had reached its limit. That was how Ava operated: swoop in, soak up Nina's joy, and grow more and more agitated as claustrophobia set in. Then she usually split.

But now she was back, flanked by a blank-faced Phoenix and an eternally cheerful Beth.

Unexpected, but perfect timing. He jabbed a finger at her. "We need to borrow your penthouse."

"You can't," Nina's sister replied in her iciest voice.

"Ava, don't be a—"

"You *can't*," Ava repeated, interrupting Rafe. "Because there are three Protectorate squads sitting on top of it. They almost ambushed us going in."

"What?" Dani rose, her hand dropping to the hilt of one of the knives on the table. "Why?"

"Because Nina is now near the top of the TechCorps' high-value targets list." Ava stripped off her gloves and folded them into her jacket pocket. "And they clearly think I'm Nina."

PHOENIX

Looking at Nina actively hurt, so Phoenix decided not to do it.

There were plenty of other people to focus on as Beth bounced back into the sitting room and claimed a seat next to Conall and Maya. She'd been reluctant to leave in the first place and was delighted to return, because unlike Phoenix and Ava, Beth *thrived* on being near the chaotic family Nina had assembled for herself. Not even a near miss with a hit squad could dim Beth's inner enthusiasm.

Sometimes she made Phoenix feel a thousand years old.

So did Nina's techie. Phoenix knew from Ava's reports that Conall was competent at his job, but she'd only needed five minutes at the bar to recognize what he was at heart: a puppy. Sweet and eager to please, with big eyes and frenetic energy around him that might as well have been a constantly wagging tail. He watched Ava with a combination of awe and terror that clearly pleased her—Ava's tendency to conflate fear with respect was a liability. Her tendency to prefer fear over respect was her personal tragedy.

Unfortunately for Ava, no one else in the room seemed particularly afraid of her. Nina's ex-Protectorate lover certainly wasn't. Phoenix had been circulating on the Hill long enough to know about the infamous captain of the Silver Devils. If Ava had bothered to *ask* before going on her reckless revenge bender, Phoenix would have told her that hiring the man was a mistake—everything about Garrett Knox's psychological profile *screamed* that he was a man looking for hope and redemption. Nina might as well be both, distilled into human form.

Of course she'd won him over. Of course he loved her. Phoenix could relate. Though even Nina paled in comparison to the liquid sunshine that had seemed to pulse through her sister Zoey's veins. Zoey had lit up every room she walked into. Even the gray, grim training rooms at the Franklin Center had sparked with possibility when Zoey leaned close and smiled.

Phoenix had loved her before she'd understood what *love* even was.

That brought the pain rushing back, so Phoenix shut it down and fell back on her Franklin Center training. Classify, calculate, control.

The sniper had crossed the room to hover protectively behind Maya. He was the one she'd focus on, if it came to a fight. The quiet, watchful one—the secret weapon. Phoenix didn't need to see Gray's file to know he'd stymied the profilers. His mask was exquisite. They'd probably thought he was disaffected, at best, and a straight-up sociopath, at worst. But she could *feel* the locked-down emotion in him, like a dormant volcano trembling beneath her feet.

But he still wasn't the most dangerous person in the room. That honor went to the icy blonde, Dani. Oh, she was *glorious*. Like a blade honed so sharp you wouldn't feel the kiss of it until she'd cut you to the bone.

If she hadn't so obviously been tangled up with Rafe, Phoenix might have propositioned her in the bar that first night. If Rafe's infatuation had appeared to be one-sided, she still might have. But even now, Dani was *aware* of him in a way that seemed to subtly shift the gravity in the room. Dani hadn't sprung into a protective posture the way Gray had, but Phoenix would bet all of Ava's money that if she lunged at Rafe, she'd end up with at least one of Dani's knives sticking out of her.

She was almost agitated enough to try it.

Nina's voice intruded again, bringing the inevitable ache with it. It was amazing how she could sound so much like Zoey, while Ava rarely did. Probably because Ava would have coolly demanded a sitrep, whereas Nina's voice was soft with worry. "Was anyone hurt?"

"No, we're fine," Beth assured her. "Just a little displaced at the moment. But I told Ava this is actually great, because while those squads are there, they're not out causing other trouble. Am I right?"

"I mean, I'd rather they're staking out an empty penthouse than *our* house," Maya said. She slid a plate of cookies toward Beth in obvious invitation. "I'm kind of surprised Ava didn't just murder them all, though."

That would have been Phoenix's preference. Three squads of bio-chemically enhanced soldiers might have been a little more than she usually liked to tackle, but the three of them likely could have pulled it off with minimal injuries. Ava would have taken the risk if Beth hadn't been with them. Not that Beth couldn't fight. Her short, curvy body hid the same genetically enhanced strength and reflexes as everyone else who had come from the Franklin Center, and what she lacked in viciousness she made up for in brutal protective instincts.

But unacknowledged feelings made people irrational—something Phoenix had hoped Ava would have figured out by now.

For a genius, Ava could be remarkably obtuse.

"It wasn't strategically optimal," was all Ava said as she shrugged out of her jacket and folded it across the back of a chair. "But it means the TechCorps is running facial recognition scans for Nina. Not just on current surveillance, but old footage, too."

"I always assumed they might be," Nina said, then sighed. "But I guess things are a little different now, after the Richter situation."

"I thought I'd purged all the recordings from that conflict," Conall said with a dark scowl. "Cara Kennedy must have swiped some video before she bolted."

"Or they found the video Lucas Taylor gave Richter," Maya pointed out. "The *why* doesn't matter. Good thing there's no ground surveil-lance in Southside. They don't have the resources to run satellites full time, and we keep shooting down the drones."

"Isn't that rather obvious?" Ava asked. "If I were looking for you, I'd focus on places where my drones were being compromised."

Rafe laughed. "It might be obvious, if that wasn't the usual state of things." He winked at Ava. "Why the hell do you think Nina settled here? These charming assholes in Five Points have been shooting down TechCorps drones for decades."

"Plan now, flirt later." Dani's flat tone proved Phoenix's instincts correct. She wasn't just protective, she was possessive. Interesting. "What are we going to do for cover if we can't use Ava's penthouse?"

Ava's brow furrowed. "Cover for what?"

"To infiltrate TechCon," Nina answered simply. "We need to make contact with a potential ally on the inside."

Beth's smile somehow grew even brighter. "Oh, that's easy! Phoenix is going."

Every gaze in the room seemed to swing toward her in unison, and Phoenix carefully kept her exasperation from showing on her face. Beth might be a B-designation, genetically designed and brutally trained for the same cool intellect that Ava possessed, but nothing about Beth was cold *or* calculating. She was a chaotic bundle of sunshine and earnest enthusiasm, and she *loved* to help people.

All people. All the time.

And she dragged Phoenix and Ava into it without hesitation.

Phoenix parted her lips, but Ava saved her from having to ask the most awkward question in her usual blunt manner. "Conall and Maya would be recognized, and Knox would give himself away as military in under five minutes."

"Gee thanks, Ava." Rafe wasn't fake-flirting anymore. He looked genuinely affronted. "But we're actually not completely inept. Dani and I are going to go."

Oh, shit.

"TechCon isn't a game," Phoenix told him. "You're talking about the sleaziest, cruelest, richest fuckers on this continent getting together to do designer drugs, plan crime, fuck the help, and trade people like us back and forth like collectible art."

"I know," Dani fired back. "I was Ex-Sec."

Phoenix froze, factoring that into her mental profile of Dani. Not just a former assassin with enhanced speed, then. She must have come out of the TechCorps, one of those wild 55 series of experiments where they took apart your body and put it back together funny just to see what would happen. If they'd made her an executive bodyguard afterward, she'd likely seen *everything*. Nothing on the Hill rattled Ex-Sec after the first six months. If you *survived* the first six months. Few seemed to.

Dani apparently had.

Phoenix blew out a soft breath. "TechCon is my hunting ground. One of the main commodities on offer is genetically enhanced—" She broke off, glancing at the end of table, where a kid sat there, a coloring sheet in front of her. Her red pencil was moving back and forth on part of a rainbow, idly coloring over the same spot. She was definitely listening.

Great. "Materials," she finished awkwardly. "I have a target this year. The person at the Franklin Center who's been selling us off when they don't want us anymore. I won't sacrifice that goal."

"No one's asking you to," Rafe said. "Get us in the door, and we'll work the room. Trust me."

That, she didn't doubt. Dani's lethal beauty would draw them in like flies to poisoned honey, and Rafe . . . Phoenix could number the men she'd found physically attractive on one hand without even using all of her fingers, but Rafe was *stunning,* and it wasn't just his body or his face. It was charisma, the thing you couldn't teach because it came from a place deep inside you that genuinely found people fascinating and delightful. Rafe could turn a smile on you and make you feel like the bright shining center of the galaxy.

Phoenix recognized the trait. C-designations were custom designed for it, for that naked vulnerable heart that loved the world no matter what abuse it heaped on you, that beat and beat and beat, pumping weakness through your veins long after the curse of feeling *so fucking much* had crushed your spirit into dust.

It was what made her so very, very good at her job. And Rafe would be, too.

But that wasn't what made up Phoenix's mind. It was Nina, staring at her with that *look* . . .

Zoey's look. Hopeful and determined. Gentle and generous. Not making demands, because she was already sure that you would be the best version of yourself. How could you be anything else when someone like Zoey loved you?

Phoenix wasn't the young woman who had loved Nina's sister anymore. But apparently she still couldn't say *no* to that face. "I'll do it," she said, breaking the tense silence. "You can stay with me, and I'll use my credentials to get you in. But if I'm going to bring you, we're building out complete personas, and I get final say over the styling and disguises. And if I think you're going to get yourselves killed, I'm pulling the plug."

Dani frowned. "Acceptable terms. Rude, but acceptable."

"Works for me," Rafe added. "Though I thought C-designations were supposed to be soft and cuddly."

His generous mouth curved in an easygoing smile, but those dark brown eyes sparked with challenge. Phoenix had been in the game too long to miss the subtle power play. With one casually dropped sentence, Rafe had made it clear he knew what she was, and moreover had the skills necessary to have extracted said information from a no-doubt unwitting and unhelpful Ava.

Maybe he wouldn't get himself killed up on the Hill, after all.

This is the tenth year in a row that my budget has been decreased while security's has been expanded. I must ask, given the fact that we control this city and everyone within several hundred miles, what has us so frightened that we require multiple standing armies to face it.

The Protectorate was created to serve the science. Now it seems like everything we produce serves the Protectorate. When did we stop innovating?

Internal Memo, January 2070

EIGHT

Dani didn't get nervous. It was a waste of her time and her energy, and she had better things to do with both. Still, as she stood in front of Rafe's bedroom door, she couldn't deny a certain *fluttery* feeling in her gut that felt a hell of a lot like nerves.

The door had a deep gouge in it. Though it was solid, sound wood, remnants of at least four layers of stripped paint still clung stubbornly to the grain. It was secondhand, of course, bought from a junk dealer or scavenged from a nearby building. The Silver Devils had directed most of their resources toward the clinic downstairs, leaving their living quarters sorely neglected.

At least Rafe *had* a bedroom. Knox and Gray hadn't bothered, since they spent their nights with Nina and Maya, anyway. Conall slept . . . *somewhere*, and Mace had installed a cot in a back room of the clinic. They had a very nice bathroom, expansive and light, with hand-glazed tile walls and floors. But that was where the indulgent amenities ended. Everything else, from the kitchen to the workout facilities, they used next door.

She was stalling. *Fuck*.

She rapped her knuckles against the door harder than she'd intended and winced at the noise. "Open up, Morales."

His voice came immediately, warm and amused. "Come on in, Dani."

She flung open the door and immediately regretted most, if not all, of her life decisions.

Rafe's room was huge, easily twice the size of hers, the wood floor bare except for one soft-looking area rug. He had a large desk against one wall, laden with books and tech, with the painting his younger sister had done hanging over it.

The only other piece of furniture in the room was the gigantic bed covered with a pristine, fluffy white duvet. It even had a headboard. Like the door, it was made of reclaimed wood, though that was where the similarities ended. This wood had been lovingly polished, with small shelves and even a reading lamp attached.

The lamp was the only light in the room. It gleamed off Rafe's chest where he lay, shirtless, propped up against that fancy headboard.

Double fuck.

He smiled and lifted his tablet in one hand. "Just doing the homework Maya gave me."

Dossiers, no doubt. She'd been handed the same files with an admonition to at least *try* and study them this time instead of winging it. "Do you have a minute?"

"Sure." He swung his legs over the edge of the bed and nodded to the chair at his desk. "Take a seat."

"I'm okay here." Close to the door. Then again, she was also close to the bed. And him. "Do you need a shirt?"

Silence. Rafe studied her for a moment, then leaned down and hooked a T-shirt from the basket of clean laundry at the foot of his bed. His muscles bunched and flexed as he dragged it over his head.

Her stomach fluttered again, but at least he was mostly dressed now. "We need to talk. Before Nina sits us down and *makes* us talk, I mean."

"About the mission?"

"Yeah, about . . ." She waved a hand between them. "This."

Silence filled the room again, heavy and tense, and all of Rafe's lazy playboy charm seemed to melt out of him. "This," he echoed, and his voice seemed lower. Rasping. *Intense.* "Are we done pretending there's not a *this* here?"

She should have waited until he was in the kitchen or the warehouse to approach him. Anyplace where she wouldn't have been staring at his headboard.

She looked away—from the bed and from him. "You know what I mean. The flirting. It's fun and all, but it's a distraction. We can't afford any of those, not up on the Hill."

"Is that all we're doing?" It didn't sound like a challenge. More like a question he wasn't sure he wanted the answer to. "Just flirting?"

Not by choice, at least not on her end. The pull had been there from the very beginning—even when she knew he was bad news, just not what kind—and she'd tried to act on that attraction. She'd propositioned him so many times that even thinking about it now made her squirm with embarrassment.

But Rafe always shut her down. Not because he didn't want her. His eyes burned with lust, and he always moved a little too close to her, as if his body was actually magnetically drawn to hers. But he didn't just want sex. He wanted *vows,* and Dani couldn't. She didn't even know if forever existed; how was she supposed to offer it to him?

No. She never made a promise she wasn't sure she could keep.

"You're the one who drew this line," she reminded him softly.

"Okay." His expression remained neutral, but she caught the flash of resignation in his eyes. "Well, we've never had a problem keeping things straight on a mission. The job is the job, right?"

"Come on, Morales. It's not the same as running an op with the rest of the crew. It's *undercover.* That shit can fuck with your head, make you mix up what's real and what isn't." She swallowed hard. "And we're going to be working together. Closely."

"It's the job, Dani." He rose and prowled toward her, and this still wasn't his easy, flirtatious playboy act. He moved with lethal grace, closing the distance between them. He was probably moving quickly, but to her, it felt like slow and inexorable motion. "Doesn't matter if we're running an op, going undercover, or sitting at the damn dinner table."

He stopped so close she could feel the heat of him all along her body. One hand splayed out against the wall next to her head, and his voice dropped to an intimate rasp. "You're deadly, and you're competent as hell, and it's *hot.* Is it going to fuck with my head? Yeah." His slow, fond smile pinned her in place, even though she knew she should put some distance between them again. "But I won't do anything that puts you at risk. Or myself. The job comes first."

"Good." It came out low, breathless, and she couldn't look away from his *mouth.* "Because it doesn't matter how important the mission is. If we come back dead, Maya's going to be pissed."

"She already brought Gray back from the brink of death," Rafe agreed. "I wouldn't put it past her to resurrect us just to murder us herself. So let's not take any chances."

He lifted his free hand, and for a heartbeat she thought he was going to touch her cheek. But he pushed back off the wall with an easy flex of muscle and held his hand out to her. "Truce? I won't poke at you."

In her mind, she knocked his hand aside, backed him toward the bed, and rode him down to the mattress. Her cheeks heated and she swayed toward him, locking her muscles as every sweaty moment of the scene played out in loving, pornographic detail. He wouldn't turn her down, not this time. Not with the taut, simmering tension that hung in the air.

But she didn't push him toward the bed, and that was the moment Dani knew they could get this done. They could infiltrate TechCon, make contact with Maya's potential ally, and make it home unscathed. They could *control* themselves.

So she grasped his hand. "Truce."

His hand was warm, his grip firm. His wicked, teasing smile was *different*, sharper somehow, as if his aggressive flirtation had always had a layer of distance built into it, and he'd stripped that away. "I notice you didn't agree not to poke at *me*."

"Because I'll inevitably do it by accident." She shrugged. "Any promise like that would be a lie."

"That's okay." He held her hand for a moment longer before releasing it. "I kinda like it."

Her skin still buzzed from the contact. "I know, Morales. Trust me, I know."

He chuckled, the sound making her stomach clench. "You wanna talk dossiers now, or save it for when we're on the Hill? If Phoenix knows our targets, she can probably give us insight." He turned back to the bed and casually sprawled across it, as if they hadn't just had an entire encounter so rife with sexual tension that Dani's bones ached.

She had to admire his ability to turn it on and off. It was the one thing she'd never managed to master, not when it came to Rafe. "Why do you think I'm not studying already? Phoenix is a C. I'm not staring at a screen until my eyes bleed when she can tell us everything we need to know."

"Fair enough." He tilted his head. "I have to admit, I'm kind of intrigued to see what a penthouse on the Hill looks like. The Board didn't exactly want Protectorate soldiers tracking blood and mud across their fancy floors."

After a moment, she pulled out the chair at his desk and sat backward on it. "Depends on the penthouse. Some of them are very sleek and modern. Stark. Others are just tacky piles of antiques and velvet furniture."

"I suppose you saw plenty as Ex-Sec."

"I saw a lot of things." Working in Executive Security was mostly boredom and monotony punctuated by short periods of fear and disgust. "I was lucky. I wasn't in for long, and I spent most of my time being studied. I was too scientifically valuable to waste on high-risk execs, so they mostly assigned me to the low-key ones. Not a lot of action, not a lot of secrets."

"Scientifically valuable," he echoed, the humor gone from his eyes. "I know what that means. Conall was *scientifically valuable* too. Knox never says it, but he burned up a lot of favors to protect him from the scientists."

"I bet." If she had a credit for every slice, burn, or electric shock they'd inflicted on her in their labs, she could flat-out *buy* the Tech-Corps, and no one would have to worry about their bullshit ever again. "They never let me keep my scars. Sometimes I wish they had."

Rafe's expression didn't change. But the tablet in his hands shattered.

For a moment, Dani stared at the bent housing and spiderwebbed screen, biting back a reflexive apology. She'd said too much, had forgotten all the things he didn't know.

She'd forgotten that her pain mattered to him.

Instead of apologizing, she rose and pushed the chair back into place. "I should go. There's a lot to do before we leave."

"Dani—"

"We'll coordinate more at breakfast." She reached the door and hauled it open, but leaving this way felt too much like fleeing. "Does that work for you?"

He nodded shortly. "Breakfast. See you then."

Now that we know they're alive, it's time to start tracing them back through the past few months. Start with known crime scenes. Pull all associated DNA and run comparisons against the entire Silver Devils squad.

Internal Memo, October 2086

NINE

Rafe thought he was prepared for the wasteful luxury of a penthouse in the heart of the Hill's most exclusive district.

He was wrong. So, so wrong.

A circuitous meander through Southside shook loose any potential surveillance. Phoenix led them to a clothing shop on the Perimeter for a quick change, then a swift trip to the roof where she summoned an AirLift.

Rafe had spent plenty of time traversing Atlanta in military transports, which tended to be starkly efficient. The high-end automated transports that zipped around the Hill were decadent by comparison, with climate-controlled interiors, leather seats with heating and cooling options, and a complimentary bar stocked with an impressive array of exclusive liquors.

Phoenix barely seemed to notice. Neither did Dani. Her gaze stayed fixed out the tinted windows, watching as the buildings around them grew taller. Sleeker. More dangerous.

Straight into the heart of the monster.

Their AirLift made a gentle turn, decelerating slowly before alighting on a brick mosaic courtyard. The doors slid open in silence, revealing a waist-height row of flowering hedges that were the only thing separating Rafe from a deadly 600-meter plunge to the street below.

"Welcome to hell," Phoenix murmured, hooking her duffle bag and slipping from the transport.

Great, *that* was encouraging.

As soon as they slipped from the vehicle, the AirLift departed, leaving the three of them standing in the bright midmorning sun. Rafe turned away from the city and took in the secluded paradise clinging to the side of concrete and glass.

Whoever had designed the courtyard had been brilliant. If he hadn't *known* he was over half a kilometer up in the air, he would have sworn he was walking into a well-maintained city park. Sturdy trees grew from camouflaged pots, their branches stretching across a path that meandered from the landing pad to a shaded area with a wrought-iron table and a few padded benches.

An outdoor kitchen area to the left held a grill and a number of other sleek, high-tech devices he could barely guess at the purpose of—one looked like it might be a miniature version of the bar from Convergence, capable of producing a dizzying array of mixed drinks at the touch of a button. And beyond that . . .

"You've got a pool."

Phoenix paused halfway around the smooth oval and stared down as if seeing it for the first time. The crystal-clear water sparkled in the sunlight, showing off the gorgeous blue tiling along the sides. "It's good for swimming laps," she said after a moment, before hoisting her bag more firmly onto her shoulder. "Feel free to use it."

"Swimming is good stress relief." Dani's voice was vague. Flat. "We'll need it."

"It's temperature controlled." Phoenix strode forward, and the glass doors on the far side of the patio ghosted open at her approach. "I'm assuming neither of you are chipped."

The skin at the back of his neck itched. Rafe clenched his fingers to avoid reaching up to brush the scar. "I had a Protectorate chip, but it's long gone."

Dani glanced at him. "Same."

"We'll have to fix that." Lights flickered on overhead as Phoenix led them into an open sitting room dominated by polished wood, sleek leather furniture, and a freestanding fireplace. To the left, a grand piano sat under a glittering chandelier of thousands of crystals. A painting of water lilies dominated the far wall—a recovered Monet, if Tessa had taught him anything.

Phoenix had already pivoted to the right. She dropped her bag on a mahogany table and tilted her head toward a bar along the back wall. It was covered with half a dozen convoluted-looking tech devices, all in black and shiny chrome. "There's a full catering kitchen if you want to cook, but I don't usually mess with it. I have drink mixers, a stocked energy drink cooler, and the in-house ordering system."

The Protectorate barracks had been graced with exactly one technological achievement in the field of cuisine—a machine that scanned their IDs from their tracking chips and delivered personally calibrated nutritional drinks that ranged in taste from vaguely tolerable sawdust to actively distasteful gravel.

All this tech for the rich, and they couldn't even manage to give the people bleeding out to protect it something half-decent to drink.

Phoenix's gaze swept over him, no doubt making note of his discomfort with those sneaky C-designation instincts. He locked his expression down and followed as she led them around the fireplace. When she pressed her hand to a barely visible scanner next to the wall, a control panel lit up, and she tapped a few buttons. "Private part of the penthouse," she explained, stepping aside. "Put your hands here and I'll add you to the system."

Dani shifted her bag to her other shoulder and pressed her right hand to the panel. A thin scar, silvered by time, tracked across the back of her hand.

They never let me keep my scars. Sometimes I wish they had.

Had the TechCorps done that to her? How long after the experimental surgery to rewire her nervous system had they realized its devastating side effects?

Devastating for Dani. She didn't feel pain like she should—a potentially lethal complication for someone constantly in dangerous situations. Rafe had seen her shrug off a bullet hole straight through her arm, had seen her bleed obliviously from cuts she didn't even know she had.

The *glee* those scientists must have felt. A bodyguard who wouldn't slow down if you riddled her with bullets, who would take a knife in the shoulder, pull it back out, and stab you with it without missing a beat. Rafe could only imagine what they'd done to her to test the limits of her endurance.

Actually, no. He couldn't. Not unless he wanted to accidentally put his fist through Phoenix's wall.

He waited until she'd reset the scanner before pressing his own hand to the cool glass. His hands were unmarked, his brown skin perfect. The TechCorps hadn't let him keep any scars, either.

They loved to hide the evidence.

A soft beep marked the end of the scan. Phoenix waved them into the hallway beyond, which proved to be more like an inner courtyard. Artificial sunlight shone through vines growing above the vaulted ceiling, giving the tiled floor a dappled effect. Small trees grew from large pots, and a pair of benches sat in the middle, near a rock fountain that burbled softly as water flowed down its multiple levels.

Phoenix gestured toward an archway to the left. "Guest wing. There are two bedrooms, a full bath, a workout room, a library, and a small kitchen. You guys can set up wherever you like in there." She pointed to the right. "My rooms. My office and my equipment rooms are in there, so you have access as well. And the path straight ahead leads to the servants' area and the private elevator. It goes to the full helipad on the roof, the ground level, or the tunnels."

"It's a nice place. Thanks for the tour." Without another word, Dani crossed through the archway to the guest wing.

Rafe couldn't bring himself to be as unbothered. *Nice* felt simultaneously insufficient and far too generous. He was standing in a casual expenditure of obscene wealth, his grubby boots out of place on this spotless tile floor, and for the first time in his life he *felt* the dizzying distance between even the better-off middle-management on the Hill and the *truly* elite.

Phoenix watched him in silence for another moment before checking her wrist. "I have a call in twenty minutes. Take an hour or so to settle in, then we can discuss the practicalities of your cover."

"Sounds good." Rafe covered his lingering discomfort with a saucy two-fingered salute and hoisted his bag over his shoulder to follow Dani.

He caught up with her as she was perusing the first bedroom down the hall. "I'll take this one," she told him. "It's closest to the access points. If someone manages to get in, I can raise the alarm."

And put herself squarely between him and any potential danger. A desperate part of him wanted to interpret the protective gesture as a sign of secret affection, but Rafe had watched Dani fling herself over people as a human shield plenty of times. Maybe it was still built into her, some rigid Executive Security training she couldn't shake.

"That's fine," he said, peeking past her into the bedroom. Instead of windows, the walls had two massive embedded screens that currently seemed to gaze out onto a crystal-clear morning over rolling vineyards.

The same artificial sunlight from the faux courtyard made the hardwood floors glow softly. A massive bed was framed by artistic side tables. One open door showed an empty walk-in closet with a vanity, the other a massive bathroom. "So," he asked, leaning against the doorjamb. "How does this rate, on the penthouse scale?"

"Middle of the road." Dani tossed her bag onto the bed and shrugged. "It screams new money, but that's exactly what we want for our cover, isn't it?"

He'd mostly been trying to break the tension. "Middle of the road?" he demanded, waving a hand to take in the whole ridiculous mess of the place. *"This?"*

"Mm-hmm. A nicer place would take up an entire top floor, have real windows in every room. But you can't even buy one of those anymore."

"Why the hell not?"

"There aren't any left." Dani kicked off her shoes and peered at the climate-control panel on the wall next to him. "They all got scooped up in the early days, and TechCorps execs have been squatting in them for decades now. No room for new blood."

"Shit." He pushed off the doorframe, took two steps deeper into the hallway, and stopped again as subtle, natural light illuminated the space in front of him. Two more steps, and another section glowed gently to life. "Is this whole damn place rigged with motion sensors?"

"And heat, if I had to guess. But it's all integrated—nothing to avoid or disable, because they're built into the walls, floors, ceilings. They're just *there*."

The sense of being *watched* stirred the hair at the back of his neck, but when he opened the next door, he abruptly reconsidered the cost-benefit analysis of a life of perpetual surveillance.

It was just a bathroom. But it was *beautiful*.

The soft lighting illuminated the pristine tile floor as he stepped inside. His reflection was multiplied into dizzying infinity by wide mirrors affixed to both walls above deep sinks. The door on the left presumably led to Dani's room, and the one on the right to the room he'd be claiming. But beyond that. . . .

Oh God, the *shower.*

He'd spent years of his life on the road, making do with rough baths in streams or, at best, the comparative luxury of a makeshift camp shower. The first thing the Silver Devils had done upon claiming their warehouse was build themselves a bathroom with multiple luxurious shower stalls. Unlimited hot water—that had been the dream.

His dream had been too small.

This shower was easily three meters across, with slate tile on the floor and walls and a bench built into the back. A half-meter metal panel was affixed to the ceiling, with soft blue lights giving the whole space a dreamy look.

Rafe couldn't stop himself. He stepped up to the control panel, tapped through the settings, and watched in awe as water cascaded from the panel in a glittering rainfall, the lights making every drop shine like crystal as steam rose from the already-hot water.

The door to Dani's bedroom opened, and her low chuckle echoed off the slate. "First time?"

"I'm rethinking my commitment to a noble do-gooder life."

"No, you're not."

Rafe stared longingly at the waterfall of twinkling water and steam. "No," he agreed, "I'm not. But I am definitely remodeling the bathroom after we've saved Atlanta."

Dani's soft smile slowly faded. "Do you have a minute?"

"Of course."

She grasped the doorframe and bit her lower lip. "I'm sorry," she said finally. "About dredging up my history with the TechCorps. It's just sometimes I forget, you know? How terrible it is to hear for the first time."

Rafe's fist clenched around the strap of his duffle bag. A little med-gel had taken care of the cuts from shattering the tablet, but he could still feel them on his palm like a ghost. He'd had years to settle into his biochemically enhanced strength, years to learn how to move carefully through the world.

Thinking about Dani in pain erased all that caution. "You don't have to apologize," he told her gently. "I'm the one who's sorry. I lost control."

"I can be careless." It sounded like another apology.

"Dani, no." It was an effort not to reach for her. Not to *touch* her, to try to soothe that haunted look from her eyes. "You weren't being careless. You were just sharing your life. You can do that, whenever you want. Or not, if you don't want to. But I made you feel bad about sharing, and that was shitty. I'm sorry."

Her throat worked, and she nodded. She opened her mouth to speak, then stopped and grinned instead. "There are no cameras in here, by the way. So you don't have to worry about that when you're lingering in the fancy shower."

He didn't know if that teasing sparkle was back because she felt better, or because she just liked imagining him lingering in the shower. Hopefully both. It would be so easy to lean in, to let his lips curve in his most devastating smile. Another minute and the steam from the shower would have his T-shirt clinging in all the perfect places.

But he'd promised not to poke at her. So he cut off the water and jerked his head toward the door to the other bedroom. "You okay sharing it with me?"

Okay, maybe he was going to poke a *little.*

Dani leaned her hip against the doorframe and crossed her arms, pushing her breasts against her thin gray T-shirt. "I could ask you the same question."

He'd deserved that.

Acknowledging it with a nod and a wink, he turned and strode the four steps required to bring him to the opposite door. Opening it revealed a bedroom much like the first, only this one's giant screens offered a view of a tropical paradise, palm trees swaying in a breeze so real he swore he should feel it.

Four steps. Not enough distance to hold the avalanche of unspoken things between them . . . and somehow still too far away.

It didn't make a damn bit of sense, but nothing he'd felt about Dani ever did. Maybe that was what had enchanted him from the start.

MAYA

Beth had been in their home for less than twenty-four hours, and Maya was already plotting how to steal her away from Ava.

It was hard to believe they were both B-designations. Or maybe it shouldn't have been—Maya knew better than to believe that you could categorize people into *types* so simply. That had been one of the Franklin Center's biggest mistakes, no doubt, the idea that nature and aptitude were easily controlled at the genetic level.

Where Ava was all cold and calculating intellect, Beth was warm, earnest genius. She'd settled at the breakfast table between Maya and Conall with an open, excited smile, and by the time they had devoured their eggs and were working their way through Knox's new cinnamon sugar muffins, it was like the three of them had been friends forever.

"Okay, so." She rubbed her hands together and wiggled her fingers in the air. "Since Phoenix is their in, a DC backstory only makes sense. The question is, what do we do with that?"

Conall broke another muffin in half and chewed a chunk of it thoughtfully. "Rafe can play just about anything. But he's got, you know . . ." A vague wave of the muffin. "That whole hot-as-fuck thing going on, which is a good distraction. Most people never clocked him as our intelligence officer, which is how he liked it."

Maya huffed. "Weaponized biceps," she muttered. But Conall wasn't wrong. Anyone who found men even mildly attractive tended to trip over their own feet when Rafe broke out his best smile. "Dani was Executive Security. She can turn off the *I might kill you* vibe when she wants, but up on the Hill it might be better to lean into it. They respect power."

"Biceps and resting murder face. Got it." Beth scribbled a quick, positively illegible note on a ragged piece of paper.

"Rafe knows tech," Conall added after devouring another piece of muffin. "More hardware than software, but enough to bullshit."

Beth's scribbling slowed to a stop, and she looked up. "Ava said there was something unique about Dani, but she didn't elaborate."

As much as she already liked Beth, Maya still hesitated. Phoenix would have to know for strategy, and it wasn't exactly a *secret*—but protectiveness was a hard habit to break. Especially when your secrets made you a target. "Dani underwent an experimental procedure at the TechCorps," Maya said finally. "To give her enhanced reflexes. It worked, for the most part. She's the fastest person you'll ever meet. But she doesn't process pain right."

"And by *doesn't process*," Conall drawled, "Maya means Dani straight up doesn't feel it. I've seen her surprised to discover she'd been shot."

Beth gasped. "Shut *up*."

"He's not exaggerating." Maya shredded her own muffin nervously. "Rafe knows this, but Phoenix should, too—it means you have to watch her. If Dani's hurt, she doesn't always realize. She can be bleeding out and not know it."

Beth bit her lip and reached over, stopping just short of laying her hand on Maya's. "Strictly need-to-know. We won't put it in any digital record."

Beth's brown eyes were so earnest. Her hand hovered over Maya's, because even in the short time she'd been here she'd clearly noticed that Maya shied away from casual touch. Another way she was nothing like Ava—Beth understood people. Maya forced herself to relax, and it wasn't hard to smile. "Nina trusts you both. That's all I need to know."

A wide grin rewarded her words. "Sweet. Okay, next order of business . . ." Beth turned as Mace shouldered through the door and stalked toward the kitchen. "Um, hi."

He grunted as he snagged a mug from the hanging rack and started filling it with coffee.

Her gaze lingered on him as she reached for her tablet. "Rafe and Dani. I noticed a little—"

"Tension," Mace muttered.

"Yes, thank you!" Beth answered brightly. "Are they . . . ?"

"Exes?" He shook his head, then frowned. "This for their cover?"

At her nod, he snorted. "Make them a couple. Easiest parts they'll ever play."

Then he exited the kitchen through the back, leaving poor Beth looking a little dazed.

Conall dropped his head to the table with a groan. "That was Mace."

"Your medic?"

"Yes." Conall sounded aggrieved. "And he's not wrong. Blunt, but not wrong."

Maya flexed her fingers, another secret catching on the tip of her tongue. Mace had been a captive of the TechCorps until a few months ago, tortured and brainwashed with every intention of turning him against his own squad.

Trauma like that didn't heal overnight. It had been a while since the last time Mace had snapped and tried to stab someone, but loud noises and unexpected movement could still trigger a violent outburst. And Beth looked *so* sweet and helpless . . .

Except she wasn't. Just because she was all smiles and sunshine didn't make her any less a genetically enhanced badass. Hell, Maya didn't even have superstrength, and *she* was far from helpless.

Before she could decide how much to tell Beth, Conall had spoken again. "Don't mind Mace. The TechCorps fucked him up a little, and he's still getting his feet back under him. He mostly stays in the clinic, outside of meals."

"Right." Beth cast one more glance toward the kitchen, then cleared her throat. "So we have a rich, glamorous couple from DC, looking to invest heavy money in some new tech. That should get them all the invites they could ever want."

Conall pulled his favorite tablet over and swiped muffin crumbs out of the way. "What kind of digital trail would a rich couple from DC have? I know y'all have access to the GhostNet and some local networks, but nothing like the kind of surveillance we have in Atlanta, right?"

Beth shook her head. "Someone with as much money as we're giving them? They could probably afford to stay off the surveillance grid entirely. Keeping a low profile in DC is a pay-to-play system, and it's *extremely* effective."

Maya shoved her own plate aside and snapped open her tablet. "So the more important you are, the less anyone knows about you? Not so different from the way it is here, I guess. No surveillance in the fancy ballrooms and secret sex parties, after all."

"Did anyone warn them about those, by the way?" Beth asked. "The secret sex parties?"

"I didn't know there *were* secret sex parties," Conall retorted. "They don't exactly invite the techs to those."

Birgitte hadn't been a popular attendee, either. Most of the elite on the Hill had considered Maya's former boss to be a cross between the morality police and a highly paid hall monitor. No one wanted the vice president of Behavior and Analysis watching them indulge their freakiest fantasies.

Dani, on the other hand, had undoubtedly had to stand guard at them. Ex-Sec was trained to be invisible, which often meant standing like a lamp or elaborate floral arrangement while crime, debauchery, or outright murder went down in front of you. "Dani knows," she stated confidently. "She'll make sure Rafe is up to speed."

"Of course—former Executive Security." Beth smacked her forehead lightly. "She probably knows more about the secret sex parties than I do." She laughed. "And I have videos."

"Wait, you have videos?"

"*Conall.*" Maya kicked him lightly under the table. "Savitri lifted your ban from Convergence. If you want to see an orgy, just go there. Trust me, most of the assholes on the Hill probably aren't even having good sex."

"It's true," Beth confirmed mournfully. "Just tragic. Plus, it's from a button cam. *Very* shaky footage."

"Okay, okay." Conall flexed his fingers. "Rich couple. Lots of disposable money. Into investing in questionable tech. This shouldn't be hard."

"Now, we lay the trail. Accounts, shell corps, and a couple of questionably legal buyouts and mergers for good measure." Beth cracked her knuckles. "Rock and roll."

As Conall and Beth settled in, exchanging quips and friendly banter, Maya decided she was *definitely* going to steal Beth.

Ava would just have to deal with it.

SECURITY MEMO

Franklin Center for Genetic Research

We still haven't been able to figure out a way to guard against the flaws in the HS genetic strain. I submit that it is time to set aside ego and put more formidable minds to the task.

Generation 16 ended in catastrophe. I suggest we share the files with Generation 17. They are intelligent enough to recognize the stakes of failure. And, perhaps, intelligent enough to avert it.

Dr. Reed, January 2078

TEN

Dani wasn't, by nature, an envious person. She just didn't see the point in wanting what other people had. Life was about playing the hell out of the hand you were dealt. It was either that, or figure out some way to get all new cards. But envy? Way too passive, and it led nowhere good. A waste of time.

But. *But.*

She coveted Phoenix's crime closet.

There were probably better terms for it—*design workshop* or *prop room* or any number of other phrases that certainly fit but couldn't begin to capture the sheer scope of its contents or function. No, the room—thirty square meters, oblong and occupying one side of the penthouse—had one singular, exquisite purpose: to facilitate crimes.

And Dani wanted it.

Shelves holding bolts of fabric lined one wall and framed a state-of-the-art garment construction machine. Another workbench held a smart mirror surrounded by various makeup items, as well as a pigment mixer that could produce single-use bottles of foundation or press palettes of powders and shadows.

Only the perfume station held no automated components, just carrier formulations and *hundreds* of vials of fragrance oils. Phoenix must have preferred to mix those by hand, tailoring them from her own experience rather than relying on programmed recipes.

There were dozens of wigs hanging on one wall, and more styling tools than Dani had ever seen in one place. Right next to those was a huge case of weapons—firearms, blades, even a handful of high-tech grenades.

"I would live in this room," Dani told her honestly.

Phoenix smiled. "It's my favorite in the penthouse."

"I can see why." The sheer amount of possibility that existed within these four walls was dizzying.

Phoenix pulled out a bolt of shimmery black fabric and brought it to the table. When the light caught it, the color seemed to shift to metallic blue. "The Franklin Center had a room like this. While Nina was combat crawling through the mud and Ava was hacking servers, this is what their sister did."

"Zoey." Dani watched as Phoenix's fingers flexed on the fabric. "You were close."

"We were in love." A short, harsh laugh. "Ava *hated* me. She's always been a possessive little shit."

Nina had probably been the opposite—transitively fond of Phoenix, happy that her sister had found love. "What was she like?"

"Zoey?" Phoenix sighed softly. "People always talk like C-designations are all sunshine and light, but we're not, you know. They didn't design us to be compassionate, they designed us to be con artists. But Zoey was all of that. She was just . . . good."

Just like Nina. It was enough to make a person wonder what might have become of Ava without all the torture and abandonment.

Phoenix glanced back at her, eyes narrowing. "Ava was right about you."

"I have no idea what you mean."

"She said you act feral, but you're a thinker. And dangerous." Phoenix made another amused noise as she lifted a tablet from the table. "She likes you, you know. She says you're the smartest one there because you're the only one who still wants to kill her. I told her that was an awkwardly revealing statement, and she went off to sulk."

"Sounds about right." Dani pulled out a chair and dropped onto it. "She's antisocial, but so am I. And there are worse things to be."

"Far worse." Phoenix flipped the tablet around and offered it to Dani, revealing half a dozen elaborate outfits that somehow combined menace, sex, and decadence. "This is the style in DC right now. I assume you and the pretty boy are comfortable showing some skin?"

Dani snorted. "He has a name, you know. And yes, we're both extremely practical when it comes to using sex as a tool." Maybe *too* practical. "You've seen him. I don't think we have much of a chance of being boring and blending in, so our best option is to go hard. Really play it up."

Phoenix waved her finger. "Flip the page. I have some potential outfits for him in there, too."

Dani complied. The sketches and photos were highly constructed and equally daring, all sleek black vinyl and shiny metallic fabrics. The garments and suggested accessories were dramatic, all right—so dramatic they would have swallowed a less commanding, confident person.

Rafe would wear them easily. Beautifully.

Dani cleared her throat and returned the tablet to its owner. "He'll make it work."

Phoenix arched one perfectly shaped brow. "Are you two . . . close?"

It was absolutely the most delicate way Dani had ever been asked if she was fucking someone. "We are not."

"Hmm."

Phoenix clearly thought she was full of shit, but before Dani could explain, Rafe strolled through the open door, barefoot. His short hair was damp, as was his skin, judging from the way his workout pants and T-shirt clung to his body. As Dani watched, an errant drop of water rolled down the side of his neck, followed the curve of his muscled throat, and disappeared beneath the V-neck of his shirt.

Goddammit.

"How was the shower, Morales?" Her traitorous voice had gone husky. "Was it everything you dreamed it would be?"

"First thing I'm doing when we get home is build one exactly like it," he replied, winking at her. Then his gaze swept the room, taking in the vast and enviable array of equipment, and his eyes brightened. "Damn, Phoenix. You have a grifting lair. How the hell did you get this place, anyway?"

Phoenix yanked the knife out of the table next to her and flicked her wrist lazily. It flashed across the room, where it thudded into a much-abused painting, piercing the subject's eye. "Meet the previous owner. He was buying broken stock from the Franklin Center and selling our blood and plasma as a magic elixir of youth and vitality. I executed a hostile takeover of his business portfolio."

"You mean you murdered him," Dani corrected.

"That, too." Phoenix strode across the room and jerked her knife from the painting. "But only after I'd established myself as his business proxy. As far as the elite on the Hill are concerned, he's debauching himself in DC while I do the hard work of running his empire from his tacky poser penthouse."

Rafe whistled softly as he stopped in front of the station laden with scents and oils. He picked up one bottle and turned it over, his gaze thoughtful. "I'm guessing it didn't come with all the pretty toys, though."

"No," Phoenix conceded. Then she grinned. "Ava may be a pain in the ass, but she *does* buy nice presents."

Ivonne and her brand-new heart probably agreed. "She has her moments," Dani admitted.

"From time to time." Phoenix returned the knife to her wall of weapons, then settled back on the garment table, her tablet in hand. "Since you're both here . . . Conall and Maya helped Beth build your identities. Meet Bette and Bryce Parker-Holmes."

A few flicks of her fingers activated the massive screen that covered the wall to her left. She pulled up two dossiers, and Dani found herself staring at life-size photos of her and Rafe displayed next to a sizable list of criminal achievements, dodgy business investments, and ruthless corporate takeovers.

"We've been busy, apparently," she observed, pleased. "And this'll check out if someone decides to call a buddy up in Washington?"

"No one who's important enough to know one of my associates would ever admit they don't," Phoenix replied with a feral smile. "It's the one nice thing about a town where only the rich can be invisible and no one wants to admit they're out of the loop."

"Good." Dani's gaze returned to the hyphenated—and *shared*—last name. "Married. Is that a DC power couple thing, or is Conall somewhere right now, laughing his ass off?"

"Conall *and* Maya," Rafe murmured.

"Maybe." Phoenix's fingers danced across her tablet. "It's not *uncommon*. Think of a DC marriage like a business merger. Shared resources, shared profits. Mutually assured destruction."

"How romantic," Rafe drawled. "Business partners with benefits."

"Pretty much." A few more taps. Phoenix gestured to Rafe, then to the 3D body scanner in the corner. Tucked into a small alcove, it almost looked like a mirrored shower stall. "I sent all of the details to the consoles in your rooms. But before you go anywhere, I need you to jump in the scanner so I can get measurements for your outfits."

Rafe slipped past Dani, so close that she could smell the warm sandalwood of his aftershave. He stepped onto the platform and stood there, completely at ease, as the machine whirred to life. Seconds later, the scan was finished. Phoenix checked the scan quality, then nodded. "My machine can construct garment bases overnight. Tomorrow, we put together Bryce's wardrobe."

"Sounds good." Rafe jumped lightly off the platform. "You mind if I study my dossier in that library?"

"Make yourself at home."

"Oh, I am."

Rafe winked at Dani and strolled out of the room. Phoenix watched him leave with an expression that seemed torn between perplexity and amusement.

"Yeah," Dani told her. "Rafe has that effect on people."

"I underestimated him." Phoenix tilted her head. "He's got a good game face."

"You won't know anything he doesn't want you to know. He's a stand-up guy, though. You can count on him."

"High praise from someone in your line of work."

"High praise from me, full stop." And she meant it. She and Rafe might have their issues, but they had zero to do with his competence or dedication. "I trust him with my life."

Phoenix nodded, but her assessing gaze lingered on Dani's face. "I noticed that Beth set you up as the scary one. You'd think she'd give the violent backstory to the ex-Protectorate soldier, but I'm guessing your friends told her something juicy."

Phoenix seemed to specialize in delicate questions that weren't really delicate at all—or maybe she just figured that was the best way to deal with Dani. "I worked for the TechCorps. Executive Security. When I bounced, I went freelance. Security never really was my style, so I adapted. Went into contract killing."

"That's a rough business." There was no judgment in her voice, just cool curiosity. "What about Nina? Unless she's changed a hell of a lot, I can't imagine she endorses it."

"I'm retired," Dani allowed. "These days, I only kill people out of necessity. Or extreme annoyance. But usually necessity."

"Don't we all?" Phoenix set her tablet aside and raised both eyebrows. "Anything else I need to know?"

Dani knew what she was asking, even if Phoenix was too careful to say it outright. She opened her mouth to explain about the TechCorps' rewiring experiment—and the permanent damage it had caused—but the words didn't come.

She didn't want to talk about it. At least, not with a virtual stranger.

"No, nothing else," she said instead. "I should go. Get to work slipping into my new life."

Phoenix straightened and turned to unroll the shiny black fabric. "I'll be in here for the rest of the day, if you need me. There's a comm system, too."

"I'll manage." There'd be plenty of time for socialization in the days to come—too much of it, in fact.

Right now, she needed to be alone.

Dani studied the information on her cover until a vague headache throbbed in her temples. The dossiers Maya had given them on the big players up on the Hill? Those were useless, as far as Dani was concerned. She'd find out everything she needed to know about those assholes the moment she walked through the doors and into their world.

But her cover was sacred, all-important. She had to slide into this persona like a custom-made dress, had to inhabit it with all the certainty and self-assurance she could muster. If she managed that, even mistakes could be shrugged off or glossed over. There was no limit to the amount of shit she could get away with.

So she flipped through screen after screen, read it aloud and repeated it to herself. Then she had the computer read it to her as she paced around her bedroom until the light from the simulated windows dimmed and vanished entirely, morphing into starlight and a lovely false cityscape.

Close to midnight, she set her tablet aside, rubbed her burning eyes, and headed for the kitchen, intent on making up for skipping dinner.

Rafe was there, four virtual screens hovering in the air in front of him. He flicked through them, glowering like they owed him money.

She hovered in the doorway, taking in the scene with amusement, longing, and an almost embarrassing fondness. "Having problems?"

His glower deepened as he waved a hand, accidentally triggering another cascade of menu options to open. "How am I supposed to figure out what I want to eat when there are this many options? How many damn restaurants are on the Hill?"

"Rookie mistake." She stepped forward to reset the system to its initial screen. Her bare arm brushed his, and she had to close her eyes for a moment before she could focus on the glimmering text. "You weren't even on the delivery menus. Those were the in-house options."

Rafe blinked. "In-house?"

"Buildings like this include meal service. There are probably two or three world-class chefs down in the kitchens right now, even at this hour."

Frowning, Rafe flicked open a selection of beef entrees that spanned seven virtual pages. "You're telling me we throw a party every time we get real meatballs down on Southside, but this building—that houses a few dozen families, max—is sitting on enough fresh food to cook anything in here?"

"Oh, it gets worse."

"Do I *want* to know?"

"No, but I bet you can guess."

His jaw worked. His fingers flexed. "They don't redistribute what they don't use to the people in need."

"Nope." She hopped up on the massive island in the middle of the kitchen. The engineered marble chilled her bare thighs, but she didn't start shivering, so she guessed it wasn't *too* cold. "They don't even throw it away. They destroy it. Wouldn't want to encourage any dumpster diving."

"Jesus, I hate these fuckers." He exhaled roughly. "Maya and Conall tried to tell me, but I never really got it. I mean, I lived on the Hill, too. I always figured it couldn't be *that* different just because you took the elevator to the hundredth floor instead of the second."

"It's a different fucking world." She nodded to the screens. "Can't go wrong with noodles. And if you like seafood, this is your moment."

It took him a few minutes to navigate to the seafood section and select a spicy lobster pasta. Then he flipped over and added a dessert sampler. "Got to get in character, right? Live this wasteful life of indulgence."

"Better make it two."

He adjusted the quantities and hit the *Send Order* button. "So what happens now? Is a butler going to show up with a tray?"

"Something like that." She crossed her legs as he leaned against the counter opposite her. "Tomorrow's the big day. How much undercover experience did you get while you were in the Protectorate, anyway?"

"Nothing this formal." His lips curved in a soft smile. "I mean, I never had days of prep and a whole team laying out a backstory. Usually it was on the spot, feeling out a target and being whoever I needed to be to get the job done. Most people are pretty easy to read, if you know what you're looking for."

He was observant, empathetic, and smart. Add in an innate knack for cold-reading a mark, and it made for a deadly effective combination. He might not have huge amounts of experience, but he was just that good.

Still, most immediate cons were blitz attacks that relied on the paralyzing element of surprise. You had to overwhelm, to take the money and run before they had a chance to process what had happened. "It's a different kind of game. It's a slower play, and it requires a lighter touch. We can't lay it on as thick as we would on the fly."

Rafe nodded. "I'll follow your lead. It fits with our cover, anyway. Conall and Maya know our strengths and played to them."

"But Phoenix is our point of contact, and she . . ." Dani swallowed hard. "She doesn't know everything."

A moment of silence, and then Rafe's expression softened. "You didn't tell her about . . ."

"The experiment? No. I don't even know *why*—I mean it's pertinent information, right? I just didn't want to talk about it. Not with her."

Rafe planted a hand on the counter next to him and boosted himself up effortlessly to sit across from her. Moonlight through the floor-to-ceiling glass windows slanted across the bare skin of his chest, turning the deep brown to a silvery play of shadows. "It's hard," he told her softly. "To talk about that shit with a stranger."

"No, you—" He didn't understand. Then again, how could he? "No one knows all of it. Not even Nina and Maya."

Another pause. "Do you want someone to know all of it?"

No, she didn't. She didn't even want *him* to know, she just wanted to tell him. Which didn't make any damn sense at all, except that maybe—just maybe—the very act of saying it aloud to another person could banish a bit of the darkness. Alleviate a little of the pain.

She had to swallow hard just to speak. "Everyone assumes I'm an orphan. It's fair—most of the kids who wind up in the experimental programs are. It's just easier for the TechCorps that way. If you die, they don't even have to pay out your signing bonus."

There was too much understanding in Rafe's dark eyes. "How old were you?"

"Eighteen. Older than most." The memories of the screaming arguments and tears rolled over Dani, threatening to choke off her words. "My parents didn't want me to sign up, but you couldn't tell me anything at that age. Still can't, I guess."

"I remember being that age. And thinking I was doing the right thing."

"I just wanted to do *something*. Be someone," she whispered. "Then it went sideways."

She knew the words didn't sufficiently describe what had happened. She remembered bits and pieces of the interminable surgery, even though she'd been under general anesthesia. She remembered fire and blood, constant flickering shades of red painted across the backs of her eyelids. And she remembered feeling pain—as it turned out, for the last time.

Those memories were the haziest. She could no longer recall what it felt like, not really, just the words people used to describe it—agonizing and stinging and sharp. But she only knew them in the abstract now.

Rafe was waiting, so she dragged herself out of her reverie. "I was in a coma for a couple of days after the surgery. My parents were so happy when I woke up that my dad actually cried."

Rafe flinched. "How long before the TechCorps realized what had happened?"

"They knew almost immediately. They never devise their tests with patient comfort in mind, so when they started checking out my reflexes and nothing seemed to bother me . . ."

Her memories of what pain was like may have faded, but she'd *never* forget the look on her mother's face when the doctors told them. The blood had drained from her face, something Dani had always chalked up to a metaphorical figure of speech until she'd watched it happen in real time. And then—

"My parents bailed," she told him bluntly. "They couldn't handle it. So they left me in the hospital, and they didn't come back."

The marble counter creaked under the force of Rafe's grip. "That is some serious bullshit, Dani. They shouldn't have done that to you."

It would be easier to keep blaming them for abandoning her, just like she had in the early days, but she'd made her peace with it. She'd become another TechCorps orphan, not because her parents had died, but because she was dead to them.

She shook her head. "It doesn't matter. I'm over it."

"It's still bullshit." Another graceful flex of muscle, and he was close enough to brace his hands on the counter on either side of her hips. No parts of their bodies touched, but Dani felt him anyway. His gaze held hers, refusing to relinquish her even when the tension grew sharp enough to slice to the bone. "You deserved better."

She believed him, that was the crazy part. When he looked at her like that, he could say the sky was green, and she would just nod in agreement.

She was nodding now, even though it made no sense. She leaned closer. "How are we going to do this, Rafe?"

He didn't pretend not to understand. "We're going to do it because the fact that we never seem to know if we want to fight or fuck sounds pretty much like how marriage works in DC. And we're going to do it because nothing matters to me more than having your back on the job. Sex can't distract me from that."

"We don't even know how to touch each other," she argued.

"I bet we can figure it out." A smile curved his lips—warm, sweet, challenging. Pure Rafe. "Touch me, Dani."

His teasing tone turned it into an open invitation, one she was determined to answer. But when she moved her hand, it wasn't to stroke his shoulder or explore the bare skin of his chest.

She reached for his cheek.

Her fingers made contact. Light, barely there. His skin was smooth and soft, so *warm,* burning her fingertips as he tilted his head into her touch. The movement dragged her fingers lightly across his jaw, to the gentle abrasion of the stubble already growing there.

There was nothing overtly sexual about it, but a bolt of heat shot through her core. "Rafe—"

A sharp *buzz* tore through the room. Rafe jerked away and spun to confront the sound. He crowded against her, pressing her against the safety of his back as he searched the room, a knife in his outstretched hand.

"Hey, it's okay." She stifled a rueful laugh as she gripped his shoulders, steadying him. "I should have warned you. It's just the food."

His muscles remained tense under her hands for another second before he relaxed with a rough chuckle. "I'm sure I'll make a great impression if I flip out and stab the oven or something. Maybe you should show me what all this shit is."

"I will," she promised. "First stop: the delivery capsule."

She slid off the island, still holding onto his arm, and steered him toward the rounded, tinted glass delivery door. It slid open at their approach, revealing plates covered with burnished metal cloches and a display that read *Delivery 1 of 2.*

"Convenient," he said in his wryest drawl as he pulled out both plates. "No chance you'll accidentally be forced to look at the people making your food."

"Nope." The door slid shut. The platform inside spun around, and the door reopened to reveal the other two plates. "As impersonal as everything else on the Hill. But wait until you taste it."

She hopped back onto the island and uncovered her meal. The scents of cheese and cream melded perfectly with the sharp spice and the briny lobster. Steam rose as she twirled her fork in the pasta and took her first bite.

Heaven. Paid for with blood, sure, but *heaven.*

Rafe dug his fork into his own meal and took a bite. An expression of bliss rolled over his face, and he actually groaned after he swallowed. "I'm definitely going to hell for eating this, but damn. Maybe Knox can learn how to make it. Nina said we could do seafood with the aquaponics, right?"

"Yeah, tilapia, not lobsters." She paused. "Think Phoenix is the type of person to keep booze in the freezer?"

Rafe studied the wall of sleek metal doors, his head tilted to one side. Carrying his plate, he walked past the delivery chute and opened what proved to be a fridge containing energy drinks and six apples. The door above it revealed a freezer with a stack of packets filled with frozen fruit and three different bottles of liquor. "Shit, this is the good stuff. Think she'll mind?"

"I hope not." Dani recognized the stylized skull & crossbones labels. O'Kane liquor. "Clem waxes poetic about this. It's distilled out in Wyoming, or some shit. Pour us a couple of whiskeys."

"Nevada," Rafe corrected absently as he set down his plate and went hunting for glasses. "Knox managed to score a couple of crates because we did a favor for one of the Mississippi trading families out of Baton Rouge. They pretty much paid for the clinic."

The whiskey went down smooth, with just a hint of smokiness. Dani hummed her approval and clinked her glass against his. "To the mission."

"To the mission," he echoed, his warm voice as smoky smooth as the liquor. "The Hill won't know what hit them."

Dani lifted her plate again. "Where were you hiding that knife, anyway?"

"Uh-uh." He grinned at her over his lobster. "I'm not giving you *all* my secrets. Besides, tell me you haven't got a couple on you."

She rolled her eyes. "Eat your rich-people food, Morales."

They lapsed into companionable silence. It was nice, just sitting there, having a meal and a drink. There was something comfortable about it, even though they weren't talking.

Something that almost felt like home.

The members of the Board invite you all to wish CEO Kyle Donovan a happy 127th birthday. His leadership has brought us through the most turbulent times in recent history, and his longevity is a promise to us all that the future is very bright, indeed.

November 2086

ELEVEN

Bette and Bryce Parker-Holmes made their TechCon debut by stepping out of a sleek AirLift into a goddamn fairy wonderland.

The massive patio on the 212th floor of the building located on the eastern side of the Hill made Phoenix's look quaint. If wealth was measured by the power to turn a bit of plascrete and steel clinging to the side of a skyscraper into a slice of paradise, tonight's host had money to burn.

The interlocking sandstone mosaic that served as a landing pad gave way to lush green grass Rafe could smell from five meters away. Tall, delicately pruned shrubs blocked out the city skyline and a nearly invisible dome sheltered the entire space from the whims of the weather, its programmable vista currently shining with constellations no one on the Hill had seen in decades.

Peach trees had been painstakingly trained to grow in arches above a walkway that wove through trees draped with strings of twinkling lights. Convenient sheltered nooks already held people whispering and giggling . . . and sometimes moaning.

Rafe scanned the entire fantastical assortment with an expression teetering between amusement and boredom, then turned his back on it to hold out his hand to Dani.

It was a good thing he wasn't seeing *her* for the first time as she slid out of the car with effortless grace. A million credits spent fetishizing the nature people on the Hill refused to get near? He could pretend to ignore that.

But Dani, dressed to kill . . .

Tonight, Phoenix had put them both in flawless white. Rafe's sleeveless tunic bared his arms and hugged his chest, tailored with interlocking silver rings that gave the faint impression of chainmail.

Dani's dress didn't need any help—Phoenix had fitted it to every curve. A five-centimeter gap in the fabric started at her right shoulder and dipped between her breasts, baring pale flesh. The gap ended high on the opposite hip, where her skirt flared open to reveal the entire length of her left leg. Rafe had tried not to stare at the delicate silver chains crisscrossing that bare skin, but the *possibilities* overwhelmed him. Were the chains decorative or structural? Integral? If he tugged one free, would the entire dress come apart like unraveling lace?

Dani met his stare with an indulgent smile, then lifted his hand and kissed the back of it.

An inappropriate warmth kindled inside him, far more dangerous than any lustful ponderings. It would be so *easy* to fall into this cover. To slide his arm around her waist as if he'd always had the right, to let his fingers tease through the loose strands of hair tumbling down her back—deep blue at the tips now, thanks to Phoenix's clever little heat wand that added and removed temporary color with a single pass.

Touching Dani was allowed. No, it was *required*. But it still felt a little like cheating. Like stealing all the intimacies he'd craved without giving her the part *she'd* wanted—the superpowered bounce-off-the-ceiling and break-the-headboard fucking.

Definitely *not* what he needed to be thinking about right now.

The few people lingering near the entrance had turned to assess them, but their condescending puzzlement vanished swiftly as Phoenix made her entrance.

If Dani was pure sophisticated sensuality, Phoenix's entire outfit screamed unchecked violence. Combat boots gave way to skintight pants of some material Rafe had never seen before—it had the shine of leather but moved with Phoenix's body like a second skin. Black bracers with gold buckles covered her arms from knuckles to elbow, and where Rafe's top gave the impression of armor, Phoenix's *was* armor—ballistic-grade fabric shaped into a corset that hugged her body and glinted in the light like obsidian with fine cracks showing lava seething beneath.

Her hair was a riot of reds, oranges, and golds, shaved along the sides and braided down the middle in a messy way that whispered of flames. Her eyes *were* flames—a side effect of the same cosmetic contacts Rafe had donned. Of course, with Phoenix, nothing was merely cosmetic—a slight tilt of Rafe's head at just the right angle activated the augmented reality setting on contact lenses and revealed a secondary layer of excess.

Fashion on the Hill transcended the physical. When he looked at Phoenix with his AR lenses engaged, virtual flames licked over her skin and singed the air around her, and the movements of her arms left eddies of fire in their wake. Dani, on the other hand, stood looking angelic in her pristine white gown while the ghostly impressions of dark wings unfurled behind her, a whisper of the angel of death. Rafe knew anyone viewing him would see the same.

The people on the Hill were a lot of things, but subtle was *not* one of them.

"Phoenix!" A woman clad in skin-tight faux leather broke free of the milling crowd. The same jewel tones of her jumpsuit—majestic purple, blue, and green—were replicated in the virtual peacock feathers that streamed behind her as she hurried forward.

Rafe didn't need an introduction to recognize the newcomer. Beryl Andilet, wife of the vice president of Emerging Bioscience, was one of the most influential hostesses on the Hill. She'd singlehandedly parlayed access to her husband into a full-time bribery business, with invites to her intimate dinner parties going for hundreds of thousands of credits.

The dossier Maya had put together for him suggested that *Emerging Bioscience* was simply code for *how do we live forever?* Rumors varied on exactly how effective their top-of-the-line treatments were at fighting the aging process. Beryl's pale skin certainly showed startlingly few lines for a woman just past seventy, and Rafe didn't think she owed her condition to a robust skin-care routine.

Whether it was plastic surgery or just the soft life of the overly privileged with cutting-edge healthcare, she barely looked forty, moved with lithe vigor, and served as a walking marketing campaign. Rafe imagined those who'd spent their lives scrabbling to have more than their share of everything only had one *real* fear—having to leave it all behind. Those people would pay millions for the mere promise of a miracle.

And Beryl let them think she held the keys to forever in her beringed hands.

The woman greeted Phoenix by pressing their palms together. "You beautiful, terrifying thing. I love this. You're fabulous, as always."

"Beryl. It's been forever." Even Phoenix's voice had changed. Gone was her usual cool, flat rhythm with the vaguest hint of a Carolinas drawl. In its place was something warm and rasping, her *R*s dropping away like she'd grown up in the Northeast. "Business has been a pain."

Beryl clucked her tongue and hummed soothingly. "Isn't it always, darling?" Her gaze flickered over Dani to linger on Rafe, and her voice took on a bright, predatory edge that Rafe recognized all too well. "You brought guests."

"Investors," Phoenix corrected, a word that made Beryl's predatory gaze flare with open, avaricious glee. "Meet Bette Parker-Holmes, and her husband, Bryce."

"Ooh." She clasped Dani's hand. "Such a pleasure, Bette. What's a stronger word than *charmed*?"

"Try *enchanted*." Dani held on to her hand just a shade too long. "*Dazzled*, perhaps?"

Beryl burst out laughing. "She's adorable! You . . ." She turned to Rafe and took a half step closer. "Are a lucky man."

"I've always thought so," Rafe agreed, curling his hand around Dani's hip in a claim just shy of overt, even as he softened his gaze and let it drift down Beryl's body. That was the line he had to walk tonight. Loyal, possessive . . . but always hinting that he might be open to intriguing offers.

From the way Beryl all but swayed into him, she was definitely pondering making a few offers, and he doubted they had much to do with business. She waved her fingers at Phoenix. "You know our host is absolutely *dying* to see you, darling. Let me introduce our new friends around."

Phoenix didn't hesitate. Introductions from Beryl would assure them immediate status and credibility, and she'd taken them at their word that they were ready. She kissed the air next to Beryl's cheek. "Make sure they meet Desmond."

"Of course." Beryl offered her arm to Dani, who accepted it with a gracious nod. "This is your first time at the exhibition, yes?"

"First time in Atlanta," Dani corrected. "Our travels usually center around resource acquisition."

"Fascinating," Beryl said breathlessly. "How did you meet? I *love* a good love story."

Dani glanced over at Rafe, the teasing glint in her eyes accentuated by the lights glimmering in the trees. "Would you like to share the tale, darling, or shall I?"

Rafe laughed, letting the low sound rumble out of his chest. "It starts with her stabbing me."

Beryl gasped, and Dani patted her hand. "Barely. Also, he deserved it."

"Maybe a little." He let his true feelings for Dani show in his eyes, knowing that for once he didn't have to worry about scaring her off. "You see, we were both interested in a certain extremely valuable asset." He let the word hang for a moment, letting Beryl use her imagination to fill in something amazing. "I knew where it was being held, but she had the skills necessary to acquire it. So I proposed an alliance."

"With every intention of betraying me at the first convenient juncture," Dani purred. "Which I knew, of course. But I still couldn't resist."

It wasn't that far off from their real origin story—everything from the way Dani had nicked him with a knife the first night they'd met to the disastrous attempt to lure Nina into danger that had ended with Knox, Gray, Conall, and Rafe caught inexorably in a trap of their own making. Conall and Maya had been clever about crafting the story, that much was certain.

With Beryl hanging on every word, Rafe delivered the grand finale. "While we were dancing around, trying to decide which of us would betray the other, a third party swept in and almost stole the prize right out from under us." Rafe gave his usual sensual smile a bloodthirsty edge. "Chasing them down together made for one thrilling courtship."

Beryl turned toward him, scandalized and fascinated. Dani rolled her eyes behind the woman's head.

Rafe managed to keep a straight face. Barely. "She keeps me at the top of my game. And it's a *very* lucrative game."

"I imagine so." Beryl exhaled. "Oh, I simply can't *wait* to show you two off."

The faux fairy forest ended abruptly at a small patio, where a set of massive glass doors had been thrown wide to the night. Beryl guided them through the doorway into a . . .

Ballroom? It was a ridiculous word, but the only one that fit. Two stories high and ringed in a balcony above, the room was a dizzying space that felt unstuck in time. Marble floors gleamed under subtly shifting light cast from chandeliers dripping with crystal-shaped LEDs. A live band sat on a raised stage, playing music amplified by concealed speakers. Servers dressed all in black carried trays of bubbling drinks and intricate appetizers, a small selection chosen from the tables lining the walls, tables which absolutely groaned under the variety of offerings.

If the lavish outdoor patio had been an attempt to recapture the nature they'd all but destroyed for everyone else, this had to be someone's cracked fantasy of living as a lord in a fancy castle, dancing and feasting while the peasants scrabbled far below.

If Rafe let himself think about it too much, he'd start crushing all these hands he had to shake. So he boxed up the part of him that cared and fell deeper into his character. Bryce Parker-Holmes wasn't just an evil son-of-a-bitch, he was a cold, calculating thinker. He was all the parts of Rafe that excelled at military intelligence, stripped free of things like his compassion and morality.

It was easier to handle the introductions like that.

And there were *so many.* Beryl glided through a crowd that seemed to revolve gently around her, summoning those with whom she wished to speak with the quirk of an eyebrow or crook of a finger.

Executives. Scientists. Innovative thinkers. Weapons dealers. Rafe catalogued them by habit even as his contacts and the mic hidden in one of his earrings recorded the whole dizzying array for later assessment. Some looked at him with naked jealousy, others with open greed.

The most forward of them pitched to him on the spot, ignoring Beryl's frowns of disapproval as they tried to get as much of their pet project out as possible.

"They're already rumored to have enhanced senses. Almost supernatural!" one junior researcher exclaimed, his pale cheeks flushed with excitement and his pupils blown wide in a way Rafe did *not* think came from cosmetic contacts. "With just a little funding, we can accelerate the process, implant as many embryos as possible into viable surrogates—"

"Irving," Beryl warned sharply.

"Psychics!" he nearly shouted, and Rafe felt his eyebrow twitch up. Irving pounced on the obvious sign of interest. "We could unlock the potential of the human mind! The military has been stuck on the Makhai Project for decades. They don't understand the potential—"

Beryl raised one finger, and the man cut off abruptly. He jerked in something approaching a bow, already backing away, but his avid gaze stayed locked on Dani and Rafe. "We'll talk! It's the future!"

And so it went. Rafe shook hands, distributed smiles, and listened to an absolute parade of lures, ranging from subtle to overt. Complete memory downloads. Genetically targeted poisons. Consciousness transfer and mind control and at least fifty-nine different ways to regain lost youth.

Rafe catalogued the list of growing horrors. He fixed faces and names in place. He watched how they moved through the crowd, sorting them into a hierarchy of influence. Most of it matched the dossiers he'd studied, but there were some surprises.

Three men in full military uniform stood stiffly in one corner. Not Protectorate or Ex-Sec—pre-Flare United States military uniforms. Rafe couldn't be sure what the stars and medals on their shoulders signified, but he knew high-ranking officers when he saw them. Generals, if Rafe had to guess.

They were almost certainly visiting from the West Coast, where the remains of the army had seized control after the Flares. It was rare for *anyone* to cross the Mississippi and the vast plains that had been hollowed out by the second Dust Bowl. Something urgent must have brought them here. Likely something dangerous.

One of the generals flicked a gaze over Rafe before dismissing him with a slight sneer, but his dark eyes lingered on Dani as she laughed at a whispered joke from Beryl. No lust or greed in that unflagging stare, just wary confusion.

Most of the people in the room couldn't see past Dani's lush smile and enticingly bared skin to the danger she represented—but even the clueless ones knew *something* about her drew the eye. They might tell themselves it was her beauty, her allure, the sensual charm she exuded like a Siren of legend.

But it was her grace. Dani moved like gravity had no claim on her, fluid and graceful, inexplicably and yet undeniably *other*. A trained soldier would note the oddity. When the general's brow furrowed, Rafe slid his fingers along Dani's waist and turned into her, blocking her from the man's scrutiny.

Best not to let his vague curiosity bloom into something more.

Fortunately, most of the denizens of the Hill were far less observant. At least three of the people who smiled at him and shook his hand had been directly involved in kill orders leveled at the Silver Devils. One had met Rafe five years ago, when Knox had been tasked with escorting a high-level scientist to a satellite laboratory in Alabama.

Rafe resisted the urge to tense as the executive, a man named Kelley, curled his fingers around Rafe's, but there was no recognition in his eyes. A simple soldier was simply beneath Kelley's notice. Not worthy of remembering a face, much less a name. To the people in this ballroom, Rafael Morales had been Recruit 66–942. An expendable, interchangeable tool that had angered them by breaking. Killing him wasn't murder. It was disposal of a useless resource.

It took every scrap of willpower in Rafe's body not to tighten his hand until he heard the crunch of bone. "Nice to meet you."

"Mmm. You came with Phoenix, didn't you?" Kelley eyed Rafe curiously over his bubbling drink. "Are you in the same business?"

As far as the people here were concerned, Phoenix's *business* was the same as the man whose penthouse and life she'd co-opted: the procurement and distribution of rare genetic materials and weapons. A clean, clinical way to describe kidnapping genetically enhanced people and selling them for experimentation . . . or parts. "Something similar," he murmured, making his tone conspiratorial. "A little less mundane. A little more lucrative."

"Indeed?" Kelley clapped Rafe on the shoulder. "We'll talk, son. I need a more robust set of test subjects if I'm ever going to crack consciousness transfer."

Rafe was surprised they weren't using Protectorate soldiers as guinea pigs already. Then again, maybe they were. Maybe that was what the man meant by *more robust*. Someone who'd been genetically manufactured by a place like the Franklin Center wasn't limited by hormonal enhancements. Their endurance was built into them at the genetic level. They could survive things that would kill someone like Rafe.

A horrifying thought that explained a *lot* about Ava's temperament.

Finally, the wave of eager new faces broke, and Rafe found himself tucked into a corner with Dani, gripping a fancy glass filled with some sort of gently smoking neon-blue cocktail.

They'd positioned themselves on instinct so that they had full coverage of the room between the two of them. Rafe lifted his glass and let the odd blue liquid just touch his lips—it actually wasn't bad, though he had a feeling the alcohol content was high enough to endanger even his metabolism.

"Regretting all the choices that landed you here?" Dani murmured.

"I've had seven of those lobster things," he shot back, forcing humor to hide his growing urge to strangle the lot of them. "I'm living my best fucking life."

"So you say." Dani pressed closer and leaned up to nuzzle his jaw. "On your three, in the next room over. It's Anderson."

Rafe waited until a waiter eased by with a tray and deposited his drink on it. Then he turned into Dani, shifting enough to get an eyeline as he brushed his lips over her temple.

The arched doorway was three meters to his right. The lighting in the next room was subdued, mostly deep blues and teals that sparkled off the guests' jewels and made the white parts of their clothing glow. Their target stood just inside.

Dr. Helen Anderson had been the vice president of Research and Development at the TechCorps for decades. Rafe could rattle off her vital stats from memory: 162 cm, Caucasian, seventy-eight years old but, like many of the higher-ups in the TechCorps, wearing those years lightly—but not quite so lightly as Beryl. Her eyes were a piercing blue that didn't come from contacts, and her uncolored silver hair was cut in a blunt, no-nonsense bob. Even her dress was subdued—a black sheath that fell to just above her knees, with matching plain black pumps.

Her only adornment was an intricate silver necklace set with a cascade of sparkling crystals that ranged from white diamond to deep sapphire. Compared to the elaborate fashion surrounding her, she looked utterly mundane. A casual observer might mistake her for nobody of importance.

Rafe never would. The rhythms of the room she was in revolved entirely around her. People hovered, eager for her attention, devastated by her disinterest. He could almost see their mental hierarchies shifting in real time as they elevated those she deigned to speak with and discarded those unworthy of her attention. In a sea of people trying incredibly hard to attract attention, she was one person too important to need—or want—it.

And, according to Maya, she was the woman who'd originally radicalized Birgitte Skovgaard. Anderson had been fighting her own quiet rebellion from within the TechCorps since the day an unstable Protectorate soldier had perpetrated a massacre that had taken out his entire squad and far too many civilians—including her favorite grandson.

She was their best hope of survival. Or, if Maya was wrong, the person who might kill them all.

Rafe turned his face into Dani's hair, steadying himself by drawing in a deep breath. She didn't smell at all like herself, but somehow the scent Phoenix had helped her develop fit her. Probably because it was sleek and mysterious and deadly—all features of Dani's personality that Rafe found perversely soothing. "No way we can get near her without everyone noticing."

"It's too soon, anyway." She tugged at his hand. "Come on, let's find another buffet. Something with cheesecake on it."

He let his laugh roll out, because he knew he had a good one. More than one head turned to follow them as he and Dani strolled across the room toward the array of tables set up against floor-to-ceiling windows. He flashed his best smile freely, knowing it was a lure he might be able to reel in later.

But halfway across the room, his gaze locked with a pair of familiar brown eyes, and his best smile froze on his lips. Icy shock shuddered down his spine, followed swiftly by denial. It couldn't be.

She couldn't be.

His stunned brain clicked over into threat-assessment mode. The woman who held his gaze was tall, her skin almost the same warm brown shade as his own. And there was plenty of that skin bared by a tight bodice covered in crystals that spilled down toward her asymmetrical skirt in all the colors of the northern lights. Loops of diamonds sparkled at her throat and glinted from the black glossy curls that framed her face like stars strewn across the midnight sky.

She was a glamorous stranger with his sister's face, and even as he tried to tell himself he must be imagining the resemblance, her eyes widened in shocked recognition.

"What is it? What's wrong?" Dani followed his gaze and amended her questions. "Do you know her?"

Across the ballroom, those familiar brown eyes narrowed. In the next moment, she resumed a polite social mask, smiled at someone passing by, and pivoted deliberately on her heel to walk away.

Dani's hand tightened around his. "Honey?"

"That's Tessa," he whispered, his lips numb. "That's my sister."

She froze, then cursed. "Shit. Okay, I'm on it." She grasped his arms and turned him toward her. "Look at me." When he met her gaze, she nodded once. "Stay here. Don't move. If anyone comes up to you, you play the game and play it *hard*. You understand me?"

If it had been anyone else—even Knox—he would have bodily moved them out of his way. Tessa, his sweet-faced little sister, was *here*. In this den of sick, greedy monsters, surrounded by danger and the promise of near-certain death.

Every muscle in his body trembled with the need to follow her, to get her away from this place. The mission could go fuck itself. The whole *world* could go fuck itself.

But Dani's gaze held him. Her fingers burned on his arms, ten perfect spots of contact that grounded him. Her blue eyes were clear chips of ice, enhanced by her dramatic makeup. She was fierce and deadly, the only person on this earth he trusted as much as himself when it came to his family.

Because Dani was a protective force of nature when it came to her people, and it didn't matter that their relationship was an awkward, twisted thing of thwarted passion and sharp edges. Rafe was one of Dani's people. He knew it in his bones.

Other partygoers were watching, so he lifted a hand to cup her cheek. Hopefully only Dani could tell that his fingers trembled on her skin. He smiled, touched her lips with his thumb for the benefit of prurient onlookers, and leaned in to whisper a single word.

"Go."

There was a trick to crossing a crowded room unimpeded. Normally, Dani would bare her teeth and growl at anyone who got in her way, but this occasion called for more subtlety.

She squared her shoulders, lengthened her stride, considered which items in the room she could use as improvised weapons, and stared straight through anyone who looked like they might approach her.

It worked. Only one person even tried to step into her path—Irving, the dickhead from earlier who'd been ranting about genetically engineered psychics. Dani brushed past him and considered where Rafe's sister might have gone.

The balcony was a definite no, unless Tessa wanted to get cornered, which Dani doubted very much. She could have tried to blend into the crowds, but Rafe was tall enough to spot her in any crush of people. There was only one place he couldn't follow—the bathroom.

It didn't take Dani long to find the facilities, and irritation gripped her as she faced down just two doors—a ladies' room, and a matching one across the hall marked GENTLEMEN. Never mind that she hadn't seen a single one of those so far at this fucking party, what kind of assbackward people hadn't moved on to private restrooms yet?

Swallowing a growl, she pushed through the door. The soft tinkle of computer-generated piano music drifted from hidden speakers as she made her way toward the mirror and searched through her small handbag for her lipstick.

Dani did a quick touch-up, then placed the engraved silver case on the counter. Though audio and video surveillance were vanishingly rare in these private spaces on the Hill, she wasn't taking any goddamn chances. The tiny jammer hidden in the bottom of the case would scramble any digital devices within range.

"You might as well come out," she said, still facing the mirror. "I'm not leaving."

One of the elegant stall doors *clicked*, and Tessa Morales stepped out. She was dressed like she belonged in a place like this, and her face was set in a polite, slightly bored mask.

But her clenched jaw gave her away. She walked to the mirror without looking at Dani, held out her hands for the sink to dispense its floral-scented foaming soap, and let the water switch on before she spoke in a low voice. "There's a kill-on-sight order on him."

What else was new? "Tell me about it. These assholes live for a good KOS order."

"Get him *out* of here."

"You know better—or you should, anyway." Dani turned to face her. "What the hell are you doing here?"

Tessa held her hands under the small dryer, her gaze still pointedly fixed on her own reflection. "I'm surviving."

Dani saw desperation every day, and it radiated from Tessa in nauseating waves. Closing a bit of the distance between them and lowering her voice, Dani tried again. "Tell me, please. I can't leave this room without some sort of answer."

The younger woman closed her eyes and gripped the edge of the counter. "A few months ago, the acting VP of Security ran my brother's DNA against samples from every crime scene in the past year. I assume they did it for all of his friends, too. But nothing popped. Nothing except trace DNA from a Monet confiscated after a robbery."

It took Dani a moment to piece together her meaning. "*Your* DNA," she murmured.

She sighed and pushed upright, her mask sliding back into place. The resemblance to Rafe was undeniable—they had the same dark eyes, the same full lips. The same perfect cheekbones and smooth brown skin. But while Rafe's mouth always looked poised to quirk into a smile, Tessa's had a tight set, as if she'd been holding back a scream for weeks.

"I'm so careful," she said quietly, each word precise and considered. "I wear gloves. I cover my hair. I don't know what slipped through. But an Ex-Sec torture squad went to the painting's owner, who turned over the gallery that sold it to him. They flipped on the fence. He probably held out a while, but eventually he gave them his supplier. And that led them straight to the forger. A likely full sibling of Recruit 66–942."

It was heartbreaking. Rafe had tried so hard to protect his family, to keep them from falling into the TechCorps' clutches . . . only to have it all blown to hell because of a drop of sweat or blood.

Or maybe even a single tear.

"*Fuck.*" Rafe was going to be pissed. Rafe was going to be *terrified.* "Who was it? Who approached you?"

"Cara Kennedy."

It was an immaculately designed trap. The rest of the Silver Devils had no ties to exploit, nothing and no one that Cara could use as leverage, but that didn't matter. Rafe was enough. Holding a knife to his baby sister's throat was a brutally effective way to flush him out of hiding—and with him would come everyone else.

Tessa's gaze flicked over Dani. "You're not Maya, are you? Because she *hates* Maya, whoever that is."

"No, but she'd gladly shoot me in the face, too." Dani's stomach twisted as a horrible new thought snaked through her brain. "The rest of your family—are they safe?"

"I don't know. We had a signal . . ." Tessa's careful mask slipped again. Pain, just for a heartbeat, swallowed by determination. "They should have bolted. Rafael knows the safe houses. He's the one who set them up. Tell him to go, find them. I'll be fine."

"You really think he's leaving here without you?"

"He doesn't have a choice," Tessa hissed. "There's a GPS-locked bomb in my head."

Of course there was. Tobias Richter had been terrifyingly thorough and not very creative—both traits he'd apparently passed on to his protégée.

"They'll blow it if I do anything suspicious, like lurk in bathrooms with strangers. So *go*, for the love of God, and take him with you."

"Is your entire family this fucking impossible to deal with?" Dani snapped, then snatched up her bag. "Watch your back and don't get dead. Leave the rest to me."

Dani didn't look back as she left the bathroom, but she paused at the end of the hall to school her features. This was still a party—a sad, frustrating excuse for one, granted, but part of her cover involved at least pretending to enjoy herself.

Even if she was surrounded by intractable, bullheaded members of the Morales clan.

She caught sight of Rafe through the crowd and smiled reassuringly, though it didn't do much to alleviate the tension in his eyes. She kept her gaze locked with his as she made her way through the throng of people, right up until she could lay her hand on his rigid arm. "Honey—"

"There you are! See, I told you we'd find her," Beryl declared triumphantly. "Bette, darling, I'd like you to meet someone very special."

Dani turned, and the tension in Rafe's eyes took on a whole new meaning.

"This is John Smith, the TechCorps' newest Board member. John, meet Bette Parker-Holmes."

The Professor smiled genially and held out his hand. "I heard you were beautiful, but the tales don't do you justice."

Dani bit back a retort, smiling out of habit as she shook his hand. "You flatter me, Mr. Smith."

"Please, do call me John."

Beryl beamed. "Oh, I just *knew* you two would hit it off."

He chuckled. "And you were right, Beryl. As always."

Dani squeezed his hand—hard.

If anything, his smile widened. "Will you dance with me, Mrs. Parker-Holmes?"

She wanted to tell him to go to hell, preferably followed by a few swift punches to the junk. But she had to simper before passing her handbag to Rafe along with a silent promise to extract as much information from the bastard as possible. He smiled that warm, lazy smile in return, and she joined the Professor—*John*—on the dance floor.

He slid his arm around her waist, his executive-perfect smile never wavering. "I wasn't sure you'd agree to this."

She laughed gaily. "Well, it was either this or stab you in the face in front of all these people."

John gasped mockingly. "You wouldn't."

"Oh, I'm still considering it."

He hummed and spun her around, making her dress flare out behind her. "You know, I think that's my favorite thing about you, Dani. You're predictable, but only when it comes to violence."

"You're pretty predictable yourself," she hissed. "When it comes to lying."

He sighed. "You're upset."

Upset was a mild word. A weak one. *Upset* was what you got when you broke your favorite coffee mug, or when the hot water heater was on the fritz. This man had come into their lives under false pretenses, lied about who he was and what he wanted. He'd taken advantage of Nina's desire to see the good in everyone.

"You used my friend. I'm not upset. I'm angry. Offended." She stepped on his foot. "I'm *fucking pissed*."

A flash of something almost like remorse darted across his classically handsome features. "Nina's a nice girl. I wouldn't ask her to do anything she wasn't ready to do."

"You cultivated her as an *asset*. She's not a person to you, she's a tool."

"She's both." He shrugged one shoulder. "That's what makes her so useful."

He spun her again, and she caught glimpses of people watching them with hungry curiosity. So she leaned in, guiding him down so that her mouth almost touched his ear. "You're a bastard. And I still haven't decided not to murder you yet."

He threw back his head for a full, booming laugh. "You are more than welcome to try."

Ugh, she didn't know what was worse—that he actually thought he might beat her in hand-to-hand combat, or that he was *right*. "Kindly shut up and dance, Professor."

"My name is John."

"Your name is *bullshit*."

He threw back his head and laughed again. Oh, well. She might be in hell, but at least all the curious onlookers would be convinced they were having a great time.

TECHCORPS PROPRIETARY DATA, L1 SECURITY CLEARANCE

We've finally achieved limited success in reconstructing Novak's destroyed research. Fatality rates for raw recruits are still universal, but almost 20 percent of Protectorate soldiers undergoing the process have survived. I suspect this is due to weaker candidates already having been weeded out of this number. Their inherent stamina and healing abilities also afford them a greater chance of surviving integration.

If you wish to push forward, we'll need to increase Protectorate recruiting dramatically to make up for the loss of soldiers.

Internal Memo, May 2085 ·

TWELVE

Somewhere between watching the Professor swing Dani around the dance floor and forcing himself to smile at a man who was hinting that he could supply Rafe with all the genetically enhanced toddlers he could ever want, Rafe's emotions shut down.

It wasn't his usual careful compartmentalization or professional distance. It wasn't even focus on the mission. It was a good thing his high-tech contacts were recording every interaction for later analysis, because he could barely remember a word he said.

He smiled. He laughed. He let his fingers linger on wrists and at waists, and let his sentences trail off into teasing innuendo. He knew that two dozen important people would be blowing up every channel of communication Phoenix had to lure him to increasingly intimate parties where increasingly powerful people would plot increasingly horrifying things.

He did the job. He was good at the job. But numbness flowed through his veins, a chilly detachment he knew couldn't be healthy.

But all the unhealthy in the world was preferable to opening his eyes and staring into the abyss he could feel opening before him. So he just . . . didn't feel.

He didn't feel as they left the party and settled into the AirLift. He didn't feel as Dani watched him with silent, worried eyes. He didn't feel as he strode into Phoenix's penthouse and waited for Conall and Phoenix to establish a secure video connection for their debriefing. He didn't even feel when Dani related the whole sordid story to the entire team, whose faces took on various expressions of horror and concern.

Rafe didn't feel until he was facing his former captain. Knox's eyes were gentle and understanding, and relief flooded Rafe as Knox took quiet, effortless control. "You set up the safe houses?"

"Two." He rattled off their addresses from memory. "Check the Peachtree Hills one first. Soon, Knox. Please."

"Conall's already pulling up maps and surveillance," Knox assured him. "We'll go tonight, and we'll bring them back safe."

It was the only thing he needed to hear. The only thing he could *cope* with hearing. Anything else might crack open the fragile hell holding his panic at bay, and he couldn't do that. Not here, in front of Phoenix.

So he fled.

He escaped the room and strode through the dark corridors, moving in an oasis of illumination as lights flickered on ahead of him and faded as he passed. The metal links on his outfit *clinked* softly as he ripped at the ties holding them, and by the time he palmed his way into his room he'd managed to tear free of the long tunic, too.

Rafe let the entire mess drop to the floor and kicked off his boots next. The gently warmed hardwood of his bedroom floor was smooth beneath his bare feet, and the vast embedded screens on his wall gazed out over a moonlit sand beach, millions of stars twinkling bright enough to touch. He could even hear a faint echo of crashing surf, no doubt pumped through invisible speakers. There was probably a setting that would bring him the tang of salt water and hot sand, too.

No one lied to themselves quite like these bastards on the Hill.

"Morales?"

He was lying to himself, too. He was pretending he could keep his eyes closed and not face the black hole trying to pull him in.

Heels clicked on the engineered wood. *"Rafe."*

He spun to face Dani. Framed in the soft glow of the hallway, she looked ethereal in her devastating gown, her hair mussed and wild, the deep blue tips kissing her arms.

She looked like she belonged here, in this glittering world of greed and lies—until his gaze found hers. He'd seen that softness directed at Maya or Nina or even a beautiful weapon, but he'd never seen those gorgeous eyes so open and gentle when she was staring at *him*.

It crashed into his heart and shattered the numbness, and the truth escaped his lips in a heartbroken whisper. "It was all for nothing."

"No." The denial was fervent, immediate. Then her shoulders fell. "Yes."

That one word, regretful and brutal, ripped the fight out of him. He sank to the edge of the endless, pristine bed, hollowed out but oddly relieved. Dani would never lie to him.

And Dani understood. Which was the only reason he could say the words out loud. "I was seventeen when my father died. Tessa was eight, and Antonio was just two. Rosa wasn't even born yet—my mother was only a few months pregnant."

She stepped closer. "What was he like—your father?"

"Smart. So fucking smart." Rafe curled his fingers into fists so tight his knuckles ached. "He was a professor before the Flares. He taught math. High-level shit. He never wanted to get tangled up with the Tech-Corps, but he still had a reputation, I guess. Scientists would hire him to consult sometimes. We weren't exactly well-off, but . . . we were comfortable. And so many people weren't, back then."

Dani kicked off her shoes, crawled onto the bed behind him, and wrapped one arm around his shoulders.

The warmth of her skin against his still sparked—they always sparked—but this time the embers eased the chill of the ice in his veins. "My mother was an artist. A children's book illustrator. She used to make stories about us—" His voice wobbled, and he closed his eyes again. "She didn't have the connections to sell to people on the Hill. Not for the kind of money you'd need to feed three kids with another on the way."

She'd worked herself sick. Doing art commissions for scraps, taking in laundry and mending on the side, struggling in their garden to grow food even when her body already ached and the exhaustion from a hard pregnancy had settled in her bones.

Dani just squeezed his shoulder, so he forced out the words. "The bonus is so big, Dani. For a Protectorate recruit? It's nothing to the TechCorps, but it was *so much* to a family like ours. Enough to keep a roof over their heads and food on the table for years. I had to do something, before she worked herself to death."

"You did the right thing." She laid her cheek on his shoulder. "You did the *only* thing."

"Maybe." He reached up to cover her hand with his, clinging to the strength she offered as he forced himself to stare at the cliff edge before him. The ground just kept crumbling beneath his feet, so he might as well jump. "And then I did terrible things."

The words hung between them for a moment, and Rafe let them. He had to face this. He had to own it.

He'd done terrible things.

Terrible things.

Terrible things.

That was why the Protectorate existed, who they were. Not the shiny propaganda vids or the parades or the ceremonies where they pinned a medal onto someone and celebrated great victories. Maybe Knox had fallen for that lie—he'd been from a safe little suburb where people mostly took care of each other and the Protectorate only rolled in if the raiders got too cocky.

But Rafe had grown up in the shadow of the Hill, in one of those deceptively shiny neighborhoods where you could never forget you had just enough because you were always one bad break from losing everything. The Protectorate leaned hard on all the communities that bordered the Perimeter, and Rafe had grown up knowing in his bones that he was one of the people they protected *against*.

Safety ended at the foot of the Hill. Everyone else was an enemy who simply hadn't fucked up enough to get swatted down yet.

Rafe had known he wasn't joining some heroic band of soldiers bent on making life better for everyone. But he'd done it anyway. He'd put his family above others. He'd carved off little bits of his soul, bleeding a little more day by day. Week by week. Year after year after year . . .

He'd done it to keep them safe.

"I did terrible things," he whispered again, "and she *still* ended up here."

"It's not your fault," Dani whispered. "Or hers—she must have had her reasons. Because the TechCorps, that's all they do, Rafe. Give us reasons. One way or another, they always get us. That's what we're trying to stop, remember?"

He gripped the edge of the bed, the expensive silk comforter crushed between his fingers. "We have to get her out. *I* have to get her out—"

"Yes. But we have to be smart about it. First things first—make sure Knox and the others have secured the rest of your family."

No hesitation at all. It should have helped, but every mistake he'd ever made dragged at him from the abyss. Every moral sacrifice, every failure. He'd gotten contacts burned. Hell, he'd gotten Luna *kidnapped*. He'd shut down union organizers who might have made things better for their families, and the fact that he'd done it without killing them like another squad might have didn't mean shit in the long run. He'd dragged out the status quo, helping the TechCorps avoid the outrage that might have sparked a full revolt.

He'd made things worse instead of better. Not always. Not even most of the time, maybe.

But enough. Enough.

For *nothing*.

"Come on." Dani tugged him up, somehow moving him, as if he wasn't nearly twice her size. "Lie down. You need to rest."

Oh *God*, no. Not sleep, where the guilt and the darkness could swallow him whole. But even though he'd already bled his messy emotions all over Dani, he couldn't quite admit that he was afraid to close his eyes and endure the silence of his own head.

She made a soft, soothing noise as she stretched out beside him, her fingers sliding through his hair. "First, your mom and the others. Then Tessa. We'll get them all out, and they'll be safe. I'll make sure of it."

Her fingernails dragged over his scalp. Her body was warm against his side. Her arm grazed his bare chest, her skin soft and smooth, and he shivered and closed his eyes.

The darkness didn't sweep over him. It couldn't, not with Dani wrapped around him, all but vibrating with protective violence. Not with her voice whispering against his ear with a tenderness he'd been yearning for since he'd met her, and could never deserve.

"Even if I have to do it myself, Rafe. We'll get them out."

He believed her, because Dani wasn't like him. Dani had never lied to herself or built a crumbling castle out of rationalizations. Dani didn't care if she was good or bad. She didn't waste time on existential angst. And whether this thing between them burned into glorious fire or exploded into shrapnel that cut bone deep, it wouldn't matter. Not to her.

Dani would still get the fucking job done.

That was why he loved her.

Cara is still showing undesirable emotional weakness. Whatever you did during her dissociation training was clearly insufficient. Repeat the process, and this time I expect results.

Internal Memo, December 2078

THIRTEEN

Dani woke up with Rafe's hand in her dress.

Not *up* her dress, or *down* it, or anything that salacious and ultimately excusable. His fingers had slipped into the gap that slashed across her midsection and were curled around her rib cage. His other arm lay under her head, and his body was half-wrapped around hers.

He was *cradling* her.

It was sweet, and it was unacceptable. She wasn't even sure how it had happened. Normally, she woke at the first hint of disturbance—it was at least half the reason Nina had soundproofed Dani's bedroom. But somehow, here she was, with fake sunlight streaming from the wall screens. She'd spent the whole night in Rafe's bed, and she hadn't even stirred, much less jerked awake the way she should have.

Slowly, she peeled his hand away and slipped out from under his arm. He didn't wake up as she slid off the bed, just rolled over to grip a pillow instead. She crept out, pausing just long enough to retrieve her shoes.

She didn't take a deep breath until she was in the bathroom, her dress crumpled on the floor and hot water streaming over her head, washing away the smeared cosmetics from the night before.

The shower had a full-body dryer function, but she grabbed a towel instead and hurried into her room. She pulled on the first pair of pants she laid her hands on—some gray sweatpants she'd stolen from Nina, so faded and threadbare they were practically white—and a black tank top. She left her hair loose and wet and went in search of coffee.

Phoenix was in the kitchen, cutting up fruit and tossing it into a blender as she chatted with a holographic projection of Beth. "There are probably a few first editions in the penthouse library. When this is over, you can box the whole thing up and give it to them, if you want. It's not like anyone on the Hill *reads* the damn things."

"Oh, that'd be great. I'll tell—" Beth cut off abruptly and turned to smile at Dani. "Good morning! You look great! I love the blue."

Belatedly, Dani realized she was talking about her hair. The color in the tips wouldn't wash out. They'd have to get the heat wand after it later. "Thanks."

Phoenix gestured to the hologram with her knife. "Beth was telling me about your big score."

"Last night?"

Beth giggled. "No, the RLOC bunker. It's *amazing.*"

The Rogue Library of Congress cache had been so stuffed with digital information and hard copy books that they were still sorting and cataloguing it. Even so, the sheer value, monetary and otherwise, of the information they'd recovered had Nina and Knox talking in wistful tones about looking for more RLOC repositories.

Wistful because of course they didn't have time to actually do it. But it was a nice thought.

"Yeah, we brought home a lot of stuff." Dani chose a mug and slid it under the sensor on the coffee maker. A moment later, a fragrant, earthy stream began to pour from the machine. "Are the bosses around?"

"Nina and Knox? They're upstairs, but they'll be back soon." Beth pointed at Dani. "*You* are a popular lady who has received a *lot* of social invitations this morning."

"How many is a lot?"

"I believe Conall called it a *metric shit ton*. Must have made quite an impression up on the Hill."

Dani groaned. "Just kill me now."

"Can't. Too many parties to attend." Beth's sympathy was apparent even on her digital visage. "We're in the process of sorting through the invites and cross-referencing them with Helen Anderson's known proclivities and social contacts. We'll let you know which events the Parker-Holmeses shouldn't miss."

"Thanks, Beth." The girl was so chipper it made Dani's teeth ache, but she was efficient and effective. Paired up with Conall and Maya, she might even be unstoppable.

"You're very welcome!"

Even Phoenix's usually severe expression melted into something fondly indulgent when she looked at Beth. "Beth is our secret weapon."

If holograms could blush, Beth did. "That's too sweet." Then she straightened. "Oh! Incoming."

She stepped to one side and vanished, only for Nina and Knox to appear in her place.

"Did you find them?" Dani demanded. "Rafe's family?"

"We secured them a few hours ago," Knox reassured her. "His younger sister and brother are resting with Tia Ivonne for the moment, but his mother wants to speak with him. Is he up?"

"I'll check." Phoenix set down her knife and strode out of the kitchen. "And the Professor?"

Nina blinked at her. "What about him?"

"Can I kill him?"

"Dani—" Nina pinched the bridge of her nose. "I get it. *Trust me,* I do. But he wasn't wrong before, when he said we needed someone on the inside. And if he sits on the fucking TechCorps Board?"

"I know, I know." It made him more than valuable to them. It made him irreplaceable. Untouchable. "But the second he's outlived his use-fulness, I am *at least* whooping his ass."

"I think he'd consider that more than fair."

Footsteps in the hallway heralded Rafe's approach. He burst into the kitchen at a run, his hair wet, still tugging a black T-shirt into place. He blinked once at the hologram—not common tech off the Hill—but his gaze immediately found Knox. "My family?"

"Fine," Knox said immediately. "The safe house was intact. You did a good job with it. We picked them up and brought them here. Hold on."

Knox looked to one side, then vanished. The woman who appeared a moment later looked like an older version of Tessa. The hologram washed out her dark skin—though Dani imagined it was the same rich shade as Rafe's—but had no problem capturing her model-sharp cheekbones, deep brown eyes, and elbow-length tumble of perfect black curls.

Did his entire family look like this, as if they'd stepped off the pages of a pre-Flare fashion magazine?

"Rafael." Her voice broke. "You've seen Tessa? Is she all right?"

If Dani hadn't seen Rafe so shattered the night before, she might have believed his smile. "She's fine, Mama. We already have a plan to get her home. You just keep Rosa and Antonio safe, okay?"

His voice was confident, reassuring. A smooth rumble of absolute lies.

And his mom *knew* it. The few lines around her eyes deepened, and her shoulders stiffened, as if bracing for a blow that could come at any moment. She sure as hell didn't look as if his reassurances had set her mind at ease. She looked fucking miserable.

Dani found herself stepping forward. "I spoke with Tessa last night. She's scared, but she's hanging in there."

Rafe shot her an irritated look, though it was swiftly replaced by that soothing smile. "We'll take care of her, I promise."

Nina spoke up. "Gray is putting the finishing touches on the apartment across the hall from Tia Ivonne's. She really wants a neighbor, and I thought you might indulge her, Señora Morales."

Rafe held his mother's gaze in silence for several moments, his eyes quietly pleading.

At last, she nodded. "Until Tessa comes home."

"Knox and Nina will protect you and the kids," Rafe promised her. "When we're done up here, we'll come home to see you. With Tessa."

"I know you will." Her hand lifted, reaching forward almost as if she could touch Rafe. "I love you."

"I love you, too." His smile wobbled. "Kiss the babies for me."

"I will."

The holograms dissolved, and Rafe's jaw clenched. He gave Dani one slashing look before pivoting and stalking from the kitchen.

Fuck. "Rafe, wait." Even though she was faster, his legs and his anger had carried him halfway down the hall before she caught up with him. "Hold on a second, would you?"

He stopped so abruptly she almost plowed into him. "Don't freak my mother out, okay? She's got enough to handle without imagining Tessa up here, terrified and living with a damn bomb in her head."

"Is it better to lie to her?"

"Maybe!" A growl of frustration ripped free of him. "And I know that's stupid, and I know I'm being an asshole. But it's the *only thing* I can do for them. Make sure they don't worry."

"It's not the only thing you can do," Dani countered. "And she's going to worry anyway, Rafe, because you and Tessa are her kids. It's her job. But one thing *I* can do is tell her what's really going on. That way, at least she's not over there, imagining something worse than reality."

He heaved another massive sigh and glared at her. "Do you have to be so damn reasonable? I'm trying to have a pointless fight with you."

"I know, I'm the worst. Want me to punch you?"

"Maybe," he rumbled. "Thank you, Dani."

"You're welcome."

He stepped closer. His jittery helplessness had dissipated, but it had been replaced by something even more dangerous: a warmth that seemed deeper than lust. He stared at her with such affection that it made Dani's stomach flip over.

He was almost looking at her like he lov—

"No time to play, kids," Phoenix's voice drifted down the hallway. "Your invites are coming in, and we need to discuss strategy."

"No rest for the weary," Dani murmured automatically. "And no fun for the wicked."

"It's the Hill." Rafe flexed his fingers, as if he was still imagining the physicality of a good, rowdy fight—or like he wanted to pull her close and just *hold* her. "They're all wicked. And I'm going to enjoy ruining their fun."

TECHCORPS PROPRIETARY DATA,
L3 SECURITY CLEARANCE

With all due respect, Rafael Morales is my intelligence officer, and an integral part of my squad. His talents would be wasted as your decorative accessory or your personal bodyguard. If you require an escort to a party, I'm sure that Executive Security will oblige you. That is their function.

Internal Memo, February 2080

FOURTEEN

Dani had thought nothing could be worse than a penthouse full of people trying to convince her to invest in technological torture or organ theft.

She was so, *so* wrong.

It started with their arrival—sans Phoenix this time. She'd seen them off at the penthouse with a wave and the beginnings of a smile, exhorting them to have fun in a way that made the idea sound not only impossible, but hilarious.

The moment they exited the AirLift, a silent servant appeared and offered up a silver platter laden with an assortment of black velvet masks. Dani reached for one automatically, her attention already on the small crowd of masked guests who'd begun to gather.

Their covetous gazes traced over Dani and Rafe, lingering far longer than mere appreciation required, and the pieces clicked into place. She turned to Rafe, one eyebrow raised, to find him already wearing his mask.

He slipped the fabric from her hands and grasped her shoulders, fingers warm on the bare skin as he turned her back to him. The velvet settled over her eyes, and she shivered as he positioned it carefully before tying it in place. His lips caressed her hair, and his whisper tickled the shell of her ear. "You got this?"

"It's the Hill's idea of a kinky sex party," she shot back. "I'm going to be bored out of my skull."

"So you've told me." He ran his fingertips down her bare arm, clasped her hand, and brought it up for a kiss. "Disappointing, really. If I was this rich, I'd throw amazing kinky sex parties."

It was a joke, but she had no doubt it was also the truth. Rafe clearly understood the finer points of consent and fun, two concepts that seemed to evade those on the Hill. They knew what physical pleasure was, sure, and they pursued it with the same single-minded intensity they usually reserved for their money. But it was bizarrely cold. Sterile. It was all about the endgame, with no regard at all for the journey.

Rafe was probably *all about* the journey. Every whisper, every sigh. Every stolen moment that existed only between lovers, the ones they'd tried for centuries to capture in poems and songs and paintings and could never get quite right.

She turned to Rafe and straightened his collar—such as it was. Like her, he was dressed all in black today, loose-fitting garments that should have hung off his body but seemed to cling to it instead, revealing more than they concealed.

It helped that his tunic was open nearly to the waist, affording a mouthwatering view of his gleaming chest and abs. Dani tried not to touch him, she really did, but she'd laid her hand on the center of his chest before she could stop herself.

She bit her lip and almost jerked her hand back, but it was too late. He covered her hand with his, pressing it tight against his skin, which burned with a heat that seemed to spread far beyond her palm.

The mask concealed his perfect cheekbones but framed his gorgeous eyes. He'd abandoned the cosmetic contacts tonight—surveillance tech of any kind was forbidden—and this close, she could see how gradually the impossibly vivid amber that ringed his pupils deepened into dark brown. His thick lashes were highlighted by a teasing smudge of eyeliner, and he was staring down at her with that *look* again, as if he could see straight into her soul. As if he knew every detail, not only about what she wanted, but what she *craved*. What she'd never even admitted to herself in the safe silence of her own head.

But the look didn't end there. It also whispered that no one else would ever come close to giving her all those things. Not the way he could.

It was dangerous. It was seductive.

Dani swayed toward him.

Several meters away, the servant cleared his throat discreetly. His gaze stayed fixed forward, not quite looking at them, but he bowed slightly and gestured with one hand, clearly indicating it was time to move along as the next car hovered close to landing.

Rafe folded his fingers around her hand, his touch warm and protective. "Shall we?"

They joined the throng of guests milling about in the exterior courtyard. Unlike the previous party, there were no lights twinkling overhead. There was nothing to illuminate the space but the light spilling from the interior of the penthouse.

They drifted through the doors. Dani hated turning her back on all those heavy stares, but they had no choice. It was either engage or keep moving.

Compared to the Baroque opulence of the venue the previous night, this place was stark, decorated in postmodern black and white with the occasional disorienting slash of red. It might not have been so bad, if not for the lighting. It was harsh, almost glaring, chilling in its brightness.

Dani sighed, and Rafe chuckled quietly at her irritation.

"I've seen sexier mausoleums," she muttered.

"Maybe it gets better in the next room," he murmured back, clearly unconvinced of the truth of his own words.

It *did* get better, but only marginally. The next room was long, with a cavernous ceiling, and featured a row of daises filled with naked, writhing bodies. "Impressive variety," Dani noted.

His gaze swept the row of revelers, and his full mouth twitched in something like amusement. "I'm sure they're doing their best."

Everyone else in the room *not* naked in a pile was riveted to the debauchery unfolding before them. Dani tugged Rafe closer in a half-embrace. "We can wander a little, case the place. Since everyone's so distracted."

He bent his head, brushing his lips to her temple in a feather-light kiss. "Might be a good time to find an office."

In addition to making contact with Anderson, they had been tasked with finding—and tapping into—a terminal hardwired with priority security access to the TechCorps' main computer system. And tonight's host just so happened to have L1 clearance, as well as a propensity to brag about his tricked-out home office.

As secondary objectives went, it was huge. Splicing into an L1 hardline would not only restore some of their lost access to TechCorps' communication systems, it would offer additional benefits. This was an *executive* line, and there was no telling what Conall could do with that.

"Next room?" Dani blinked innocently up at Rafe. "Should be just about time for the whips and chains."

Either she was psychic, or horny people on the Hill were just that predictable. The next room was, indeed, lined with X-shaped racks and padded benches, all with individuals bound to them. The slap of leather against skin was constant, receding into a dull roar under the sharp rise and fall of cries.

Some of Rafe's good humor had faded. His face showed nothing but pleasant interest, but she could feel the stiffness in him as they drifted deeper into the room.

What part of it bothered him? "Are you all right?"

His fingers flexed on the small of her back before he tugged, spinning them gently into the shadow of one of the massive columns. The carved marble pressed cool against her skin as Rafe splayed a hand above her head and leaned in close. "I know the blond on the rack in the middle," he murmured against her cheek. "66–1035. He's Protectorate."

Startled, Dani shook her head. "No."

Rafe made a dark noise, laughter with a slicing edge. "Happens more than you'd think. We can take a lot of damage, and consent's a tricky thing when your biochemical implant is basically a ticking time bomb. Saying *no* to the execs doesn't usually end well."

Amazingly, it hadn't been an issue in Executive Security—probably because the bastards kept their bodyguards around specifically for their ability to kill just about anyone and didn't dare risk it.

Or maybe she just hadn't stuck around long enough for anyone to try it.

"I'm sorry, Rafe." It wasn't enough, but it was all she had.

His soft exhalation stirred her hair. "They never really got a shot at me. I was barely out of training when Knox swept me up, and he had enough influence to protect all of us. But most people don't have a Knox."

"No, they don't." She tugged at his tunic, eager to get him away from the spectacle—and from anyone who might recognize him, even under his mask. "Let's go find a fucking drink and some fresh air. In that order."

It only took a few minutes to find a tray full of champagne flutes and a closed balcony door. It took Dani a few more just to soak in the view.

She'd almost forgotten it, the steel and glass spires rising into the sky like the shoots of some exotic alien plant. In the daytime, sunlight glinted off everything in a blinding blaze. At night, it looked like something even more alien, glowing and alive, with the steady blinking light of drones and AirLifts buzzing back and forth like worker bees maintaining a hive.

It was beautiful in a way that nothing in Five Points or the rest of Atlanta could ever hope to be—and it was twice as treacherous.

Dani drained one of her flutes and reached for the second she'd grabbed for herself. "Have you ever seen a Venus flytrap?"

"Not up close and personal."

"That's what this place is. It's gorgeous, in its own way. But if you get too close, it gobbles you right up."

"Most of the time." Rafe leaned against the side of the balcony, sipping his champagne. "You escaped."

It was a nice thought, so she let him keep it. "I wonder if it would work for me." She turned around and nodded toward the door. "Whipping. The pain, I mean."

He tilted his head and considered her. "You've never told me how it works. I know you don't seem to feel pain, but . . ." His voice dropped, the final words coming out in a suggestive rumble. "I know you feel touch."

Her cheeks heated, and she tilted her face to the cool night breeze. "I get off just fine, if that's what you're asking."

"It's not."

It was so *hard* to describe. "I feel pressure, if I'm paying attention. That's why fights can be dangerous, because there's so much going on. And blades, those are so sharp there's no pressure to feel." She paused. "And I have all the physical effects of pain—I get sweaty and fidgety, even light-headed and nauseated. It just . . . doesn't hurt."

He moved closer and trailed one fingertip from her elbow up to her shoulder. It was a slow, careful caress that made her think about entire days spent in bed.

She shuddered, and her nipples hardened against the slinky fabric of her dress.

Rafe smiled. "See? You felt that."

Dani had to swallow hard in order to speak. "But isn't it about endorphins? The BDSM stuff?"

"It doesn't have to be. Pain carries its own kind of catharsis, but sometimes . . ." His fingertip traced a delicate path across her shoulder. "Sometimes it's about surrendering to sensation, whatever that happens to be."

She felt almost hypnotized, like she had on the arrival platform. "I've never trusted anyone enough for that."

"You can trust me." Another teasing smile. "I trust you. Hell, you can tie me up anytime, cupcake."

"No way. That would take even *more* trust."

"True enough." His fingers drifted up to her cheek, but whatever he was about to say died as the door whispered open again.

It was Helen fucking Anderson, vice president of TechCorps R&D, alone except for a half-filled highball glass and a scowl.

When she caught sight of them, her scowl deepened for a split second before smoothing into a polite, vague almost-smile. "Lovely evening, isn't it?"

Dani's heart rate spiked as adrenaline coursed through her. This was it, their best chance for making priority contact and delivering the message that could draw Anderson into their circle—or get them killed.

The risks didn't matter. She and Rafe both understood them well enough. They had to try.

Dani sipped her champagne and smiled. "It's a bit warmer than back home."

"Oh? Where is that?"

"DC. We're in town for the technology exhibition."

Another tight smile. Anderson was nearing her limit for meaningless small talk. She'd probably come out on the balcony to be alone, and they were fucking up her plans.

That was fine. All they needed was another minute.

"The exhibition must be so thrilling for you, being in research and development," she observed. When one of the woman's perfect silver brows rose in an arch, Dani nodded. "Why, of course I know who you are. I'm Bette Parker-Holmes, and this is my husband, Bryce."

Rafe deployed that stunning smile. "An honor."

Dani flipped a business card out of her clutch and passed it to Anderson. The contact information on it routed to Phoenix's penthouse—

after passing around the world a couple dozen times. "You should visit us next time you're in town. At least, through the winter. Come spring, we'll be back in Europe."

"How nice," Anderson said with strained courtesy.

She'd practiced the words until they echoed in her brain. They both had. It had to be precisely, exactly right, so there was no way Anderson could chalk it up to coincidence.

"I love Paris in the springtime." Dani smiled and leaned against Rafe's side. "At dusk, you can see the reflection of the Eiffel Tower's lights on the Seine. Nothing compares."

A heartbeat. Two. Birgitte's documentation had also held the answering phrase—*whether blue or gray be her skies.* Those words would signal their message had been received, loud and clear.

Dani watched. Rafe tensed slightly beside her as Anderson sipped her drink and tucked their business card into her tiny handbag. She didn't react at all, not even a flinch or a flash of something in her eyes. If anything, she looked like she was stifling a fucking *yawn.*

Maybe she'd forgotten. Maybe Birgitte's information had been wrong and she'd never even known the code.

Or maybe Helen Anderson was just *that* damn good at the game. It would explain how she'd managed to survive and advance where others in Birgitte's revolution had fallen.

Rafe finally broke the tense silence. "Maybe we could—"

He cut off abruptly as Anderson held up a hand. She waved her fingers slightly, and followed the gesture up with a verbal dismissal, as if she doubted they were intelligent enough to understand. "I'm sure you want to return to the party, now."

Rafe glanced at Dani, but all she could do was shrug. Either Anderson had gotten the message or she hadn't, but they were certainly being told to get lost.

Inside, she deposited her empty flutes on a table in the hall and backed into a secluded corner. "What do you think?"

"If she's playing it cool, she's stone cold," he replied softly. "But at least she didn't call security on us."

"There is that," Dani agreed. "Ready to address our secondary mission objective?"

"Way preferable to a boring orgy." He held out his hand. "Let's do some crime."

Finally, the fun part. "Yes, let's."

Rafe had prepared for subterfuge. He'd spent his morning studying the penthouse's blueprints, identifying potential secondary and tertiary access points to the central hardline in case the office proved too dangerous to approach. He'd dug through Phoenix's anti-surveillance equipment and found pieces that would disable smart home tracking— one was embedded under his cuff links, the other rested against Dani's collarbones in a delicate necklace of sparkling crystal and twisted wire.

With Conall's gleeful guidance, he'd loaded up a chip with a dozen hacking programs. He'd refreshed his memory on circumventing biometric security, and had even found a set of lockpicks that Dani currently wore in a sheath on her thigh.

Preparation was how he coped with stress. It was a strategy he'd learned from Knox, whose contingencies had contingencies coming out of their contingencies, though for Rafe it had a narrowed focus: supplies and intelligence. He procured the information necessary to understand the scope of a job, and then the tools necessary to complete it.

So he'd come with a mental map of the home and every scrap of tech they might need. Phoenix had sworn it wouldn't be necessary, but he hadn't quite believed her. Maybe he hadn't *wanted* to believe her.

The TechCorps executives were creatures of legend, the monsters they all feared. Their power had to be immense, their plans flawless. It should take every scrap of courage and all his available wits to best them.

He hadn't wanted to believe that the people who ruled so cruelly over Atlanta could be this *incompetent.*

"I told you we wouldn't use any of that stuff." Dani slid one drawer shut on the file cabinet and moved on to search the next.

Rafe huffed as he unscrewed the last bolt on the metal plate that hid the office wiring. "Turning off security so you can play naked hide-and-seek with all of Atlanta's other most powerful jackasses is some truly questionable risk-assessment."

"It's more than that." She slapped a file folder on the desk and flipped it open. "These people think they're untouchable."

"I suppose they pretty much have been." With the wires exposed, he slipped open his tool kit and found the clip Conall had sent with him to splice into the hardline. "They have the food, they have the water, they have the electricity."

"And they have all the dirty secrets. Where'd you put that camera?"

"Here, try this." He slipped the slim document scanner from his case and held it up. "I stole it from Phoenix. I might see if she'll let me keep it. She does have nice toys."

"True." Dani expanded the telescoping scanner to the proper length, pressed the button on the end, and waved it over the paper. "It's enough to turn a girl's head."

"Stop trying to make me jealous." A flick of his wrist opened his knife so he could get on with his work. Conall had put them all through relentless training in stripping every possible kind of wire in every conceivable scenario, up to and including half-dead or in the dark. Or both.

Splicing into well-maintained top-of-the line wires in a comfortable office with Dani's perfume surrounding him ranked as one of his more pleasant infiltration experiences. Within minutes, he'd secured access, with Conall's clever wireless transponder tucked in with the wires. "Almost done here. Anything useful in the files?"

"Oh, all *kinds* of shit. I might even need your help." She looked up, her eyes sparkling. "Guess who found a stash of blackmail material?"

Both of Rafe's eyebrows tried to climb straight into his hairline. "He's keeping it in an *unlocked file folder*?" After a moment's thought, he shook his head. "No, of course he is. Give me some highlights while I close up here."

"Most of these involve embezzling. Some adultery. This one lied about his credentials to secure a job. It's fairly standard stuff." She barked out a laugh. "Wait. He's pretty sure the Professor's hiding something."

"Uh-oh."

"Relax, he thinks it's a sex thing. Something real kinky." She shook her head. "Well, if this guy suddenly turns up dead from a mysterious accident or heart attack, we'll know why. He tried to play a player."

Rafe had barely had the bandwidth to process the Professor's double-dealing last night, not with the revelation of Tessa's presence seeping through his veins like acid. Compartmentalization had done its job, but he *still* didn't know what to think about the Professor's convoluted game. Except for one thing. "If he pops up in the kitchen again, Maya is going to put a fork through his face."

"Not if I beat her to it."

Rafe imagined the ass-kicking line that would form the next time the Professor showed up in Southside would be truly inspiring—and that the Professor was smart enough to know that. He'd likely stay where he held all the power for the time being.

Most people did.

It only took a minute to restore the metal panel and pack up his tools. The entire case slid easily into his boot, and he smoothed his skin-hugging trousers back into place before rising to stand next to Dani. "Got it all scanned?"

"Almost. I just need—" The words cut off as she cocked her head to one side. *"Fuck."*

The next few moments were a blur. Dani threw the file into the empty executive chair, then shoved Rafe after it. Before he could speak, she'd climbed on top of him, her skirt rucking up around her hips. He gripped her for balance as the chair tilted back and found her bare thighs under his hands, skin so soft and warm his head spun in an attempt to catch up.

The door handle jiggled, but he barely had time to register the sound before Dani yanked on the zipper holding the top of her dress together. The fabric fell away, pooling around them.

The click of the electronic lock disengaging snapped him out of his daze. Instinct kicked in, and he ran his hand up her spine, tangling his fingers in her hair. One soft tug was all it took, because she was already moving toward him. His face found the vulnerable curve of her throat, his lips already parted. Her breathing hitched, and her hips rocked against his, and he didn't need to fake the groan that left him as the door swung open.

God, she felt good.

"Oh! My apologies," a man's voice stammered.

With unfeigned reluctance, Rafe looked up. It wasn't a server, but it definitely wasn't the owner of the penthouse, either. Probably an assistant, sent to fetch something or take care of some forgotten task.

Dani twisted with a supercilious sigh, turning her upper body toward the door. "What do you want?"

The man's discomfort spiked, and his cheeks flamed. "Nothing, it's—it's just that this office . . . It's off-limits to guests."

"First you interrupt us, and now you're kicking us out?" Her tone was cool, calm, shot through with a white-hot thread of danger.

Rafe saw the conflict play out in the man's nervous eyes. He weighed the potential threat to his presumed employer against the violent promise in Dani's voice. Of the two, leaving strangers in his boss's office was riskier . . . but angering a guest was likelier to get him fired immediately.

The man came to the same obvious conclusion. "No, please, I . . . was just leaving. Enjoy your night." The door clicked shut behind him as he practically fled.

Dani turned back to Rafe. "Rich bitch voice," she murmured. "Works every time."

She sounded incredibly casual. As if she wasn't naked to the waist, her breasts pressed to all the skin bared by his very risqué tunic. As if her squirming and pure adrenaline hadn't had predictable results—she was straddling an undeniable erection, a fact that might have been more embarrassing if he couldn't feel her tightly pebbled nipples against his chest.

Pure physical response. Nothing to see here.

Well, nothing he was *going* to see. He kept his gaze locked to hers as he guided the fabric of her dress back up her body. "You know, you could have just kissed me. That is the time-honored cover."

"At an orgy? Not good enough. Besides—" She zipped her dress. "When I kiss you? It's not going to be to maintain our cover. It's just going to be for us."

When, not *if*.

When.

Anticipation burned in his blood, but he kept his hands steady as he smoothed her disheveled hair, letting his fingertips trail all the way to the ends. "I can't wait."

"Could have fooled me," she teased, straightening his lapels. Then she slid off his lap. "Come on, we'd better get out of here anyway. No telling who'll wander in next."

Rafe rose and retrieved the file, holding it while Dani scanned the last few pages. She moved with her usual grace, but her cheeks were flushed and her breathing a little fast, and an inappropriate part of him reveled in it.

At least he wasn't the only one feeling unsteady.

With their blackmail secured, they packed up their supplies and slipped back into the hallway. Rafe worried briefly about cooling his body's excitement, but he shouldn't have.

Wandering back into the least joyful orgy imaginable was like a bucket of ice water straight to the face. Every executive screamed *threat* to his instincts on a cellular level, and the only thing he wanted to do to Dani now was wrap her in his coat to protect her from their hungry gazes.

He resisted. Barely. But he indulged himself enough to tuck Dani close to his side and accepted another glass of champagne, mostly to wash the metallic taste out of his mouth.

It was impossible not to compare the performative debauchery playing out in front of them to the gleeful depravity on display at a place like Convergence. Power and trust. That was the heart of it. A criminal nightclub like the one owned by Savitri, the self-crowned queen of Atlanta's digital underworld, might seem like an unlikely place to let down your guard. But those granted access to her inner circle were also brought under her protection. The pursuit of pleasure was an end in and of itself, yours *and* that of your partners, and if power came into it at all, it was just the spice. Another path to bliss.

Power was all that mattered here, but for all their reckless abandonment of security, there was precious little trust. Sex was just another variable in their intricate social hierarchy, a tool they used to climb higher or the knife they slipped into a competitor's back. His skin crawled at the competitive tension in the room, at the knowledge that some of the fixed smiles belonged to people there under duress.

At the reminder that this so easily could have been his destiny.

He'd been twenty-three when the Silver Devils formed, just old enough to see the danger ahead of him. His brains had earned him his place in military intelligence, but it was his perfect cheekbones and bedroom eyes and carefully honed weapon of a body that would have made him the Protectorate's favorite honey trap. Knox had prevented that by seeing the potential in him. Knox had literally saved him.

Because a decade subjected to the whims of these coldhearted bastards would have burned the soul right out of him.

A woman in a lavender evening gown sidled up beside him. She was older, but with the sort of ageless beauty that made it impossible to really pinpoint *how* old. Deep brown hair curled around her shoulders, and only the tiniest of lines formed between her perfectly shaped brows as she frowned.

"Are you as bored as I am?" she asked without looking away from the scene before them.

A frisson of warning tightened his grip on Dani's waist. He'd thought his mask was perfect, but perhaps it had slipped. Consciously, he relaxed into an easy smile. "How could anyone be bored on a night like this?"

"Oh, no need for that. I won't spill your secrets, love. And I'm not making a pass at you, either." The woman turned to face them, her gaze roving over them both. "Though you and your lady are both exquisite."

"Then what can we do for you?" Dani asked coolly.

"Actually, it's what I can do for you." She pressed a card into Rafe's hand with a wink. "You won't be disappointed. Neither will your wife."

The card was unrelieved black, made of the highest quality paper. Rafe flipped it over, and a shimmery outline caught the light—a single orchid, rendered in holographic purples and golds. Precious little context, but Rafe could connect the dots. "I take it you offer services for a more . . . discerning clientele?"

The woman inclined her head.

There was no name on the card, as if anyone who mattered would already know who she was. It wasn't so different than the gambit that had launched Dani and Rafe onto the Hill—the people up here would go to truly astounding lengths to avoid looking like they were out of the loop.

Rafe recognized the game, but he still had to play his part. With deliberate indifference, he passed the card off to Dani and gave the woman a curt nod. "Perhaps we'll meet again, in that case."

"I certainly hope we do." She drifted away, melting into the crowd.

Dani growled. "I hate this fucking place."

In that, they were in firm agreement. "Have we made enough of an appearance, do you think?"

"Fuck, yes. Let's get out of here."

Of course, it wasn't that easy. Three more enterprising owners of what he assumed were extremely exclusive brothels tried to lure them in by passing them discreet cards. And the man who'd been babbling about psychics the first night actually broke off from his sexual escapades to chase them across the ballroom wearing nothing but a mask, a sight that might have amused Rafe if the bastard hadn't been standing there in gold body glitter, trying to convince Rafe to procure genetically enhanced surrogates for his experiments.

Summoning the guards might have saved them from hearing the entire sales pitch, but neither Dani nor Rafe could afford the extra attention. So they listened. They forced smiles. They played the damn game.

And Rafe hated them all.

By the time they broke free, Dani's grip on his arm was tight enough to leave bruises and he was entertaining active fantasies of burning the entire building down. The only thing that kept him going was knowing Dani's safety rested on his ability to fake it.

Luckily, that was all the motivation he needed.

Dedicated.
Motivated.
Educated.
Elevated.

Protectors.

This week only: Signing Bonuses Doubled

100,000 credits

FIFTEEN

When they returned to the penthouse, it was empty. A terse message on Dani's private terminal proclaimed that Phoenix had "stuff to do" and would be back later.

Dani regarded the words as she stripped down, kicking her shoes and dress into a pile near the foot of her bed. She should have felt even a hint of curiosity as to Phoenix's whereabouts—she was on the Hill to gather intel, after all. But all she felt was numb, worn thin by dealing with the TechCorps' elite.

She claimed the shower first, hoping to wash away the evening along with the makeup and glitter dust. But the unsettled feeling lingered. Even after she'd scrubbed her skin bright pink, it *clung*.

This place was worse than filth. Dirt, you could wash away. But being on the Hill stained your soul. She needed more than a shower. She needed to be *immersed*.

She almost went straight to the pool naked, but after grinding up against Rafe tonight, skin to skin, there was only one place that would go. So she pulled her swimsuit out of the closet instead.

She'd packed the bikini just in case—though technically Dani supposed it was actually a one-piece. It was fancy enough to suffice for these fuckers on the Hill, and she liked the design and the way it felt. It was made of soft fabric and straps, all connected with little silver rings.

The pool glittered under the patio lights, muted gold that complemented the patterned blue tile. Soft sounds emanated from hidden speakers, noises of birdcalls and rolling waves—completely out of place, considering the trees ringing the outer edge of the courtyard. The overall effect was disorienting and fake, the kind of thing Dani hated. A perfectly clean box of treated water next to trees that couldn't possibly exist near the make-believe beach.

Right now, she didn't care.

She dove in, bracing herself for water that was either too cold or too warm. But it was just cool enough to be refreshing without making her teeth chatter, and she breathed a sigh of relief that bubbled to the surface.

She stayed under, enjoying the muted roar of the water in her ears and the gentle buoyancy cradling her limbs, until a burning need for air drove her to the surface.

A dark figure sat on the tiled edge at the deep end of the pool, his familiar silhouette backlit by the glowing lights of the city behind him. "I guess we had the same idea."

"I guess so." At least she had an excuse for sounding so breathless. "It's hard to wash this place off, isn't it?"

"Yeah." Rafe's voice was a low rumble. "But if you need space, I can go hit the bags or something. It's up to you."

The safest option was for him to be someplace else—but was it what she wanted? They'd been pushing one another away for so long that it felt like a habit, the *only* thing to do. But it hadn't helped matters, and it was getting harder and harder to do.

"No." She swam a little farther away, giving him some space. "It's fine. You can stay."

Rafe slipped into the pool in silence, disappearing beneath the rippling waves much the same way she had, as if only the complete embrace of the water could wash away whatever lingered inside. When he broke free of the surface again, he was just out of arm's reach. "We need to talk, don't we?"

Her heart jumped, beat faster. "Probably."

He floated in silence for an endless moment, his hands making gentle waves through the water. "You were right," he said finally, exhaling on a sigh. "It's harder than I thought. The long con. It's getting in my head."

It was an out, whether he realized it or not. She could reassure him that the proximity and the uncertainty were fucking with his mind, that once they were back at home, on solid ground, things would be clearer. They'd make sense. He'd see that the situation had magnified his feelings, blowing them way out of proportion until all he could see or hear or feel was something manufactured. As fake as the scene around them.

She opened her mouth, but what came out instead was a confession. "I'm so tired, Rafe. I'm tired of fighting myself."

Water rippled over her skin as he drifted closer. "I know how you feel."

"It doesn't seem like you do." The closer he came, the faster and harder the truth beat in her chest. "How are you not scared of this?"

He made a low noise. "I'm fucking terrified, Dani. We're two trains on the same track, headed toward each other at top speed. And you can't escape me now. If we crash and burn, it won't matter. Your family, my family—they're *ours*. You're stuck with me."

That was the whole problem, how intertwined their lives already were. If things went bad, there was no walking away. They'd still be in each other's lives—inescapably, permanently. It didn't matter what they'd done or how wildly they'd hurt each other.

It was too much pressure. It had kept Dani paralyzed for months, frozen in the hesitant, fearful space between taking the risk and turning away. But right now, here, surrounded by water and soft light and the smell of the same soap on their skin, it sounded like something else.

"Do you promise?" she whispered.

He was close enough to touch now. His fingertips grazed her jaw, leaving tingles in their wake. "It's the only thing I *can* promise," he replied just as softly. "I'm not going anywhere. Even if you break my heart and stomp on the pieces. You're worth it."

She had to close her eyes against the earnest sincerity shining on his face. "You don't get it. That's exactly what I've been trying to avoid. I don't *want* to hurt you."

"I'm a big boy, Dani. I get to decide what risks I'm willing to take." His thumb brushed her lower lip. "And you're *worth it*."

It shouldn't be a risk he *had* to take. A better person would swear not to hurt him, even if they had to lie.

But Dani never, ever lied. "You're worth it, too."

He curled his hand around the back of her head, his large fingers incredibly gentle as he tugged her closer. A swell lifted her, and she wrapped her arms around his neck, clinging to him as his breath warmed her wet skin.

"Rafe." Her lips brushed his cheek as she spoke, and the low noise he made in the back of his throat left her shivering.

His fingers wove beneath the straps of her bikini, burning as he stroked her skin. "Kiss me."

Dani opened her eyes. He was so *close*, staring at her with an intensity that belied the slow, casual movements of his fingers on her back. She might have wondered which emotion was real, but the fine tremor in his hands left no doubt.

She licked his lower lip.

This time, there was nothing subtle about his groan. Water sloshed around them as he drove her back toward the edge of the pool until her back hit the cool tile. His breath feathered over her lips, and then he was *kissing her,* open and starving. Like he'd been holding back for a lifetime.

Dani knew what that was like. She wrapped her legs around him, pulling him closer as his tongue slicked over hers. She poured everything into the kiss—every teasing remark, every glancing brush of hands. Every time she'd wanted to touch him but hadn't allowed herself the freedom.

She was free now. She slid her hands over his shoulders, digging her fingertips into the smooth skin and clenching muscle. She tilted her hips, and he slipped one hand down to curl beneath her thigh, encouraging her to grind against him as he dug his teeth into her lower lip, then soothed the sting with a slow lick.

Dani broke the kiss, her head spinning. "Fuck, this is a terrible idea."

"Is it?" His mouth brushed her jaw, tracing to the curve of her throat. "Maybe the terrible idea was fighting it for this long."

"Not the kissing." Or, she hoped, the inevitable fucking. "We're going to drown."

"Do you know how long Protectorate trainees can hold their breath?" She could *feel* his wicked smile, his lips curved against the spot where her pulse fluttered rapidly. "I'll show you."

It was Dani's turn to groan.

He licked her pulse, teasing her even as his hips rolled against hers beneath the water. "I won't let you drown, sweetheart. Just hold on for the ride."

"I think you've forgotten who you're grinding against." She bit his earlobe and dug her nails into his back. He shuddered, his hiss of pleasure hot against her skin.

When he lifted his head to meet her gaze, his brown eyes practically glowed in the golden light. "I could never forget," he rasped, his thumb sweeping up the inside of her thigh. *"Never."*

Well, damn. Dani slanted her mouth over his again, claiming him as her chest . . . ached. There was no other word for it. It couldn't possibly be a physical pain, but it sure as hell felt like her faded memories of a tender, bruised spot. Right in the vicinity of her heart.

The rest of her body? That was *singing.* In spite of the feverish impatience of his kiss, Rafe's hands moved like they had all the time in the world. Like he'd been planning this from the first moment they'd locked eyes in Clem's bar.

He touched her everywhere. A taunting brush of his thumb along her inner thigh was followed by teasing circles across her hip. His fingers danced up her body, exploring the skin bared by her bikini and tracing the patterns of the interlocking straps.

He hooked one finger under the strap at her shoulder and dragged it down. She sucked in a breath as his lips followed, blazing a path down her throat as he bared her breasts. Then he lifted her half out of the pool and closed his lips on her nipple while water cascaded around them.

The shock of it stole her breath, cool, wet skin versus the heat of his mouth, and she whimpered. His tongue flicked over her, circled her, and sensation threatened to overwhelm her.

She pushed at his shoulders, desperate to maintain control, but the thought shattered as he sucked her nipple deeper into his mouth. Her back arched, and instead of shoving him away, she dragged him closer.

"Please," she whispered, beyond caring about anything but his hands and his mouth on her skin. *"Please."*

Rafe kissed his way back up her chest and throat as he let her sink back into the water. But this time she came down straddling his thigh, his fingers already tracing her abdomen above the low elastic of her bikini.

His mouth found her ear for a low, commanding rumble. "Tell me what you need."

Her hips bucked in a silent plea. She opened her mouth to make it a real one, but a soft buzz cut her off. It was followed by a serene digital voice announcing an incoming landing, and exhorting them to clear the area. Dani glanced over and glimpsed the flashing red glow of landing lights through the trees.

Rafe buried his face against her throat with a groan. "Goddammit, Phoenix."

Frustration burned in Dani's core. "We can be quick, right?"

His low chuckle was full of promise, even as he nudged the top of her swimsuit back into place. "When I make you come for the first time, it will not be *quick*."

"*Not* helping."

"I know," he said, sliding the strap back over her shoulder. "Trust me. I know."

The click of boots on stone gave them just enough time to break apart before Phoenix appeared from the tree-shaded walkway, clad in another of her fabulous costumes that looked like flames devouring the darkness.

Instead of striding past them into the house, she came to the edge of the pool and braced both hands on her hips. "I don't know what the hell you two got up to tonight, but an invitation to the Free Thinkers' Salon just hit your inbox."

Rafe raised an eyebrow. "Is that . . . good?"

"That's *insane*," Phoenix shot back. "I've been trying to crack that party for three solid years. Even Beryl can't get an invite. Everyone who attends either sits on the TechCorps Board or basically owns their own feudal empire. That's some rarefied fucking air."

Dani shared a concerned look with Rafe. It could have been the Professor's doing, but she doubted it. He wouldn't potentially endanger his own plans, not for their sakes. Which meant it had to be Anderson, and she would certainly be there. But *why*? Because she understood their message after all and wanted to assist them? Or because she got the message, all right, but helping them was the last thing on her mind?

They could be about to fulfill their primary mission . . . or walk into certain death.

"It's a risk," she whispered.

"Exactly the kind of risk we signed up for," he countered.

That was true enough. This was their mission, their purpose. So she offered him a shrug. "I'm game if you are, Morales."

"I'm always up for violence and anarchy." He grinned. "You know Knox and Nina will murder us if we don't let them help strategize, though."

Some of her lingering ardor cooled. Something this huge meant a virtual roundtable discussion, possibly including everyone. It would take hours, if not the rest of the night, to develop plans and run through contingencies.

So much for sneaking off to Rafe's bed tonight.

She braced her hands on the tile and levered herself up to sit on the edge of the pool. "No time like the present. Let's go fill them in."

She reached to help him out of the water. He didn't need her help, but he took her hand anyway. When they were both out of the pool, standing at its edge, Rafe drew her closer and kissed the tip of her nose.

It was soft, sweet, the kind of caress that warmed her, even in the winter breeze. When he kissed her like that, she couldn't even be upset by the thwarted desire that still thrummed in her veins.

Fuck, she was in deep. And she didn't even care anymore.

**TECHCORPS PROPRIETARY
INTERNAL COMMUNICATION**

Anderson, Helen: Kyle?

Anderson, Helen: Kyle, are you available?

Anderson, Helen: Kyle, it's been forty-eight hours. If we reach seventy-two without a response, I'm coming up there.

Donovan, Kyle: I'm trying a new regeneration therapy this week. If you need anything, speak to Vargo.

Executive Internal Network

SIXTEEN

Superelite meant superexclusive, which posed several problems they hadn't encountered yet.

The first was a matter of scale. So far, Dani and Rafe had relied on a crush of guests, the large attendance of the various parties allowing them to blend in if they needed to avoid close scrutiny. But this was a rather intimate dinner party, at least by Hill standards, with no more than two dozen guests waiting to gain entrance.

The second issue centered around the fact that these were all *very* important people—mainly TechCorps executives. It was enough to make Dani nervous, though she knew logically that none of them would recognize her, even if she'd been on their Executive Security detail. To them, their guards were invisible, disposable, and forgettable. Equipment, not people.

Still, she was ridiculously grateful for the way Rafe squeezed her hand in reassurance as a stone-faced employee scanned their invitation code and then gestured them through.

The guests were gathering in a study decorated in deep, rich shades of green and brown. The furniture was surprisingly tasteful, with strong, classic lines. It was a warm room, beautiful in a comfortable, understated way.

Rafe squeezed her hand a bit harder, and she turned instinctively. The Professor was approaching them, impeccably turned out in a tailored suit. It was as old-fashioned as his usual attire, but instead of looking dated, the whole effect was just like the furniture—classic.

Dani greeted him warmly, with a smile she knew showed a few too many teeth. "John."

"Bette. You managed to secure an invitation to the Salon." Ice clinked as he raised his glass in salute. "I'm impressed."

"When will you learn not to underestimate me?"

He laughed. "Apparently too late for my own good."

Rafe's game face was flawless, his smile so warm Dani would have thought he was greeting an old friend if she couldn't practically feel the ridges of his fingerprints as he clung to her hand. "It's good to see you again, John."

Another man was making his way toward them. He was dressed in black, with a tunic fastened all the way up to his chin, smiling broadly. As if he hadn't a care in the world.

Dani knew who he was—Kristof Vargo. She'd once spent three miserable weeks on his detail. He wasn't the worst of the bunch, by far, but he was the kind of guy who talked big and kept three times as many guards as anyone else. A coward.

A coward who liked to *talk*. Dani herself had been subjected to multiple rants about how the future was shining, all they had to do to grab it was fully divorce themselves from antiquated ideas about how things had worked in the past.

If she had to guess, she'd say the guy would love to be a fucking dictator.

Vargo greeted John, who immediately turned to Dani and Rafe. "Have you been introduced to our esteemed host? Kristof Vargo, chief operating officer. This is Bette Parker-Holmes and her husband, Bryce. Tech investors from DC."

"I've heard so much. Wonderful to finally meet you, Bette." Vargo looked Dani straight in the eye, then lifted her hand and placed a slimy kiss on the back of it. "May I call you Bette?"

Not a hint of recognition. Of course. "You may."

"Wonderful," he said again. He reached for Rafe's hand next, dropping a kiss to the back of it, as well. "Bryce."

"Charmed," Rafe replied, managing to sound like he meant it.

"I've taken the liberty of seating the two of you near the head of the table. Well, near me. I hope you find the arrangements to your satisfaction." His tone made it clear he expected them to be more than pleased. He expected them to grovel in gratitude.

Dani forced out the words, though she had no real idea *what* she was saying. She was busy playing out the situation in her head, all the probabilities and possibilities. How much intelligence they could gather during the meal if they were extra careful—

The Professor laughed. "I daresay she's excited by the idea."

"As well she should be. You'll join us, won't you, John?" Vargo grinned at Dani and Rafe. "It's not every day you get to have dinner with the vice president of Recruitment and Retention."

Dani arched an eyebrow, hoping it looked impressed rather than incredulous.

"And, if I may . . ." Vargo leaned closer and dropped his voice. "Soon-to-be chief information officer."

"That's *not* a lock, Kristof," John protested.

"Ah, but it will be. At least, if I have anything to say about it."

Dani swallowed a laugh. He already sat on the fucking Board, but he was still hustling. Whatever he had planned for the TechCorps, it was bigger than she'd imagined. Deep cover had its limits, after all—you were always safer at the lowest level of power and exposure that allowed you to complete your mission. You got where you needed to be, and then you kept a low profile.

If the Professor was shooting for CIO, it meant he wanted to be within touching distance of the top. And Dani wasn't sure whether to be amused or frightened by the idea.

"Never mind that," John demurred. "You're basically our acting CEO. Donovan's name might still be on the door, but he spends all his time in treatments. Everyone knows you're the man in charge, doing the real work."

Sneaky bastard, putting it out there like that. No one had actually seen Kyle Donovan in years, and though rumors had swirled about the reason, it was still a mystery why the aging TechCorps' CEO had all but vanished from the public eye. Since the man was well over a hundred years old, the most popular theories involved death—he was dead and the Board wouldn't admit it, he was lingering at death's door. Even that he'd died and been reanimated, for fuck's sake.

One theory that didn't get much traction was that he was busy try-ing *not* to die. Rejuvenation treatments, like the ones that kept Beryl in such divine condition, were common among the wealthy of Atlanta.

But even though medicine and technology had come a long way since Donovan's childhood before the Flares, they still took *time*.

Someone of Kyle Donovan's advanced age could very well be spending all of his time getting infusions, undergoing laser surgeries, and sitting through gene therapy sessions.

"Now, now, John," Vargo was saying. "If that were the case, I'd have all the filth in this city cleaned up already. But I can only do so much."

Dani's stomach actually turned. If she had to listen to another second of his prattle, she'd punch him in the throat. "Excuse me, please," she murmured, then headed for the bathroom.

She needed to steel herself for dinner, or Maya would have to share her reputation for fork-stabbings.

A server discreetly pointed her in the right direction, down a wide but dim hallway lined with pre-Flare artwork that just pissed her off even more. Selling just *one* of these paintings could have fed and clothed an entire Southside neighborhood for a month or more, but here they were instead—trophies in some asshole's hallway.

Christ, she was starting to sound like Rafe. She'd thought she was past that, way too accustomed to the selfishness and greed to be shocked by it or rail against it.

Guess not.

She turned the corner and crashed into someone. Her bag slipped from her hand, and she barely stopped herself from making a grab for it and calling even more attention to herself.

It hit the floor with a rattle, followed by a guilty gasp. "Oh, I'm *so* sorry. Here, let me help you."

Dani knelt along with the woman. She was unremarkable—neither old nor young, lovely without being striking, dressed in clothes that were fashionable but not eye-catching. The only thing that stood out about her was her hair, which was a beautiful bright copper shade that certainly didn't come from a heat wand.

"You don't have to do this," Dani told her. She wasn't worried, because there was nothing incriminating in her bag, but the woman looked so distraught she couldn't help it. "I'm fine, really."

"But I insist!" She shoveled lipsticks and compacts back into the clutch. "Whether blue or gray be her skies."

It came out of nowhere, a seeming non sequitur that made Dani falter for a moment before she managed to cover her shock. It was the designated response to Birgitte's code phrase, the one Maya had told them to expect if Anderson was going to play ball.

The woman held out the bag. Dani accepted the proffered clutch and rose, still trying to grasp what was happening. "Thank you."

"My pleasure." The woman winked at her, then sauntered off down the hallway.

Dani watched her go, then dug through the clutch. In moments, she'd found it—a small, unmarked chip about half the size of a credit chit. She didn't know what was on it, but it had to be huge.

After all, Maya knew *so much,* all intelligence that Birgitte gathered before her death. Anderson had been operating for decades longer. How much more would she know?

Dani was still staring at the chip when she heard her name. *Her* name, not her alias, a low careful whisper as familiar as the touch at her shoulder. "Everything okay?"

She held out her hand wordlessly.

His fingers closed around the chip and her hand, relief naked in his eyes. "Anderson came through?"

She nodded and huffed out a helpless laugh. "We did it."

Rafe drew the chip carefully from her grasp and tucked it into the tiny shielded compartment built into the expensive digital wrist cuff Phoenix had given him. Then he framed her face with trembling hands and bent his head. His lips found hers, soft and full of promise and celebration.

When it ended, he lifted his lips just far enough to whisper, "Let's figure out an awesome excuse and get the fuck *out* of here."

"Next, we'll find your sister," she agreed, "and *go home.*"

They were late being seated for dinner, and Dani murmured her apologies to Vargo, who waved it away.

"You're far from alone, and at least you arrived on time. Meanwhile, Ross has yet to so much as darken my door."

"Andrew Ross?" Dani asked, unfolding her napkin across her lap. "The new VP of Security?"

Vargo was pleased. "That's the one. I do love a beautiful, well-informed woman."

Dani rested her hand against the handle of her dinner knife and smiled.

"Spoke too soon, Kristof." John nodded over the rim of his glass. "There he is now."

The man who had just walked into the dining room was exactly what Dani had pictured from Maya's description of him as an evil bureaucrat. He had a humorless face and a serious mien that precisely fit his reputation for efficient competence balanced by a lack of creativity.

Rafe's baby sister was on his arm.

Next to Dani, Rafe went rigid. He didn't utter a sound, and his expression didn't change, but he tensed almost to the point of trembling, and his eyes . . .

They burned with a silent desperation that hurt to see.

She started to reach for his hand, a reassuring touch that could easily masquerade as affection. But Tessa moved, and Dani caught sight of the man behind her.

She froze. It felt almost literal, her blood turning to ice in her veins even as sweat broke out on her forehead.

Julian Marshall was senior Executive Security. A trainer, because that was what they did with you if you somehow managed to survive a decade of putting yourself between executives and blades or bullets. They made you teach the new recruits how to do it, too, as if it had anything to do with skill instead of pure dumb luck. He'd trained Dani, scolded and beaten her until she'd absorbed all of his lessons.

Marshall had always paid special attention to Dani—after all, he was the only other survivor of the nerve rewiring procedure that had ruined her life.

She tried to move—to turn her head, to look down, to do anything but stare at the man who'd turned her into a killer. She couldn't keep staring, because as good as she was at remembering faces, Marshall was better, he'd always been better—

With a curious sort of detachment, Dani realized she was panicking. Her chest rose and fell faster and faster, drawing in short, sharp breaths that did nothing to ease the tightness in her chest. And she still couldn't move.

She *had* to move.

Below the table, Rafe squeezed her knee.

It jolted her out of her paralysis, but it was too late. Marshall's eyes, cold and gray, locked with hers. They widened in shock, then narrowed in recognition and—

Consternation? Yes. He stared at her for what felt like endless moments, clearly torn. Maybe he wasn't certain it was her, or he felt guilty for the role he'd played in her training. Or maybe it was something closer to kinship, a hesitation to betray a fellow soldier.

Whatever the cause, it ended with a blink. Marshall was nothing if not dedicated to the job. He raised one hand to activate his subdural comms, and Dani didn't need to be able to read lips to know what he was doing.

Lockdown. They'd have to fight their way out.

**TECHCORPS INTERNAL
EXECUTIVE COMMUNICATION**

From: Vargo, Kristof
To: Young, Charlotte
Date: 2086–07–15

I require a detailed upgrade to security in both my private penthouse and public offices, as well as installation of secure safe rooms in both locations. Consider this your first and only priority.

SEVENTEEN

In a fight, the world often slowed to crystalline clarity. Rafe usually had time to assess, to consider, and to plan before he reacted.

All of that fell apart when Dani was around.

The adrenaline that had surged through him when his baby sister strolled into the room with a man who turned Dani into a trembling statue should have been sufficient to prime Rafe for battle. Anyone who could terrify Dani was the most dangerous person in the room.

That was as far as Rafe's assessment got before Dani vaulted onto the table.

The first peal of the alarm screeched through the room, accented by the sound of shattering crockery as Dani slid across the table so fast even his heightened awareness could barely follow her. Her foot took the closest guard in the chin, cracking his neck with a surgical kick before she skidded off the table to bear his body to the ground.

Rafe started to shove his chair back. A loud, automated voice joined the blare of the alarm.

"*Lo*—"

Dani surfaced on the other side of the table in a whirl of silk, a pistol clutched in one hand. The Ex-Sec bodyguard who'd triggered the alarm lunged toward her with a speed that rivaled her own, but she had too much of a head start.

Dani leveled her weapon at the VP of Security and pulled the trigger.

"—*ck*—"

The bullet shredded the man's throat. Blood splattered Tessa's shocked face.

As Rafe cleared his chair, the Ex-Sec bodyguard reversed course faster than any human should have been able to, diving to catch his charge before he hit the floor.

Somewhere down the table, a man screamed.

"—do—"

Rafe lunged to the end of the table and grabbed Tessa, hauling her away from the two men. Dani was already charging toward the door, a whirlwind of destruction.

The first guard who turned toward her took a bullet between the eyes.

The second hadn't even processed what was happening when she shot him.

"—wn—"

At the head of the gathering, Kristof Vargo finally realized his guests were in danger and did the predictable thing—he dove under the table.

A second screamer joined the first.

Dani swept down and stripped the guards of their visible weapons, tossing one of the pistols back without looking. Rafe snatched it out of the air, adrenaline burning through him.

"Engaged."

And just like that, they were in sync, fighting as a single unit with one mission. They dove out of the dining room and through the study to the foyer, where they startled the two guards left to monitor the penthouse's entrance.

Just two, because the betrayals they expected at a gathering of equals came in the forms of corporate espionage and subtle blackmail, not bullets to the throat. Besides, Ex-Sec would be holding down all potential exits from the building.

First things first. Get out of the penthouse, Morales.

He could hear the words in Dani's wry voice, and he knew what she'd do next. He turned Tessa toward the wall, shielding her with his body as Dani took out the guards with perfect shots to the head that had dropped them where they stood.

"Out." Dani grabbed a stun stick from one of the guards and threw open the front door.

Rafe hustled Tessa through it, into the hallway that housed the elevator. They'd arrived via AirLift, but Rafe had studied the building schematics and security out of habit. He jabbed the elevator call button, just in case, but a polite robotic voice with a slight accent informed him that the building was in lockdown.

He released Tessa and pried open the elevator doors as Dani used the stun stick to bar the penthouse door.

"How close is the car?" she demanded.

He peered down into the darkness of the elevator shaft, lit only by strips of red emergency lights. "A good twenty floors down."

Tessa grabbed him by the jacket. "I still have this thing in my head. They're going to *blow it up*, Rafe."

His heart clenched painfully, but Dani only shook her head. "Listen. Marshall's busy trying to save his VP, and no one else even noticed we brought you with us. We have time, but we need to use it, okay? Can you stay calm?"

Tessa blinked, her eyes wide and a little wild . . . then she nodded.

"Good." Dani turned to Rafe. "The stairs will be a killbox. Do you know how to access the service corridors?"

This building wasn't terribly different from Phoenix's—they didn't like to see the help scurrying about. So there was an entire system of mostly interior corridors used only by cleaning and maintenance staff. "Follow me."

The discreet door had no handles and was set almost flush with the wall. It was meant to be accessed through a keycard waved over a hidden sensor. They didn't have a keycard, not that it mattered. The damn thing wouldn't open during a lockdown, anyway.

Rafe was suddenly glad for his overpreparation. He pulled his toolkit from his boot and slipped a steel prybar from it. It was tiny, useful mostly for prying open wedged windows and such. But it would do for this.

He handed it to Dani. "Get me started?"

She slipped the end of the bar into the slim crevice between the door and the wall and pushed hard. It shifted, popping open just enough for Rafe to get his fingers under the edge.

If she let go, or her fingers slipped, he'd lose his. But he didn't hesitate. Rafe grasped the door and wrenched it back, the muscles in his back and legs straining from the effort.

The door popped open and banged against the wall. Dani readied a pistol, then began leading them through the plain gray corridors.

Every so often, they'd pass a utilitarian door marked with an equally utilitarian sign designating it as a mechanical or laundry room. Finally, Dani stopped in front of one marked JANITORIAL.

"This'll have to do." She tried the knob, which gave easily, and ushered them in.

Inside, she dropped her weapons and started tearing strips off the bottom of her fancy gown. "Are there any sterile blades in your kit, Morales?"

"Wait." Tessa held up both hands, her eyes widening in alarm. "You want to cut my neck open here, in a mop closet? While we're being chased by bad guys?"

"Tessa." Dani took her by the shoulders. "The circumstances are suboptimal—"

She snorted.

"And it's going to hurt," Dani continued. "But I promise you, I'll be quick. And when it's over, it's over. No more worrying about the thing in your head."

Tessa hesitated, then looked up at Rafe.

"I trust her, Tessa." Her hands were trembling, so he folded his around them, trying to *will* strength into her. "Not just with my life. I trust her with yours, okay?"

Tessa inhaled a shuddering breath. Her jewel-studded hair shook around her face, blood matting the perfect curls. Her face looked wan under her makeup, and there was blood smeared across her cheeks, too. But she rallied, clutching his hands hard enough to make his fingers ache as she squeezed her eyes shut. "Okay. Do it."

He wasn't sure he could free his hands from her desperate grip if he had to, so he nodded to Dani. "In my kit," he said softly. "There are sterile wipes, too. And medical tape."

She nodded and pulled the kit from his boot. Moving fast, she laid out everything she would need within easy reach. With one wipe, she carefully cleaned the blade, a tiny pair of forceps, and her hands, then hesitated. "Tessa, he might need to hold more than your hands. If you move or jerk while I'm doing this . . ."

Tessa shuddered again, her fingers spasming. She released him and wrapped her arms around herself, her eyes still shut tight, as if she could lock out the world.

Rage made it hard to think as Rafe wrapped an arm around her body, pinning her against his chest with her arms trapped between them. Every tiny, jerky breath she took only twisted his anger tighter, and as he smoothed his hand under her hair to guide her forehead to rest against his shoulder, he made a list of people who were going to die for putting her through this.

Vargo, definitely.

That VP of Security, if he made it through the night.

His bodyguard, for good measure.

Cara Kennedy, too, if he got a chance.

Tessa whimpered, and he made a soothing sound as he held the back of her head steady. He met Dani's eyes and nodded once.

She moved fast, speaking softly as she made a small, neat incision. "The good thing about these is that they insert them with a pressure injector. Quick to go in, and quick to come out." She pressed on the skin on either side of the cut. Tessa winced, but a small piece of metal now protruded from the incision.

Locking the forceps around the metallic object, Dani pulled gently. The foreign body slid free of Tessa's skin, trailing thin filaments of bloody wire after it. Dani laid it down carefully, then pressed the folded length of fabric she'd torn from her dress against the cut on Tessa's neck. A strip of tape secured it.

"There you go," Rafe murmured, stroking his sister's back as she shuddered. "It's gone. You're okay, Tessa." She pushed back and wiped at her tear-streaked face. Rafe wanted to take the time to wash away the blood, but getting her out alive was all that mattered right now. He squeezed her upper arms. "You steady?"

She squared her shoulders, the sudden stubborn set of her jaw reminding him deeply of their mother. "If my head's not going to explode, let's get the hell out of here."

"Good idea." Dani dropped the deadly little device down the stainless steel sink drain, then made a noise of exasperation and ripped off the rest of her torn, cumbersome skirt. When she straightened, the excess fabric discarded, her dress fell just above her knees, loose and flowing.

She snatched up her weapons as Rafe gathered his kit, wiping the knife clean of Tessa's blood with gritted teeth. Before he packed the kit away, he pulled out the emergency communications devices, handed one to Dani, and slipped the other into his ear. "Conall?"

No immediate response, but the alert would keep beeping back at their base until Conall acknowledged the message. Rafe herded Tessa out of the closet, following close after Dani. She took a right, heading farther down the endless corridor. They'd just turned the corner when a muffled explosion shook the floors beneath them.

Someone had finally noticed that Tessa was missing.

Soft static sounded in Rafe's ear. "Uh, Rafe?" Conall's voice came. "Did something just blow up wherever you are?"

Clenching his jaw, he hurried his steps, half-carrying his sister with him. "Yeah, the bomb that was in my sister's head until about sixty seconds ago. Dani also shot the new VP of Security in the throat at the chief operating officer's dinner table, and we need an exit right now."

"Dani did *what*?"

"Storytime later, Con. Exit now." Rafe's stomach lurched. "And get Ava or Beth to contact Phoenix. She needs to know our cover's blown."

"Fuck fuckity *fuck*. Okay." The furious sound of typing filled the momentary silence. "Beth's on it. I'm pulling up building schematics and your comm tracker. And you're . . . in the walls?"

"Service corridors," Rafe growled.

"Right, right. Okay, hold on . . ."

Rafe caught Tessa as she stumbled, then stopped next to Dani as they hit the end of the hallway. "We just hit an intersection, Con. Left or right?"

"Left," came the swift reply. "Follow it to the end and go through the kitchens. They have exterior access. There should be a delivery AirLift on the platform, you can steal that no problem."

"Got it."

Rafe pivoted left and relayed Conall's instructions. "Just a little farther, Tessa."

She bent, tore off her high heels and tossed them behind her. "I can do this."

Dani held his gaze, and he let it steady him. Through the kitchens, steal a car. That was easy. Rafe could have done it in his sleep. Together with Dani? Child's play. The two of them had handled so much worse.

The brightly lit corridor seemed to stretch out forever. Dani took the lead, and Rafe followed, one hand at Tessa's back. Her breathing was unsteady and forced, but she had her skirts gripped in tight-knuckled fists as she kept pace with him, their family's immense stubbornness carrying her through.

Rafe had never been so fucking proud in his life.

The doors to the kitchen loomed up ahead, and the tension in him started to unravel. Dani hauled open the door and Rafe spun through, his weapon in hand, ignoring the startled screech of the closest kitchen worker as he swept the room.

On the far side of the kitchen, the wide door to the loading dock—and the landing pad—slid open. The captain of the Red Eagles stepped in, his entire Protectorate squad hard on his heels.

So much for easy. Shit was about to get seriously ugly.

If you had to get into a knock-down, drag-out fight, there were worse places to do it than in an industrial kitchen.

For one thing, they tended to be wide-open spaces above the waist, which was good for visibility, while the countertops funneled movement into makeshift corridors. Plus, there were weapons everywhere. Knives, hot surfaces and liquids—hell, even a kitchen towel could be repurposed as a garrote, in a pinch.

Not to mention the crowds.

A handful of the kitchen staff hit the deck as soon as they saw the squad enter with weapons drawn. The rest started screaming. Some ran and some stood, stock-still, as the Protectorate commander waved his assault rifle and shouted for them to *move*.

Yeah, good luck with that, Dani thought ruefully.

The rest of the squad surged forward. Rafe pushed Tessa behind him, and Dani ran ahead to meet the brunt of the attack. One soldier launched a punch at her midsection. She took the blow, then leaned back, out of range, when he tried to follow it with an elbow to her face. Instead, she grabbed his arm and pushed it up, knocking him off balance.

He fell back, arms flailing to break his fall, and landed on a lit stove. One of the chefs who'd been frozen with fear began screaming. The noise was quickly eclipsed by the Protectorate soldier as he wrenched himself up off the stove, the back and sleeve of his uniform engulfed by fire.

There was a pot rack above the long steel counter beside the stove. Dani jumped up, grabbed its edge, and kicked out hard, driving the screeching man into one of his comrades. They both went down, kicking and batting at the flames, while a third member of the squad broke off his attack to help them.

They weren't even looking at Dani when she shot them.

A fourth member of the Red Eagles—Dani had just enough time to discern the insignia patch on the first soldier's uniform before it burned away—pulled a handful of throwing knives from his tactical pants. He hurled them all at once, straight at Rafe's head.

Rafe saw it coming. He snatched up a baking sheet and used it as a shield to deflect the wickedly sharp blades. Then he flung it so hard Dani could hear it whistle through the air. It caught the man in the throat, and he went down with a grunt and a wheeze.

"Look out!" Tessa yelled.

A bullet zipped by her head as the commander lunged for Dani, his rifle raised. She sidestepped his attack and kicked him in the back. He stumbled toward Rafe, who grabbed him by the collar and slammed his head into the counter with a hollow thud. He jerked back, reaching for the pistol in the holster at his side.

Tessa got to him first. She'd snatched up a heavy cast-iron skillet, and she swung it with a heave and a grunt. She hit the commander so hard that bone crunched, and he collapsed to the floor. The skillet fell from Tessa's shaking hands, and Rafe hauled her close, checking her for injuries.

The screaming had stopped. Dani didn't know whether all the kitchen staff had fled, or whether they were hiding, terrified to make any noise. It didn't matter anyway.

The door to the loading dock was sealed. Without the codes to bypass a lockdown, the access panel was useless. Dani tugged at the seam between the doors with increasing desperation, but it didn't budge.

"Let me," Rafe murmured, sliding his hands over hers.

The simple touch grounded her. Dani dropped her hands and leaned against the wall. "When we get out of here . . ."

"No more undercover work, not for a good, long while," he agreed readily. "Stand back."

His arms flexed, his tendons standing out in sharp relief as he gripped the edges of the door and pulled *hard*. The doors groaned and squealed as the metal shifted. Five centimeters. Ten.

Dani grabbed a huge empty stockpot from a nearby counter. As soon as the gap in the doors was wide enough, she wedged it between them. When Rafe released the doors, just a little, the thick metal gave a bit but held.

She waved Tessa on, then ducked through the gap herself, only to stop short. "Oh, fuck."

The landing pad was empty.

Rafe tossed a couple of handguns and a rifle through the doorway. He kicked the stockpot out of the doorway behind him, sealing off the kitchen. "What?" Then he turned and echoed her curse. "*Fuck*."

Dani snatched up the rifle and activated her comm device with a vicious slap. "Problem, Conall. There's no goddamn AirLift here to steal."

"*Really?* Shit. Must be part of their lockdown protocols."

"Find us another way, Con, and fast," Rafe gritted. "Or we'll just have to jump off this building and hope for the best."

"If you need a ride," Phoenix's voice came over the comms, "maybe I can help."

Relief left Dani a little dizzy. "How fast can you get here?"

"Just got the coordinates. Give me five minutes."

The door to the kitchen slid open, and three soldiers marched through. Their heads turned in perfect unison, zeroing in on Rafe.

"Hurry," Dani whispered as another trio of men stepped out behind the first. "We've got trouble."

There was a small alcove near the edge of the building, a purely architectural feature that nonetheless made for good cover. Rafe edged back until he could push Tessa toward it, then rejoined Dani.

His casual words belied his tense frame. "Problem, guys?"

The soldier in the middle of the front row blinked at him. "We demand your immediate surrender," he said flatly. "You will be disarmed, taken into custody, and questioned."

"Huh." His robotic affect left Dani gripping the rifle even tighter. "How about no?"

The six of them turned to regard her. Dani's blood went cold as they just . . . stared.

"What the hell, Rafe?" she breathed.

"I don't *know*," he replied. "This is . . ."

The soldier who'd spoken before tilted his head, then nodded once. "Your denial has been noted. We will proceed with your apprehension."

They *moved*. Dani lifted the rifle out of sheer reflex, but managed to squeeze off only half a dozen shots. She hit three—two in the head, and another in the shoulder. He jerked back and froze, his face a rictus of pain, but the hesitation and the grimace lasted only a moment before his expression smoothed and he continued his advance.

The others didn't even seem to notice.

She and Rafe fought back-to-back to fend off the attack. It was all a blur, even for Dani. These fuckers were so *fast*. Not only did they manage to disarm her, they kept landing kicks and punches—not enough to take her down, but plenty sufficient to knock her off balance. Rafe was faring a little better, not because he was avoiding the blows, but because he was a freaking wall who could absorb every hit.

And their opponents were *good,* blocks and parries flowing into jabs and strikes like currents of water. It wasn't even their individual movements that were so graceful, but the fact that they worked together smoothly, like dancers orbiting around one another.

Shit. She tended to get poetic when she was feeling overwhelmed.

She almost missed when the blades came out. Rafe hissed in pain, and she looked over just in time to see a slice well across his arm.

Too late, she turned back—and directly into a blow to the side of the face. It knocked her head back, and she swayed on her feet as her ears rang. A steely hand locked around her wrist, and she growled as she twisted free.

Seriously, *fuck* these guys.

Dani reached for the nearest hand holding a knife. She grabbed the man's thumb and yanked it back so hard she felt the bone give way, and the knife dropped into her outstretched hand.

She let the next attacker come at her, then ducked out of the way at the last minute, swinging around to bury the blade between his shoulders. He shook her off with a roar, and she staggered into Rafe and the soldier who was trying to maneuver him into a headlock.

The man she'd stabbed pulled a pistol and leveled it at her. Dani stared at it—he couldn't use it without possibly hitting his squadmate, who was right behind her.

His finger tightened on the trigger, and the man at her back dove out of the way, as if issued a silent command. She tried to move just as the sound of the gunshot exploded through the chill evening air, and she felt the pressure of the bullet graze her arm.

"Dani, no!"

Rafe shoved her out of the way, *hard*. She went flying, hit the concrete, and skidded to a stop just in time to watch him take the second shot straight to the gut.

Tessa screamed.

Dani scrambled over to him and pressed both hands to the blood welling up from his side, every fiber of her being focused on *him*. "Rafe! Rafe, don't you *dare*—"

The deafening whir of a hovercraft filled her ears a moment before bright lights cut through the darkness.

Phoenix.

Dani threw herself over Rafe as Phoenix began firing the AirLift's automatic guns. Bullets tore through the remaining soldiers as shell casings rained down on the concrete. It was over in moments, the comparative stillness echoing in Dani's ears.

When the alarm and warning message that indicated an incoming landing gave way to actual stillness, Dani lifted her head. "I have never been so glad to see anyone in my entire fucking *life*, Phoenix."

Phoenix hopped out of the AirLift and wrapped an arm around Tessa's shoulders. "I accept clean trade credits as payments. And gifts, but only really good ones. You got him?"

Rafe groaned as he tried to sit up. "I can make it."

"Come on." Dani looped his arm around her neck and helped him up. They limped their way to the AirLift, where Tessa already huddled in the back. Dani urged Rafe in, as well, where he collapsed heavily on the large back seat.

Dani climbed in after him and shut the door. She held her breath until Phoenix took off, then released it on a sigh. "Sorry we blew your cover."

"Eh, shit happens. Is everyone okay?"

"I think so. We . . ." Dani's gaze fell on the AirLift's biometric panel, which was smeared with blood. A dripping trail of it led to a severed hand lying on the floorboard.

Phoenix glanced down. "It's okay. Dr. Long didn't need it anymore."

Rafe reached out. "Tessa—"

She scooted forward and gripped his hand. "I'm here, Rafe. It's okay."

He nodded, his face ashen. "Dani?"

"I'm here, too." She put more pressure on his bleeding abdomen. "Don't try to talk, all right?"

"No, I have to . . ." He raised his other hand to her cheek. "Don't let go of me."

His eyes rolled back, and he went limp. Tessa stifled a sob, but a quick check of the pulse at the base of his throat confirmed that he'd only lost consciousness.

Dani kept her fingers on the spot, counting its reassuring thumps.

I won't. I promise I won't.

CLASSIFIED BEHAVIOR EVALUATION

Franklin Center for Genetic Research

At this point, it's clear that something about the genetic enhancements specific to B-designations tends to destabilize the HS strain in increasingly unmanageable ways. Neurodivergence seems to intensify in correlation to their intellectual potential. Given the danger presented by 16-B, I recommend we enact contingency protocols with future generations.

Dr. Keller, February 2082

EIGHTEEN

One thing Rafe had forgotten: how *irritable* Mace got when he had to patch up the squad.

He leaned over Rafe, glowering at every slice he and Beth uncovered as they peeled off his tunic. "Oh, this one's nice," he growled. "This one almost took out your liver."

"But it didn't," Rafe retorted. "You're welcome."

Mace grumbled something else, earning him a stern look from Beth. "Leave him be, James," she admonished. "He's been through so much, poor thing."

"Yeah, *James*," Rafe echoed, forcing his usual humor. "Leave me be."

Mace glared at him with enough irritation to fuel a small nation, but his grumpy mutter as he carefully revealed the next wound was blessedly unintelligible.

Just as well. Rafe didn't have the heart for banter tonight. Not with Dani sitting across the room, enduring her own cataloguing of injuries as Nina and Ava passed each other first-aid supplies.

She might not be able to feel the pain of her cuts and bruises and bullet grazes, but the blood streaking her pale skin twisted him in knots. So did the look in her eyes—a barely contained wildness that only grew with every wound Mace uncovered, as if she could feel every stab and scrape and ache on Rafe's body.

Even Tessa was handling it better than Dani. He'd expected hysteria, once they hit safety. Tears, at the very least. But she'd endured Mace's ministrations in silence, let him affix a bandage to the back of her neck, and quietly asked if there was somewhere she could clean up.

Maya had gathered her up with promises of a hot shower and clean clothes, and Rafe had been forced to grapple with the truth that his baby sister was either a stone-cold badass, or he'd failed so spectacularly at sheltering his family that even a deadly flight from the Hill and getting a bomb cut out of her head in a janitor's closet couldn't rattle her.

Either way, he had to stop thinking of her as a baby.

Mace held out one hand. "Okay, first I'm gonna need—"

"Pressure dressings." Beth slapped a paper-wrapped package into his hand. "I'll get the antiseptic and zip strips. Do you want imaging or manual exploration?"

Mace blinked at her. "Manual."

"I'll get the forceps, then. And some lidocaine." She practically bounced over to the supply closet.

Mace shook his head, then turned his attention back to Rafe. "You gonna tell me who got the drop on you this thoroughly?"

Rafe bit back a hiss as Mace examined a shallow but painful slice across his ribs, but Dani flinched as if she'd heard it anyway. "Fuck if I know," he said hastily, trying to distract them both. "It was six guys, but they didn't overwhelm us with numbers. I've never seen anyone move the way they did. Maybe Ava and Nina come close, but this was more than that. They were perfectly coordinated, and they adapted to my style so fast, it was like I was fighting myself. I'm lucky I still *have* a liver."

Knox exchanged a worried glance with Nina. "We heard about this. It's what Savitri was working on before she defected. Conall?"

Conall didn't look up from his tablet, where he was still running safety diagnostics on the chip Dani had brought home. "The Guardian Project. Savitri told Maya about it, so we did some digging. Integrated artificial intelligence, basically. It was their Protectorate version 2.0. An *improvement*," his voice dripped with sarcasm, "on our implants. All the same superpowers, without the pesky free will."

Queasiness churned through Rafe, unrelated to the shiver of pain as Mace uncovered another wound.

All Protectorate soldiers agreed to biochemical enhancement. The recruitment videos always went long on the ability to lift a car or run for days and tended to leave out the need for constant biochemical adjustment and the occasional emotional fracture, but Rafe had more or less understood the deal before he signed on the dotted line.

Scary brain surgery, brutal training. Superpowers and super paychecks. A lifetime of following orders, *or else.*

But he'd still had a *choice*. Every step of the way, he'd had a choice. The fact that he was sitting here, a defector, free of their grasp was proof enough of that.

And probably good motivation for the TechCorps to make sure it never happened again.

Knox was frowning. "I thought you said Savitri was pretty sure they couldn't finish the project without her."

"She was," Conall said, returning his attention to his work. "But it's been . . . what? Six years? They were bound to figure it out eventually."

Savitri could be arrogant to a fault—though, Rafe acknowledged, when you were as brilliant as Savitri, it could be difficult to tell the difference between arrogance and accurate self-assessment. Hell, he'd learned that lesson tonight. When faced with only a handful of soldiers, Rafe had been confident he could cut his way through without breaking a sweat.

But betting against the TechCorps when power and greed were on the line was a dangerous game.

"I'm guessing they figured it out," Rafe said as Beth returned with the medical supplies. "I'm not saying we're doomed or anything, but it's a game changer. We were the best Protectorate squad by miles. We could plow through Ex-Sec, too. But a handful of these guys nearly stopped me and Dani cold, and I'd bet there's a lot more than a handful out there."

"Maybe," Dani said, finally breaking her pale, trembling silence. "Maybe not. I've talked with Adam about it a little. He's run all the projections, done all the calculations. He wasn't real optimistic about their chances. Maybe they've just had a few lucky wins."

"And maybe they're playing the numbers harder than we realize," Nina murmured. "How much of the Protectorate would they risk if the potential payoff was this high? How much of Executive Security?"

No one answered. No one *needed* to answer. The TechCorps had manufactured a nearly endless supply of kids, desperate like Rafe had been desperate, willing to sign over their bodies and their futures for enough credits to support the people they loved.

And the TechCorps would use them up. Brutally.

Beth's gentle hand at his shoulder warned him before Mace began injecting lidocaine into the edges of his gunshot wound. Beth seemed to have the same medical training as Ava, likely from the same source—the Franklin Center had certainly given their superbrilliant B-designations a versatile skill set—but her gentle caretaking was a far cry from Ava's brusque competence.

Rafe almost felt a little guilty as Beth and Mace bent over him to address his worst injuries. Dani was enduring Ava's terse ministrations with barely contained irritation, and the entire room felt tense enough to snap when Conall broke the silence with a sudden whoop of triumph.

"Motherfucker, I am a goddamn *genius*."

Knox raised an eyebrow. "You've had success, I take it?"

"Of course." Conall was practically dancing from foot to foot as he scrolled through his tablet. "Some of this is still encrypted, and Maya will have to help me with it. But I cracked enough to know this is the fucking motherlode."

Even with the painkillers, Rafe had to grit his teeth as Mace began to dig around in his side with the forceps, exploring the wound. "Tell me it was worth getting my ass beat down."

"I don't know," Conall drawled. "You think private security schematics for half the Board and what I'm pretty sure are secret recordings of their meetings are worth it?"

Across the room, Dani exhaled roughly. "Then we did it."

"We did it," Rafe echoed, and some hidden tension unraveled so abruptly, he almost laughed. But in the next heartbeat, a thought slammed into him so hard he struggled to sit up. "Wait, *fuck*. What about the thing Phoenix was working on?"

Beth pressed him back to the bed with surprising strength and a gentle smile. "Don't worry about that. She always has about fifteen different plans in place, just in case. She may have lost this mark, but she'll find another."

Ava made an amused sound. It was the closest Rafe had ever heard the woman come to laughing. "And she'll use your busted cover to solidify her power base, one way or another. The Franklin Center never quite understood the terrifying potential of an angry C-designation."

She sounded approving. Of course she did. Ava respected power and violence and very little else, as far as Rafe could tell. Except Nina. Even now they stood on either side of Dani, physically identical in every way. But emotionally . . . Nina's warmth and generosity of spirit practically shone from her eyes, and Ava made a room chillier just by stepping into it.

The strength in Beth's hand was a good reminder that she came from the same place. She'd had two sisters once, too. An A-designation like Nina, someone focused on warfare and combat, and a C-designation like Phoenix, all empathy and psy-ops, a true emotional manipulator. Beth was like everyone in this room—a product of scientific experimentation and genetic tinkering. A weapon, broken free of the hand who had created it.

Broken free . . . like the Guardians couldn't.

Even if they'd done nothing else wrong, Rafe would bring the Tech-Corps down for that. He'd destroy them so that no more sixteen-year-olds, desperate to help feed their families, would sign on to have their minds destroyed.

He was still trying to figure out *how* he was going to do that when Tessa returned, scrubbed clean and wearing one of Gray's oversized sweatshirts, her hair wrapped in one of Maya's head scarves. She hovered next to the bed and curled her fingers around the hand Rafe lifted to her, her gaze taking in his many injuries. Guilt pinched her face. "Rafe, I—"

"Don't," he told her softly. "We'll talk about it later, okay? This isn't your fault."

"But I—"

Rafe cut her off again. "We made our plans to do this before I even knew you were on the Hill. The chances were always there that we'd get made. What matters is that we found you, and we're all in one piece."

She let her gaze catalog his various injuries and then pinned him with a disbelieving look so reminiscent of their mother, Rafe choked on a laugh. "More or less in one piece."

"Uh-huh." She squeezed his hand. "Thank you, Rafe."

She said his nickname the way their mother always had. Two syllables, almost rolling the *r,* and the *a* short. They hadn't spoken much Spanish in the house growing up—their father had never been very good at it. He'd worked to learn for his wife, though, and Rafe could remember their gentle laughter when he messed up the pronunciation or mixed up words. It had been one of Rafe's earliest lessons about love— the point wasn't perfection, but caring enough to *try,* even if you looked foolish. Maybe especially if you looked foolish.

His gaze swung back across the room to Dani as if pulled by gravity. She'd locked down some of her outward anxiety the second Tessa stepped into the room, but Rafe could still see the trembling energy surging just beneath the skin. At least Nina's face seemed more relaxed as she smoothed med-gel onto Dani's abdomen. If none of the injuries required more serious treatment, she'd truly escaped the worst of it. She'd be fine by midnight and virtually unscathed by tomorrow morning.

Physically, anyway.

"Rafe . . ."

For a second, he thought it was Tessa again. But she released his hand with a soft cry, and the tears he'd been expecting finally burst free as she bolted across the room and flung herself into their mother's open arms.

"Shh, Tessa. I'm here." Celia Morales was tall enough to easily meet Rafe's gaze over her daughter's head, and for the first time Rafe could remember, she looked . . . not old, maybe, but *older*. Tired in a way she'd likely never let him see before, and Dani's words from the penthouse came back to him in a rush.

He'd told himself his family was happy and blissful without him, because he'd needed to believe it. He'd needed their joy to justify his own eroding sense of self—and his mother had been far too smart not to see that. They'd all been playing a game for years, keeping up appearances to protect one another, a relentless circle of well-meaning lies.

Knox cleared his throat. "All right, let's clear out and get to work. Maya, you can help Conall. Nina?"

"Ava and I are mostly done." She tossed an empty med-gel tube into the waste bin. "Just a matter of—"

Dani vaulted off the gurney and vanished into the back of the clinic.

"—bandages," Nina finished dryly. "But I don't suppose she really needs those."

"I'm not going anywhere," Mace pronounced. "You can have all the confidentiality you want, but I have a job to do, and I'm going to do it."

"Come on, James." Beth tugged at the back of his shirt until he met her gaze, then she smiled and tilted her head back and forth. "There's enough time for this."

He hesitated, then sighed. "Fine. You have fifteen minutes, and you're getting regen when I come back, no matter how much you bitch about it."

Regeneration therapy would mean a clean bill of health by midnight, even if the newly grown skin would itch like hell for a day or two. A luxury few could afford, but Rafe wouldn't turn it down. Not now.

As soon as the door closed behind Mace and Beth, Rafe gritted his teeth and swung into an upright position. "Mom, I'm sorry—"

"Shh." Tessa's bout of weeping had subsided, and Celia wiped her daughter's tears away before guiding her to take the seat next to Rafe's bed. Then her warm hands were on his face, as soft and soothing as he remembered from childhood, and she stroked his cheeks as tears misted her own eyes. "I never should have let you do that foolish thing."

"As I recall, you didn't *let* me." The TechCorps didn't exactly care about parental consent, and Rafe's thumbprint had been affixed to the binding contract before his mother had any idea what he intended. "You found out when I handed you my bonus."

"And I should have snatched you up by the scruff of the neck and left Atlanta." She sighed and closed her eyes. "But what's done is done. We all did what we thought we had to. Including your sister."

"Including—?" Rafe frowned and glanced at Tessa, who was suddenly *very* calm and very intent on studying the fraying cuff on her borrowed sweatshirt. "What did Tessa do?"

She looked up, startled. "Dani didn't tell you?"

"Tell me *what*?"

"Your sister," Celia said in a voice that somehow managed to be both proud and exasperated, "is one of Atlanta's top art forgers."

For several endless seconds, Rafe didn't even know what to say. It seemed like a joke, but his mother certainly wasn't laughing, and Tessa was practically squirming in her chair. God knew she'd always been talented, but *forgery*?

Then the implications hit him, and no number of bullet holes and knife wounds could match the pain shredding from his gut straight to his heart.

Tessa had done what she thought she had to do. Crime. Because . . . "The money I was sending wasn't enough."

His mother stroked his cheek again, infinitely gentle. "You kept us going for so long, baby. But it was never your job to do." A slashing look at Tessa. "It wasn't hers, either."

Tessa actually flinched. But a second later she firmed her shoulders and lifted her chin. "You're not the only one who gets to sacrifice for the family, Rafael," she told him, eyes sparking with the stubbornness they'd both inherited. "Rosa and Antonio needed things I could get for them. So I did it. And I'd do it again."

"Even though you ended up with a bomb in your head?" he demanded.

"At least mine's gone now," she retorted. "*You've* still got whatever it is they put in your brain. Though I'm surprised they had room with all the self-righteous hypocrisy rattling around in there."

"*Enough.*" His mother's tone snapped Rafe's teeth together on his retort, and Tessa resumed studying the frayed threads of her sweatshirt sleeve, radiating innocence as their mother spoke again.

"You both did what you felt you had to. I hate this world sometimes." Her voice had dropped to a near whisper. "I hate that we lost your father. I hate that I couldn't make a home that felt safe for you both. And I hate that you felt responsible for taking care of me instead of the other way around. I'm sorry. To both of you."

He wanted to protest. But the hurt inside him dwindled to nothing next to the pain shivering through her words, and the world seemed to vibrate around him for a heartbeat before it *flipped*. He saw what Dani had been trying to tell him, what he would have known the whole damn time if it hadn't been *his* family.

His lies had never protected his mother. She'd lived for more than a decade with the failure and shame, with the knowledge that her baby boy had gone out to bleed and hurt and carve up his own heart because she couldn't protect their family. And then she'd watched her daughter do the same damn thing.

"It's okay, Mama," he said softly, lifting a hand to cup the one still cradling his face. "We *all* did our best."

"We did." Reaching out, Celia framed Tessa's face, too. "But now we're going to do something different. From now on, you two are in charge of your own lives, and nothing else. Rosa and Antonio are my responsibility, not yours."

"Mama—"

"Mom—"

"No." The *tone* was back, and that look Rafe knew so well from his childhood. When Celia Morales's usually sunny smile vanished beneath her *this-means-business* expression, everyone in the neighborhood had jumped to obey. "I talked to Nina when she brought us here. We've come to an agreement."

Tessa still looked rebellious, but Rafe's jolt of panic dissipated.

His mother had made the classic mistake. She'd strayed too close to Nina's orbit.

"You're going to be helping at the new community center?" Rafe guessed. "That would be the perfect place for Rosa."

"Yes." His mother finally let her hands fall away from their faces as she crossed her arms over her chest. "Rosa will be helping with the garden. Antonio will assist with construction until he decides if he'd like to continue an apprenticeship with the local mechanic."

"And you?" If anyone in Atlanta could value the skills that his mother had honed before the Flares, surely it was Nina. "You know, they work on publishing books for people in the neighborhood. You could do that again."

"Nina mentioned it." Celia smiled. "It's certainly on the table. But for now, I'm going to help Nina organize childcare and classes. Art classes, especially. And reading. It will be good work."

And she'd be so good at it. Rafe could envision it so easily, because he could *remember* it. Sitting at her feet, savoring the warm humor in her voice as she read a book, the crackle of paper as she turned the pages, the vivid artwork spilling across them, art she'd created. Stories she'd written. Stories about him, and then Tessa, and eventually baby Antonio. Stories where they had adventures and saved the day.

No wonder he'd grown up with such a damn hero complex. She'd been telling him he could do anything his whole damn life.

Ignoring the ache of his wounds, he leaned forward to hug her. "I think it's perfect. Nina is good people. You can trust her."

"Of course I can. Because you do."

Having Mace poking his fingers into holes in his abdomen hadn't managed to drive tears from him, but now his eyes stung. He pulled back as Tessa rose to her feet, her gaze still unsettled.

"What about me?" she whispered. "What do I do?"

Their mother pulled her in close and kissed Tessa's wrapped hair. "Whatever you want, sweetheart. That's the point."

It was clearly too much for Tessa to process, and Rafe ignored the burn in his side to throw an arm around her, too. "Don't decide now," he told her. "You've kind of had a big night. Gun fights, daring escapes, Dani cutting a bomb out of you in a supply closet."

She made a huffing sound that broke into laughter edged in tears, and poked him lightly in the shoulder. "You're not as funny as you think."

"I'm hilarious. Ask anyone."

"Children." His mother leaned in to kiss his cheek, then wrapped her arm more securely around Tessa. "It's time to let the doctor see to you. We'll be here in the morning."

He watched them go, the words circling in his head, the meaning of it finally sinking through the adrenaline of the night and the growing pain of his many, *many* injuries.

His family was safe.

Relief hollowed him out as he let Mace and Beth push him back to the bed. But instead of sinking into the feeling, his brain kept circling back to the look in Dani's eyes, the way she'd all but bolted from the room, a creature so frantic for escape she'd gnaw off a limb to get away.

The word *family* had expanded beyond the people who shared his blood a long time ago. And he wouldn't be able to rest until he knew everyone was okay.

Especially Dani.

Recruit 66–942 has an unusual rapport with support staff. While this could simply be his natural personality and the impact his appearance has on others, it's worth being aware of the fact that he may well be subverting lower level employees. To what purpose? On that, I can offer no insight.

Recruit Analysis, August 2079

NINETEEN

Dani couldn't sleep.

Midnight had come and gone, and her bed beckoned, but she couldn't sit still, much less lie down. Every time she tried, she felt like she was going to explode if she didn't *move*.

So she did. She paced, tracing and retracing a tight *U* around the bed. She opened her window to let in some fresh air, and when that wasn't enough, she leaned out of it, mindful of the taut pull of newly mended skin on her abdomen and back.

It helped, but not enough.

Finally, she settled on breaking down and cleaning her favorite handguns. She was sure it made for an odd sight, her sitting in her underwear with pistol parts strewn all over the desk, but it helped. She was able to check out mentally, but she had a task to occupy her shaking hands as she waited for the inevitable crash.

Dani was used to this pattern: the high of battle, followed by adrenaline singing in her blood long after the last blow had landed. It always ended—the human body could only sustain that kind of physiological frenzy for so long. But tonight, it seemed like it wouldn't stop.

Finally, as she replaced the barrel and slide of the last pistol, she understood. Her hands weren't shaking from leftover adrenaline.

It was fear.

Instinctively, she shoved the thought away, then drew it back for closer examination. Yes, she was scared. She wasn't usually—not having the immediate physical feedback of pain made it easy to think of a fight in abstract, binary terms. Win or lose. True/false.

Live or die.

One outcome was acceptable. The other was not. Even with Nina and Maya on the line, the calculation was simple. The best way to keep them safe was to win the fight. Dani didn't have time to think about anything else.

Something about Rafe was different. Something about him changed the game.

As if merely thinking about him had conjured him from thin air, he knocked softly on her door. She wasn't sure how she knew it was him, but it was as if she could feel the way his body called to hers even through solid wood and drywall.

She rose and crossed the room. But when she reached the door, she only leaned her forehead against it.

A soft *thump* sounded from the other side, and she could almost envision him mirroring her with only the wood separating them, his forehead pressed to the door, his hand splayed not far from hers. "You don't have to let me in," came the soft words, warm and entreating. "Just . . . tell me you're okay."

"I can't." Her chest and her throat burned as she opened the door. "I'm not okay."

He filled the doorway, one hand gripping the top of the doorframe. He'd thrown on a coat before crossing between their buildings, but it gaped open, revealing his bare chest, half a dozen adhesive bandages over his superficial wounds, and newly healed skin at his abdomen.

He loomed there, his chest rising and falling with every deep breath, looking for all the world as if he was clutching at the doorway to stop himself from bursting through. His deep brown eyes reflected the same wild need that tore at her, and his hands—

His hands were trembling, too.

Dani reached for him.

That was all it took. Rafe crashed into the room like a wave breaking, sweeping her along with him. The door thudded shut at his kick, but she was already in his arms, feet dangling off the floor until she scrambled to wrap her thighs around his hips.

Rafe buried his face against her throat. His arms locked around her body, holding her so close, she swore she could feel their hearts pounding together. Every shaking exhale stirred the hair at her neck, but for endless moments all he did was hold her, one hand smoothing up her spine and over her shoulder as if reassuring himself she was in one piece.

"You could have died." The words left her in a helpless rush. "How am I supposed to be okay?"

"I didn't." His fingertips dragged over her scalp as he cradled the back of her head, his fingers tangled in hair still tipped in blue. "I'm okay, Dani. I'm hard to kill, I promise."

"*Not* helping."

He tugged gently at her hair, coaxing her head back so she could meet his eyes. "I'm okay, Dani," he whispered again. "I'm here. You can examine every inch of me, if you want."

She nodded, holding his gaze as they moved back toward her bed. She pushed his coat from his shoulders on the way, letting it fall to the floor. He spun, drawing her into his lap as he dropped to sit on the edge of her bed.

She skimmed quickly over the bandages and zip sutures, lingering instead on the areas Mace had considered serious enough for regen therapy. The shiny skin was warm under her fingertips, and he shuddered as her hand slipped from his side around to his back.

"The bullet went through cleanly?" she asked softly. "No fragmentation, no organ damage?"

"None." His fingers trailed up her arm, over skin already knit together thanks to the med-gel Nina had meticulously applied. "You didn't need any regen?"

Her eyes drifted shut. "No, just the gel."

His exploration continued, as slow and thorough as hers. He ghosted a gentle touch over the newly healed skin on her back, and shivered under her touch. "They were so fast, and they could barely land a hit on you. You're fucking incredible."

The reminder brought back flashes of the fight, and the goose bumps that rose on her arms weren't entirely due to his stroking fingers. "I don't want to think about them. If I do, I'll have to think about how you threw yourself in front of a bullet meant for me."

"Then don't think about it." His knuckles ghosted up her spine until they found the band of her bra, and he traced the edge of it. "Think about me, here with you. Safe."

It eased a little of her trembling, and she opened her eyes again. He was so *close*, his lips mere inches away, his skin growing hot under her hands.

He wasn't just here. He was *hers*.

Dani kissed him. The moment her mouth touched his, she knew it wouldn't be enough, so she deepened the kiss, exploring his tongue with hers. He tasted like tea and honey, and she swallowed a moan.

This wasn't enough, either.

She didn't realize she was moving against him until he made a soothing sound, his hands stroking up her back and over her shoulders. He framed her face so tenderly it stole her breath as he tilted her head back. His mouth slanted over hers, slowing the reckless rhythm of her lips on his. Not frantic. Not hurried.

A promise. Silent but unmistakable, reinforced by the brutal gentleness of his kiss, the heat of his body curling around hers, the way his thumbs stroked over her cheeks as he licked his way deeper into her mouth.

I'm not going anywhere.

He brushed the band of her bra again, and sheer impatience had her breaking the kiss to drag it over her head. "Hurry," she panted.

Rafe chuckled, but this time when his fingers slid down her arms, he caught her wrists and guided them behind her back, where he easily caged them both in one large hand. "Have you ever gone slow, Dani?" He traced his free hand back up her arm and used it to brush her hair back, baring her shoulder for the teasing brush of his lips. "Has anyone ever convinced you to just sit with the pleasure? To *feel* it?"

If anyone had tried, they would have been spending the night alone— and that was a best-case scenario. Dani was into plenty of things, but denial wasn't one of them.

She wiggled and flexed her arms as she opened her mouth to tell him so, but his grip on her wrists tightened. Not too much—the pressure was still comparatively light, but there was something . . . *implacable* about it. As if he'd hold her just as tightly as he had to. No more and no less.

It wasn't a game she usually played. It was similar to being bound, but more reactive and intimate, and it required way more trust than she typically offered—or asked of—her sexual partners.

Then again, this was *Rafe*. And it didn't feel like a game with him, not at all.

Finally, she answered his question. "Fast for you *is* slow for me, remember? But I'm willing to give it a shot."

She felt his smile, his lips curving against her skin. He dropped a taunting trail of kisses across her collarbone, and the heat of his breath feathered across the spot where her pulse pounded in her throat. "I wonder . . ." he murmured.

He closed his teeth on her neck. The pressure sizzled up her spine, arching her back, and she moaned his name. He just hummed against her skin, and soothed her with a soft kiss before working his way to her ear and nipping her again.

It was a strange mix of spontaneous caresses and methodical reconnaissance. A kiss here, a stroke of his tongue there. He revisited spots that made her shiver, lingering until her head spun. He figured out that she would chase the lighter touches, eager for more, and that harder ones made her go still, breathless. And then he discovered that alternating the two would drive her *wild*.

Dani squirmed on his lap, trying to press her hips closer to his. But he held her back with a wordless promise whispered against the curve of her breast before his lips closed around her aching nipple.

Don't fight it. Just feel *it.*

She bent her head to his, resting her cheek against his temple, and let it carry her away. The building heat. The suction, gentle and demanding in turn. Even the soft, hypnotic friction of skin on skin. All of it melted into a Siren call of pleasure, and she surrendered to it.

Finally, he released her hands and gripped her hips. The world tilted in a blur, and she landed on her back in the center of her rumpled bed. Rafe's clever fingers hooked her underwear and dragged her last remaining scrap of clothing down her legs as he rose and stepped away. He stood at the end of the bed, and Dani blinked as he lowered his hands and began to unfasten his jeans.

"Absolutely not," she rasped. "I get to do that."

His lips curved in that mischievous smile that always drove her crazy. But he obediently held his hands out to his side. "Come and get me, sweetheart."

Oh, he had *no idea* what he'd done.

Dani rolled to her hands and knees and slowly stalked to the end of the bed. When she reached the edge, she straightened, hooking her fingers through one of his belt loops. "You know," she drawled, "I thought you'd be more of a talker."

"I can talk," he replied, his voice a low rasp. "If the occasion calls for it. Is that what you like? Dirty words?"

"Sometimes." She let her hair brush his abdomen as she toyed with the button on his jeans.

Rafe plunged his fingers into her hair, tangling the strands around his fingers just tight enough that she could feel the tingle along her scalp. "Maybe I can't think of anything right now except finally watching you curl your fingers around my cock."

"That's convenient." She leaned closer, pulling against his grip on her hair until she could press her lips to the center of his chest. "You talk a big game until the game's going down. And then . . ." She eased his zipper down. "You lose your incredibly sexy voice."

"My incredibly sexy voice?" he echoed hoarsely. "I don't hear that one often."

"Probably because people are too stunned by the visuals to notice. But trust me." She slipped her hands into the warm, supple denim and toyed with the waistband of his underwear. "It's hot."

He shuddered under her touch, and this time the tightening of his fingers seemed reflexive. A rumble left him, his voice edged in a growl. "I swear to God, Dani, if you don't put your hands on me soon—"

"Rafael Morales, the world's sexiest hypocrite, can torment his lovers for *days,* but he can't"—she wrapped her fingers around him—"*take it.*"

He groaned, his hips jerking. His erection filled her hand, hard and hot, and when he stared down at her, it was like the dark amber of his eyes blazed from within. "You want me to talk?" he rumbled, his fingers flexing in her hair. "I could tell you about the shower I took after I almost got my fingers inside you in that pool."

She had cursed that *almost* at the time, but now she was glad that Phoenix had interrupted things before they could go too far. This was better. Here, cocooned in the familiar safety of her bedroom, Dani could let go, be free in a way she never could have up on the Hill.

She bit his lower lip, then soothed the spot with her tongue. "Tell me."

He shuddered again, and let his head fall back. "I leaned against that tile and closed my eyes, and I imagined you were in there with me. Water dripping down your body. All hot and steamy and slippery. I pinned you to the wall and made you come all over my fingers until you were begging for more. But when I let you go . . ." A low, hoarse chuckle, and his hips swayed forward again, pushing against her fingers. "Even in my imagination, you're impossible. You got down on your knees, just like this . . ."

"Like this?" She pushed him back—slowly, gently—and slid to the floor at his feet. "Or like this?"

Another shudder. "Like that."

She released him, but only to tug the denim down his legs and pull it free of his bare feet. "And then?"

"And then you made *me* beg," he rumbled. "Made me beg for every lick and stroke. Made me beg for you to suck me so fucking deep."

It captured the push and pull of their relationship so perfectly that she had to hide a smile against his muscled thigh. And it made the fantasy feel so real that it drew her in effortlessly, as if it was spinning out before her.

Sweat and steam pearling on his skin before being rinsed away by the cascading water. Stone tile against her back, as warm as Rafe and as rough as his ardor. Blinding pleasure and *relief,* the end to months of tension and denial.

Dani muffled a moan against his hip. "What did you do?"

"Oh, I begged." The tug of his fingers in her hair sparked tingles, but his voice was liquid sex. "I wrapped my fingers around my dick and begged for you to take me."

She held up both hands, then dropped them to her lap and arched one eyebrow.

He laughed, low and hot. His thumbs swept out to stroke her cheek, and he let one trail down to trace the curve of her lower lip. "Please," he whispered. "You glorious, dangerous, murderous goddess." He pressed his thumb to her lips, edging just the tip inside when she parted them. "Let me feel the tongue I've been dreaming about for months."

"Flattery?" She licked his thumb. "It's working."

"Let me feel these lips," he whispered. He slid his thumb deeper, stroking her tongue, then eased free and gripped his erection. "Unless you're bored of this fantasy. Because there's one where I get on *my* knees and see how loud you scream when you're riding three fingers and my tongue."

"Now who's getting impatient?" Dani closed her mouth around the head of his cock with a soft hum.

His reaction was everything she could have wanted. The low moan, the shudder, the way his hand gripped her hair—still so careful, in spite of his enormous strength. He swayed as she stroked her tongue over him, and her name escaped him as a choked whisper. "Dani. *Fuck.*"

She had to tell him her full name one of these days, discover what it sounded like in his low, mellifluous voice. Which syllables he would stress and which he would roll together, fast and intimate, like two lovers stumbling home together at the end of the night.

She *craved* it, maybe as much as she craved this—the helpless thrust of his hips, the way the fine tremor running through his body grew in intensity with each passing breath torn from his lungs. The way the pleas began to fall from his lips in earnest when she took him deeper.

"Fuck." His fingers tightened again, trying to drag her back. "Dani, I'm close—"

She dug her nails into the back of his leg. He jerked, then came with a shudder and a groan, flooding her mouth. It was a perfect moment of abandon, of absolute vulnerability, and Dani soothed him by rubbing the back of her hand over his hip.

It took him a few glorious moments to force his eyes open. He looked pleasure-drunk and debauched, and her heart skipped as he leaned down to haul her to her feet. His mouth covered hers, swallowing her startled noise, and he kissed her with lazy passion that clashed with the way his fingers flexed on her hips.

He lifted her and tossed her onto the bed. Dani bounced once, but then Rafe was looming over her, cutting off her startled laugh. "Hi," she whispered.

"Hi," he murmured back. His body pressed hers to the bed. "Have you heard what they say about fucking Protectorate soldiers?"

"Can you be more specific? Because they say all *kinds* of things, honey."

He laughed and ran a hand down her side, hooking her thigh over his hips. "They say . . ." He dropped a kiss to her chin. "That we never get tired." His lips ghosted over the curve of one breast before sliding lower. "That we can go all night." She felt his teeth this time, just the lightest teasing pressure on her hip, before he gave her a teasing lick. "That we're always ready for round two. Or three. Or ten."

"I see. And are these—" Her words cut off in a rush as he kissed the inside of her thigh, and she had to clear her throat. "Are these things they say true?"

"Not always." The width of his shoulders pressed her thighs wide as he settled between them. He grinned at her up the length of her body, his breath teasing across hypersensitive skin. "I'm an overachiever, though. And currently *inspired*."

Inspired was a good word for it. He started slow, using his tongue to explore all the spots that would make her arch and moan. With all the teasing, she was already on edge, and Rafe used her arousal to his full advantage. He fell into a maddening rhythm that brought her closer and closer to orgasm before easing her back.

It was torture. It was bliss. Dani clutched at the comforter and tried to move against Rafe's mouth, but he held her still with an iron grip on her hips. Soon, she was past moaning, past pleading, holding her breath in tense, trembling silence.

She came the moment he thrust his fingers inside her, but he didn't let the clenching pleasure subside. He kept pushing her, driving her from one peak to the next, until she was practically sobbing, her entire world shaking apart at the seams, with *Rafe* there to fill it.

"Shh. . . ." She wasn't even sure when he'd climbed back up her body. Everything was shivering aftershocks, the brush of his hot skin over hers enough to shake her close to the edge. Rafe cupped her cheek with one hand, whispering her name until she managed to focus on his eyes.

His hips were wedged between hers. The hard length of his erection ground down on her clit, almost enough to push her back into orgasm on its own. "Are you with me, sweetheart?"

"I'm here." Her voice sounded like she'd been screaming, and Dani spared a light-headed moment of silent thanks for soundproofed bedrooms. "I think."

"Need a break?"

"Morales?" His concern was so adorable that she didn't even try to quell the amused affection in her words. "Shut up and fuck me."

Dark laughter rolled over her like honey as he guided her legs around his hips and drove into her. The shock of it dragged a rough curse from her throat, and she wrapped her arms around him, too, and held on tight, just in case he was thinking of pulling away. But he didn't. He only thrust deeper, his hips grinding against hers, his groans melding with her breathless encouragement.

It didn't matter that she'd just come so much and so hard she was still dizzy with it. The desperate need surged again, and she sank her teeth into Rafe's shoulder as he moved above her.

Strong. Relentless. She'd seen him bend metal and smash through concrete, she *knew* the strength in his body. But somehow he found the perfect edge, where every thrust sank deep enough to jolt sparks through her, where the bed creaked under the force of his every movement, but he was still gentle. *Careful.* He fucked her with unyielding focus, giving her pleasure layered across pleasure, sensation building to the point of dizzying madness.

Almost. Dani wrapped her hands around the wrought-iron bars of her headboard and pushed back against his next thrust. It blazed through her, and she whimpered.

"Just like that," he whispered. "Just feel me."

She came with a choked cry, every muscle in her body tensing against the sudden release of such mind-bending pleasure. She shuddered and shook, clung to Rafe as he followed her over the edge with a helpless groan.

For a moment, it seemed like everything was still, quiet. Right with the world.

Then Rafe rolled to the bed with a shaky groan. Dani blinked up at the ceiling, her vision literally wavering as she gasped for breath. "Holy shit."

Rafe's laugh was every bit as breathless. "You're right. We *definitely* would have drowned in the pool."

"It might have been worth it, after all."

The bed dipped as he rolled onto his side, and he slipped one arm around her to gather her close. "Without a doubt. But I prefer surviving so we can do it again."

She nestled her face against the damp skin of his shoulder and hummed her agreement. "Can't cuddle if you drown, either." It wasn't usually her favorite thing—she liked her space—but with Rafe, she'd make an exception.

"Mmm." He stroked his fingers through her hair, guiding it back from her face, but caught the end and held it up with another soft chuckle. "You know, I kind of like the blue."

Dani wrinkled her nose. "Really?"

"Absolutely." His fingers continued their soothing caress, smoothing her disheveled hair back into place. "In your fancy dress with your best *fuck you* glare, you're the ultimate ice queen. Beautiful and deadly . . ." His lips brushed her forehead. "And I'm the only one who gets to see how hot you really burn."

Her stomach did a funny little flip, and she bit her lip to hide a smile. "Sleep or get out, Morales. Choose wisely."

She felt his answering smile against her forehead before he kissed her again. "Good night, Dani."

KNOX

Knox had planned a lot of battles over more than two decades in the Protectorate. He'd meticulously plotted out everything from tiny one-man ops to full-scale minor revolutions, and in every instance, his main weapon had been information.

He loved information. He loved the way his mind felt as he scanned intelligence briefings and psychological profiles, as he pored over maps and weapons assessments. It was like pouring the pieces of a massive puzzle onto a pristine mental table, and something inside him could always find the right pieces to assemble a picture that made sense.

Information was usually precious. Today, he felt like Vice President Helen Anderson had backed a dump truck up to his brain and buried it in so much horrifying *truth* that he couldn't clear enough space to find the puzzle, much less assemble the picture.

Even Maya seemed overwhelmed. They sat across from each other in the basement command center, half a dozen tablets scattered between them. Maya rubbed at her temples absently as she listened to whatever was piping through to her ear cuffs—probably the latest decrypted Board meeting.

Knox didn't envy her that task. She was the only one who could listen to them all and process the information, but he'd scanned enough transcripts to know that Board meetings were grim affairs mostly given over to bickering over company priorities and arguments about the best ways to subdue an increasingly restless population.

"Oh, this is a good one."

Knox's gaze swung automatically to Conall, who was seated at the head of the table with a holographic display that shimmered illegibly from Knox's angle. "What have you got?"

"Security info on the COO. Kristof Vargo." Conall whistled. "This is one paranoid fucker. He had a safe room installed in his office. Custom designed."

"Let me see it."

Conall made a flicking gesture and tapped something out. A moment later, the tablet in front of Knox *dinged,* and he pulled up the schematics.

Safe room seemed insufficient to describe the new additions to Vargo's HQ penthouse. The entire thing was a goddamn fortress, four rooms of reinforced steel and plascrete likely to survive a direct drone strike. You'd have to collapse the entire building beneath him to kill him—and that was if he didn't use the AirLift escape pod embedded in the wall of the bedroom. The damn thing even had a water recycler and enough food to last him a year, not to mention O_2 scrubbers and an elaborate poison detection system, plus multiple high-tech unseverable hardline connections.

"Be flattered," Conall added. "This is the system he hired Charlie to upgrade after you went rogue. This is how much you scared him."

Charlie had been Conall's main competition in the elite ranks of the tech trainees. These days, she lived a posh life as the chief security consultant to the Board . . . and had a *very* profitable side hustle as the best hacker in the cybercrime underworld. "Any chance Charlie wants to tell us how to beat this?"

Conall snorted. "Doubtful. Charlie doesn't crime where she eats."

Mace tossed a tablet onto a stack of them on the table, shaking his head. "What's the point?"

Gray grimaced. "Jesus, Mace."

"No, I'm not being a shit. It's a serious question." He pinned Knox with a searching gaze. "This is too much information to sort through without an angle. So what are we trying to do here? Pick off these execs, one by one? Run a little guerrilla warfare campaign? Or hit the Tech-Corps where it counts?"

Trust Mace to slice to the heart of the issue. Until this point, they'd been doing what they could against an implacable enemy. The fight had been about survival in the face of crushing odds, and playing the long game. But the potential involvement of multiple Board members—and, if Dani and Rafe were correct in their assessment of John's upward trajectory, someone even closer to power than a vice president—changed the dynamics.

If they wanted, this game could get short. Fast.

"Now *that* sounds like a question for your intelligence officer." Beth looked up from the tablet in her hands. "Wait, where *is* your intelligence officer?"

Conall snickered. "I suggest you don't try to find out, unless you want to open a random door and get the full glory of his naked ass. I'll admit, it is a *fine* ass . . ."

"But if you look at it too long, Dani might stab you," Maya finished without looking up.

"Oh. *Oh.*" Beth dropped the tablet and clutched both hands to her chest with a smile. "Aww! That's so romantic. Falling in love on the eve of war, trying to squeeze in as much time together as possible before—" She cut off as Rainbow came down the stairs with Nina, carrying a basket of sandwiches. "You know."

"We heard you already," Nina told her. "Here. Have a peanut butter and jam sandwich."

"I helped make them," Rainbow added, plucking two out of the basket and carrying them to Knox. She put them down in front of him with a serious look that made affection bloom like an ache in his chest. "You can't forget to eat."

"You are absolutely right." He nudged the chair next to him back in quiet invitation, and she scrambled happily up into it and leaned her elbows on the table to peer at his tablet.

"Are you planning an infiltration?" she asked as Knox bit into the sandwich, and he was glad that chewing gave him time to check his instinctive need to lie to her. She was so small, it was hard to remember that her tiny body held twice the strength of a fully grown man. It was hard to remember that even though she was probably no more than seven or eight, she'd been studying schematics and battle plans from the time she was old enough to form words.

Nina must have been like this. So small. So smart. A ready smile and an open heart and a brain full of warfare, because the people who'd created her didn't think of her as a *person,* as a child who deserved a childhood.

Somehow, Knox had to find the line for Rainbow. To build a safe space for her to be a kid without patronizing her or excluding her.

"We're not planning yet." He broke off a piece of his sandwich and held it out. "We're still assessing all the intel we have and trying to decide what we want to do with it."

Nina's expression was grave as she placed her hands on Rainbow's shoulders. "We know what we have to do with it. Beth was right—it's going to be war. It has to be."

Ava spoke up for the first time from where she sat in the corner, as far from Knox as she could get, with her legs crossed and a tablet balanced on her knee. "War is fine, and all. With the number of strategists we have in this room, it's likely we could decimate their leadership. But what then?"

"Anything's got to be better than what we have now." Gray shoved away a stack of printouts and braced his elbows on the table. "People living in fear, crushed under poverty and hunger and deprivation—all conditions that the TechCorps have manufactured? I'd take a fucking power vacuum any day."

"But that's easy for you to say, Gray," Beth whispered. "It's easy for any of us to say, even Rainbow. We'd be all right. Not everyone has that."

"A power vacuum wouldn't last a week on the Hill." Ava pinned Gray with a withering look. "And you wouldn't like the kinds of people most likely to fill it. Ask Rafe, if you can pry him off Dani. He just got a close look at the heirs to power."

"Ava's right," Maya said reluctantly. "She's being a complete asshole—*again*—but she's not *wrong*." She sighed, rubbing at her temples again. "There are people on the Hill we could work with, I think. But I don't know *who*, outside the obvious."

The frustration in her voice was so intense, Gray reached out a soothing hand to rub at her shoulder. Maya wasn't used to *not knowing* any more than Knox was, but Maya's solution was right in front of her. Dozens of hours of Board meetings that she could listen to, synthesize, and . . .

His internal landscape shifted. The jumble of pieces spread out before them wouldn't form a picture because they weren't *one* puzzle. "Okay," Knox said, feeling the ground firm up beneath him. "Maya, you focus on the Board meetings and other recordings. We need to *know* every one of those executives. Who we might be able to trust, and who we *definitely* can't."

"I can do that."

"Good. Ava—"

"I don't take orders from you, Captain Knox."

He must have been wearing her down, because it lacked Ava's usual vehemence. Or maybe that was due to Beth's presence—one exasperated look from her had Ava grinding her teeth and glaring at Knox as if he'd been the one to get her in trouble. "I'll help, though. The Tech-Corps serves no purpose for me in its current incarnation. I might as well replace them with something useful."

"We appreciate your generosity." Knox had to resist the urge to poke at her further. Ava glared at him suspiciously, but he only smiled. "If you could offer Maya any insights from your interactions with the executives, that would be helpful."

She nodded curtly and resumed her perusal of her tablet, pointedly ignoring him.

That was fine. Knox turned to Nina. "What comes next matters, but you know what we have to do first."

She held his gaze for a moment, then turned to the rest of the group. "Practical planning starts now. I want contingencies for every possible move the TechCorps might make—ignoring the shit out of us, cutting off supply lines, full-scale infantry invasion. Even bombing us right off the face of the planet. I want so many contingencies even Knox won't know what to do with them all, okay?"

"Now we're talking," Mace muttered.

"No, now we're *working*," Nina countered. "So get to it, Doc. Rainbow and I are going to figure out how to get the community center up and running ahead of schedule, so we'll be around if you need anything."

"Talk to Rafe's family." Knox leaned down to kiss the top of Rainbow's head. "Celia told me that her son's been apprenticed to a mechanic, and her younger daughter is a gifted gardener. I'm sure they'd be a big help."

"If they're settled in." Nina took the basket from Rainbow with a smile. "Let's go check. Maybe Señora Celia made some *desserts*."

Knox watched the two of them disappear up the stairs before turning to the rest of the table. His gaze swept the group. "Conall, start with a full security evaluation. I want all of our vulnerabilities *and* all of theirs."

"Got it."

"Mace, we need to be prepared for mass casualties. And if you need Rafe to get the necessary supplies, tell him to put his pants back on and get to it."

He grinned. "I think I can handle it."

"Good. Beth, I don't give *you* orders, either . . ."

"But I'm here to help!" she chirped. "Might I suggest we focus my efforts on the comprehensive survey of potential TechCorps retaliatory measures? Phoenix is still playing cleanup right now, but I can use her data, along with what we received from VP Anderson, to make conjectures based not only on their capabilities, but on their overall willingness to deploy resources."

Knox would have to remember not to underestimate Beth's razor-sharp B-designation training just because she was a bouncing bundle of pure sunlight and smiles. "That would be extremely helpful."

"Oh, I know! We'll put together a histogram for each factor. Then we can index for best-and worst-case scenarios, plus everything in between." She high-fived Conall. "It'll be great."

Ava glared at Knox again. He pretended he couldn't see it and looked at Gray. "I need you to assess the Board's personal security. Pull Dani in, when she shows up. If we need to take one of them out, I want a plan."

Gray rubbed his chin. "Access will be tricky, with everyone on high alert, but we'll figure it out."

Knox stared down at the scattered tablets and exhaled. He'd been wary about moving too fast, but everything inside him whispered that Anderson wouldn't have dumped this sort of data if the TechCorps weren't at an internal crisis point.

They were going to do something bad. Soon. And Knox would be ready.

It was time to call in reinforcements.

**TECHCORPS PROPRIETARY DATA,
L1 SECURITY CLEARANCE**

Authorization approved. Weapons hot in two hours.

Internal Memo, December 2086

TWENTY

Even with preparation for war all around him, today was, without exaggeration, the best day of Rafe's life.

He'd woken curled around Dani—the third time in a row—and the fact that she'd started *cuddling* with him in her sleep meant lazy mornings filled with soft skin and softer kisses, the intimacy of it enough to steal his breath. He'd known they'd be hot together—only a fool could have missed the spark—but she *trusted* him, and that shook him to the bone.

They'd parted ways outside her door, and Rafe had slammed from one kind of fantasy straight into another.

His family was settling into the unfinished apartment across the hall from Ivonne and Luna. He'd walked in to find Rosa and Antonio bickering over what they were going to watch on the new flatscreen Gray had installed for them while Tessa sat at the table, sketching. The aroma of spicy sausage and scrambled eggs filled the air, and his mother kissed his cheek with a warm smile before pressing him into a chair at the head of the table.

Breakfast with his family, without fear clouding every movement—something that had seemed even more out of reach last week than a cuddly, sweetly trusting Dani.

Rafe currently had too many blessings to count, and a ticking clock at the back of his head reminding him that they could all too soon be swept away.

He did his work—feeling out contacts and sourcing supplies—but his mind kept drifting back home.

To her.

When he returned, he hoped to find Dani so they could work off an entire day of sexual restraint, but she disappeared after dinner on an unstated mission. The frenetic energy in the command center was too much for his nerves to handle, and as much as he was enjoying family time, he couldn't quite justify waking them up at midnight to chat.

So he found himself back in Nina's workout room, abandoning the weight and cardio machines for the custom heavy bag that could actually sustain the force of one of his amped-up punches. Not because he needed it—he had his own specially designed bag hanging in the basement of their warehouse—but because Dani would have to come past the workout room to get to her bed.

He was laying a trap. A shirtless, sweaty trap.

And he knew it really *was* the best day of his life when she fell into it. "Oh, fuck *you*."

Rafe gave the bag one last solid *thwack*, then caught it as it rebounded. He turned slowly, letting Dani get a good look at all of his flexing muscles. She leaned against the open doorway, dressed in street clothes—jeans, boots, and a big, fleecy sweater the same color as her eyes.

She eyed him up and down, a lazy perusal that started and ended in the vicinity of his bare chest. "Rough day?"

"Oh, you know." He purposefully stretched his arms over his head. "Feeling out two dozen contacts, trying to make sure we have all the tech and weapons and meds we're going to need. Nothing to really get the blood pumping."

"Mmm. No wonder you're in here, blowing off steam." She blinked innocently at him. "That *is* why you're here, right? Nothing at all to do with the fact that my room is right down the hall."

"I guess there's only one way to find out." He started unwrapping the tape from his right hand, eyes never leaving hers. "Does that door lock?"

She stepped in and slid the door shut behind her. "Does it matter?"

Conall had already gotten an eyeful when he'd stumbled across them doing some late-night *strategizing* in the war room, and Maya had very nearly caught them violating the warehouse. As if they'd been the first to do it—Rafe knew damn well that Gray stayed up late with Maya *scanning books* all the time.

Anyone who failed to knock on a closed door got what they deserved at this point. "Nope."

"Thought so." She slipped the strap of a corduroy bag off her shoulder and dropped it by the wall. "Don't let me interrupt."

He tossed aside the tape from his hands and flexed his fingers. "You're the one always wanting to take a swing at me, cupcake. Seems like the perfect opportunity. I'm all warmed up."

Dani squinted at him, then relented with a shrug and tugged off one boot. "I'd say to be careful what you wish for, but something tells me you've given this a *lot* of thought."

Denying it was pointless. A good half of his most feverish fantasies started in this room, him fighting all-out against Dani and her blisteringly hot assassin reflexes, and the best part was never being quite sure which of them would end up on top. "C'mon, Dani. You've never wondered if you're fast enough to take me down?"

"Oh, I've wondered." With her boots and socks gone, she reached for her sweater. She took her time peeling it over her head, leaving her in her jeans and a strappy black sports bra. "Pondering the possibilities has carried me through quite a few long-distance runs."

Maybe someday he'd get tired of the way she moved. Effortless grace and sleek danger, a promise and a challenge wrapped in one. Sometimes he couldn't tell if the shiver of reaction that gripped him when she walked toward him was pure physical chemistry, or his battle instincts screaming a warning.

Probably both. That was his favorite part.

He backed toward the center of the sparring mat as she approached, enjoying the way the mirrors reflected her back at him. "Let's go, sweetheart. Try me."

"Oh, *please.*" She drew out the word as she slowly circled him. "I don't throw myself at brick walls, Morales."

"Brick?" he huffed, spreading his arms wide as he pivoted to keep his gaze on her. "Marble, at least. Bronze. Something a little more impressive than mundane brick."

"Steel? Steel is sexy."

"Steel," he murmured, then lunged for her.

It was pointless, he knew as soon as he moved. He was fast, but she was ... smoke. His muscles had barely flexed to launch him into movement before she was spinning away with a grin. Floating like she had all the time in the world to evade his hopeless attempt to lay hands on her.

"Maybe we should make a wager," she said lightly.

He lunged again, coming close enough that the end of her ponytail grazed his fingertips before she was gone. He let the growl trapped in his chest rumble free. "Like what?"

"Something high-stakes. Wide open." She bounced a little bit closer, then twisted away again. "Winner's choice—nothing off-limits."

"Oh, did we have limits?" Rafe pivoted again, watching her eyes. When he lunged, she danced away to the left. The third time in a row she'd gone left. Useful. "I didn't think we had any limits last night . . ."

Her eyes gleamed with humor and affection. "Careful, now."

"One minute." Another lunge. Another graceful dodge to his left. It matched the flow of their circling, and she was right-handed. He'd seen her lead with her right side in plenty of fights. "If I can't catch you in sixty seconds, you win. But if I've got you pinned . . ." He let his eyes make the promise.

"If you *get* me pinned, or *keep* me pinned?" Dani stretched her neck. "It's an important distinction."

"Oh, if I put hands on you tonight, cupcake, I am *not* letting go."

"Deal."

Rafe pivoted again. "Computer, set a timer for one minute."

The soft, slightly accented voice of the training room computer responded immediately. "Timer set, one minute. Starting . . . now."

Dani, underneath him. No limits.

Rafe smiled, pivoted to the left, and lunged. Dani's warm, husky laughter as she escaped heated his blood. His fingertips tingled. He could feel her already, writhing beneath him, begging in a hoarse voice for a release he'd withhold until the force of it shattered them both.

Her eyes sparkled as she danced around him. Rafe pivoted, watching until her gaze slipped to his chest, and he knew she'd see the clues, the flexing of muscles.

The trap.

He feinted, starting to lunge. At the last second he jackknifed to the left, crashing into her escape trajectory. It was messy—she was *so damn fast*—but they both went down to the mat, his body half over hers. He scrambled to find her hands—

But she was already fighting back. She arched beneath him, jammed a knee into his side, and sank her teeth into the inside of his arm.

Rafe yelped in surprise, jerking away even as the pain sizzled into something hotter. Even that tiny window was too much. Dani heaved her body with surprising strength, using her momentum to roll them over. She ended up straddling his hips, thighs splayed wide, and having her grinding down against his dick was *not* helping his focus.

"Mmm." She braced her hands on his chest and rocked against him. "This feels strangely like winning."

He grabbed her hips in an iron grip, mostly to retain his sanity. "I didn't know we were playing dirty."

"We always are, sweetheart."

"You really think you can keep me pinned for another thirty seconds?"

"Don't know." Her hands began to drift down. "You tell me."

Her fingertips skimming the bare skin of his chest only stirred arousal deeper. It didn't matter that she couldn't rock against him—just having her hips under his hands made him want to drive up against her. Fighting and fucking—there'd never been enough of a line between the two where Dani was concerned.

And letting her stay on top had its delightful possibilities, too. Dani, having her unrestrained way with him . . .

But neither of them would savor it the same if he *let* her win.

With an easy flex of muscle, he rolled them over. His hips settled between her thighs like he belonged there, and he braced his hands on either side of her head. "Earn it," he whispered. "Twenty seconds."

Dani arched against him again, but this time it didn't feel like she was trying to dislodge his weight. She moaned softly, then slid one hand down between them and popped open the button on her jeans.

Trap. His brain registered it even as his body reacted, lifting instinctively just enough to give her fingers room to maneuver. She tugged at the zipper, and he eased back a little more.

Then she slipped her hand into the denim.

"*Fuck.*" He pushed himself up higher, but all he could see was her wrist disappearing beneath those damned jeans he was seriously considering ripping off her body.

Ten seconds. Ten seconds to victory.

Dani moaned.

Groaning, Rafe rolled them both again. Dani ended up straddling him, her hand lost inside her jeans. Rafe grabbed either side of the zipper and yanked with all of his strength, tearing the fabric apart at the seams.

She gasped and shimmied out of the ruined jeans. "You could have just taken them off—"

Rafe cut her off by hooking a finger under the waistband of her underwear. "Unless you want the same thing to happen . . ."

She stripped out of the rest of her clothes with lightning speed, then stretched out over him, burying her face in his neck.

"One minute," the computer announced.

"You win," she whispered, then bit him.

The sting of it sizzled through him, hotter than her whispered surrender. A thousand utterly filthy possibilities tumbled through his mind, but one need surpassed them all. Sinking a hand into her hair, he dragged her head up and seized her lips in a blistering kiss.

Dani moaned into the kiss as she tilted her head to his, her hands framing his face, as if she had to hold him close because the idea of letting go was unbearable.

He knew how she felt.

He kissed her until his entire body hummed with the pleasure of it. He kissed her as he slid one hand down her spine to cup her ass, urging her to rock against him. His thin workout pants might as well not be there when she ground down against him, hot and already wet, as turned on by their sparring as he was.

He shuddered and bit her lip. "I win?" he asked hoarsely.

She ran her fingernails down the side of his neck. "Anything you want."

All he wanted was her.

He rolled them again, and rose to his knees. He gave himself a bare moment to admire how she looked stretched out naked before him, all flushed skin and glazed eyes. Then he gripped her hips and flipped her onto her knees in front of him. She'd barely gotten her hands underneath her when he leaned over her, covering her back with his chest and bracing one arm along hers. "Look up."

She met his gaze in the mirrored wall with a noise that was half moan, half chuckle. "You are a brilliant man with brilliant ideas."

"I know." He found her ear with his lips, and let his warm chuckle tickle her skin. "Now where were we before I ripped your jeans off . . ."

"I think right about . . . here." She lifted her hand to his mouth.

He licked the tips of her fingers, savoring the way she shuddered as he let his teeth scrape over her index finger. Soft touches, that was the key to Dani. Her body had built defenses against pain, but she melted under the gentlest graze of teeth or a fingernail tracing over skin.

He sucked her finger deep just to hear her moan, then covered her hand with his own and guided it down her body. The mirror reflected her back at them—her flushed cheeks and wild hair, her sleek body. Her hand, trembling as he let his fall away.

But she didn't hesitate. Her fingertips found her clit, stroking with eager need, and all of his plans for a slow, brutally gentle seduction shattered.

He didn't just want her. He *needed* her.

"Don't stop," he ordered hoarsely before rising upright again. She moaned in protest at the loss of his body against hers, but her fingers kept their frantic pace, and he could feel the trembling in her thighs. She was close. So fucking close.

Too close. He couldn't even find the self-control to take off his pants. Dani moaned again, and he had the fabric shoved halfway down his hips and his dick in his hand. She trembled when he gripped her hip, and then he was thrusting into her, a groan of absolute bliss tearing free of him as he sank deep.

She came immediately, her hand sliding out from under her. She collapsed to the mat as she bucked and shuddered, her body squeezing him so tight he almost lost it. Shuddering, he dropped forward, one hand slapping down on the mat next to her. He slid his other arm beneath her body and hauled her up against his chest.

"Dani." Another buck of his hips had her whimpering, and he pressed his mouth to her temple. "Dani, look."

Her glazed gaze found his in the mirror. The sight of it was visceral—their bodies locked together, one of her arms trapped under his, her fingers still trembling against her slick flesh. Plenty of his fantasies had ended like this, with him buried deep inside her on the training room floor as he fucked her through half a dozen orgasms.

But she'd never looked at him like this in his fantasies. Even in the darkest, deepest recesses of his own heart, he'd never imagined she'd be so . . .

Open. Adoring.

His.

"You," her voice cracked, "are so fucking beautiful."

Shuddering, he fucked into her again, never breaking their gaze in the mirror. Words fell from his lips with every thrust, and he didn't care if they revealed too much. He couldn't have stopped them, not with her body clenching around him, not with her gasps and wordless pleas, not when her eyes never left his.

When she came the third time, he closed his eyes and buried his face in her hair as his body jerked toward the precipice. "That's it," he groaned. "Let me feel you. Let me—"

Release crashed over him, stealing the fatal confession. He groaned against her, the words echoing in his bones. In his heart.

Let me love you.

She went limp in his arms, clinging to him for support as she panted for breath. Even Rafe's arm felt unsteady. It took a moment to regain the coordination to lift them both, and they ended up in a limb-tangled sprawl on their sides with Dani's ponytail tickling his face.

His attempt at a laugh came out more like a groan. "Dear God, woman. I think you broke me."

"*Me?* This was all your doing."

"No, I had *plans*." He nudged her hair out of the way and pressed a kiss to the back of her neck. "And then you started playing *filthy*."

"I ruined your plans?" She rolled over in his arms, a sweetly curious smile curving her lips. "What were they?"

"Uh-uh. You'll just have to find out." He grinned. "Next time you lose."

"You're really not going to tell me?" Dani gasped in mock outrage and poked him in the side. "You shredded a perfectly good pair of jeans. You owe me."

"I'll buy you another pair." He caught her hand and brought it up to kiss her palm. "And for the record, I didn't even get out of my pants. That's how much you ruined my damn plans."

"Well, now I'm not sorry." She pressed her lips to his jaw with a satisfied hum. "You got what you deserved."

Hot sex on the training room floor followed by a playful, cuddly Dani. *Best day* didn't even cover it anymore. The joy in his chest expanded until it was very nearly an ache, and Rafe slipped his fingers through her ponytail, curling the tousled strands of hair around his fingers.

They hadn't talked about what they were doing, as if by mutual silent agreement. Like they both understood that trying to draw lines and rules around this glorious messy thing between them was likely the swiftest way to destroy it. And, with war looming, did it even matter? They could all be dead in a week. Or tomorrow.

But Rafe might ruin it anyway. He almost had, this time. Those words hovered on the tip of his tongue even now, the words that terrified him because he had been so sure they would terrify her.

Love.

Maybe he'd read her all wrong. Dani certainly wasn't withholding anything now. It could be that she'd simply recategorized him in her head, and now he occupied the same space in her estimation as Maya and Nina. He had to have earned the melty eyes and the sweet affection somehow.

It had to be new. Because if she'd felt this way about him all along, if he'd wasted all this time and they *did* die tomorrow? He would be so fucking pissed.

He'd been so sure she was only interested in sex, not *him*. But maybe *he'd* been the one letting fear hold them back.

"You're thinking too hard," Dani murmured against his skin. "If you're thinking this hard, I didn't wreck you nearly as much as you claim I did."

"No, I—"

A quick blow rattled the door, too forceful to even be called a knock, followed by Nina's terse, oddly thick voice. "Get dressed."

Rafe hurriedly tugged his pants into place, and Dani sat up, a frown creasing her brow. "What is it?"

Nina slid open the door, her face uncharacteristically pale. "The Board made its first move. They hit Montgomery Farms."

"Fuck." Dani paused while reaching for her sweater. "They sent in troops?"

Nina's shaky exhale kindled dread in the pit of Rafe's stomach. Then she spoke, and the dread exploded.

"I wish. The bastards bombed them."

**TECHCORPS PROPRIETARY
INTERNAL COMMUNICATION**

Anderson, Helen: This was done in violation of every rule we have on proper use of force.

Vargo, Kristof: This was a necessary security action, approved by the CEO, and carried out with the full support of the new acting VP of Security.

Anderson, Helen: It was barbaric, gratuitous, and foolish. What possible purpose could it have served?

Vargo, Kristof: Stick to science, Helen. You never were any good at politics.

Executive Internal Network

TWENTY-ONE

Montgomery Farms at night was usually serene, the air full of peeping frogs and lightning bugs, lit only by moonlight and the gentle golden glow through warehouse and cabin windows.

Tonight, the sky blazed as Gray pulled their tactical truck to a stop near the main warehouse that served as a communal building for Jaden's people. It had been blown in half by an impact, the metal roof peeled away like the skin of an orange while the wood and canvas walls burned, spitting flame and ash into the night breeze.

She hoped against hope that it had been empty when the bombs hit, but she knew better. Communal buildings in places like this were never really empty, even in the middle of the night.

Dani's chest hurt, and not because of the smoke.

People milled about—some running, *screaming*, and others staring blankly at the carnage, shock deadening their expressions into an awful jumble of confusion and horror. It was a scene of such anarchy that she didn't even know where to start.

Knox jumped out of the truck, already pointing and handing out orders. "Mace! Grab a team and set up here."

The medic nodded, already pulling big silver cases loaded with supplies from the back of the truck. "Ava, Beth—you're with me. You, too, Rafe."

For a heartbeat, it looked like Rafe would argue. His entire body was already tensed as if to leap toward the nearest burning building. But he jerked himself back and spun toward the truck to help unload the medical supplies.

Nina took over. "Everyone else is search and rescue. Be as safe as you can—if you get hurt, you're down for the count. And remember, this is triage." Her jaw clenched. "If you can't help them, you have to move on."

The words made Dani a little dizzy, even though she knew they were nothing but the truth. They were going to find bodies in some of these tents and buildings, everyone knew and accepted that. But finding someone alive, fading fast or hurt so badly that no amount of intervention would save them . . .

That was the hardest part, walking away from someone who was going to die but hadn't yet. Leaving them to their fate. It was harder than running straight into hellish scenes of flame and carnage, harder than locking down worry and fear. Harder than swallowing her own tears and screams to soothe people.

Dani led an older woman with a gash over one eye toward the area where the field hospital was beginning to take shape. Gray met her halfway, taking the woman's shoulders and meeting Dani's gaze over her head.

"You're the fastest," he told her quietly. "Find Jaden."

Oh God, *Jaden*. Dani dreaded it, because he had to be hurt. If he wasn't, he'd be the one taking charge of the people who were okay, making some sort of sense of the chaos.

But she nodded and took off, past a line of people who'd formed a bucket brigade to try and quench the worst of the fires. It was a futile effort—the fire was burning through the buildings and tent cabins like they were tissue paper, but it kept them occupied.

While they had something to do, maybe they wouldn't go mad with grief.

Dani caught sight of a tent cabin set apart from the others. Its canvas roof had been punched through, and it looked as though some of the wooden beams supporting the structure had caved in, but it wasn't burning.

Why wasn't it burning?

When she pushed through the door, all she heard at first was the creaking of wood under strain, as if the beams that still stood were about to give way. Then, under that noise and the commotion outside . . .

The steady *beep* of an armed drone.

It lay on top of splintered wood and shredded canvas. The drone had crashed through the tent with its payload still attached, locked and loaded and ready to explode at any moment. It happened sometimes, usually when the drone collided with a tree or a bird or even another drone. And the sheer uncertainty of a live, unexploded round always made the situation very, very dangerous.

Dani began to slowly turn, ready to run like hell the moment she cleared the doorway.

"Was wondering when you guys would show up."

Dakota. Dani froze, her gaze following the sound to the back of the tent, past the drone. The woman lay in the darkness, pinned under the main support beam, one end of it sitting heavily on her leg.

The other end rested against the drone.

Oh, fuck.

"At first, I thought moving might be a bad idea," Dakota said, her voice mostly even, with just the slightest hint of a tremor. "Then I tried it anyway, but it wasn't enough to get my leg free."

Dani didn't censor herself. "Fuck. Fuck fuck *fuck*."

Dakota grimaced, fighting to hold back either laughter or tears. "I concur with your assessment of the situation."

Dani held up both hands. "Okay, just . . . don't move."

"Wouldn't dream of it."

She ran through the options in her head, and they *sucked*. It was either move the drone or move the beam, and neither was safe to do—even with the bomb blankets and other gear Knox had packed into the truck. These bombs were loaded with enough plastic explosive to blow straight through any kind of potential containment, and in these close quarters, that was tantamount to suicide.

Dakota seemed to have figured that out already. "You should go. Make sure people stay away."

"Like hell. Nina would have my head. You two may not be an item anymore, but she's still pretty fond of you." Dani carefully picked her way through the debris and peeled off her jacket. "And Jaden—Christ, don't get me started on what he'll do to me if I let you die."

Dakota released her breath on a choked sigh. "Jaden's okay, then?"

"Don't know for sure, but you know I'd lay money on that cranky bastard. He's too stubborn to go out like this."

This time, Dakota's smile was real—a little sad and tinged with regret, but *real*. "True."

Dani eased her light jacket around the end of the beam closest to Dakota and slowly twisted the fabric, turning it into a handle. If she gripped the bare wood, shards of it would cut into her flesh. She might not be able to feel it, but blood was still slippery.

"Okay," she whispered. "I'm going to lift it a bit at a time. The *moment* you can free your leg, roll free and get the fuck out of here. Crawl if you have to."

"What about you?"

"I'm hard to kill, and I'm not afraid." The truth and a lie.

Dakota huffed, and Dani began to lift the beam. It creaked and groaned, but her gaze never, ever left the drone. It shifted slightly, and she froze, her heart pounding in her ears for long moments before she realized it wasn't going to blow up.

She kept lifting. Dakota braced her arms on the floor, her whole body shaking with strain as she pulled. The seconds ticked past, each one loaded with terrible possibility—

Finally, with a sharp hiss of pain, Dakota scooted back, pulling her limp, bruised leg from under the beam. "I'm out!"

Under any other circumstances, that would be Dani's cue to drop the beam. Instead, she remained still, unmoving. "Go."

"But you—"

"I can move a lot faster than you, Dakota. I have a shot. But you need to be *out of here* before I take it."

She nodded, scrambled to her feet, and limped out of the tent. At least she *could* move. It made Dani's job a lot easier.

Funny, how the definition of *Dani's job* in a situation like this had suddenly expanded to include *staying alive*. It had never been her main focus before. Not that she had a death wish—she liked living a lot, especially with things like ice cream and dancing and attractive people around—but she'd always known she'd bite it sometime, and it wouldn't be old age that got her.

But she had to care now, and *be careful*. Her dying would break Rafe's heart, and she refused to do it. Not if she could help it.

She began to lower the beam, centimeter by excruciatingly slow centimeter.

A scuffle outside heralded Knox shouldering through the door with an expression of pure military assessment tempered with exasperation.

His gaze landed on the drone, and he unfurled a ballistic containment circle with one hand. "You couldn't wait for backup?"

"Oh, you know." Relief made her knees wobble. "I'm a problem child."

He laid the circle around the wrecked drone and its bomb, then slowly laid the suppressive blanket over it. Should the bomb explode, the circle would funnel the worst of the force upward and into the blanket, hopefully containing the blast.

But systems like this were meant for dealing with improvised devices like pipe bombs, as well as other low-yield explosions. Not for this.

Dani's hands kept shaking, but she didn't move, and she didn't lower the beam any more. "Go on, Knox."

He arched an eyebrow in disbelief.

"Trust me, I've got this." She jerked her head toward the door. "Just . . . clear me a path."

He finally relented and disappeared out into the night, wedging the door open as he went. Dani waited for a slow count of ten, then raised the beam higher, over her head, and unwound her jacket in favor of bracing the wood with her bare hands.

Go big or go home, right?

She took a deep breath, then let go of the beam, turned, and *ran.* Everything seemed to be happening in especially slow, agonizing motion—the creak of wood, her jacket flapping in her hand, even the heavy fall of her boots hitting the cabin floor.

Dani gritted her teeth and braced herself for the impact of a premature blast. She dove through the open doorway and hit the ground instead. A roll brought her back to her feet, and she kept moving, glancing back over her shoulder to gauge the distance she'd put between herself and likely death.

She hit a wide chest, and a pair of strong arms snatched her off her feet. Rafe dropped them both facedown on the ground, his body shielding hers.

Dani covered her ears with her hands and pressed her face to the grass as the bomb exploded. The concussive blast shook the earth and rattled her bones, even under the protective weight of Rafe's body.

"Fucking goddamn hell," he growled against her ear. "Dani, *what the fuck?*"

"Unexploded ordnance," she choked. "It's a real pain in the ass."

"*You're* a real pain in my ass," he retorted, and she realized he was trembling.

She turned her head to his arm and whispered against his skin. "It's okay. I'm okay."

He pulled her to her feet. "You're letting Mace check you out."

Dani didn't argue.

The medic turned out to be busy. He had Dakota stretched out on a portable gurney while he examined her leg. Jaden stood next to the makeshift bed, though *standing* was too static a word for the way he paced and fidgeted. His skin was scratched and his clothing torn, but otherwise he seemed unharmed.

Then he glanced up, and the lost, desolate look in his eyes nearly stopped Dani cold. The high of rescuing Dakota faded, and she hurried toward Jaden, pulling her hand free of Rafe's grasp.

"Who?" she asked.

"Lucas," Jaden rasped. "We were in the kitchens when the strike hit. It was just *annihilation*. Part of the roof fell, and he shoved me out of the way. It knocked me out, but it got him, Dani. It got him."

The common building, the one she'd first seen when they arrived, split in half and burning to ash. Even then, she'd thought that no one inside when the blast hit could have lived.

She turned for it, heedless of Nina's protests.

Rafe was there a heartbeat later, one hand reaching for her shoulder. "Dani, wait—"

She shook him off. "I have to *know*, Rafe."

The interior of the warehouse was dark where the flames had died down, and glowing coals and debris littered the ruined floor. Dani picked her way through it toward the back of the building, grateful that the worst of the thick, choking smoke had been blown away.

She found Lucas lying under a tangle of wood and twisted stainless steel that used to be a long food-prep counter, his half-open eyes stared blankly past her.

Dani couldn't look away from them.

She'd never understood being unsure if someone was dead or not. Even before all the telltale visible signs began to set in, there was a particular stillness in death, an absolute surcease of movement that couldn't be replicated by anything else.

You owe Jaden. You owe him your entire worthless life.

She jerked her gaze away from that dead, accusing stare, crouched beside the body, and reached for the collar of his shirt. Her fingers brushed his throat, and she almost recoiled from the unfathomable chill of his skin.

She'd forgotten how quickly corpses began to cool, and how just a few degrees could set off such primal alarm bells in the brain.

Rafe didn't touch her again, but his voice came from just behind her. "Dani, we need to go."

"Hang on, I have to . . ." She finally found the leather cord around his neck and snapped it free. A medal slid free of Lucas's shirt, some pre-Flare military thing he'd told her had belonged to his grandfather.

She clutched it in her fist and rose. "He said his mother gave him this. I should make sure it gets back to his sister—just in case that part was true."

She owed him that much—from one monster to another.

TECHCORPS PROPRIETARY DATA, L1 SECURITY CLEARANCE

COO Vargo acted with my authority. If you have a problem with his actions, you may call for a vote of no confidence in my leadership. Or you may fall in line. These are your options.

Message from the CEO, December 2086

TWENTY-TWO

Rafe couldn't make himself step into the community center.

The building Nina had secured on Poplar was massive. Not tall so much as *wide*—it covered an entire city block, rising four stories into the air. Graceful stone arches welcomed you inside, and floor-to-ceiling windows—newly replaced with tough plexiglass instead of fragile glass— lined the entire front.

Two nights ago, over hot chocolate, Nina and Rafe's mother had discussed having her paint seasonal murals on each window with the neighborhood children.

Now it was filled with grief and death.

The heavy crate on his shoulder shouldn't have been enough to weigh him down. It was barely a hundred kilograms, nothing for a man who could bench press a car.

But Rafe was *tired*. Not in his body, but in his heart.

Sighing, he caught the door and tugged it open. Sound washed over him in a visceral wave—the low hum of voices, the beep of equipment, and above it all the soul-shredding sound of children crying for parents they'd never see again.

Hardening his heart, he brought the box to where Nina was overseeing the organization and distribution of supplies at a long table. "Fluids," he told her, settling the crate down. "Something the TechCorps used to give us. Electrolytes and vitamins, but it tastes decent enough. The kids'll probably drink it."

"Thanks." Nina opened the box, picked up a bottle, and examined the label. "Have Gray and Conall finished bringing over the cots and heaters?"

"Maya pulled Conall back into analyzing the data from the TechCorps.

But Antonio is helping Gray, and Rosa and Tessa made sure everyone's got blankets and enough clothing." It still felt surreal to talk about his family openly after so many years of caution, but the pleasure of it was hollow when he'd watched thirteen-year-old Rosa tuck blankets around blank-eyed refugees, her young face so serious. When he'd watched fifteen-year-old Antonio take on the responsibilities of a man twice his age without blinking, installing the heaters with a silent efficiency that somehow made Rafe proud and broke his heart at the same time.

And nothing could feel good about watching his mother hold sobbing orphans as Tessa bathed soot from their small faces and hands so they could check them for injuries.

Nothing felt good at all, right now.

"*Rafe.*"

Rafe blinked and forced his eyes to focus on Nina again. "Sorry. What do you need me to do next?"

"Take a break," she instructed. "Before you fall over, or worse."

Pride made him want to argue. So did guilt. Every moment he'd stolen for himself over the last few days burned beneath his skin, a silent accusation. Every time he'd kissed Dani was a minute he could have been holed up in the command center, clawing through their newly revealed data for a hint, a whisper, for *anything* that could have stopped this—

He was the fucking military intelligence officer. Somehow, he should have known.

Nina opened her mouth again, and he cut her off. "Fine, fine. I'll be good, Mom."

"Don't pull that shit with me, or I'll tell your *actual* mother."

Rafe backed away, both hands raised in mock surrender. "I'll take a break. But you better get one soon, too."

Nina dropped the bottle back into the box and closed it. "Take an hour—*at least.*"

He saluted in silence and pivoted away. But he didn't go to the makeshift area where they'd set up food and strong coffee and pillows on the floor. And he didn't turn back to the door, even though it was only a couple of blocks back to the comfort of his own bed.

Rafe walked past a line of cots until he found the stairs in the middle of the building. They rose up to a second-floor balcony that circled the main atrium, giving him an all-too-clear view of the surviving residents of Montgomery Farms scattered across the first floor, struggling to piece together what was left of their shattered lives.

Forcing himself to look away, he climbed to the third floor, and then the fourth. A door at the end of a dark hallway led to a narrow set of concrete steps so shadowed he pressed his palm to the cool wall to ground himself as he ascended to the thin crack of light at the top.

Someone had already propped open the door to the roof. Until he slipped through and let the door bump carefully back against the can of paint holding it open, he hadn't even known he had a goal beyond escaping the pain and grief and claustrophobic *guilt* of it all.

But he always had a goal. One goal.

Rafe stepped out onto a cement roof into the brisk night air, and the tension twisting through him somehow both relaxed and intensified.

Dani sat on a folding metal chair, her feet propped on the low wall edging the roof. She had her knees pulled up to her chin, and her arms wrapped around her legs. Her hair was loose, and it danced around her face as she stared out at the darkened sky.

Another chair lay abandoned on the rooftop. Rafe picked it up and set it next to Dani's, but didn't sink into it. Not yet. "Do you mind company?"

She didn't answer.

The urge to wrap his arms around her was painful. But she hadn't met his eyes since they'd found Lucas. She hadn't spoken to anyone unless answering a basic question. She'd walked through the necessary tasks in front of her like a robot, like someone had scooped out the fundamental parts of her that were Dani and left behind a shell.

"Dani . . ." His fingers tightened on the back of the chair, leaving grooves in the thin metal. But he wouldn't touch her. Not like this. Not until he knew she wanted him to. "Talk to me. Please."

Her head turned, tilted. Moonlight illuminated the wet tracks of tears on her cheeks as she looked up at him.

"Oh, sweetheart." He crouched down next to her chair and let one thumb graze her cheek, wiping away tears. "I'm so sorry."

"I was just thinking," she said thickly, "that I don't know what to do."

"About what?"

"About you. Me." She shook her head. "Everything."

Her words lashed through him like ice cracking beneath his boots. He'd crept out onto the barely frozen lake of her heart, knowing that Dani might not be ready, knowing that the next step might send him crashing through the ice and into the freezing depths.

Maybe the smart thing would be to turn around and flee back to shore. But he'd promised her he wasn't going anywhere. He'd promised her she was worth it.

Tensed against the next thunder-sharp crack of ice, he edged forward. "Tell me, Dani. Whatever it is, you can tell me."

Her gaze locked with his, and she frowned. "No. Rafe, *no*. That's not—I'm not doing that. Maybe I should—for your sake—but I can't."

So she wasn't up here trying to figure out how to dump him on his ass. It should have firmed up his footing, but if anything it felt more tenuous. Fingers still whisper-gentle, he stroked her hair back from her face. "Then what is it?"

"You won't get it. You can't, because you're a good person." She practically shook with emotion. "You're like Nina, or Knox. Even when you fuck up, you were always trying to do the right thing."

The chair legs scraped over the roof as she rose and paced to the corner of the building. She hesitated, then turned, and the words seemed to break free, like water thundering through a broken dam.

"Do you know why I can't stand to look at people like Ava and Lucas? Do you, *really*? It's because I *am* them," she spat. "We don't do what's right. We do what's easy, and we don't care what kind of carnage we leave in our wake, because we're already gone."

The ice beneath shattered, plunging him into chilling darkness. Because Dani wasn't struggling with loving him.

Dani was struggling with loving herself.

Easy words bubbled up, a hundred of them, a *deluge*, a wave he could ride back to the surface. He wanted to deny everything, swear to her that she *was* good, that she was fierce and wonderful and loveable and *loved*.

But his words couldn't fix this. Only Dani's could, and she was still talking, her words quick and disjointed.

"Everyone thinks it was the surgery. But not feeling pain doesn't make you a different person. It just makes you *arrogant*." Dani's chest heaved. "Marshall did his job. He always does. By the time I finished my Ex-Sec training, I was a machine. A weapon. All they had to do was point me at a target. And I didn't care. I didn't leave Executive Security because the TechCorps ranks are full of evil assholes. I bailed because I didn't want to take a bullet for someone who didn't even know my goddamn name.

"And what did I do then?" She drove her hands through her hair. She was sobbing now, but the words kept coming. "I didn't get out and try to make the world better. I didn't *fight* for anything. I killed people for money—that's it. Hell, even *Ava's* a better person than I am. At least she's been cleaning house. I just took my contracts and didn't think about them too hard. And I only stopped because I ran into Nina and Maya."

The first people who had ever loved her. Because Dani hadn't had sisters like Nina, or a loving family like Knox and Rafe. Just distant parents who'd been so horrified by her, they'd taken money to make her go away. There'd been no lessons to counteract the ones pounded into her by the TechCorps. Nothing but pain and rejection, then cruelty and neglect.

Maybe Gray would know what to say to her. Rafe could only open his arms in silent invitation.

She stumbled into his embrace, shaking with the force of her pain. But instead of leaning into him, she clutched at his shirt. "I didn't have to kill Boyd when we were on the road, either. Nina did the good thing—she made a deal with him so he'd leave you all alone. But I didn't know, Rafe. I didn't know if he'd hold up his end of the bargain. It was too great a chance to take with your life."

At first, the words made no sense. She was talking like she'd killed Boyd *for him,* but they'd only just met. They barely knew each other then.

"I had to protect you, but I'm not Nina. I'm not *good.* So I killed him, because I couldn't let him hurt you."

Jesus Christ.

"I'm sorry," he whispered, pulling her to his chest and stroking her hair. "I'm sorry, sweetheart."

The words made her cry harder, but she didn't pull away. He held her until the sobs wracking her body gave way to trembling, then swept an arm under her legs and hoisted her against his chest.

She turned into him, burying her face against his throat. Hot tears still fell, silent now, and he cradled her close as he nudged open the door and kicked the paint can out of the way so it would shut firmly behind them.

Navigating the dark stairs with his arms full of exhausted Dani wasn't easy, but he got them down to the second floor and found one of the recently refurbished rooms, swept clean and waiting. Tessa had left a stack of blankets and pillows near the doorway, which made it easy to set up a comfortable little nest for the two of them.

It was a far cry from the lush, massive bed in Phoenix's penthouse. There were no silk sheets, no carefully manufactured white noise drowning out the city with sounds of the distant ocean. Even with the door closed, he could hear the murmur of voices drifting up from the atrium, the echo of footsteps, the sounds of doors closing and machines humming.

It didn't matter. He tucked Dani beneath the soft blanket and wrapped her in his arms, his fingers stroking her back as she clung to him, too exhausted to weep. And as he stroked her hair, he confronted the truth.

He'd gotten Dani wrong from the beginning.

Those walls he'd smashed up against had seemed impenetrable, and so *familiar*. The generation born in the decade after the Flares had come into a world of chaos and famine, their earliest memories those of hunger and desperation. So many of them had learned to harden their hearts. To protect themselves.

He'd assumed Dani was the same. Hard on the outside, but fragile at her core, erecting steel barriers to keep anyone from crushing her.

But Dani didn't care about herself. She'd built walls to cage what she imagined lived inside her, like a labyrinth trapping a monster at its heart. Where he saw a fiercely dangerous woman unwavering in her protection of those she loved, she just saw a wild beast straining at the leash, as likely to maim friend as foe.

She'd been his from the beginning, but it didn't feel like victory. Not when she lay broken and wrung out against him, her cheeks still wet with tears.

Rafe couldn't fix it. But he could hold her, just like she'd held him through that terrible night when he'd faced his own inner darkness.

Maybe, together, they could help each other stagger into the light.

ENCRYPTED GHOSTNET
PRIVATE CHANNEL #PERSEPHONE

Anderson, Helen: There's no way Kyle wrote that memo. It doesn't even sound like him.
Young, Charlotte: So what are you going to do about it?

TWENTY-THREE

The war room had descended into chaos.

Apparently, after Dani and Rafe's disastrous flight from the Hill, Knox had called Syd. She'd breezed into town the previous night, her taciturn right-hand man at her . . . well, right hand. She'd smiled, he'd glared, and the specter of impending war had solidified a little.

Savitri had arrived this morning with Adam, her *own* taciturn shadow. Dani would have been willing to bet that no one had called her, she'd just known that shit was going down, and it was time to rally the troops.

Then Jaden and Dakota had come over from the community center after lunch. Though Mace had repaired as much of the damage as possible to Dakota's leg, she still had numerous soft-tissue injuries that required stabilization. But instead of something simple, the robotic leg brace she wore was top-of-the-line, the very latest in assistive technology.

Dani wondered if Ava had somehow gotten her hands on it, or if Jaden had taken care of that himself.

Jaden looked even worse. Bruises had formed under his dark skin, marring the smooth, deep brown with mottled purple. The left side of his face was swollen, heightening the severe effect of his angry expression.

And he was *definitely* angry.

"It's easy to talk about slowing down to strategize when *your* people aren't the ones who just got bombed off the map," he growled at Savitri, who seemed unbothered even when he leaned both fists on the table and bent toward her. "I want to go over there and blow up *their* homes, see how they like it."

"She's not wrong," Gray interjected. "You go off, half-cocked, and it won't be the TechCorps brass suffering. It'll be the rest of your people."

"And the innocents on the Hill," Maya added. Jaden opened his mouth again, and she cut him off with a sharp gesture. "And *don't* tell me there aren't any. Most of the people in those buildings are just trying to survive, same as you, and the TechCorps treats them like they're disposable. We're *better* than that. Or we're supposed to be."

"Maybe," Syd said, crossing her arms over her chest. "But I speak from experience. The first time they bomb a bunch of civilians? That's a line they have to cross. From now on, crossing it's just gonna get easier and easier for them. They're not going to stop."

Nina's serious but calm expression didn't change. "Which is why we're here, discussing our next move. We can't ignore this, but we don't have the luxury of acting rashly, either. We have to stand and move *together*."

Rafe shifted against the wall next to Dani, turning his shoulder to it so that he was almost facing her. His fingers brushed her arm, then slid down to wrap around her hand. Easy, automatic. Like blinking or breathing.

Maybe it *was* like that for him. Maybe she'd become such an integral part of his existence that touching her wasn't even something he actively chose to do. His body simply gravitated toward hers.

Dani glanced over, and he favored her with a tense but gentle smile. Then he shifted again, pulling her slightly closer.

She'd been so *mortified* to wake up in his arms with rough, itchy eyes and dried salt on her cheeks. She wasn't sure what had caused her to break down the way she had. It wasn't that she'd said anything wrong or untrue, but to say it—no, *scream* it—at Rafe like that . . .

It could only have been the circumstances. Dani was normally in control of her emotions, but every time she closed her eyes, even to blink, she saw Lucas's dead green eyes staring back at her. They'd all been raw, scraped and cut by the wanton death and destruction out at the Farms, and she was certainly no exception.

Grief did funny things to everyone.

But Rafe hadn't seemed to mind the ugly emotional scene. In fact, he seemed to prefer it to her silence. Not that he enjoyed her pain, far from it, but he wanted to be close to her, and she supposed that wasn't limited to physical contact.

She smiled back at him.

"You're being a fool." Ava's cool voice cut off another rumbling demand from Jaden. "Your pathological need for vengeance is making you act recklessly."

"Says the pot to the kettle," Conall mumbled, sotto voce.

Ava narrowed her eyes at him, but she didn't disagree. "Precisely. I know how rash actions under the influence of grief can lead to regret. You have access to multiple trained tacticians. Sit down and listen to us."

Jaden's chest heaved. He looked like he wanted to pick Ava up and shake her. Ava stared back, daring him to try. But one gentle touch to the shoulder from Dakota, and Jaden shuddered and dropped heavily into his seat. "Fine. Fuck it. How do we *hurt* them?"

"By taking away what they love most." Beth sounded uncharacteristically bloodthirsty. "Their power. If we remove them from the equation, not only do they suffer, they also can't hurt anyone else."

A sharp alarm cut through the tension—the one wired to the exterior basement door. Half a dozen people reached for weapons simultaneously, an action that looked so perfectly choreographed Dani almost laughed.

Conall jerked a tablet toward him, then frowned at it. "What the . . . ? It's Charlie."

Charlotte Young—also known as Persephone—was a hacker who handled high-level computer security for the TechCorps. She and Conall had competed for the top spot back in their training program. He considered her something of a nemesis, while Dani was moderately sure Charlie didn't consider him at all.

Charlie and Maya were friendly, though, and Maya was the one who rose from the table with a frown. "Let her in."

"I don't *have* to," Conall grumbled. "She just—"

"Let myself in," Charlie said from the doorway. The last time Dani had seen her, she'd been in full leather and punk chic, fully embracing her alter ego as queen of the criminal underworld.

Today she looked like Charlotte Young, private security consultant to the most elite assholes on the Hill. Her elbow-length braids were secured into a prim crown around her head, and her perfectly tailored black slacks gave way to a vivid yellow silk blouse that made her brown skin glow.

She stepped forward, nodded once to Savitri, and then slashed a glance at Conall. "You got a projector down here?"

At Maya's nod, Conall slid a palm-sized box down the table. Charlie set it upright, gestured for Mace and Gray to move aside, and pointed it at the far wall. "I'm sorry to crash your party, Maya," she said, tapping at her wrist. "But you need to see this. *Now.*"

A video began to play, scored by tense music with sad, plinking piano notes. It was drone footage of Montgomery Farms, sweeping aerial views that showed the horrifying extent of the carnage in the aftermath of the bombing. A grave voice detailed the destruction, so eye-rollingly sincere that Dani almost tuned it out.

Then she heard the words *terrorist action,* and her full attention snapped back to the video just in time to see the images give way to surveillance footage. Nina flashed across the wall, beating the crap out of someone with a whirl of kicks and punches. It ended on a still frame—a close-up of Nina's face. The next clip showed Maya, her pretty features fixed in a glower as she fired two pistols at once. It also ended with a still shot.

The third clip popped up, and Dani gritted her teeth. It was from the building where Richter had laid a trap for them, when he'd captured Maya and Gray. In it, Dani had hopped onto an Ex-Sec grunt's back to stab him, only adrenaline had kept him upright far longer than she'd anticipated. The end result looked almost cartoonish, a deadly, bloody parody of a piggyback ride.

"Oh shit," Conall cursed. "I can't believe I missed *that* because I was bleeding out in a van. That's *amazing.*"

Normally, Maya would have punched him in the shoulder. But her gaze was fixed on the screen, her expression stricken as her vital stats flashed up next to her picture.

Marjorie Chevalier

AWOL—Data Courier

Terrorist

2 million credit reward for information leading to capture

Gray wrapped his arms around her and pulled her to his chest. She started, then reached up to grip his arm, her expression hardening to anger and determination.

The still of Nina popped up beside it, with a similar—if incorrect—description.

Ainsley Moore

Foreign Spy

Terrorist

2 million credit reward for information leading to capture

"They still think you're me." Ava studied the image critically.

Dani couldn't help it. "You and the Professor both *suck* at picking out fake names."

"It has a *meaning*," Ava replied stiffly. "It was symbolic, at the time. Ainsley means *alone.*"

The words faded under the rush of blood in Dani's ears as the third image—*hers*—appeared.

Danijela Volkova

AWOL—Executive Security

Terrorist

2 million credit reward for information leading to capture

It hurt. Why did it hurt? Had she really, honestly thought that Julian Marshall—the man who'd taught her all the quickest and most efficient ways to murder a person—might try to protect her by keeping her identity a secret?

Stupid, Dani.

Rafe's arm tightened around her. "Are you okay?"

"No," she admitted. "That's six million fucking credits. This is bad. Apocalyptically bad."

"It's not great." Charlie cut off the video as it began to loop again. "But I wouldn't call it apocalyptic. A few people have probably seen it, but not many. It seems someone has been using the GhostNet to launch a DDOS attack on any server they try to stream it from. Very mysterious."

The way she said it was almost teasing. Dani looked around the room, but no one seemed to get the joke. No one except for Maya, whose eyes had gone wide.

The silence dragged on to the point of awkwardness, and Charlie looked at Maya, both eyebrows climbing halfway to her hairline. "You didn't tell *any* of them? Not even Dani and Nina?"

"I would have if it had been relevant," Maya replied evenly. "But do you know how many secrets I have in my head? If I tried to share them all, I wouldn't have time to eat or sleep."

"Fair enough." Charlie's gaze swept the room, as if assessing each of them for worthiness. She didn't look incredibly comforted, especially when her eyes landed on Conall, but she sighed and braced her hands on her hips. "I founded the GhostNet."

"Bull*shit*," Conall exclaimed, half rising. "That was over ten fucking years ago. You would have been—"

"Seventeen." Charlie shrugged, as if the invention of a sprawling network that piggybacked off TechCorps satellites and gave shelter to criminals and revolutionaries was no big deal. "You were busy trying to be the top of our class. I was securing my exit strategy. It's your fault, really."

"*Mine?*"

"Mmm. I watched them put that implant in your head." She shuddered. "That was *not* going to be me. So I made alternate arrangements."

That was one way to put it, though Dani couldn't argue with the results. Conall was still tethered to the TechCorps—at least in theory—while Charlie was free to take her GhostNet profits and vanish herself off to a life of incognito luxury.

None of which explained why she was *here*. "You could have messaged to tell us you were saving our asses from bounty hunters," Dani pointed out. "So what's really up, Charlie?"

Charlie acknowledged her point with a nod. "I'm here on behalf of a . . . mutual acquaintance." She gestured to the wide screen embedded in the far wall. "Do you mind if I bring her in?"

Understanding tightened Maya's eyes. "Anyone who doesn't want their face recognized by a TechCorps VP should leave the room now."

Savitri tensed, and Syd's lieutenant, Max, grimaced. But no one rose or turned away.

Maya gestured to Charlie, who tapped on her wrist again. A few moments later, the elegant face of Vice President Helen Anderson filled the far screen.

Her gaze drifted from side to side, no doubt categorizing the people sitting around the table. Her lips pursed as she slid past Rafe and Dani, and her brow furrowed when she got to Savitri. But a heartbeat later her expression smoothed, and she focused squarely on Maya. "Marjorie. I was surprised to hear from you after so long. You seem well."

"I was better a few days ago," Maya replied evenly. "Before y'all started dropping bombs on babies."

"Yes, that was an unfortunate escalation." Her gaze flicked to the side so fast most people probably wouldn't have noticed, but Dani had the strong impression the woman had glanced at her. "Chief Operating Officer Vargo was already advocating for harsher punitive actions to bring the outlying areas into line, and I'm afraid that having the VP of Security shot in the throat over his dining room table radicalized him somewhat."

Dani smiled and raised her middle finger.

Anderson's mouth flattened into a stern line. But her voice was smooth as silk as she continued. "When I had my information sent to you, Marjorie, I assumed we'd have plenty of time. But while Ms. Volkova's actions certainly contributed to the current crisis, I'm afraid an old friend of yours is responsible for the current pace of acceleration."

"Cara Kennedy," Maya said flatly.

"Indeed. She's ingratiated herself to Vargo and seems to hold considerable sway over him." Another twist of her lips. "The fact that Ms. Kennedy served as Tobias Richter's data courier for decades makes her extremely valuable to a man with Vargo's political ambitions."

Of course it did. Cara was a walking repository of blackmail material. If he played his cards right, he could be CEO in truth, not just in theory.

Maya cut right to the heart of it. "So Richter had dirt on everyone, and Vargo is trying to blackmail his way into the CEO seat. Let me guess—it was her idea to pin the bombing on us."

"She does seem to harbor a particular animosity toward you, personally," Anderson acknowledged. "She claims you killed Tobias Richter."

Maya glanced back at Gray, her lips quirked. "Sorry I stole your thunder."

He shrugged one shoulder. "It's okay. I didn't do it for the glory."

Anderson cleared her throat. "The relevant point is this: Vargo's decision to bomb Montgomery Farms is deeply unpopular. The fractures on the Board are very close to erupting. While I can't be happy about the situation that led us to this moment, we have been presented with a unique opportunity."

"A coup." Knox stared at the screen with his arms crossed over his chest, his expression blank. "You're reaching out for our help because you want to facilitate a coup."

"A restructuring of power and priorities," Anderson corrected smoothly. "Under Vargo and Richter's joint leadership, security and military objectives were given a disproportionate amount of funding and attention. Our focus should be science and intellectual discovery, not playacting as conquering feudal lords."

Knox opened his mouth again, but stayed silent when Maya held up a hand. "You want us to remove the obstacles in your path," she said, her voice cool and confident. "We can do that. But we're going to need a few promises in return."

"Surely there will be time to discuss this after we settle the situation," Anderson protested.

Maya didn't back down. "I imagine that you're only taking this kind of risk and contacting us directly because your life is in significant and imminent peril."

Anderson hesitated, then inclined her head. "Vargo won't be able to consolidate the Board behind him unless he removes me from the equation. I hold too much influence. Research and Development is the heart of the TechCorps, in spite of their best efforts to undermine our true mission."

"Then it's time to negotiate." Maya waved a hand, indicating the room around her. "We can scatter. We can hide, bide our time, and tear him down after he's weak from fighting you. You need us."

It was a bluff, and most of the people in the room knew it. There was nowhere *to* hide. It was a damn miracle the TechCorps hadn't found them already, and if Vargo put Cara Kennedy in charge of searching?

She'd turn Atlanta upside down and rip it apart to find them.

Some of them—Ava, Dani herself, even Mace—might be able to

accept the inevitable collateral damage as that war played out, but it would shred Maya's heart to stand by and watch helplessly when she could *act*.

But Helen Anderson clearly believed. Her reluctant smile held a surprising edge of fond pride. "Birgitte taught you well."

"She had her moments."

"Because *I* taught *her* well." Anderson quirked one perfect eyebrow. "What are your terms?"

"Three promises," Maya said without hesitation, holding up one finger. "I want a strict policy of noninterference off the Hill. No military or security patrols in outlying neighborhoods."

Anderson frowned. "Not even to stop crime?"

"That's not what they're doing out here, and we both know it. Communities have been policing themselves for decades, so let us do it *without* swooping in to make things worse."

That provoked a slight frown, but Anderson only said, "Number two?"

Maya held up a second finger. "No standing in the way, directly or indirectly, of community organizing or communities forming their own governing structures."

The pause was longer this time. Anderson tilted her head, seeming to consider. "And your final demand?"

Maya held up a third finger. "I want a five-year plan to transition utility infrastructure back into public control."

Anderson scoffed. "You don't have the skills or technology to manage it."

"Maybe not," Maya retorted. "But we try or fail on our own. If communities want to negotiate with you for service, that's fine. But it will be a *choice*."

"Fine. *But—*" Anderson held up a hand. "I intend to implement community stabilizing measures on the Hill. Healthcare and basic income, universal education—the sort of cost-effective, logical programs that lead to a strong and healthy workforce. If my influence grows because I offer security instead of chaos, you can't blame me."

"Hey, offer all the carrots you want," Maya agreed. "But no more sticks."

Silence ticked on for nearly a minute as Anderson and Maya stared at each other. Finally, Anderson nodded. "Agreed. Now, as a show of good faith, I'd like to personally invite you to return to the Hill and serve as my personal advisor."

Maya sputtered out a laugh. "Oh *fuck,* no. I listened to every fucking Board meeting you sent us. I heard your proposals for fixing Atlanta. They were decent, and that's why I'm willing to trust you. But I am *never* going back."

"That's a pity. You could achieve amazing things."

"I *am* achieving amazing things," Maya retorted. "Right where I am."

"Touché." The older woman's face softened for a moment. "Birgitte would be proud of you, I think."

"Fuck yeah, she would." Maya's sudden smile was radiant. "I'm pretty damn awesome. And my friends and I are about to save your ass."

"I certainly hope so." Anderson's gaze shifted to Charlie. "How long can you hold them off?"

Charlie frowned as her gaze lost focus. "I can probably keep them busy and distracted for seventy-two hours. After that, things get dicey."

"Can you stay and coordinate with Marjorie's team?"

"If you cover for me on the Hill."

"Consider it done." Anderson gave them all a chilly smile. "Seventy-two hours."

The screen went dark, and Maya immediately collapsed into her chair, looking somewhat dazed. "Did I just do that?"

Nina nodded slowly. "I think you did."

"Holy shit." She blinked, then winced. "Um, I told her we can take out Vargo. We can, right?"

All eyes swung toward Rafe and Dani.

Dani quickly ran through the possible approaches, but there weren't many. Even fewer that stood a chance of working. "He'll be holed up in his safe room by now. We can't get in . . . but we can get him out. Just need to squeeze him a little."

Nina leaned past Conall and tapped his tablet. A 3D rendering of TechCorps HQ materialized in the center of the table. "Show me."

Dani stepped away from the wall and snagged a tablet from the end of the table. She zoomed in and highlighted the reinforced area on the northeast corner of the building. "This is Vargo's safe room. It has an emergency exit, but we can take that out of play. And then . . ." Another tap, and the floors of the building began to light up red, one after another, starting at the bottom. "We squeeze."

Rafe leaned over the table. "Like a tube of toothpaste."

"He'll come out," Dani muttered. "The only thing worse than a threat to his life is a threat to his precious power. If he thinks HQ is falling into enemy hands, he'll act. And then we can take him."

"I can work with that," Knox said, his gaze already unfocused, as if he could *see* battles raging across the holographic image. "We'll need to—"

The buzz of the door cut him off. Conall swept up his tablet again, and his face paled. "Uh, there's an angry mob at our door. Clem's at the front. With her shotgun."

Well, *fuck*.

"News travels fast," Gray observed flatly.

Nina's jaw clenched. "I'll go—"

Dani cut her off. "No, I'll handle it. I'm too fast for her to shoot in the face. Besides, Clem likes me best."

It was a lie, on both counts. But having their neighbors, people they called *friends,* ready to turn on them for something as crass as money would break Nina's heart, just as it would Maya's. At least Dani could deal with that part.

She made plans as she headed upstairs. She could disarm Clem, yank her inside, and reengage the locks. That would give her time to talk some sense into Clem—and without their leader, the mob might just disperse.

Either that, or they'd go home to call the Protectorate.

Dani's hands were steady as she unlocked the door, her eyes dry as she pulled it open. "Folks. Clementine. How can I help you?"

Clem's hands tightened on her shotgun. Her lined face was severe. "We saw the vids," she said shortly.

"And you headed right over."

"'Course we did." Her frown deepened. "And we're ready. Just tell us who to shoot."

A murmur of agreement rose from the gathered crowd, almost drowned out by the relief buzzing in Dani's ears. She threw her arms around Clem, burying her face in the woman's graying auburn hair.

They weren't here to turn on them. They'd come to help.

TECHCORPS PROPRIETARY
INTERNAL COMMUNICATIONS

Alert: Executive Security Breach

Recruit 55–312 has murdered her charge and abandoned her post. All security access has been revoked, and a Protectorate squad dispatched to arrest her.

Executive Internal Network

TWENTY-FOUR

It was hard to have a proper brood around the house these days.

Between the Devils next door, Jaden's people split between the basement shelter and the community center, and the neighborhood folks coming and going at all hours, the place was getting *crowded*. All her usual spots were definitively occupied.

Dani resorted to her bedroom. She didn't like to brood there—it was a place for sleeping, resting, recharging. A private oasis in the middle of what was sometimes a topsy-turvy world.

Brooding marred that perfect calm.

Of course, so did her best friends bursting in to make sure she wasn't *too alone*.

"You're brooding," Nina proclaimed.

"I'm *trying*."

Nina sat on the edge of the bed, while Maya threw herself dramatically across the foot of it. "Don't worry," she told Dani sympathetically. "You're doing a really good job."

Dani groaned. "No, I'm not. Because of you guys, and Clem and all the others, and *Rafe*. You broke me. I can't even brood properly anymore."

"It's overrated," Nina offered. "Knox has been so much happier since he stopped having to brood."

His elevated sense of well-being had other, far more base physical causes, but Dani kept her mouth shut. Besides, it had nothing to do with her foul mood. "Do you think Anderson was right?"

"About what?"

"Did I do the wrong thing?" She'd run over the facts endlessly since the meeting, trying to envision a scenario where leaving Vargo's dinner party had gone smoothly. She couldn't see a way . . . but that didn't mean there wasn't one. "Did I get us in trouble?"

"You did the only thing you could." Maya rolled onto her side and propped her head on her hand. "We knew it was a risk that you'd get IDed if we sent you up there, but it was our only shot."

"If there had been another way—"

"You heard Maya. There wasn't. The moment Marshall recognized you, you were in survival mode." Nina patted her hand. "You got Rafe and his sister out. You got *yourself* out. I call that good."

Maya made a rude noise. "If you want to blame someone, blame the fucking Professor. He's been playing all of us from the beginning, and I still can't figure out *why*."

"I have my suspicions," Nina admitted. "Only I have no idea how we play into his plans, except that we do—and that we're on the same page."

For now. The words were unspoken but tangible. And it would have to be enough.

Maya sighed and flopped back over onto her back. "I know how you feel, though. I mean, I just reinvented Atlanta's system of government on the fly. Did I do the right thing? How do I even *know*?"

"You don't yet. None of us do." Nina shrugged and laughed helplessly. "We're all doing our best. That's all there is."

"That's all there is," Maya agreed.

It was dangerous, even with Anderson on the inside and Charlie's help against the considerable security measures threaded throughout the TechCorps' main building. There was no guarantee they'd even manage to breach the building, much less complete their mission. And the potential losses . . .

It didn't matter. That's what *that's all there is* truly meant. If they went out in a few days, hey. At least they'd go down fighting.

"We do our best, then get up the next day and do our best again." Maya reached out to pat Dani's leg. "Tessa is kind of awesome, you know. She's been helping out with the kids from the Farms. They love her. And she's here because of you. You did that, and no one else could have."

Rafe's family was *baffling*. Even when they were arguing, there was a sense of absolute, unending love between them all, something inseverable, even by the worst actions and deeds. When she closed her eyes and tried to imagine Celia turning away from any of her children, the image simply refused to form.

It was also humbling, in a way, because Celia showed every intention of showering the rest of them with that unconditional love and acceptance.

"Rafe's family is nice," Dani said finally, drawing her knees up to her chest. "I'm glad we were able to bring them here. For everyone's sake." But especially for Rafe's.

Nina watched her intently, something serious and searching dancing behind her eyes. But when she opened her mouth, a scraping noise from the window interrupted her.

Maya jerked upright, then cursed and scrambled to the window. As soon as it swung open, she held out her arms, staggering back a step as Rainbow hopped into them. "Bo," she chided. "I thought we talked about not climbing the outside of the building at night."

"But daytime is harder," the girl protested. "The brick is too hot, and people yell if they see me."

Maya rolled her eyes and tossed Bo onto the bed, where she bounced with a grin. "You are exactly like your Aunt Dani, aren't you?"

"*Yes.*" She snuggled against Dani's side. "Are you talking about the siege?"

Dani's heart thumped a little too hard at the casual way the word rolled from the kid's tongue. "No, we're talking about people. Right now, about Rafe's family."

Rainbow nodded approvingly. "His mom is so nice. She drew me some pictures, just like in Maya's storybooks."

"Aww, Bo. That's amazing." Maya climbed back onto the bed with a smile. "Rosa told me that she has storybooks her mom drew when Rafe was little. Stories about him going on adventures. That's how she knew all about her big brother even though he was already gone when she was born. Maybe she'll draw one for us, if we ask."

The idea of little storybook Rafe was adorable, but it was also a little heartbreaking. No wonder he'd joined the Protectorate with legitimate delusions about saving the world. He'd grown up being told that was his destiny.

Maybe it still could be.

"We'll ask her in a few days," Dani promised. "After."

"After." Rainbow nodded solemnly. "What do I do?"

"About what, bug?"

"I know how to do things," she said earnestly. "I can fight, too."

The painful thump in Dani's chest turned into a staccato beat at the thought of Rainbow running into danger. "*No*. Listen to me, Bo—"

"You have the most important job of all," Nina interjected. "One we can't trust to anyone else."

Maya rose onto her knees and watched Rainbow seriously. "We need someone to go into the bomb shelter with the kids from Montgomery Farms. They're not like us, Rainbow. They didn't grow up learning the kinds of things we learned. They're going to be scared, and if anything happens, they won't know what to do. You can help them stay calm, and protect them."

Rainbow's eyes narrowed in assessment, as if she was trying to discern whether Maya was being truthful. Finally, she nodded. "I can do that. But they have to listen to me."

"They will." Nina smiled and brushed her hair back. It was growing so fast it had started to flop over onto her face. "It's your op, so you're in charge of planning and supplies."

That seemed to appease her. "Okay. I'm *very* good at logistics."

In that moment, she looked and sounded so much like the Professor—like *John*—that Dani was torn between laughter and tears. "I bet you are, bug."

Maya saw it, too. But she smiled and squeezed Rainbow's hand. "When we're finished here, I'll help you start your requisition list, okay?"

"Okay." She toyed with Maya's ring, the one Gray had fashioned for her out of a goddamn *fork,* of all things. "Should I leave now?"

"Nope." Dani nudged her with one foot. "We're hanging out."

Rainbow wrinkled her nose, then brightened. "Can I practice braiding your hair?"

"Sure." Dani tugged the elastic from her ponytail.

The girl scrambled up the bed to sit behind Dani, already reaching for the brush on the bedside table. "How fancy?"

"As fancy as you can get. Dazzle me."

Nina grinned. "This is going to take a while."

By the time Rainbow finished twisting and plaiting Dani's hair, it would be locked in a style so intricate it would take ages to unravel it. "That's okay. We have time."

As Rainbow began drawing the brush through Dani's hair, Nina settled into a cross-legged sitting position and propped her elbows on her knees. Maya shifted as well, moving until she could rest her head on Nina's thigh.

Nina took a deep breath, as if steeling herself. "Is it just my imagination, or is Ava kind of into Mace?"

Maya burst out laughing.

Yes. For this, Dani would always have time.

With less than forty-eight hours left before they blew up the world as they knew it, Rafe found himself with an overabundance of protective energy and far too few targets to expend it on.

Dani was his first choice. But Dani had gotten skittish since their emotional night at the community center. Not just with him, but with everyone, as if she'd had to lock down her emotions to cope with the task ahead. Putting fractures in a protective wall she might need to survive the next few days wouldn't do either of them any good, so Rafe was willing to wait for her to come to him.

His family had been the next obvious target. But Rafe had been forced to face a stark reality—his siblings, far from being the helpless and sheltered children they'd fixed themselves as in his sporadic memories—were fiercely competent and incredibly tough. He supposed that was inevitable. Only a fool would imagine that Celia Morales would have raised anything other than passionate crusaders for fairness and equality.

Celia had taken all three of them to the community center, where they were helping the refugees from Montgomery Farms cope with their tragedy.

That left Rafe's protective instincts with an extremely narrow window of victims. Luckily, they were the ones he'd been practicing on for a decade.

Conall always got a certain look when he'd been working for too long. Rafe knew the signs well. His hair standing straight up because he kept scrubbing a hand over it was the warning sign. Muttering to himself was yellow alert.

When Conall's leg started bouncing hard enough to shake the table, Rafe plucked the tablet from his hands and replaced it with a deck of cards. "Shuffle," he ordered, picking up the three other tablets within arm's reach. "You're taking a break before your brain starts to smoke."

Conall glared at him. "I still have my contacts in, you know. I could just transfer my work and keep going."

"You *want* me to wrestle you to the ground and take them out?"

"Fuck you," Conall muttered. But a moment later, he popped open the deck of cards and the sound of the thin cardboard rectangles sliding against each other replaced his borderline-manic mutters.

With one down, Rafe swung around on Knox. But his former captain had already set aside his list of contingency plans. "Rafe is right," he said in a firm voice. "We need to pace ourselves. Our preparations are on schedule."

Gray snorted. "As much as you can schedule a coup, I guess." He left the ammunition canister he'd been inventorying behind and dropped onto a chair at the table. "Deal me in. And someone find some of that whiskey. The good stuff."

The common room in the Silver Devils' building had suffered from their tendency to hang out with the ladies in their far better furnished warehouse. Weapons and tech had their own organizational structures and storage, and the large table in the center gave them room to eat, plan, and perform personal tasks. But Rafe had to dig through three stacks of reinforced cardboard cases before he found the single remaining bottle of the expensive O'Kane whiskey.

"This is the last of it." He brought it to the table with five collapsible glasses. Not exactly the crystal tumblers folks used on the Hill, but a ritual the Devils had enacted plenty of times on missions. "I suppose if there's any time to drink the good stuff, though, it's now."

Gray cracked open the seal on the bottle. "We all need a little distraction."

"Oh, do we?" Conall gave Knox a teasing look over the cards. "Knox has been *distracting* himself and Nina in every goddamn place imaginable. The only place left is in the middle of the street."

"Leave the man alone," Mace grumbled as he took the bottle and filled his glass first.

"You want to change the topic?" Conall flicked a card across the table to bump into Mace's hand. "Because I would *love* to discuss how Beth gets away with telling you what to do without so much as a single grunt or glare."

His only answer was a withering stare . . . until the tops of his ears started to turn pink.

Oh, boy. Mace. *Blushing.* That was truly some end-of-the-world shit, which was appropriate for the night.

Rafe leaned over and plucked the bottle of whiskey from Mace's hands. "You need to be careful, man. Beth and Ava have some sort of relationship, and until you know for sure what it is? I'm just saying, that woman is a scary kind of possessive. And jealous. Ask Knox."

"She certainly can be," Knox agreed. "If it wouldn't make Nina sad, she'd stab me without thinking twice about it."

"She's already had a knife to my throat," Mace informed them archly. "If she wanted to use it, she would have done so. Also, shut the fuck up."

Conall flicked out the final card and slammed the deck onto the table. "Excuse me, you got into a *knife fight* with the evil genius clone and didn't tell us about it?"

"Because it wasn't a fight." Mace sorted through his hand, arranging his cards. "It was more like a polite introduction."

Gray's shoulders heaved with silent laughter.

Conall turned to Rafe with a clear *Are you hearing this?* expression. Rafe sipped his whiskey, savoring the exquisite burn of it. The shit really *was* good. "I don't know what you want me to say, Con. Compared to how Ava usually introduces herself, that was damn near cuddly."

"Oh my *God*," Conall whispered in awed horror. "Does Ava like Mace?"

"I don't think Ava *likes* anyone," Knox replied easily. "I also think you're talking even more than usual. Almost like you're trying to distract us from something."

"Probably the Max thing." Mace looked up, a slow, fairly evil smile curving his lips. "Because that *is* a thing, right? You and Max?"

"Maybe it should be. World might be ending—again." Gray's expression turned thoughtful. "You'd hate to miss out, wouldn't you?"

Rafe almost choked on his whiskey when Conall flushed. Syd and Max ran an underground resistance for the genetically altered, which included a heavy dose of rescuing children. They'd come onto the scene a few months ago when they'd arrived to take the rest of Rainbow's fellow clones to a remote farm where they could live semi-normal lives and hopefully find grown-ups with superpowers who understood them.

Max seemed to have exactly two modes: teaching advanced science to fascinated children, or scowling at adults like he was two seconds from murdering them. Rafe supposed it was inevitable that the latter would draw Conall in like a moth dive-bombing the nearest flame.

But Conall fell in and out of love every twenty minutes. For a crush to have this kind of staying power, it had to be *serious*.

"I'm not dignifying any of this with a response," Conall said loftily, examining his cards. "What are we betting this time? Chores seem a little lightweight when we're on the eve of the next apocalypse."

Gray acknowledged his point with a nod. "Money and credits seem equally inconsequential, then."

"There's only one thing worth betting tonight." Knox put down two of his cards and let his fingers rest on top of them. "The future."

"The future?" Conall echoed in confusion.

"One thing you're going to do after this is over." He said it with the kind of conviction Rafe remembered from their earliest years as a squad, back when Knox had *believed* with everything in him that he could shift the world if he pushed hard enough. The Protectorate had broken him down in the end, but it seemed Nina had patched his heart back together with her love and unflagging optimism.

And Nina was clearly at the center of any future he could imagine. Knox smiled. "When this is over, I'm going to help Nina make her community center everything we've dreamed it can be."

Gray tilted his head back. "I'm going to take Maya someplace. Show her something she's always wanted to see."

Conall sighed and slapped down four of the cards from his hand. "Fine, you absolute assholes. *When* I survive this mess, I'm gonna jump that hot motherfucker's grumpy bones."

It took Mace a little longer to answer. "When this is over, I'm starting a vaccination program. For the kids."

"Great," Conall grumbled. "I say I'm gonna get laid and he says he's gonna save babies. Way to show me up."

"Can't help that I'm a better person than you."

The bickering felt *natural*, like something that had been broken forever had finally healed itself. Knox, feeling optimistic again. Mace, not just alive but slowly coming back from the months he'd spent locked away and tortured in the heart of the TechCorps. This family Knox had made for them in spite of everything had been the heart of Rafe's world for over a decade.

He *loved* these men. Loved them deep in his bones, with the kind of loyalty time couldn't wear away. Most of them had never had a family the way he had, but his love for his mother and siblings didn't change the way he felt about the Silver Devils. If anything, it made that love effortless.

Love would never be effortless for Dani. She'd been abandoned by the people who should have sheltered her, shattered by the people she'd trusted to teach her. Rafe couldn't heal those wounds for her, any more than she could reach inside him and quiet his guilt over the things he'd done to survive.

But he could love her. He could love her with all the reckless, effortless love he had, until she was ready to believe she deserved it. And then he'd keep loving her.

Because he couldn't dream of a future that didn't include her.

Silence filled the table. They were all looking at him, waiting for his bet. He barely glanced at his cards—winning this game didn't matter. It was all about the words, spoken like a promise. "Dani," he told them. "Dani's my future. I want to go on wild adventures with her."

"Undercover on the Hill's not wild enough for you?" Mace teased.

"Wrong kind of wild," Rafe retorted. "I've had enough of ballrooms and boardrooms. I want to see what else is out there. Nina's building her library. Maybe Dani and I can find things to go in it."

Knox lifted his drink, a fond smile curving his lips. "I think it's a good dream."

"Not dreams," Conall reminded them. "Promises. That's the bet, right?"

"That's the bet." Knox held out his drink until they all matched the gesture. "To the future."

"The future," they echoed, and when the whiskey burned its way straight to his middle this time, Rafe embraced the heat, and the promise.

A future free of the TechCorps. A future with Dani.

That was worth fighting for.

CONALL

In the privacy of his own mind, Conall had no problem admitting the truth.

Charlie was a fucking *genius*.

Their little competition had started within months of Conall's arrival on the Hill, ten years old and high on the status of having unprecedented aptitude scores. He'd been petted and praised so much in that first month, and the praise had been motivation enough to continue to excel.

No one had ever praised Conall before. No one had ever really noticed him much at all, as long as he stayed out of trouble. His parents had done their best, but both had worked multiple jobs just to keep a roof over their heads and food in the bellies of the nine children under their care.

His collection of siblings might not have *technically* been his full brothers and sisters—some were cousins, and others neighborhood orphans—but Conall had loved them all the same. He'd been happy to know his signing bonus would buy them all a little security, and over the years he'd nudged credits and opportunities their way whenever he found a chance.

But they'd never understood him. Not like his peers in his elite classes. Not like Charlie.

She'd jabbed at him from the beginning. However hard he excelled, Charlie always seemed to be right behind him, the prickle at the back of his neck that inspired him to study harder, run faster, be *better*. It was humbling to discover he'd been pushing himself at a full-on sprint, and she'd been loping along lazily behind him, careful not to overtake him and attract the full interest of the TechCorps.

Hers had proven the wiser path, in the end. Spurred on by his competitiveness, Conall had allowed them to put a chip in his head at fifteen.

No, that wasn't entirely fair. In retrospect, he knew *allowed* was a generous term. The TechCorps would have gotten their way in the end, one way or another. But Conall hadn't even fought it. He'd wanted the advantages—the faster processing, the enhanced memory, the sharper cognition. The stamina and strength and all of that was a bonus, sure.

But Conall had wanted to be the *best*.

He was older and wiser now. Staring down the most dangerous mission of his life, Conall didn't give a shit who was smarter. He just wanted to survive. More, he wanted the people he loved to survive, too.

Charlie's brilliance was going to help with that. Thanks to her, he had fifteen wrist cuffs laid out on the table, each one well on its way to becoming a skeleton key to the entirety of TechCorps HQ. With Charlie's security back doors and Conall's hardware upgrades, anyone wearing one of these cuffs would have CEO-level access to every door in the building.

Maybe they were *both* brilliant.

"Need some help?"

The familiar rumbling baritone sent goose bumps racing up Conall's arms and glued his tongue to the roof of his mouth. He almost missed the tiny screw he was attempting to fasten back in place, and he used that tedious task as an excuse not to look up and get the full glorious impact of Max as he no doubt prowled into Conall's workspace. "I'm almost done."

His voice got even deeper. "Is that a no?"

Oh, for the love of sweet baby Jesus on a donkey in a blizzard. Conall could talk big about jumping this man's bones, but he couldn't even lay eyes on him without feeling his ability to form full sentences evaporate. Surely it should be against some natural law to genetically engineer a man with that voice, that body, and *that brain*.

The tiny screw on the wristband was already tight. If he kept fiddling with it, he'd just strip it. And he couldn't think about stripping. Or tight things, for that matter. Or screwing. Or—

Fuck.

Conall forced himself to look up, and it was as bad as he'd feared. Max was like Syd, a product of one of the privatized military bases on the East Coast who'd taken the genetic experiments of their predecessors and run with them. Of course, the problem with optimizing for brains *and* brawn was that you ended up with Max—someone too fucking smart to put up with your bullshit and too fucking strong to contain.

And, apparently, too fucking hot to stare at straight on. Piercing blue eyes and tanned skin, combined with a muscular build only Rafe could ever hope to compete with, short cropped hair, and a neatly trimmed beard with an inexplicably glorious spattering of silver.

"Hi," Conall said helplessly.

The corner of Max's mouth kicked up. "Hi."

Oh no. He was smiling. Even his *smile* was devastating. Conall flailed for something to say, something smart or witty or even just coherent. Instead he held up the final wrist cuff. "I finished them."

"All right, then." Max pulled a stool out from under the workbench and sat. "What's next on the list?"

Okay, apparently being incapable of words wasn't going to scare him off. There was something comforting in that. Conall slid the cuff to rest next to the long row of them and refocused his attention on work. "I want to install some new sensors on our van before I drive it up onto the Hill," he said, sliding a tablet with his list of tasks toward him. "Last time we tangled with the TechCorps, I got shot in the abdomen."

"Very nearly the *least* fun place to get shot."

"Right?" Without thinking, Conall grabbed the edge of his T-shirt and dragged it up, showing off the thin, almost faded line across his abdomen. "Mace is good, though. You can't even tell Rafe was doing surgery on me in the back of a van. Barely even a scar."

Max reached out.

Conall realized what he'd actually done a heartbeat before Max touched him, and then it was too late for rational thought. Max rubbed his thumb over Conall's stomach, close to but not quite touching the scar. Then he looked up and met his gaze, his thumb still moving slowly across Conall's skin.

Well, it hadn't exactly been a smooth flirtation, but there was at least a 50/50 shot the TechCorps would drive a drone straight into him before tomorrow was over. Who had time to be subtle at the end of the world?

Conall dropped a hand to cover Max's. "Want to come help me put sensors on the van?"

"Yes," he answered immediately.

"To be clear, you know that was code for *help me put sensors on the van* but also *make out a ton.*"

Max arched an eyebrow.

Conall forged ahead. "And possibly take off all of our clothes and fuck like it's the end of the world."

"Okay." Max stood and held out his hand. "I can work with *possibly.*"

Maybe Conall wasn't so bad at flirting after all.

TECHCORPS PROPRIETARY
INTERNAL COMMUNICATIONS

Executive Security Alert: No Contact

The squad tasked with apprehending Recruit 55–312 has not made base contact in ninety-six hours.

List as MIA until status confirmed.

Executive Internal Network

TWENTY-FIVE

Rafe never slept well the night before an op.

He hadn't been the only one. While Gray usually put himself to sleep through force of disciplined habit, Mace had always struggled with sleeplessness before a big mission, and Conall veered wildly between staying up half the night in jittery preparation and crashing out like a snuffed candle. Knox always insisted on lying peacefully in his tent and feigning sleep in a show of confident reassurance, but all the Devils knew he stayed up most of the night, playing out contingencies across the backs of his eyeballs.

Rafe didn't have any contingencies to play out. He didn't have any mission prep left. Tomorrow at sundown, they would storm the Tech-Corps headquarters. They'd live, or they'd die.

And he was pacing his rooms, praying Dani would come to him. He'd been wrong about her before, God knew, but every instinct inside him screamed that she *would* come. He had to be patient and sit very still, the same as you would with any wild creature whose trust you were trying to earn.

It was hard. God, it had never been this hard before. If this was his last night alive, he *had* to spend it with her.

But he trusted her.

Rafe hit the far side of his room and pivoted, flexing his fingers. Five more minutes. Five more minutes, and if she didn't—

The knock made him jump nearly out of his skin, but then Dani's voice followed, soft and tentative. "It's me."

Thank *God*.

Rafe rushed to the door and jerked it open, relief washing over him in a wave. Dani stood there, already dressed for bed, wearing a hastily donned jacket and slippers.

His self-control snapped. He grabbed her and dragged her over the threshold, giving in for one endless moment to the need to just *hold* her. He kicked the door shut without looking, then fell back against it, his face buried in her hair, his arms tight around her body. "I'm so glad you're here."

She clutched at his arms. "You knew I would come, didn't you?"

"I hoped." He couldn't help the low laugh that shook through him. "If I hadn't been mostly sure, I would have been on your doorstep two hours ago."

She pulled away just enough to look up at him. "That would have been okay, too."

Rafe slid his hands over her hair, smoothing it down. "There's a lot going on right now. I didn't want to get in the way or distract you. You're the heart of our plan."

"Fuck the plan," she said firmly. "That's tomorrow. Tonight is for *us*."

Rafe lifted her easily and carried her into the room. "And what are we going to do with our night?"

"Whatever we want." She gazed down at him. "Are you all right?"

"I'm as okay as you can be on a night like this." He dropped to the edge of the bed with Dani cradled on his lap. "I can admit it. I'm a little scared."

"We're going into battle tomorrow night. You'd have to be crazy not to be scared."

"Battle is easy," he countered. "I know how to hold myself in a fight. But the stakes have never been this high before. This is it, tomorrow. This is the whole game. If we can't take out Vargo—"

Dani laid her finger over his lips. "I know." She slid her finger away and kissed him quickly. The spark between them ignited, and his fear melted away as he gripped her hips and hauled her closer, sinking into the now familiar bliss of kissing her.

He slipped his hands up and under her jacket, coaxing it off her arms to fall away. But when he reached for her shirt, she grasped his hands.

"It was never about you," she told him haltingly. "All the bad stuff, the things I had upside down and backward—that was me, not you."

The vulnerability in her eyes stole his breath. He curled his fingers around hers, gentle and supportive. "It wasn't you," he whispered. "It wasn't me, either. It was your scars. I've got some, too. Sometimes they hurt like hell, and all we can do is scream until it stops."

She nodded slowly, still solemn. "I love you."

His heart lurched. He'd wanted these words *so much*, and somehow still wasn't ready to hear them. But there was only one response that mattered, the one he'd been biting back forever. "I love you, too."

"You don't have to say it—"

It was his turn to press a finger to her lips. "If I hadn't been worried about scaring you off, I would have said it to you a long time ago. I *love* you, Dani. When you're sweet and when you're hot and even when you think you're a monster. I love you."

Her smile was brilliant, warm—and brief. It faded into another grave look, and she framed his face with her hands. "Then promise me something."

Uh-oh. *That* sounded like trouble. "What?"

"If something goes wrong tomorrow, and it looks like I might not make it out . . ." She swallowed hard, and the familiar rush of words escaped her. "Let it go. Don't risk yourself just for me. You have so many people counting on you, Rafe. You have to come back—for their sakes."

"Oh, sure," he said, covering her hands with his. "If you promise me the same. No risking your life for me."

She hesitated.

"We both have so many people counting on us," Rafe told her gently. "You have Nina, and Maya, and Rainbow. You have this whole damn neighborhood. People who saw a chance to live easy for the rest of their lives if they turned you over to the TechCorps, and showed up with shotguns to protect you instead."

She opened her mouth, but Rafe silenced her with a shake of his head. "Before we go in there, I need to know you see it, Dani. I need to know that you *understand*. It's not just me. You are *loved*."

"Okay," she whispered. "We'll protect each other."

"To the bitter end," he agreed, stroking the backs of her hands with his thumbs. "The best way to protect the people depending on us is to take this bastard out. And we can do fucking *anything* if we're working together."

"Anything." There was that dazzling smile again, and Dani still wore it when she leaned in and kissed him again.

There were no more words. Not serious ones, anyway. Just smiles, and laughter, and murmurs of encouragement as Rafe stripped away Dani's clothing and let her tug away his own.

He'd imagined something frantic. Something wild and desperate, tinged with fear that this could be the last time. But as he slid over her, slid *into* her, Rafe realized that no part of him believed it would be. Arrogant, to be sure. Maybe reckless.

But how could he feel anything but invincible when Dani wrapped her arms and legs around him and panted those two words against his cheek with every thrust? *Love you. Love you. Love you.*

She'd take apart the world to protect him. She'd bleed and kill and die, if that was what it took. And he would do the same.

Because together, they really could do anything. And if they went down tomorrow, it would be in a blaze of glory, saving everything they loved.

Together. The way it should be.

KNOX

When Nina wanted to distract Knox from last-minute battle planning, she did it directly and enthusiastically. She'd done it three times last night before they both collapsed into exhausted sleep.

He was still there, enjoying an *extremely* pleasant dream, when the tablet next to their bed started screeching an alarm.

Knox jerked upright, adrenaline snapping him to full alertness immediately. Nina was still faster. She dove across him to snatch up the tablet from the side table.

"It's Charlie's code." Nina brushed her hair out of her face and tapped the tablet to open an encrypted line of video communication. "Charlie? Are you okay?"

"Nothing is okay," came the short reply, somewhat breathless. "I need you all out of bed, *now*. Vargo is moving against Anderson. And he's mobilizing the Protectorate."

"What? *Why?*" Nina demanded. "Do we have a leak?"

Knox rolled from bed and reached for his pants as Charlie answered. "Not on our end. But from the internal chatter I'm hearing, Vargo must have realized how shaky his support is. Unfortunately, the bastard is *paranoid*. And not entirely stupid."

"Dammit. Is Anderson safe?"

"I don't know. I lost contact thirty minutes ago. I'm still working the cameras, but we have to assume the worst—that she's dead, or Vargo has her."

Nina swore again, then rubbed a hand over her face. "We'll be ready to move out by dawn. Hang in there."

Charlie terminated the connection without responding. Knox dragged a clean shirt over his head as the building alarms cut off, too.

"This is going to be a lot messier if Anderson is dead. Without her, all of our assurances are off the table."

"There's still John." Nina chewed on her thumbnail for a moment before reaching for her shirt. "We don't know what his endgame is, but it's almost certainly not the status quo. Maybe we can reason with him."

Reasoning with the Professor had not gone well for *any* of them so far, but Knox had to concede that at least someone who'd dealt with the indignities of being treated like intellectual property instead of a person might be an improvement.

Might.

He sat down next to Nina on the bed and grabbed his tactical boots. "If Vargo's mobilizing the Protectorate, we're looking at a pitched battle just to get into the building. We're definitely going to have to change our approach. But Charlie makes it possible."

"Hey." Nina rose and stepped close, standing between his feet. "There's only one Protectorate squad, current or former, that I wouldn't want to go up against in battle."

Her fingers framed his face, and Knox savored her touch. He closed his eyes, breathed in the familiar scent of her soap and shampoo, and let her confidence in him steady his racing thoughts. "We're the best," he agreed. "And the three of you ran circles around us. The TechCorps doesn't have a chance."

"Not a single one." She brushed a delicate kiss to his brow. "Come on. We need to get the others moving. You want to sound the alarm?"

There was no time to waste, but Knox didn't care. He caught Nina and hauled her down into his lap for one breathless, perfect kiss. Not a last kiss, but a promise that there would be a million more kisses to come.

Then they broke apart, and he triggered the alarm to call his people— and their allies—to war.

CLASSIFIED BEHAVIOR EVALUATION

Franklin Center for Genetic Research

EF-Gen14-B continues to resist desensitization training. She's the first subject in history to score higher than HS-Gen16-B on aptitude and reasoning tests, but she fails even remedial disassociation and logic tests. It is incredibly frustrating to see such potential marred by such weakness.

Dr. Keller, June 2073

TWENTY-SIX

It had been five years since Dani had been this close to the headquarters building that housed the beating, festering heart of the Tech-Corps.

When she'd run, she'd *run*, never once looking back. Of course, she'd been up on the Hill since—even before her undercover assignment, she'd had to run drops and pickups in the neighborhood. Once, she'd even had to track down a contact who had gotten cold feet after promising to come through on a job, just to talk some sense into him.

But she'd never gotten this close.

They'd stopped on a small rise several hundred meters from HQ, the perfect place to observe the situation before heading in. The building towered before them, a thousand meters of glass, steel, and suffering. And, surrounding it like a protective moat, stood an entire fucking battalion of Protectorate soldiers.

"Can't be more than five hundred of them," Dani remarked casually to Syd, who stood beside her, glowering down from their vantage point at the world in general. "Piece of cake."

"Easy, peasy, lemon squeezy," Syd growled in potential agreement.

Knox lowered his binoculars. "There are elite squads mixed in with the rank-and-file infantry. I recognize some of them."

Mace had his own set of lenses, and he kept staring through them at the gathered defensive forces. "Surprised they have any six-six squads left after the way Dani ran through them this fall."

"Flatterer."

"Maya, Gray, go ahead and peel off," Nina ordered. "You know your objectives. Everyone else, we're going in together."

Everyone else covered a lot of ground. Jaden stood next to Nina, righteous anger pulsing from him in waves, with Adam beside him, as blank and emotionless as the computer that ran his brain. Both were accompanied by fighters from their respective communities—though Dakota and Savitri had remained behind, sheltered in place with the rest of Five Points.

Ava stood in a small cluster with Beth and Phoenix. They were dressed identically in custom ballistic armor—though Beth's sunny expression and scant height almost made the black tactical jumpsuit look like a costume.

Syd had brought Max, of course. Interestingly, he kept glancing back through the trees to the mobile command center where Conall and Charlie had set up shop, to fight the battle as only they could. She touched the lightweight cuff on her wrist, the one Conall had sworn would open any interior door in the headquarters building, and smiled.

The smile faded when she peered up at the two lonely drones that hovered above their heads. They were armed, programmed to lay down suppressing fire to cover their advance. "Any more aerial support on deck?"

Charlie's voice tinkled merrily in her ear. "Oh, I wouldn't worry about that, Ms. Volkova."

Knox stowed his binoculars and drew his sidearm. "Keep your comms on and open. The plan's solid, but plans can change."

Rafe grinned. "Yes, Dad."

Dani nudged him with her elbow. "Behave. And *be careful.*"

His grin only widened. "You know it."

Dani felt her lips curving into an answering smile. It should have felt out of place, like gallows humor carrying them through their fear. But she honestly felt *good.* Lighter somehow, as if the sheer relief of finally moving against the TechCorps outstripped any trepidation.

"On my count," Nina called out. "Three, two—"

Dani took off down the hill, her heavy braid bouncing off her shoulders with every bound. She expected to be dodging bullets by the time she covered a quarter of the distance to the Protectorate line, but they simply stood there, watching the advance.

Maybe they were cocky about the sheer, overwhelming size of their force—the Protectorate troops outnumbered them twenty-five to one, so perhaps they assumed Nina and Knox were undertaking a battle that was simply impossible to win.

Or maybe they were counting on all their support drones to do the heavy lifting for them. There were *dozens* of them, their autotargeting lasers dappling the courtyard as they jumped around, searching for something to shoot.

Dani gritted her teeth. She could dodge a lot, but not that.

Halfway there. She broke into the middle of the courtyard, then skidded to a halt when the Protectorate drones suddenly reversed position, their lasers zeroing in on the uniformed chests of the infantry soldiers.

For a split second, no one moved.

Laser fire erupted. Dani dove behind one of the marble columns encircling the courtyard just in time to see Adam and Max do the same. Agonized screams rose from the Protectorate line, followed closely by gunfire.

A cluster of soldiers broke rank and ran past Dani. A drone chased them straight through the courtyard, firing frantically at their backs. After the drone cut them down, it circled back and headed right for the other soldiers—ignoring everyone else, including her.

Realization hit Dani like one of those laser blasts. Charlie—brilliant, deadly Charlie—had tasked the drones with firing on the fucking *camouflage pattern* all the Protectorate forces wore.

"Charlie," she muttered, "you are an evil genius."

"Trust me, I know."

The sound of laser fire dwindled, and Max gestured forward, both eyebrows raised in query. Dani nodded, and the three of them moved forward.

The unbelievable carnage almost stopped Dani in her tracks again. At least a third of the battalion lay dead or gravely injured. But it wasn't the blood or even the gore that really turned her stomach.

It was the remaining soldiers. Some were desperately trying to drag their wounded comrades out of harm's way, while others simply stepped over them, as if the bodies were debris instead of dead or dying human beings.

None of this had to happen, and it was always inevitable. That dichotomy was the true hell of the Protectorate, of Executive Security. Of the TechCorps as a whole. Their ranks weren't filled with cackling villains, but with people—good, bad, or indifferent. Some were like Rafe, who had joined up out of desperation and need, while others truly believed the lies. There was no reasoning with them. They would follow their orders, as flawed and wrong as those orders were.

And there was no telling them apart on the battlefield.

A man charged at her, swinging the butt of his rifle toward her face. Dani recognized him—Captain Richard Osgood, commander of the Red Arrows. Popularly known as Tricky Dick, and third on her current list of potential targets.

Might as well mark him off now.

Dani ducked the rifle, caught it by the barrel, and pushed it through its spinning arc to strike Osgood in the face. He staggered back, releasing the firearm, and she followed through by clubbing him in the knees with it.

Bone crunched, and he went down. Dani gave him another good whack—this time on the head. When he didn't try to get up, she dropped his rifle on his chest and moved on. Dead or alive, Dani didn't care. As long as he was out of the fight.

She moved between the dangers—blows intended for her face, weapons meant for any bit of vulnerable skin available. She dodged an ill-advised bullet, fired from a shaking corporal's pistol, that found its way instead into his comrade's upper thigh.

She could pass through the entire fight like this, untouched even in the heart of it, but it didn't seem fair. Not when everyone else was working so hard.

She watched as Max bashed two men's heads together, then turned and tangled another's rifle strap around his neck, choking the soldier with his own weapon. Nina and Knox fought together, back-to-back. Mace had taken up a stunstick, but was using it more as a baton than for its intended purpose, each swing short and brutal.

She spotted Rafe through the chaos, fighting with one of the elite soldiers, who was armed with a knife. Dani watched with approval as Rafe twisted the man's wrist, disarming him with one quick, effective motion.

The warm glow vanished, drowned by a swell of fear, when she saw a man running toward Rafe's back, a wickedly sharp bayonet affixed to his rifle.

Dani didn't think. She launched herself toward the scene unfolding in front of her, intent on intervening however she could, even if it meant putting her own body between Rafe and that blade.

She went low, beneath his outstretched weapon, and swept his legs out from under him. He pitched forward, and she hopped on his back, pinning him to the ground as she wrenched his rifle from his hands. She drove the bayonet through his back, into his heart, twisting it just in case.

Rafe hauled her to her feet. "Thanks."

"Hey, when I said I'd watch your back, I meant it."

He grinned. "Flirt with me on your own time, Volkova. We're in the middle of a fight here."

Any rejoinder she could have offered was cut short by a loud *boom* that seemed to shake the very ground. Dani looked up, shading her eyes against the early morning sunlight as she tracked five cylindrical objects across the blue and gold sky.

Missiles.

"They're headed for Southside," Mace growled.

Knox touched his earpiece. "Charlie? What the hell's happening?"

"Shit," she answered, her voice frantic. "Shit, shit, *fuck*. Vargo must have forged a CEO override."

"Can you abort the launch?"

"I have the codes to do it, but no time. Even if Conall and I—"

"Give them to me," Adam cut in.

"What can you—"

"Do it," Knox ordered.

Dani watched, sick and spellbound, as Adam tilted his head back. His eyes darted back and forth beneath his closed lids as his hands curled into fists.

The missiles looped around, turning nearly one hundred and eighty degrees to a heading due east.

Out toward the ocean.

Dani felt sicker than ever, the queasy sensation warring with her relief. Adam had not only gained access to the missile guidance over the span of a few heartbeats, he'd altered their course.

With his fucking brain.

That was one single Guardian. She and Rafe had almost died at the hands of a few more.

What could an entire platoon of those motherfuckers do?

MACE

He was getting too old for this shit.

Granted, the fighting had never been Mace's favorite part of running operations. He was more at home with a stethoscope or a scalpel in his hands, and never had he felt that more acutely than now, when he was close to opening his clinic. For the first time, he had a real base of operations, a place where he could do more than the bare minimum, offer some sort of continuity of care.

But he'd never get to use it if they didn't win this fight. So Mace sidestepped an outstretched blade, twisted his attacker around, and snapped his neck.

He was *definitely* getting too old for this shit.

"Sweet move," someone said approvingly.

It was Beth, Ava's friend who smiled all the time. What was she even doing out here? Even in tactical gear, she was all sunshine and light. Out of place on a battlefield, surrounded by blood and carnage.

"Get back," he growled. "It's too dangerous out here."

She waved a hand at her ear and shook her head. "What?"

"I *said*, it's too dangerous out—"

She held up a finger, as if to tell him to hold that thought, turned, and bashed two Protectorate soldiers' heads together. Another rushed at her, and she punched him in the throat, then dragged him down into a swift, efficient knee to the face.

She turned back to Mace and brushed her hair out of her face. "Sorry, you were saying?"

What the hell kind of a place *was* the Franklin Center? "Nothing. Not a damn thing."

"Oh. Okay."

A flurry of coordinated movement drew his attention. A phalanx of soldiers emerged from the side of the building—an even dozen moving in close formation. Something about the way they marched sent a cold prickle racing up Mace's spine.

It was *too* coordinated, every movement almost synchronized. Robotic, even.

"Aw, hell. You know that trick Adam just pulled with rerouting the missiles?" At Mace's nod, Beth gestured toward the formation of soldiers with a flourish. "That's these guys. Guardians."

Then they posed more of a threat than the rest of the troops on the field combined. "Then you should—"

"Time to go to work," Beth said brightly, then waved at Ava's approach. "Nina and Phoenix?"

"On their way." Ava straightened her collar and favored Beth with a look that almost resembled a smile. "Ready?"

"To fight beside you? *Always.*"

The four women rushed the Guardians. During their advance, Ava flicked her wrist, deploying a handful of small silver spheres that arced with electricity when they came close to the soldiers, scattering their tight formation.

Then they attacked, and Mace stopped wondering what kind of place the Franklin Center was, because he knew. It was the kind of place that took pain and blood and promise and turned it into even more pain, more blood. The four of them cut through the Guardians like a focused laser, zeroing in on the tiniest of weaknesses and exploiting them until only death and silence remained.

It was deadly poetry, and Mace couldn't look away.

Deep in the woods, where only the birds could find it, stood a cabin. It wasn't the tallest cabin, or the strongest. The walls were made of wood and the roof was made of straw, and sometimes it creaked at night when the winter winds blew. But the cabin was special, because the boy and the girl who lived there were special. Tessa was an artist who could form the clouds into a brush and paint with sunlight, and Rafael was as tall as the trees themselves, and always willing to help anyone who needed it . . .

untitled picture book by Celia Morales

TWENTY-SEVEN

Rafe had never loved the lift drones.

It wasn't that he questioned their reliability. One of the clever little devices could shoot a grown man a kilometer straight up in about a minute, and they beat the hell out of any of the alternatives. But as he stepped onto the narrow platform and clipped the safety harness to his belt, he couldn't help but feel nostalgia for grappling hooks.

Granted, a grappling hook wasn't about to get them to the roof of the TechCorps. And since someone inside had triggered some sort of lockdown that bricked every elevator below the fiftieth floor, the only way up was . . . *up*.

"Y'all are gonna have to stand close together," Charlie's voice came over his comms. "This is easier if you center your weight."

Dani pressed her body to his and hooked one arm through his safety harness.

"Okay, here we go."

He was never ready for that first jolt. The drone took off fast enough to rip the breath from his lungs, and Rafe locked his arm more tightly around Dani. The wind grabbed at the end of her braid, flicking it wildly, but her cheeks were flushed and her eyes bright. No fear in her.

Trust Dani to enjoy being flung halfway to heaven. "Enjoying the ride?"

"You're not?"

He laughed and hid his face against her hair. Mostly to keep from looking down. "Not all of us love this level of adrenaline. Or heights."

She touched his jaw. "It won't be long now."

Until they reached the top? Or until they reached the end? Rafe could have pulled back to look into her eyes and read the truth there, but he wasn't sure he wanted to know. If Dani didn't expect to walk back out of the TechCorps . . .

Well, too fucking bad for Dani. Rafe had already bet on their future.

Raising a hand, he covered her fingers with his, twining them together as the rising sun reflected off the glass windows that rushed by.

Too soon, and not nearly soon enough, their rapid acceleration slowed. Charlie brought the drone over the edge of the roof and set them down neatly on one of the massive landing pads. Rafe's hand was steady as he unclipped them from the drone, but letting go of Dani was harder.

She gave him an encouraging smile, then stepped away to peer over the edge. "We're going to have to make a hole, Charlie. Floor 245, maybe?"

"On it."

While Charlie disappeared to disengage the lockdown bars over the windows beneath them, Rafe helped Dani secure the end of her retractable rappelling cord to one of the fixed points on the roof's edge. It was smooth, easy work, as if they'd done it a thousand times before. They didn't need to speak, but as Dani tugged to check his harness connection, Rafe couldn't stop himself.

Just in case. Because sometimes bets fell through.

"I love you." He caught her face between his hands and captured her mouth, trying to put a lifetime of wanting into a single kiss.

She kissed him back, her tongue sweeping over his, lingering even when he reluctantly began to pull away. She stood there, her eyes closed, the first hints of a smile curving her lips.

"Well, that's decided, then," she said finally.

"What's decided?"

"We're definitely making it through this shit." She gave his harness one last yank to tighten it. "Because I am *not* ready to give that up."

Joy bubbled up in a giddy rush, and he laughed as he tightened her harness. "Damn right, we're gonna live. Do you know how many things we have left on our bucket list? We haven't even gone to a *good* orgy yet."

She rolled her eyes and climbed up on the low wall edging the roof. "Baby steps, Morales. Got a fight to finish first." Then she fell back, over the edge.

Dani made it look effortless. Rafe climbed up with a good deal more trepidation. This high in the sky, the ground barely seemed real. They were in the literal clouds. Halfway to heaven, for real.

Oh, well. He'd follow Dani over a cliff or straight to hell.

Time to do both.

He jumped, letting the rope catch his weight as he braced his boots against the metal bars covering the top windows. Dani had already descended to the window Charlie had unsecured and was busy pulling something from her vest. Rafe focused on her as he rappelled down to join her.

She used a small handheld laser to carve a rough square through the reinforced glass. When she finished, she knocked it in with one firm kick, and then they were inside.

The room looked like the kind of conference space used for private, in-person meetings. A long polished table was ringed by a dozen plush leather chairs. Rafe drew his sidearm to cover Dani as she swept the room, but he wasn't surprised to find it empty.

He wasn't surprised to find the hallway outside empty, either.

By the time they'd cleared the sixth room, however, it started to seem odd. He didn't know which executive or vice president had claimed this penthouse, but he'd expected *some* resistance, even if it was just from a random bodyguard or a Protectorate squad doing a sweep.

No one stood between them and the stairs, so they went up. Even the stairwell was nice on the executive floors, the walls finished with a faux fresco in shades of understated gold, each polished wooden stair subtly lit from underneath with a soft glow. At each landing, a brass plaque affixed above a chip scanner identified the floor in graceful script.

246.

247.

248.

Rafe hesitated just below the next landing, checking the stairwell for cameras. But it was like all those fancy parties—rich people didn't like their movements tracked. "You ready?"

"You know it," Dani replied, flashing the smile that always made him weak in the knees. Even here, about to kick down a door belonging to the chief operating officer of the TechCorps.

Of course, Dani didn't need to do anything so uncivilized as kick. She waved her wrist cuff over the scanner, and a green light flashed immediately, unlocking the door with a soft click. Rafe reached past her to grab the handle. "On three. One, two . . ."

He jerked open the door and Dani swung around the open doorway in a blur. He followed, sweeping for enemies in the opposite direction.

An empty hallway stretched out in front of him. No Ex-Sec guarding the stairs. Not even common guards. "Check the safe room?"

Dani nodded, and oriented herself. "This way."

Rafe followed hard on her heels, clearing each intersection with her, his nerves wound increasingly tight as they passed through empty corridors and checked abandoned rooms. Some showed signs of a hurried retreat—loose papers, overturned chairs, tech left scattered across tables.

But no people. Not even when they swept through the massive open doors to the safe room. They cleared each part of it methodically, just in case, but a certainty had already settled in Rafe's gut.

"We squeezed," he said as they returned to the main area. "And he popped. Straight up."

Dani tilted her head back, staring at the ceiling, and Rafe knew she felt it, too. "The CEO's penthouse."

The one place they knew the least about. Even Charlie had never been allowed inside. No one knew what the security measures were, or who was inside. With its own private helipad carrier, Vargo could have stuffed this palace with his own private army.

And it didn't matter. They were in too deep now. If they retreated and left Vargo alive, he'd wipe Southside right off the map. He might even level a few more Atlanta neighborhoods just to drive the lesson home. "So. How do we get there?"

"There's only one way, from inside." Dani pivoted and strode back the way they'd come. "The CEO's elevator."

She said it like she knew what would be waiting for them. Like she was stalking toward her destiny.

Maybe even like she was saying goodbye.

When they cleared the corner, Rafe knew why.

Julian Marshall stood in front of the elevator, his expression blank. He barely flicked his gaze at Rafe, as if he was beneath the man's notice. No, his entire focus was locked on Dani.

Rafe's finger itched on the trigger, but he didn't raise his gun. Marshall moved like Dani. Like smoke. Shooting at him would mean wasting bullets he was going to need. But maybe if Dani distracted him, he could—

"I'm the only one who can fight him," Dani told him, as if she could hear his thoughts. Then again, she didn't need to hear them. She *knew* him, knew he wouldn't abandon her to this fight. Not unless the mission was on the line.

No, not unless the damn *world* was on the line.

She removed her comms earpiece and stowed it in her tactical pants. "I'll be right behind you," she whispered.

He reached out to touch her, but she was already gone, a blur of black tactical gear and blond hair that clashed with Marshall in the middle of the hallway.

All Rafe could do was wait for his shot at the CEO's elevator, and do what they'd promised. Get the job done.

Whatever the cost.

CONALL

Conall missed Maya.

They'd developed a comfortable routine during their many hours together running support in the van. He didn't exactly *resent* that she'd become a magical sharpshooter who could take out fancy bodyguards in the dark. Nor did he envy her the personal animosity of Cara Kennedy.

But his grudging admission that Charlie was brilliant didn't make sharing the confined space inside the van any easier.

For one thing, Charlie scorned his old-fashioned keyboards. She wasn't tremendously impressed by the limitations of monitors, either. She operated the display embedded in her smart glasses with a combination of subvocal commands, eye movements, and tiny hand gestures registered by the sixteen perfectly polished gold rings that circled each of her fingers at the base and just above the first knuckle.

Doing security for the anxious executives on the Hill apparently paid *very* well.

But the most annoying thing about Charlie was that she was so efficient, she kept fixing all the problems before he could help with them.

"Hold on," she said, tapping the comm device in her left ear. She held up a finger, demanding Conall's silence, then tapped the one in her right. Her voice shifted to a sleek, professional tone. "I traced the hackers to the hundredth floor. They're splicing directly into the security mainframe. Divert at least three squads to pin them down. We need to regain control. *Now.*"

She tapped the comm again, then grinned at Conall. "That should keep them off our backs for a bit. If you want to have some fun, wait until the squads get to one hundred and then trigger the floor-wide lockdown. They'll all be trapped."

"You know, you're a little scary," he muttered as he pulled up the cameras for the hundredth floor.

"Hey, they're the ones who decided to bomb some harmless fucking farmers," Charlie retorted, her fingers flickering through the air so fast they seemed to blur. "I had no plans to become a revolutionary, you know."

"Oh, bullshit." Conall pulled up the internal TechCorps tracking database and checked to make sure Cara Kennedy was still parked in place, then tapped his comms twice. "We're still good on Kennedy."

"Got it," Gray replied. "We're almost in place."

With that resolved, Conall flipped back to watching the squads make their way to the hundredth floor to bust hackers who weren't there. "You're a liar," he told Charlie, picking their conversation back up. "You started an illegal network under the TechCorps' nose, piggybacking off their satellites, and sold access to every political dissident and criminal who could pay you. You're telling me that's not revolutionary?"

"That was just correcting a power imbalance." Charlie's eyes flicked back and forth as she processed whatever was scrolling past on her glasses. "I was never all in with Anderson or Skovgaard, you know. Not at first. I just wanted to have enough money that no one could hurt me. But doing security for those bastards . . ."

She trailed off, and Conall didn't push her. He had a pretty vivid imagination when it came to the horrible shit the execs on the Hill could get up to professionally, but he did not want to *imagine* what they did for recreation.

On his camera, three elite squads converged on the hundredth floor. Conall let them crack the elevators and sweep inward, clearing each room methodically, and waited until they reached the server room. A few keystrokes engaged total lockdown. Metal grates slammed down over the windows, and blast doors slammed into place over the elevators and stairs.

Watching them scramble to figure out what was going on would have been funny, if his new proximity alerts hadn't chosen that moment to screech a warning.

"Fuck." He shoved across to the opposite side of the van, where his newly installed cameras showed all approaches. After the last time, *no one* was coming at him by surprise. Gut wounds were for suckers.

His foresight paid off. The rear camera showed a familiar Protectorate squad approaching silently. The Iron Dragons had featured prominently on Dani's hit list over the last few months, but they rarely ventured off the Hill. Their captain, Jackson Miller, had been a favorite of Tobias Richter's—the bully he sent out when someone within the company needed to be brought back into line through intimidation or outright violence.

Jackson had a fist in the air, halting his squad. Chris, Dan, Nic, and Tyler clustered behind him, all four of them looking not just ready, but *eager* to do serious violence.

Fuck. Fuck fuck *fuck*.

"Charlie, get down." The sides of the van were bulletproof, but Conall knew that the *proof* part only lasted until it met a scary enough bullet. He locked a hand on her shoulder before she could protest and shoved her to the floor. "You can keep working down here. Stay down and do not open these doors for anything."

Her gaze caught on the camera display, and concern furrowed her brow. "Can you take them alone?"

"Please," he scoffed, showing a bravado he certainly didn't feel. But Charlie wasn't enhanced at all. No superstrength, no enhanced stamina or healing—and no weapons training. "I'm a fucking Silver Devil. You do what you do best, and let *me* do what *we* do best."

She fell silent as he climbed past her, his brain racing as he considered his tactical advantages.

Surprise. And . . .

Well, mostly surprise.

He was outgunned, outmanned, severely outmuscled, and about to be flanked. He had a civilian to protect, at least three different in-progress ops that needed support—

And all five of those bastards were still standing behind his 10,000 kilogram armored van.

Conall didn't stop to think. The electric engine was silent, and he knew from experience how fast the thing could accelerate. "Hang on," he muttered to Charlie, then slid into the driver's seat. She scrambled to brace herself against the table as he switched into reverse and slammed a boot down on the accelerator.

The tires spun for a second before they caught traction, and the van lurched backward. The passenger side-view mirror showed a blur of camouflage right before the first solid *thump*. Shouted curses turned to screams of pain as the van lurched, but the reinforced wheels had carried the van over broken roads and uneven terrain, and they carried the van over the Iron Dragons, too.

Bump. Bump. Bump.

Well, *most* of the Iron Dragons.

Conall slammed the van into park and dove out of the front seat, bringing the sawed-off shotgun Gray loved to keep between the front seats with him. Not Conall's usual weapon, but when Chris popped up on the other side of the van, Conall squeezed the trigger and couldn't fault Gray's choices.

Chris went down in a spray of buckshot and blood, and Conall whipped around the front of the van, scanning for his next opponent. Two sets of boots stuck out from beneath the van, one still twitching. But when he rounded to the passenger side, he only saw Chris sprawled out, staring skyward.

Fuck.

Gunfire erupted behind him. Conall ducked behind the van as pain erupted just below his elbow. His right hand went numb, and the shotgun almost fell to the ground. He shifted his grip to his left and popped back up, firing in the direction of the footsteps.

Jackson Miller took a full round of buckshot to the throat. Blood splattered as the force of it nearly decapitated him, and Conall silently apologized to Gray for doubting him. Shotguns were fucking *amazing*.

The captain of the Iron Dragons was down, but Conall didn't relax until he'd circled the van and accounted for all of the bodies. Only then did he haul open the back door, only to come face-to-face with Charlie holding a pistol.

"Don't shoot," he told her. With the adrenaline from the fight fading, the stabbing pain in his arm was enough to make him grind his teeth together. God, he was going to get so much shit for getting shot *again*. And the bullet was still in there, which meant digging around himself or trying to talk Charlie into doing it.

Given the slightly queasy look on her face, Charlie was *not* going to be volunteering to do field surgery. She set the gun aside with a trembling hand, and Conall bit back a smile. She might be a genius, but she wasn't good at *everything*. "Don't worry," he told her. "Toss that first-aid kit my way and cover for me while—"

The explosion came out of nowhere. Pain shredded Conall's world, and the ringing in his ears was so loud it blacked out everything else.

Almost everything else.

"Mace! Get here, *now*."

Blackness. Hellfire. He was burning, *burning alive—*

"—the round was still in his forearm, and it just fucking *exploded—*"

Sound drifted in and out, carried to Conall on waves of agony. His eyes felt like lead. Maybe it wasn't dark. Maybe he just had his eyes closed.

"—fuck, fuck, *fuck—*"

Open. Open your eyes. Come on, Conall. Open your damn eyes.

"Come on, Conall. You're the best, remember. You are *not* dying on me."

It was the hardest thing he'd ever done, and the light burned as hot as the agony climbing up his right side. Conall squinted against it, forcing himself to blink. A dark blur above him came into focus—Charlie's face, stricken with terror.

Charlie, afraid. Conall had never seen *that* before. That couldn't be good.

"Oh, thank God, he's looking at me." A surprisingly gentle hand, sticky with blood, touched his cheek. Charlie bent over him, her eyes commanding. "Stay with me, Conall. Mace is coming, okay? I'm giving you something for the pain—"

He barely felt the pressure injector. But he felt what followed—the blissful, dizzying *surcease*. Like a cool wind blowing down his body, chasing away the fire and pain, leaving him floating.

He wanted to reach for Charlie, but he forced himself to lie still. Because his brain understood something his body still didn't. Even drugged, even in agony, his biochemically enhanced brain had put all the pieces together, because that was what Conall did. "It's gone, isn't it?"

Charlie didn't pretend not to understand. "From the elbow down, yes."

Well, that wasn't ideal.

Conall lifted his left hand—his only hand, for now—and gripped Charlie's shoulder. "I saved you because you're the one who can get my family out of there alive. So as soon as Mace gets here, get back in that fucking van and *get them out alive.*"

"Conall—"

"Just remember who's number one," he muttered. The drugs were really kicking in now. Floating seemed like a great idea. Mace would be here soon, and everything would be fine. "And when this is over, you owe me a kickass arm."

"I'll build you a dozen," Charlie promised. "The most expensive tech the world has ever seen."

Not exactly the dream he'd wanted, but Conall let it carry him into the seductive, drug-wrapped stillness.

TECHCORPS PROPRIETARY
INTERNAL COMMUNICATIONS

Executive Security Alert: KIA

A box containing human remains was delivered to HQ Reception at 0900. The remains have been positively identified as those of a Protectorate squad commander. His squad was the one tasked with apprehending Recruit 55–312.

All squad members have been updated to status: Killed in Action.

No further squads will be dispatched.

Executive Internal Network

TWENTY-EIGHT

Two things struck Dani as she grappled with Julian Marshall.

First, that this fight had always been inevitable. Even when she'd thought she'd escaped the TechCorps' clutches, the prison that was Executive Security, she'd always been bound to wind up right back here.

Second, that fighting someone who'd trained you was a pain in the ass. They knew all your moves because they'd taught you all your moves, so you had to either get real creative or real lucky.

Marshall's elbow caught her chin, snapping her head back.

Okay, maybe *three* things struck Dani. But it was worth it when she caught sight of Rafe slipping into the CEO's elevator. No matter what happened to her now, he'd get it done.

Marshall slammed her against the wall, his forearm across her throat. "What's funny, Volkova?"

He'd pushed her up onto her tiptoes. "Am I laughing?"

"You're smiling." He frowned. "Maybe you *are* as mad as the rest of them."

Little black spots were starting to swim at the edges of her vision, so she drove a knee up toward his crotch. He dodged the blow easily, but had to release her to do so.

Dani rolled away, panting for breath. "I think you're kind of nuts."

"You have no idea." He landed a kick to her ribs, the force of it jarring her entire body. "We're the only ones." He knelt and grabbed her braid, wrapping it around his hand. "The only ones who didn't go mad."

Keep him talking, Dani. Keep him busy. "From the torture?"

Marshall hauled her head back and peered down into her eyes. "From the pain."

Something about the words caught at the edges of Dani's consciousness, like fine silk snagging on barbed wire.

"It's unending," he almost crooned. "Agonizing. Fire in every vein, every *cell*. Constant, grinding torment, so nauseating you'd do anything to stop it. Peel off your skin, shove every drug known to man down your throat, even jump off a fucking bridge. *Just to make it stop for a single moment.*"

The sob rose, unbidden, and escaped before Dani had a chance to choke it back.

He slammed her face down into the floor. Her cheekbone struck the hard marble so hard she saw stars, and the entire right side of her face throbbed.

Ached.

Jesus Christ. It fucking *hurt*.

She lashed out, but Marshall caught her arm and wrenched it up behind her back.

"It's always there," he continued, as if they were having a casual conversation. "If it wasn't, you'd do things like constantly bite your tongue or get eye infections because you don't realize you're scratching your corneas with grit. But you don't. You feel the pain, all the time, but somehow . . . you ignore it." He jerked her up until her face was mere centimeters from his. "*How* do you ignore it?"

Dani froze, pinned in place by the desperation in Marshall's flat gray eyes, and a horrifying realization washed over her.

He wasn't like her at all. He wasn't immune to pain. It was all he felt, all the time.

His voice shook as he repeated himself. "Tell me how you ignore it, or I'll let the doctors slice you into tiny pieces to find out."

Desperation was dangerous. It was deadly.

Dani opened her mouth, but instead of answering, she slammed her forehead against Marshall's as hard as she could. He fell back, but recovered quickly. He grabbed her as she shot to her feet, then threw her against the wall.

Blinding pain ripped through her as her shoulder dislocated, as if the very mention of its existence made it real. She gasped, tears pricking her eyes.

Marshall descended on her. She'd always thought he was hard on her during training because he wanted her to be the best, most effective Executive Security guard and assassin she could be. Now, seeing the rage burning in his eyes, she knew the truth.

He simply hated her. And she was running out of time.

He tossed her against the opposite wall, and pain splintered through her ribs. But when he dove at her again, she ducked and slammed him to the floor.

It was in the top zipper pocket of her tactical pants, a thin wire suitable for use as an emergency saw—or a garrote.

She dropped on top of Marshall and wrapped it around his neck, pulling it taut as he thrashed and bucked. He flipped over, smashing her over and over into the hard floor beneath them, trying to dislodge her. Blood flowed over her hands and arms—his, hers, she didn't know anymore.

All she knew was not to let go.

She held on as his movements slowed, as his body went limp, and for long minutes after, until her burning lungs demanded air. She shoved him off of her, using adrenaline and militant self-preservation more than anything to free herself of his dead weight.

Her bloody and bleeding hands slipped on the floor as she tried to climb to her feet. She couldn't get a deep breath, either, could only cough and wheeze as she tried to draw oxygen into her lungs.

The CEO's elevator was only ten meters away, a straight shot down the wide hallway. Dani had to get to Rafe, would *crawl* the distance if she had to. She dragged herself across the slick floor, but the edges of her vision grayed out more and more with every labored breath.

She made it halfway there before the darkness claimed her.

MAYA

Maya couldn't count the number of times she'd lounged in the climate-controlled cab of an AirLift as it ascended to one of the penthouse patios that dotted the top floors of the TechCorps headquarters. Hundreds, likely. Perhaps thousands.

None had been quite like this, though.

For one thing, this wasn't exactly a normal AirLift. Gray had hot-wired this one over at the building next door, overriding its computer and ripping out all guidance and navigation, so only he could control where it went.

For another, Maya's outfit was all wrong. Instead of carefully tailored silk, she was wearing tactical gear and a new bulletproof vest. The thigh holsters were also new, and not as comfortable *or* as sexy as Dani made them look. She hadn't been a huge fan of them in the beginning, but Gray had run her through drills drawing her pistols until she could do it upside-down in her sleep.

Hopefully she wouldn't need them today, but best to be prepared.

The AirLift settled on the late Tobias Richter's patio, and Maya scrubbed her hands on her pants to hide her nerves. "We still good?"

"You've got a clear approach," came Gray's immediate reply, his smooth, gorgeous voice whispering through her comms like her own personal guardian angel speaking directly into her head.

She could get used to that.

It was Gray's presence that gave her the courage to climb out of the automated vehicle. As she strode across the patio, it took off with a soft whir, the wind of its passing disturbing the modest pool gracing one side of Richter's patio. Water lapped against the tiles, the sound of it a vivid sensory memory.

If she closed her eyes and breathed in the scent of chlorine, it would be too easy to fall back into the crystal clarity of the past. How many summer afternoons had she spent out here, lounging on those chairs with Cara Kennedy while assistants brought them frothy fruit drinks with crushed ice and little umbrellas?

A different life. A *false* life. The memory of Cara's laugh twisted, jerking her sideways into the memory of Cara's perfume as she tore a bag off Maya's head, revealing a concrete room. The bite of plastic digging into her wrists was as painful as it had been on the day it had happened, the day Cara had stood by while Tobias Richter tortured Maya and Gray.

The day Gray had killed the former VP of Security. The man who'd raised Cara, the terrifying monster she'd loved as her only father.

For Cara, this was about revenge. For Maya, it couldn't be personal. She was the only one who recognized the full danger of letting Tobias Richter's data courier roam free with a head full of deadly secrets. If they wanted to preserve their future, Cara had to be neutralized.

And Maya was bait she couldn't resist.

This early, the kitchen and dining room facing the patio were empty. Thanks to Conall, Maya knew that Cara was still holed up inside her suite within the penthouse, but there was an easy way to draw her out.

Maya drew two round devices about the width of her palm from her vest pockets and peeled the tape off the back. Bulletproof glass made up the entire front wall of the penthouse, floor to ceiling, with a wide set of glass French doors centered in the middle. Maya secured one of the larger circles to either side of the doors, then affixed smaller ones to each door. One tap to the back of each set them to beeping, and she backed up to a safe distance.

The hum started low in her bones. She gritted her teeth as it rose, probably easily ignored if you didn't happen to be a data courier with enhanced auditory processing. No doubt Cara could hear *something* from inside, but she wouldn't guess what it was in time.

Within a minute, the little devices had matched their resonance to the glass they were attached to. For one amazing moment it almost looked like the glass had become liquid, roiling and shivering with the vibrating sound.

Then they shattered. Shards of glass rained down, crashing against the rock mosaic pathways and bouncing over the protective walls. A waterfall of tinkling glass bounced against the windows as it spilled over the edge, plummeting hundreds of meters to the ground.

That would get everyone's attention.

It wouldn't hurt to throw a little more fuel on the fire though. Maya raised her voice. "Hey, Cara! I heard you wanted to see me!"

Heavy footsteps inside the building were followed by the arrival of half a dozen Ex-Sec soldiers in full tactical gear. Maya tensed, her hands drifting to her pistols on instinct, but Gray's voice whispered in her ear. "I've got you."

God, the sound of that man made her feel invincible.

The soldiers milled hesitantly, a few reaching for their sidearms before Cara's annoyed voice lashed through the room. "No lethal force, you idiots. That's Skovgaard's data courier. Do not do anything to risk her brain."

Cara arrived to stand in the missing doorway, her heeled boots crunching on the shattered glass. Even with the sun barely up, she was dressed perfectly, in her favorite jewel-toned silk to set off her pale skin and bright red hair. She gave Maya a withering look from head to toe, a superior smile curling her lips. "Kevlar does *not* flatter your figure, darling."

Maya let the bitterness roll off her. This wasn't personal. This wasn't revenge. "I can't let you stay here, Cara. If you come with me, I'll take you somewhere safe until this is over. I can get you help."

"*Let* me?" Cara scoffed. She spread both hands, indicating the half-dozen Ex-Sec soldiers who'd moved up on either side of her. "I have the power here. Why don't *you* come inside like a good little girl, and we can wait until Vargo has crushed your pathetic little revolt. If you apologize, I might even put in a good word for you."

Maya's fingers curled toward her palms, the only sign of anger she'd allow herself. Not personal. *Not personal.* "Last chance, Cara."

Cara raised her right hand, and flicked a finger forward in imperious command. "Hit her once. A knee, maybe. That might make her see reason."

The soldier directly to her left started to raise his pistol. Maya threw out a hand. "I wouldn't, if I were you," she warned him. "I have some very powerful friends."

"Who, Helen Anderson?" Cara actually scoffed. "She's firmly under Vargo's thumb by now. I'm your only friend with any real power, and you're going to *recognize* that."

Maya could have pointed out that a *friend* wouldn't consider shooting her in the knee, but she'd long given up hope on teaching Cara the definition of love. No one raised by the previous VP of Security had a chance of understanding it.

"I warned you," Maya said instead, and let her hands fall.

A crack sounded in the distance behind her, echoing louder through her comms. Almost simultaneously, the man's head exploded.

Blood splattered Cara's pale skin and perfect silk blouse. The Ex-Sec soldier on her other side reached for his sidearm and barely got it clear of the holster. A bullet slammed through his forehead, splattering more blood across Cara even as her first scream split the morning air.

Chaos erupted.

Maya dove to the ground as one of the remaining bodyguards laid down a spray of covering fire. Gray silenced him with another expert sniper shot, but not before Cara's screams cut off abruptly. Maya raised her head and glimpsed one of the men lifting her body in his arms, ignoring her flailing commands.

Executive Security had one overriding directive above everything else—protect the VIP. Maya swore as another rain of bullets started, chipping the mosaic walkway beneath her. She rolled behind a low stone wall. "I need to get in there."

"I've got you," came Gray's calm voice, followed by another crack. A body thumped just beyond the wall. Maya drew in a steadying breath, pulled her pistol, and braced herself.

One final crack. She was lunging to her feet before its echo faded, sprinting past the final falling body. Her boots slipped when she hit the broken glass, but she caught herself and slapped at her comms. "Charlie!"

Charlie's voice came immediately. "What do you need?"

"Lock down all exterior exits at Richter's penthouse," she told her, following the sounds of Cara's increasingly enraged demands deeper into the hauntingly familiar dining room. "I have Cara and one Ex-Sec in here."

"Got it." Another heartbeat. "Done."

She hit her comms again. "You still watching me?"

"Always," came Gray's swift response.

The warm confidence of his voice grounded her. "Good, I—"

A gunshot came from deeper into the penthouse, and Maya froze. Queasy certainty slammed into her, even before Cara stalked into the dining room, her guard's gun held in one shaky hand, her eyes wild.

Cara had snapped.

"No one tells me what to do anymore," Cara whispered. Straggly pieces of her red hair stuck to her face, caught in the spray of blood. She looked feverish, *desperate,* and Maya knew what she should do. Raise her sidearm and end this, before Cara could hurt anyone else. Cara certainly wouldn't hesitate to do the same. She'd made that clear enough.

But Cara had been an infant handed to a monster, who'd twisted and terrified her until the only way she knew how to love was with jealousy and punishment. She'd been raised to disassociate from her own senses, to lock down emotions to preserve her brain, to optimize its efficiency for other people's use.

She'd been abused. She'd been tortured.

Then again, so had Maya.

"Don't *look* at me like that," Cara hissed, lifting her stolen gun. With the way her arm was shaking, Maya wasn't sure she could aim it properly, but this close it didn't exactly matter. "Don't *pity* me."

"I can't help it," Maya replied softly. "I *was* you. I know you, Cara. Maybe I still love parts of you. The parts that could have been better."

Her chest heaved. "He has to have been right," Cara all but panted, her voice shaking with the conviction of it. "I helped him, Maya. I helped him make the world better."

Maya stepped closer. The gun was wavering. She reached out and folded her fingers over Cara's, gently pushing it down until it pointed at the floor. "You helped make the world better for some people," she agreed. "But just a few. For a lot of people, it got worse."

"Birgitte was lying to you," Cara whispered. "Birgitte—"

"It wasn't Birgitte." Maya tightened her fingers on Cara's hand. "I've lived in the world, Cara. They lied to us about it. They lied to us about almost everything."

Silence, except for Cara's panting breath. Then her hand jerked, trying to bring the gun back up. Not to point at Maya, but at herself.

"Decommission me," she begged. "Just decommission me. If they get their hands on me—"

One of the pockets on her tactical vest held a pressure injector. She whipped it free and jabbed it into the side of Cara's neck. Her eyes widened in shock, but a heartbeat later she slumped so fast, her dead weight carried Maya down to the floor.

She sat there for a shuddering breath, her arms around Cara's limp body, her heart an aching throb in her chest. "Did I do the right thing?" she whispered to the man who loved her enough to tell her the hard truth. "She could be so dangerous."

"You need to trust your judgment," Gray murmured back, and she could hear the sharp clicks of him disassembling his sniper rifle. "Trust yourself, Maya. I do."

She had learned to trust herself, too. Face-to-face with Anderson, she'd been ready to bargain with the fate of their world on the line. But Cara was different.

Cara *was* personal, and Maya had been a damn fool to pretend otherwise.

Maya wet her lips and tasted the tang of sweat and the salt of tears, though she couldn't remember crying. Maybe it had been that last terrible moment, the blank fear in Cara's eyes as she struggled to get the gun to her head.

Decommission me.

No one had ever taught Cara that she was more than a tool to be discarded when she broke. Maya knew someone who could help with that. On Syd's farm, Cara would be safely away from the temptation to meddle in politics and far beyond the TechCorps' grasp. If she learned how to embrace a life on the outside, maybe she could have a second chance.

"I think I know what to do with her," Maya told him, shifting the weight of Cara's boneless body in her arms. "But you're definitely going to need to come get us."

She heard the hum of an AirLift over her comms, and Gray's chuckle soothed her lingering nerves. "I'm on my way."

SECURITY MEMO

Franklin Center for Genetic Research

It's been over seventy-two hours since Dr. Long last made contact. I'm growing concerned.

Dr. Reed, December 2086

TWENTY-NINE

The CEO's elevator had exactly the sort of understated opulence Rafe was starting to expect from the executives on the Hill. Everything gilded within the bounds of good taste, enhanced with the very latest tech, and for some reason sporting a strange surplus of decorative molding.

That last bit was useful, as it turned out.

The moment Rafe had scanned his wrist cuff to send the elevator to the top floor, someone up there had undoubtedly been alerted that the elevator was on the move. Rafe had no intention of standing where his welcome party would be shooting.

His dedication to leg day certainly paid off. His muscles weren't even trembling as he braced himself above the door. The wall panels actually gave his toes a nice ledge to rest on, and the lack of glaring mirrors and shiny walls common in elevators on the lower floors made it less likely a stray reflection would give him away.

It was the most you could hope for as a single soldier mounting a reckless solo assault on a fortified position.

A soft chime announced his arrival on level 250. The *actual* penthouse, the very pinnacle of the TechCorps HQ.

Home of its reclusive CEO.

The doors slid open, and half a dozen laser sights pinged off the wall beneath him. Rafe froze in place, not even breathing as the barrel of a rifle inched through the doors. A soldier followed—Ex-Sec, thank *God*—jumpy as hell and swinging his weapon from left to right before turning to face his compatriots.

Rafe dropped behind him and hauled his new human shield tightly back into place.

Gunfire erupted immediately. The body in front of him jerked, as bullets slammed into his armor. Rafe borrowed Nina's favorite trick and raised the man's arm—and his rifle with it, firing on the others.

Three of the guards were down by the time Rafe cleared the elevator. He flung his human shield at the remaining two, bowling them over. He finished each with a single shot, then tossed his empty sidearm and swept up another rifle.

When no other footsteps came running, he ducked back against the wall and chanced his comms. "Charlie?"

"Where are you?"

"Two-fifty. Don't suppose you have eyes on Vargo?"

"I don't have eyes on *anything*." Charlie sounded frustrated. "I've tried every trick I can think of, but I think there are literally just . . . no cameras. At all."

Honestly, he wasn't surprised. Surveillance certainly seemed to diminish as your power increased on the Hill. Why would the man who ruled over it all deign to have his personal life invaded in the same way he invaded everyone else's?

Which didn't help Rafe. He scooped up a second rifle and looped it over his shoulder. "Any idea where I should go?"

"I've been looking at the schematics. Best guess, there's some kind of control room in the center of the penthouse. It's pulling a *ton* of power."

"And I get there . . . ?"

"From the elevator? Hard left, then hard left again. The first hallway on the right should be a straight shot to . . . whatever it is."

Rafe raised his gun and moved to the intersection, his senses on high alert. The expensive rug beneath his boots absorbed the sound of his footsteps, which meant they'd do the same for anyone else who was lurking out there.

But no one interrupted him as he traversed the hallway, and for the first time he truly understood in his *gut* what Dani had been talking about when she called Phoenix's penthouse mid-range. Everything about Phoenix's place had been trying too hard—the extravagance too opulent, the technological conveniences aggressive.

This place didn't need fancy lights, because even the hallway had windows staring out over the literal clouds. Paintings covered the tastefully painted walls in between them, casually displayed classics he'd seen in Tessa's books.

The thought that perhaps she'd painted some of them gave him a temporary thrill, but his amusement died swiftly when he reached the final corner and pulled a mirror from one pocket to peek around the edge.

There was a control center there, all right. A hallway wide enough to drive a tactical van down led straight to it. And filling that hallway . . .

Guardians. Five of them. A full fucking squad.

Charlie's voice crackled in his ear. "Did you find it?"

Rafe leaned back against the wall. "Yes," he replied softly. "And I'm gonna have to go silent. Send backup if you can."

"Rafe, wait—"

He disabled his comms. No one needed to hear what was about to go down—especially Dani. She had her own battle to fight, her own monster to slay.

And Rafe had a grenade.

He pulled the pin as he reconstructed what he'd seen. Five soldiers, all armed with semiautomatic rifles. Clustered closely enough that he might do some damage if he got lucky. And if none of them were fast enough to kick the grenade back. Or selfless enough to throw themselves on it. Or—

He shut off the litany of worst-case scenarios. Attacking now was reckless. He should wait for backup. Chances were good he was about to get his ass stomped. But *someone* had to get to Vargo before he did something truly unhinged.

He spared one heartbeat to hope Dani was okay, then tossed the grenade.

The explosion shuddered through the enclosed space. Rafe whipped around the corner and opened fire through the smoke.

He didn't let himself think about the odds. He didn't let himself think about how much Knox was going to yell at him for charging five Guardians all by himself.

He thought about Rainbow, huddled somewhere in a bunker with the traumatized kids from Montgomery Farms. He thought about the future that assholes like the ones at TechCon had planned for her—the life they'd given *him*.

Existing only as a tool, a killer.

An experiment. A test run for all the enhancements they longed to have for themselves, but not until they could be sure there were no awful side effects.

He thought about all the shiny Protectorate bonuses they'd never had to pay out because the surgery still killed so many—and how that was why they kept doing it. Starving the city, making people desperate. Making them hurt until they'd sign over their bodies as resources for this damn place to burn through in their quest for power and immortality.

He thought about Rosa, and Antonio, and even Tessa, who were still young enough to thrive.

But only if he got to the other end of this hallway and through those doors to stop the twitchy motherfucker inside from figuring out a way to burn down the world.

The Guardians scattered as he fired on them, but his reprieve was short-lived. There were four still on their feet, more than enough to swarm a lone soldier.

It barely even hurt. He took the blows, the bullets slamming into his body armor, and kept moving. Somehow, he'd make it to his destination. He had to.

But he was slowing down, dragged to a halt by pain and steely, clutching hands. He tried to fight them off, tried to get free—

He saw the fist coming toward him. He just couldn't stop it.

But someone else did.

A huge body in tactical gear slammed into one of his opponents, carrying him to the ground, at the same time a familiar voice shouted, "Rafe, *down*."

Falling to the floor was the easiest thing he'd ever done.

He hit the blood-splattered marble and rolled in time to see Nina flying through the air like a literal goddess. She grabbed the chandelier above them and twisted with breathtaking precision, slamming both steel-toed boots into the lead Guardian's chest so hard he flew back into the wall.

A knife whipped through the air, passing just under her feet, and slammed into the man's throat, pinning him to the wall as blood fountained around it. Nina dropped to the ground and whipped around, kicking out at the man Knox had tackled.

Rafe lifted his head just enough to see Phoenix whipping another knife as Ava launched herself after her sister. Giddy relief rattled his bruised chest. Even the near-certainty of a couple of broken ribs couldn't stop him from laughing out loud.

The fucking cavalry had arrived.

Rafe rolled until his back hit the wall. Pushing up to his knees hurt so much it drove a string of curses from his lips, but there was an increasingly desperate man behind that door, likely getting ready to do something crazy.

And Rafe was ready to end this dance.

Locking down the pain, he staggered to his feet. Ava and Phoenix spun past him, violent poetry in motion. The Guardians couldn't adapt fast enough to their discordant styles, but somehow the women knew how to mesh them together. It was glorious. It was absolute anarchy.

It was the perfect distraction.

Rafe waited until they'd cleared a path and *ran*. Pain jabbed in his sides with every footstep, but he didn't care. His hacked wristband hit the scanner, and he had a terrified moment to fear it wouldn't work.

The light turned green. The doors slid apart.

Rafe found himself staring at the business end of a semiautomatic from two meters away.

It exploded, but he was already moving. One swift dodge to the side, then back to jam a hand under Vargo's wrist, pointing the weapon uselessly at the ceiling. The COO might have the best healthcare known to man, but he hadn't risked *his* precious body with any experimental tech.

It was child's play to strip the gun from his grip and toss it aside, even beat to hell and back. It was even easier to catch Vargo by the throat and lift him until his feet scrabbled for purchase on the control center floor.

Rafe stole a second to scan the room, but Vargo was alone. A single plush leather chair sat at a polished mahogany desk in the middle. And on every wall . . .

No, those weren't monitors on the walls. The walls *were* monitors. Floor-to-ceiling displays on three sides, showcasing a dizzying array of camera angles. Not just from within the TechCorps but all across the Hill, and even the bordering suburbs.

From the top of the TechCorps HQ, you could see all of Atlanta.

"Mr. Morales," Vargo croaked. Rafe's fingers tightened reflexively, and the man spluttered, his face turning red. Rafe relaxed his grip immediately.

If he killed the man, it was going to be on purpose.

"That's better," Vargo wheezed. "We figured out who you were after the fact. Should have realized as soon as you grabbed the girl."

"My sister, you mean?" Rafe let his voice drop to a warning rumble. "I'd be careful what I said next, if I were you."

"We never harmed her." Vargo actually sounded like he meant it. "We offered her a *life*. Work that challenged her artistic skills. Access to a proper education. Clothing worthy of her beauty and every comfort imaginable. Was she so much better, scraping and scrabbling for survival?"

"Well, for one, she didn't have a bomb in her head."

"An essential precaution." Vargo started to lift his hand, but froze when Rafe hoisted him another inch. His toes barely scraped the carpet. "One that won't be necessary this time."

"This time?" Rafe demanded. "You think we're negotiating right now?"

"I think life is a negotiation, Mr. Morales." Vargo flicked his fingers, indicating the room around him. "You had a taste of what this life is like. Will you really condemn your siblings to the exhaustion of daily toil? You could have a penthouse of your own, enough credits so that your grandchildren's grandchildren never have to work a day. I can arrange that."

"What, so I just betray all my friends, and you set me and my family up as your pets in your gilded zoo?" Rafe scoffed. "You think that's tempting?"

Even with Rafe's fingers digging bruises into his throat, the man somehow managed to smile. "Who said anything about betraying your friends? The offer is extended to anyone you care about. I'll even sign a pardon for 66–615. Knox, I believe you call him? Full pardons for your entire squad, and honorable discharge with full pensions. I'm sure we can negotiate a retirement settlement worthy of your consideration."

Vargo's eyes gleamed. And Rafe didn't even doubt him. The man didn't have to lie. He could do all of that and more with just a wave of his hand. Erase their crimes, restore Knox's medals and honors. Throw enough money at them to let them live the high life for decades.

He'd probably spent more in his life on fancy cuff links than it would cost to buy them all off.

And for one terrible moment, Rafe could feel it. The stabbing pain in his ribs, the ache in his body, the *exhaustion* of always looking over his shoulder, of worrying about his implant going haywire, of knowing that the people he loved were in danger because he *was* the danger.

All of it, wiped away in a heartbeat. All he had to do was make a deal with the devil.

Again.

At seventeen, he'd pressed his thumb on the dotted line. He'd done it for his family, to keep them safe. He'd carved off pieces of his soul he could never get back. He'd hurt people, racking up debts it would take a lifetime to repay. In the end, his family had gotten hurt anyway.

That was how these deals worked. Even if you went in with the best of intentions, evil was pervasive. It had a way of seeping into your life, no matter what, contaminating those intentions until nothing good was left. And there would always be someone like Vargo waiting around the next corner, ready to strike. Not because men like him were strong, but because they were *everywhere.*

Rafe wasn't fucking around with the devil anymore.

Vargo must have seen it in his eyes. His smug triumph melted into rage, and searing pain cut through Rafe's side. Whatever defiant thing Vargo was about to say came out as a gurgle when Rafe tightened his hand, crushing the man's throat.

His body went limp. His head lolled, that grotesquely furious expression frozen on his face even in death. Rafe opened his fingers and let the body fall, then glanced down to the black hilt of the knife sticking out of his side.

That . . . was not good.

"Rafe!"

The room wobbled as he turned. Ava was kneeling over the final Guardian, delivering a killing blow. His gaze skipped across the people in the hallway—Knox, Ava, Phoenix, Nina.

Knox, Ava, Phoenix, Nina.

Knox, Ava, Phoenix—

"Rafe?" Knox sounded concerned as he stepped forward. "Are you—?"

"Dani," he blurted out. That was why his gaze kept jumping around. Someone was missing, someone who would have flown up the stairs to have his back—if she had been able. "Where's Dani?"

Nina came up beside Knox, her face gentle and worried. "Beth is keeping her stable. We're going to have to AirLift her out of here, but Maya and Gray are working it out."

Fuck. He had to get to her. He took two steps and listed into Knox, who caught him by the shoulder. "Hold on, man. You're in no shape to move, either."

No, he wasn't. Not with that fire burning through his entire side every time he took a step. He looked down again and gripped the hilt of the knife.

"Rafe, no—"

"What are you—?"

"I need to see Dani," he muttered, jerking it free. Blood gushed up over his fingers, and he blinked in confusion. Knox's curses filled the air, but Rafe tried to shake him off. "Dani—"

Nina's face was a frantic blur, and then the floor was coming up to meet him. Nina caught him in gentle arms, and her voice was the one that chased him into unconsciousness. "We'll take you to her, I promise."

Maybe they were going out in a blaze of glory after all.

TECHCORPS PROPRIETARY
INTERNAL COMMUNICATIONS

Silias: Can anyone get a drone to the roof? I think something's
   going down in the CEO penthouse.
Wardlow: The drones are still compromised.
Jessica: And putting cameras on 250 is against every fucking rule.
Charlie: I'm on it, y'all.
Wardlow: Do you need help?
Charlie: Whoever handles what's going on up there is going to
   have to face the Board and explain themselves. If any of y'all
   want to take over . . .
Silias: Nope.
Wardlow: Fuck no.
Jessica: You're the boss.
Charlie: I better be, by the time this is over.

Department of Executive Security

Security Server Logs Auto-Delete after 12 Hours

THIRTY

Hospital beds *sucked*.

For starters, they were built like little cages, and Dani hated feeling trapped. They also weren't comfortable in the slightest. Even with the sort of decent mattresses Mace had sourced, they were too narrow. Every time Dani moved, she ended up smashing an elbow or a foot against the bed rails.

Very inconvenient, considering that shit *hurt* now.

Oh, she was going to have one hell of a time getting used to that. Granted, it was unreliable, her newfound appreciation for pain—the same stimulus would hurt like hell sometimes, but not others. And there was no predicting when it would come and when it would go.

Not that they could possibly know, since Mace refused to agree to any real testing. It was tantamount to torture, he claimed—something she couldn't really dispute, despite her willingness as a subject. And besides, she had some healing to do first, since she had, according to Mace, "more internal injuries than a grapefruit dropped from orbit."

He did have a way with words sometimes, but Dani forgave him—especially since he'd given her complete details about Rafe's condition without making her ask.

"You look reassuringly grumpy," came a familiar voice from the doorway. Savitri stood there, dressed in clean scrubs and wearing her hair in a messy ponytail. She had a tablet in one hand, and was scanning the information on it as she stepped into the room. "You took a hell of a beating."

"Yes, I did. And also, you are not my doctor," Dani added. "How is Conall?"

"He lost the arm." Savitri sighed. "We surgically amputated above the elbow, but there are plenty of healthy nerves for us to interface with his new prosthesis. If he ever finishes designing it. Right now, he has five top contenders for his everyday arm."

Leave it to Conall to get super picky about it. Then again, Dani probably would be, too. "Is it time for more meds or something? Fair warning, I think I've officially run out of veins for you guys to stab."

Savitri pulled up the stool next to Dani's bed. "You're famous, you know. I mean not *you,* personally, but your case. You're patient 55-X. We all studied you."

"Was I at least interesting?"

"Fascinating. They had us trying to work out why you were impervious—no." She corrected herself. "Why you were *indifferent* to the pain that incapacitated the other test subjects."

"Incapacitated them how?" Dani had heard Marshall's side of the story, but she needed more. A clearer picture.

Savitri hesitated, then nodded. "There was a spate of suicides. They tried implementing safety protocols, but the isolation—the lack of distraction . . ."

She didn't have to finish for Dani to understand. Left alone in padded rooms with their suffering, the other subjects had gone mad.

"They'd use their own fingers as weapons to self-inflict wounds. They'd dislocate their shoulders and wiggle out of their straitjackets." Savitri's voice trembled. "They were in constant, horrible agony. Nothing could stop them from trying to end it. Eventually, they were euthanized."

Dani shuddered, horrified. Not by their collective desperation, but by the unbearable pain that could have been hers, as well. "Did you ever come up with any theories?"

"Just one. I kept it to myself." Savitri leaned closer. "I think your brain just . . . chooses not to process it."

"Chooses not to process it," Dani repeated slowly.

Savitri nodded. "The same way it knows to flip the images your eye perceives because they're upside down, or how you don't walk around staring at your own nose all day."

"As simple as that, huh?"

"There's nothing simple about it, Dani. The brain is a marvelous, miraculous thing, and there's still so much we don't know about it. Plus, the real question remains: why couldn't everyone just ignore the pain?" She shrugged. "You *were* in a coma after your surgery; maybe that's the key. Your brain might have grown accustomed to the pain and categorized it as background noise while you were still unconscious."

It was too much to take in all at once, and Dani sank back against the pillows.

"You haven't asked me about Rafe," Savitri observed.

Dani's cheeks heated.

"Oh, I see. You already grilled Mace." She smiled, wistful and a little sad. "You two are . . . good together. It's nice to see."

"Oh God, are you getting *mushy* on me?"

"Maybe a little." The beautiful woman grinned. "Just promise that when the two of you are feeling better, you'll come see me at the club. In the VIP section."

The very *naked* VIP section. "How can I?" Dani grumbled. "You've seen all my internal organs. That's just weird now."

A gentle but firm knock on the wall interrupted their laughter. It was Rafe's mom, standing just inside the doorway, looking happy, if tired.

"Right." Savitri lifted her tablet and started for the door. "Take care of yourself, Dani."

Dani rattled the bed rail a little. "Do I have a choice?"

"I certainly hope not," Celia Morales commented dryly as Savitri slipped past her. "For my son's sake, if nothing else."

Dani blushed, chastened. "I'm following orders, I promise."

"That's more than I can say for Rafe." This time the woman sounded aggrieved, but she still wore a gentle smile as she stopped next to Dani's bed. "He woke up a little while ago. We told him you're awake and doing well, but I wouldn't be surprised if he comes to see you as soon as Mace has turned his back on him." She heaved a long-suffering sigh. "My children can be *incredibly* stubborn."

"A trait that came from absolutely nowhere, I'm sure."

Celia laughed. "Their father was surprisingly even-tempered, if you can believe it. But the most charismatic man who ever drew breath. Rafael has always been too charming for his own good. But the part that always terrified me was his heart. He loves so readily, and so completely."

"Even recklessly," Dani agreed. "But if he didn't, he wouldn't be *him*. And that would be a shame."

"It would." Rafe's mother reached out to touch Dani's cheek, her fingertips gentle. "That's why I'm glad he found you. Someone who sees who he is, and wants to protect him and his heart."

"On all counts." This whole conversation was starting to make her nervous. She didn't know how to do heart-to-heart parent talks. "But is it enough?"

"Do you love him?"

Yeah, she was *definitely* nervous, but she managed a nod. "I do."

"Then it's everything." Celia raised her hands to the chain around her neck and unhooked it. The pendant she pulled from beneath her blouse was small, burnished antique silver set with a chunk of some precious stone that shimmered blue and green and bronze, with black cracks across it.

Moving gently, she lifted Dani's hand and let the necklace pool in her palm. "My mother-in-law gave this to me the night before we got married. She'd gotten it from *her* mother-in-law, who'd worn it all her life. I suppose that makes it a family heirloom." Celia closed Dani's fingers over the pendant. "Welcome to the family, Dani."

Dani shook her head and pushed their joined hands back toward Celia. "No, I can't. Give it to Tessa, or Rosa, or—"

"They'll get treasures of their own." Rafe's mother gave her fingers a fond pat. "This is tradition. You don't have to wear it, if you don't want. But from now on, it's yours. And you'll know you're part of this family, welcomed and loved."

Tears pricked Dani's eyes, not only at the generosity of the gesture, but by the sure and complete knowledge that Celia truly meant it. Rafe's family was hers now, too.

It was still new, this feeling of unconditional acceptance, but it didn't seem so foreign to Dani, not anymore. Not after Nina and Maya. After *Rafe*.

"Are you in here making Dani cry, Mom?" Rafe leaned against the wall by the open doorway, dressed in clean scrub pants, but with no shirt to hide his bandages and bruises.

"I don't cry," Dani sniffled.

"Uh-huh." Rafe stepped into the room with none of his usual grace.

Every step looked like it hurt, but he made it to her bedside without pitching over. "Are you gonna tattle on me to Mace?"

"No, I know you better than that." Celia leaned down to kiss Dani's forehead, then turned and went up on her toes to kiss her son's cheek. "There's barely room for both of you in that bed, but you might as well get in before you fall over on your face."

"Yes, Mama."

Celia's lips quirked in a smile as she started for the door. "That's what I like to hear."

When they were alone, the door shut gently behind her, Rafe gave Dani an unsteady smile. "Is there room on there for me?"

His question had nothing to do with the size of the bed, she knew. In answer, she lowered one side rail and beckoned. "We'll have to smoosh."

He climbed in and curled around her with a soft hiss of pain. "Remind me not to try to fight five of those Guardians on my own ever again."

"Don't worry." She carefully pulled his arm over her waist and relaxed into the solid warmth of his body. "I don't think there are even five of them left."

"Thank God." He huffed. "Or thank the Franklin Center. I suppose I have to be nice to Ava for a while. She saved my life."

"Pretty sure she'd rather have you pretend it never happened."

"I'd like to pretend most of it never happened, too." His fingers found her hair, teasing gently through the strands. "Leaving you behind to face Marshall was the hardest thing I've ever done in my life. I don't want to do it again."

She'd faced Marshall alone for so many reasons—because he was too fast, too vicious. Because he would have killed Rafe in a heartbeat, just to remind Dani what being alone felt like.

But mostly, she'd done it because it was her fight.

"I had to," she whispered, either in explanation or apology. Or maybe even comfort. "But just that once. I don't think there will ever be another fight where you have to leave me. Not like that."

"Do you want to talk about it?" he asked softly. "About . . . him?"

"No." That part of Dani's life was over, well and truly in the past, and now was no time to look back. "Your mom gave me this." She opened her hand to show him the pendant on its fine silver chain. "So I think you have to marry me now."

He touched the necklace, tracing the silver setting on the stone. "I was going to ask for one of her rings to give to you. I guess she figured it out on her own." A small, utterly sweet smile curved his lips. "Does this mean you want to go on wild adventures with me for the rest of your life?"

She didn't have to think about it, not exactly. But as questions went, it merited serious consideration. "You know I'll follow you anywhere. As long as this is still home."

"Always. This is where our family is." He huffed out another laugh. "Besides, Nina has her hooks firmly in my mother. They are making *plans* together. So many plans."

Good. Nina deserved to see her plans for the community come to fruition. And Rafe's mother deserved to feel the relief and warmth kindled by not being scared all the time.

Fear. It had ruled over Five Points, over Southside, over the entirety of Atlanta, for too damn long. It was time for them to feel a little hope.

She snuggled closer to Rafe, until she could feel his heart beating under her ear. "What will we do first? You and me."

His chest rumbled under her cheek as he started listing ideas. "I want to go to Baton Rouge again. That's the heart of trade in the Southeast, and you can find *anything* there. And maybe cross the Mississippi someday, too. Gray says he tried to go up to the Canadian Territories and they turned him back, but he never tried Old Mexico . . ."

She closed her eyes and let the timbre and cadence not only of his voice, but of his vision for their future lull her to sleep.

ENCRYPTED GHOSTNET
PRIVATE CHANNEL #VI67201

Violette: Did I hear this right? You're retiring???

D: Maybe. Taking a break, at least.

Violette: Shit, you're my best contractor! Break a girl's heart, why don't you?

Violette: Are you at least up for pulling occasional jobs? Keep the skills fresh?

D: We'll see. No promises, but we'll see.

THIRTY-ONE

In all her worries and concerns over the fallout from Vargo's attempted coup, there was one problem Dani hadn't seen coming.

No one wanted to be in charge of the TechCorps.

So there she was, stuck in HQ on one of the nosebleed executive floors she'd been infiltrating only a few short weeks ago, sitting at a conference table so shiny she could see her own disgruntled reflection in it.

It was *not* how she wanted to spend her afternoon.

Nina and Knox sat on the other side of the table, along with Jaden and Savitri. Dani shared her side with Rafe, Gray, and Maya. They all had to divide their attention between Helen Anderson at one end of the table, and John Smith at the other.

They were the only two Board members present. Dani didn't know where the others were, or if there were even any left, but it didn't matter. They were as incidental to the rebuilding process as they had been to Vargo during the coup. Mere background noise. Static.

All the power to be had at TechCorps HQ these days was right here in this fucking room.

"The science is all I care about," Anderson said, her tone firm. "As the chief science officer, I can oversee a shift in our priorities, away from militarization and back toward medical and technical innovation."

John pinched the bridge of his nose. "This was *your* internal revolution, Helen. You really should step into the CEO position."

"That was never my goal," she replied in a cool voice. "And, frankly, no one else in this company is qualified for the CSO position."

The Professor certainly was, being something of a genius science experiment himself. Then again, it seemed he still hadn't shared that fact with Anderson—or anyone else at the TechCorps.

"Besides," Anderson continued, "I assumed *you* wanted to be CEO. You've certainly maneuvered aggressively for power during your tenure here."

Jesus Christ, she'd shit a brick if she knew the truth.

"I want the position that best suits my skills and temperament," he shot back.

A dark suspicion gripped Dani. "You want the job Vargo promised you. You want CIO."

"That would be foolish," she said mildly. "In light of the revelation that Ms. Young is the sole architect of GhostNet, I find it painfully obvious that she's the most qualified person to serve as chief information officer."

Charlie pushed away from the wall and strode to the table, stopping next to Anderson. She stood with her arms crossed over her chest, her eyes narrowed as she studied John. "I've always been the most qualified," she said after a moment. "But I was pretty sure I'd have to fight you for it."

Nina arched an eyebrow. "Looks like it's CEO for you, after all, John."

"No. I want Richter's old spot."

It made a twisted sort of sense to Dani. It wasn't a label as rigid as those bestowed upon the chief executives. As VP of Security, he would have the opportunity to touch every single aspect of the TechCorps' day-to-day operations. All the intel, all the surveillance footage. The dossiers, the communications. Hell, he could know every time someone entered or left the building, if that was what he wanted.

You wily bastard.

"You're passing up the chance to run the company?" Gray asked skeptically.

"It's not an altogether altruistic choice," John explained. "It's the safest one. Right now, the organization is unstable. If another coup were to take place, the CEO would be the first to die."

Dani snorted. "Tell that to Kyle Donovan. He survived this last one somehow."

"Yeah, for some definitions of the word," Nina muttered. "As far as I know, he hasn't regained consciousness once in the last three weeks."

But John's eyes had already lit up. "No, Dani's right, and it's brilliant. We *do* have a CEO. If Donovan retains leadership . . ."

"Then it's not a coup at all." Savitri spoke up for the first time, from where she lounged in a black suit jacket cut to show off plenty of skin. "It's a corporate restructuring."

"A rich-people coup," Maya corrected. "I don't care who's got their name on the letterhead. I care who has the power, and whether or not you're going to honor the agreement you made with me."

Anderson tapped her fingers on the table. "John, as our new VP of Security, can you commit to limiting our sphere of influence to the Hill? No policing or security patrols, and no interfering with community attempts to organize their own governing bodies?"

He hesitated. "Instability isn't good for anyone. But I'm not interested in running the neighborhoods off the Hill. As long as they're handling their business—"

"We will be," Nina cut in. "The people don't need policing, John. They need support."

After a moment, he relented with a shrug. "As long as it works, and it gets done."

"And the utilities?" Maya pressed. "I want a five-year plan to transition them back to public control."

"Maya—"

"Do it," Charlie interrupted, pinning Anderson with a look. "Power, water, network access. You know damn well we have the technology to let communities maintain their own sustainable infrastructure. We don't have to give it away for free, but we *can* sell it to them for a reasonable price. If you're not willing to let go of control over their survival, then this is all a fucking lie, and I'm not signing on to it."

Anderson's polite mask didn't falter, but Dani could *feel* the woman's exasperation. "Are we going to regret giving you this seat at this table?"

"Absolutely," Charlie replied easily. "But not as much as you'd regret *not* giving it to me. You made a promise, Helen. Keep it."

"Fine." Anderson met Maya's gaze squarely. "A one-year grace period with continued access to our infrastructure, and a four-year transition period where we don't withdraw until the community has either transitioned to private management or arranged for a contract with us. Will that suffice?"

"We can work with it," Maya said.

Anderson looked around the table. "Anything else?"

Dani didn't plan to speak. After all, this wasn't her gig. She was around for security purposes, to gather intelligence and handle people who caused problems. She wasn't there to make plans or big decisions.

But then she glanced at Rafe. He stared back at her, and she thought about the look in his eyes when he'd talked about taking care of his family, how he would have done anything to ensure their survival.

He nodded and squeezed her hand, and she took a deep breath. "You're going to overhaul recruitment."

Anderson frowned. "For Protectorate service?"

"Yeah. *And* for TechCorps experiments."

John eyed her shrewdly. "That'll slow down Helen's beloved scientific advancement. Significantly."

The woman's jaw *had* tightened, but Dani just shook her head. "It's not only the right thing to do, it'll be necessary. Do you even realize how many people sign up solely because they need the bonuses? You must, or those incentives wouldn't exist. And if you really, *truly* plan to make life better for people in Atlanta, you can't bank on that desperation anymore. So you'll have to figure out something else."

"We can discuss the situation." Anderson turned to look at Knox. "I was actually hoping you might be interested in offering your expertise."

"On recruitment?" Knox asked warily.

"On the Protectorate in general," Anderson corrected. "You are, without a doubt, a sterling example of what the program *could* have been. Tobias Richter failed to appreciate that. You could reform the program. I'm sure John will agree to give you a great deal of latitude in recruitment and—"

Gray burst out laughing.

But Nina wasn't amused. She rose and leaned over the table, her white-knuckled fists braced on its mirror-shiny surface. "*No.* The Protectorate tried to kill him already, and I'm not giving them another chance. You can forget it."

Knox looked like someone had offered him the weight of the universe to carry. Stark lines bracketed his eyes as he reached out a hand to touch Nina's arm. "If John wants my advice on how to restructure, he can ask for it," Knox said carefully.

John held up a hand. "Stand down, Captain. Not that I don't appreciate your willingness to help, but Nina's right. You've done enough."

Huh. Maybe the man wasn't completely heartless, after all.

Anderson waited until Nina had resumed her seat before scanning the table. "Do the rest of you feel the same way? I must admit, I'm a little surprised. Maya, you could have considerable influence as the heir to Birgitte's successful rebellion. And Dani . . ."

Rafe tensed, and she squeezed his hand again. "And Dani *what?*" she asked softly.

Anderson's gaze lingered on her. "Your rather eclectic skill set could be of particular use. You would be paid *very* generously."

Her *skill set* had brought her to the Hill, not once, but twice. She'd been surrounded by apathy, greed, and lies, all wrapped up in glamorous clothes and sparkling lights.

But that wasn't who she was. It never had been, but it especially wasn't now. She had a family, one she'd chosen rather than being born into it. She had a community, a home. A place to belong.

She had *love.* And Anderson would never, ever understand that.

"I can read really fast," Dani told her. "Like, inhumanly fast. I can juggle, too. Can't cook worth a damn, but I can sing. And I'm a really good listener. *That's* my skill set, Anderson. Nothing the TechCorps would be remotely interested in."

After a brief hesitation, Anderson nodded. "Fair enough. If that's all you need from me . . ." She nodded to Jaden. "We'd like to discuss what the TechCorps can do to address our culpability in your recent tragedy."

Jaden glared at her with the full force of his still-simmering rage. "You mean how you killed my people? You'd like to *address* that?"

"Yes," Anderson said, unperturbed. "And Savitri, I'd like to go over some consulting opportunities with you, if you're open to it. The rest of you can enjoy your day."

Dismissed. Normally, the ease with which Anderson had absently discharged them might have offended Dani. Today, she was too eager to get the fuck out of there to let it bother her.

John caught up with them at the door. "You don't want to work on the Hill," he acknowledged, "but how about a freelance job every now and then?"

"Do your own dirty work," Dani growled.

But Nina only shrugged. "Maybe. It depends."

"On?"

"You know. The details of the job, how busy we are, my mood, whether you guys are holding up your ends of these bargains." She smiled and leaned closer into Knox's side. "Lots of things."

"Right." The corner of his mouth ticked up, and he tossed Knox a lazy salute. "See you around."

It was so bizarre, seeing the offices bustling with people instead of deserted in the middle of a lockdown. Hell, if Dani hadn't *been* there, in the thick of the siege, she might not have believed the HQ building had suffered an invasion. She certainly wouldn't have noticed.

They'd cleaned up in record time. All the bloodstains were gone, and the broken windows had been replaced. Even the bullet holes had been patched, the walls repainted.

Just like it had never happened.

The six of them piled into the elevator, but an arm plunged through the door before it could close. Charlie followed, standing just inside the doors to block them from closing again. "I wanted to ask, how's Conall?"

"He's recovering," Knox said seriously. "Mace is keeping an eye on him just to be safe, but he seems optimistic. He's still on some pretty heavy drugs, though."

"And designing increasingly elaborate arms he expects you to help program," Maya added.

"And pay for." Rafe raised an eyebrow. "Which should be pretty easy on a chief officer's salary."

"I'll buy him whatever he wants. But that's not why I asked." Charlie waved a hand, as if a ridiculous amount of money meant nothing to her. "The GhostNet still matters. Maybe not as much as it did, but we're always going to need alternatives to the official network. I won't have time to run it, though. I was kind of hoping Conall might be interested."

Dani snorted. Offering Conall control of GhostNet would be like waving an antique bottle of bourbon in front of one of the old-timers at Clem's bar. They'd snatch it up so fast you'd be lucky to keep all your fingers.

"He's interested," Dani told her. "You don't even have to ask."

Charlie grinned. "Tell him to call me when he's feeling better. He can help me keep these assholes honest. Or at least slightly nervous."

"I'll tell him," Knox promised.

Maya nodded agreement. "Thanks, Charlie."

The other woman shrugged and stepped back. "I got the easy job. You're the ones who have to go reinvent democracy. Have fun with that."

The shiny reflective doors slid shut, and the elevator beeped as it started its smooth descent. Rafe frowned at their reflection. "Is that what we're doing? Reinventing democracy?"

"Because it went so well last time," Gray mumbled. *"Fuuuuuuck."*

"We're not talking about fixing the whole damn country." Knox leaned back against the wall, his face thoughtful. "The people around Atlanta have been trying to form communities this whole time. We know that. We were the ones sent out to stop them."

"Nina's basically been the mayor of Five Points for years," Maya added. "Nothing will really change, except now the TechCorps won't come in and shoot anyone who tries to set up a town council. We can just make stuff a little more . . . official."

Nina lifted her head from where she'd leaned it back against the elevator wall. "I don't want to be mayor. I just want to open my community center."

Knox wrapped a hand around hers. "Then that's what we'll do. Someone else can be in charge. I'm done compromising." He lifted their joined hands and kissed the back of Nina's fingers. "I want to build something. Your library is a good dream."

Rafe's smile seemed to light up the whole damn elevator. "I'm down for building things. As long as I don't have to go back to the Hill." His hand found the small of Dani's back, a gentle caress before he slid his fingers around her hip and tugged her closer to his side. "Someone very smart once told me this place is like a Venus flytrap. It'll eat you alive if you let it. And I, for one, don't plan on giving it a chance."

SECURITY MEMO

Franklin Center for Genetic Research

Attached is the latest video from the TechCorps coup. I believe we can all agree this is a worst-case scenario. Four of our most dangerous rogue subjects, all presumably now enjoying Tech-Corps connections at the highest levels.

If we don't act judiciously, this could mean our destruction.

Dr. Reed, December 2086

THIRTY-TWO

ONE MONTH LATER

A sex worker, a punk rocker, a data courier, and a creaky-jointed pre-Flare vet walk into a bar . . .

Rafe bit his lip to hide a smile as he leaned back against the wall next to Gray and watched the first official meeting of the Five Points Neighborhood Council come to order.

It wasn't a particularly glamorous setting for the area's first attempt at democracy in almost fifty years. Several mismatched tables in Clem's bar had been pushed together at the back of the room to give the newly elected council members a place to address the concerned citizens who'd come to lodge complaints and requests. Interested parties were scattered across the room in beat-up chairs or leaning on pool tables, and most of them had mugs of beer or hard cider in spite of the early afternoon hour.

Rafe supposed that was inevitable after they'd elected the bar's owner as their first mayor.

The council itself was an eclectic bunch. Clem sat at the center, her auburn and steel-gray hair pulled up in its usual messy knot. Maya sat to her right, looking extremely comfortable for someone who'd never intended to run for leadership and had been completely shell-shocked when people started shouting her name during the riotous election last month.

Next to Maya was Sam, the old-timer who'd lived in Southside since before the Flares and knew every person and every thing that was happening in the neighborhood. His bones may ache in the winter, but there was nothing wrong with his sharp eyes or sharper brain.

Cheryl had claimed the seat directly to Clem's left. Rafe knew less about her, aside from the fact that she was the one who'd organized Southside's sex workers and set up safe check-ins and, recently, medical assistance at the new clinic. Plenty of people underestimated her because of her job, but Rafe certainly didn't. What Cheryl didn't know about the shit going down around Five Points wasn't worth knowing.

The final addition to the council was Rowan, the startlingly talented violinist who was starting to make a name for themself on the Hill thanks to a few clever music videos Conall had recently leaked onto the vid network. They were dressed in their usual punk rock glam, with electric blue hair and dramatic eyeliner, which probably should have looked out of place at a serious governmental meeting but somehow . . . didn't.

Five Points was dabbling in democracy, but they were going to do it *their* way.

Next to Rafe, Gray leaned against the wall in his best *severe bodyguard pose,* the entire stance ruined by the softness in his eyes and the impossibly proud smile that kept curving his usually stern mouth. He gazed at Maya like she was the most amazing thing he'd ever seen, and a year ago Rafe would have bet most of his life's savings on the fact that no person could crack the blank nothingness with which Gray met the world.

Rafe had rarely been so happy to be so wrong.

He nudged Gray as the meeting got underway, and dropped his voice to a low murmur. "She's doing amazing."

Gray smiled. "Because she *is* amazing."

"I'm headed out," he whispered, and Gray acknowledged him with an absent nod, his entire focus already returned to Maya as she answered someone's question about their plans for starting a formal school for the children.

It was fucking adorable.

Outside the bar, the bright afternoon sun couldn't heat up the crisp January air. Sam had sworn his weather bones were predicting snow by the end of the week. It didn't happen often in Atlanta, but Rafe found himself hoping they got a solid snowstorm. Enough to teach Rainbow about snowball fights and snow angels, the way *his* father had during an improbable February blizzard during Rafe's youth.

Enough to chase Dani through the frosty outdoors and then warm up with a long afternoon in bed.

That thought kept him warm as he traversed the blocks to the new community center.

When the rumblings about an election had started, Rafe had half-expected Nina to end up as the new mayor of Five Points, if not all of Southside. She'd been serving as community leader in an unofficial capacity for so long, it seemed inevitable. But Nina had dodged any attempts to co-opt her into the new civilian government, insistent that she already had a job.

The results stood before Rafe. The newly launched community center.

Cheerful paintings covered the front windows, some sort of story about a cartoonish blue dragon who made friends with a snowman. His mother and Tessa's work showed clearly in the dragon's delicate scales and elegant wings, but there was something impossibly wholesome about the childishly sketched snowman whose number of arms seemed to vary from window to window. They were pure joy and innocence, such a far cry from the night after the bombing of Montgomery Farms that the memory of that dark night seemed softened.

Warmth washed over him as he opened the glass doors, and the *sound* slammed into him—a bright chorus of giggles as pure as the paintings outside. Rafe reached the main atrium to find most of the youngest children in Five Points gathered around on pillows, staring up in rapt fascination at Rafe's mother.

Her warm voice flowed over him, the words unnecessary when he knew the cadence of her storytelling in his heart. Especially when she was reading them the book she'd created for Rafe and Tessa when she'd been tiny, an adventure where two children roamed across the wilderness making improbable friends with woodland creatures before discovering a secret village deep in the heart of the woods.

She turned the page, and the children gasped as the illustrated version of Tessa came face-to-face with a towering brown bear. Rafe hid a smile and slid around them, his heart lifting as he glanced through a door and caught sight of Luna laughing as she bent to position a book on the scanner for Tai, who thanked her with a kiss. Through the next doorway he saw people browsing the shelves for a book to borrow.

Nina finally had her library.

Moving their treasure-trove of supplies from the warehouse to the new community center had been surprisingly easy. Plenty of the residents of Five Points had shown up to help, turning moving day into a veritable street party. Food carts had popped up, and opportunistic vendors with warm drinks. Rowan had arrived with their violin to provide music while kids ran wild and Nina oversaw it all with a smile that never faded.

Rafe didn't blame her. He smiled, too, as he climbed to the second floor. Beth's voice drifted from one of the open doors, where she'd gathered a half-dozen curious teenagers for an afternoon of science experiments. Across the hallway, Tessa's new art studio had twice as many art students—some *far* from children—busily working on self-portraits as she wandered the room, giving pointers.

His heart impossibly lighter, Rafe continued to the third floor.

The hum from the previous biofuel generators was gone now that Conall and Antonio had finished converting the entire building to solar power. Every door on the third floor led into a brightly lit wonderland of hydroponic gardening. He heard his youngest sister singing through one door, her bright voice joyful as she tended to the plants, but he didn't interrupt her.

He didn't feel the need to snatch at any chance to see her, because family wasn't just about stolen minutes anymore. Family was game night with Dani teasing his sisters and Antonio swearing they were cheating. It was breakfasts with his mother making Dani's favorites and dinners with all of them around the huge table they'd set up in the warehouse. It was squabbling and laughing and *living,* and Nina and Knox overseeing the whole thing like the parents of an increasingly riotous brood.

Rafe ascended to the fourth floor.

Hammering came from the far side of the building, most likely Knox working on finishing more of the rooms. He and Nina had a dozen more ideas for what to do with each one, everything from a computer lab to conference rooms to workout rooms and places for lessons of every kind imaginable. Rafe admired their creativity—and their energy—but the more they all settled into a routine, the more antsy he got.

Which was why he headed to the roof, a small tablet gripped in one hand.

The paint can was propping open the roof door again. Rafe slipped out into the brilliant sunlight, the cloudless sky a gorgeous blue expanse above him.

Dani stood at the edge of the roof, bundled up in a big puffy coat and a hat Conall had knitted as part of his physical therapy. When she turned to face him, her nose was red from the cold, but she smiled anyway. "Hi."

"Hey. How's the neighborhood looking?"

"Busy." She gestured down toward a small brown clearing—a vacant lot between two buildings. People were hard at work, turning and fertilizing the soil in preparation for the coming spring. "I stopped when I came by earlier and asked them what they're going to plant. Flowers, Rafe." She met his gaze. "When's the last time anyone in the neighborhood planted something we couldn't eat?"

Rafe wrapped an arm around her and stared down at the lot. Stakes had been laid out, marking off a path. A few others looked like they might be placeholders for benches, and even trees. Conall was there, testing out his new prosthesis by lifting small boulders under the direction of a tiny drill sergeant in a brightly colored coat and a knitted cap just like Dani's. Conall pretended to stagger under the weight of his load before hoisting it high and tossing it aside, and Rainbow's giggles drifted up to them on the wind as she moved on to the next rock.

They were clearing a park. Not the manufactured luxury the people on the Hill had hoarded on their skyscrapers, but dirt and fresh air and flowers and all the things that came with them—bumblebees and butterflies, maybe. Afternoons sitting on a bench and breathing in the scent.

Rest and hope.

His heart full, Rafe kissed the top of Dani's hair. Then he handed her the tablet. "I have a present for you. Not for now, but when spring rolls around . . ."

She activated the screen and peered down at it. "Another Rogue Library of Congress bunker?" she asked softly. "In . . . Where's Dallas, anyway?"

"What used to be Texas. It's west of the Mississippi, down by Old

Mexico." He grinned at her. "It would make for one hell of an adventure. Or a honeymoon."

She laughed, the sound carrying through the cold, clear air like a bell. "A honeymoon, huh? Which one of us is going to learn safecracking?"

"I'm sure Nina will teach you as a wedding gift." Her earlobe peeked out beneath the hat, pink with cold, and he pressed a kiss to it as he murmured against her ear. "You do have *great* reflexes."

She caught him by the jacket lapel before he could move away and kissed him properly. "Thank you. This is the best present anyone's ever given me."

"It is pretty amazing, isn't it?" Her adorably pink nose was cold against his cheek, but he didn't care. He just pulled her closer, fluffy jacket and all. "You know Nina and Knox are just gonna keep expanding this place, though. I can think of a worse life than finding treasures and books to fill all the rooms they make."

"The RLOC bunker isn't the present." She stowed the tablet inside her coat. "It's you."

Her eyes sparkled as she stared up at him, soft and adoring, everything he'd craved from the first moment he'd met her. But he'd been a fool, too. Because Dani wasn't just excitement and laughter and gleeful kisses. She was the darkness inside her, too—a blade honed to a killing edge. A monster who would savage anyone who threatened the people she loved.

And she'd been savaging people from the very beginning. That bastard Boyd, in a run-down town in the wilderness right after they met. He'd threatened Rafe, and Dani had eliminated him. No questions, no hesitation. And after she'd found out about Rafe's betrayal, she'd still shown up to protect him from the TechCorps.

She'd broken into his bedroom and ordered him to flee Atlanta to save himself, and when he hadn't done that, she'd helped Nina fake his death.

The darkness inside Dani had been saying *you're mine* from the beginning, and Rafe had been oblivious.

Never again. He loved her bright and shiny parts and her sharp and deadly edges. He loved being hers, and he *adored* knowing she was his.

He'd bet on a future with her, and he'd won big.

"Come on," he whispered against her cheek. "Let's go find some trouble."

She laughed, just like he'd hoped. Warm and bright. Joyful. His. "I thought you'd never ask."

SECURITY MEMO

Franklin Center for Genetic Research

Initiate Operation Gemini.

Dr. Reed, January 2087

HS-Gen17-A

HS-Gen17-A was the perfect soldier.

Thinking that wasn't hubris or ego. It was simple truth, an assessment of her own skills and talents, combined with the work she'd put in to achieve that goal. Imperfection simply was not an option. Not when the lives of her sisters depended on her overcoming the flaws inherent in her genetic code.

HS-Gen16-A had broken under pressure and caused the death of her cluster. 17-A would not make the same mistakes. And that was how she thought of herself, even in the safety of her own head—17-A.

That had been her predecessor's initial mistake. *Nina* had thought of herself as a person, first. That was the danger of choosing a name. Oh, most of the initiates at the Franklin Center did it. Their full designations could be a mouthful, and it was one of the few small rebellions that was not just allowed but gently encouraged. Choosing names often bound a cluster together, letting them create their own identity.

She already had an identity. 17-A. The warrior of the seventeenth iteration of the HS genetic strain. The leader, on whose shoulders the full responsibility for her cluster rested.

17-B had argued once that it seemed irrational to make the A-designation the leader when the B-designations were the strategic thinkers and tacticians. 17-C was the one who'd pointed out the deeper truth: their hierarchy was a stratification of priorities and values, revealing how the Franklin Center truly felt about strength and power. A, B, C. First, second, third. Leader, second-in-command, follower.

Physical prowess, intellectual skill, and emotional fluency.

17-A acknowledged the truth of that. Brawn had often been valued by militaristic societies over brains, far preferred to the softer power of emotion. But she had seen a different truth, as well.

She was the leader because she was the strongest. The one most able to take the hits, to use her body as a shield for her team. To do what had to be done to keep her sisters safe.

Today was the perfect example. 17-C was still emotionally compromised by the . . . *situation* with their sister. She wouldn't have been able to maintain a perfect warrior façade in the face of three of the most senior trainers at the Franklin Center.

17-A could. Because she was the perfect soldier.

"HS-Gen17-A," started Baudin, breaking the tense silence. Dr. Baudin was a solid woman in her late sixties, her hair wrapped in a sleek bun. Her skin was an indeterminate light brown, exactly like her hair and eyes. *Average* was the word that had always come to mind—average height, average build, average intellect.

But she was the most senior scientist and trainer overseeing A-designation trainees, so 17-A sat straighter in her chair. "Yes, ma'am."

"We've broken certain protocols with you over the years," the woman said, tapping on the computer embedded in the table in front of her. The massive debriefing screen on the wall at her back flickered to life, showing a stilled video of a city in the midst of battle. Atlanta, most likely, given the comparatively clean streets and relative level of technology.

Baudin didn't look away from 17-A as she continued. "We don't usually brief trainees on previous generations of their genetic legacy, to preserve scientific integrity. But in your case, an exception seemed prudent. Given the unprecedented potential of your particular strain, we thought arming you with history might prevent the rather spectacular flaws of previous iterations."

She paused, and let the silence say the words that hung heavy in the rooms.

And yet, you are still flawed. So very, very flawed.

17-A stared ahead and refused to feel the sting of that quiet condemnation. Her sister's life depended on her ability to traverse this political minefield. "I'm sorry for our failures, ma'am."

"I'm aware. Fortunately for you, the fact that you have spent most of your life studying the HS-Gen16 files gives us a unique solution to a recent problem."

Baudin waved her hand over the tablet, and the video began to play on the briefing monitor. Chaos at first, a battle where the drones had clearly turned on the people who'd expected to use them. Their attack pattern seemed sporadic at first, but a moment later 17-A realized why—someone had hacked them to only target people wearing the TechCorps' distinctive camouflage.

Clever. Exactly the sort of thing 17-B might have suggested—whenever people outsourced their thinking to an algorithm, there was a chance to exploit it against them.

Then a familiar face swept into frame, and 17-A's stomach dropped. Nina.

Baudin paused the video, and 17-A stared at the face that would be hers if she managed to survive into her thirties. And it *was* Nina, she had no doubt. Anyone who'd grown up at the Franklin Center swiftly learned that the outside was the least consequential way to recognize a person. No one who'd trained with her would ever mistake 17-C or 17-B for her. They moved differently, sat differently, smiled differently, *breathed* differently.

The woman on the screen stood like Nina. More, she stood like an A-designation. 17-A could feel that stance in her bones—the weight of it, the balance. There was a confidence and an ease in knowing how every muscle in your body worked, and what you could do when they worked together in ways those born normally couldn't begin to comprehend.

"You recognize her?" Baudin asked unnecessarily. But that was the Franklin Center—there was always another test.

"Yes, ma'am. It appears to be HS-Gen16-A."

"Mmm."

The video continued for long enough for a second HS-Gen16 to move into frame. Even if she hadn't known that their C-designation had died, she would have recognized this woman in a heartbeat. HS-Gen16-B. Ava. Cold and brilliant and so deeply fractured. There was a feverish light to her gaze, even in its frozen hatred. Something wild, barely contained.

Just like 17-B.

Careful. Careful . . .

"Is this video recent?" she asked, watching as the women were joined by two more Franklin Center graduates—faces 17-A only knew from her growing mental dossier of Ava's revenge spree. Those had *not* been included in her briefing packets on HS-Gen16, but Baudin hadn't been wrong. The HS strain did have incredible potential.

17-B could be an incredibly stealthy hacker.

"This is from one month ago," Baudin told her. "As you know, we always suspected HS-Gen16-A had gone to ground in TechCorps territory. At the time, given our sometimes fraught relationship with them, it didn't seem prudent to trespass. But things have changed in Atlanta. And now that we're certain HS-Gen16-B has joined her . . ."

Baudin slid a thin tablet across the desk.

"An offer," Baudin told her. "A compromise. Given your particular expertise, your cluster may be the only people with the skills to extricate the Gen16 defectors without triggering a political incident."

17-A's heart jumped. A mission that took all three of them out of the Franklin Center could be the chance she needed. Generation 17 could vanish into the wilderness, and Generation 16 could burn this cursed place to the ground, if they wanted.

"I can draw up mission specs," she said, controlling her excitement. "The three of us—"

"Two," Baudin interrupted. "HS-Gen17-C will, of course, be a vital asset to your mission. But given the recent . . ."

"Incident," said the man next to her, biting out each syllable from between grinding teeth. Dr. Phillips was *not* having a good week. Good. 17-A wished him misery of it.

"Yes, the incident." Baudin cleared her throat. "It seems for the best that HS-Gen17-B remain with us. However, once you've brought us proof that Generation 16 has been terminated, the Franklin Center has agreed to grant the three of you honorable discharges, with full pensions paid in a lump sum. The three of you will be free to pursue your own paths in life."

In other words, the Franklin Center was holding her sister hostage. And the only way to get them all out alive was to kill Nina and Ava.

17-A picked up the tablet. She'd spent her entire life learning from

Nina's detailed catalogue of missteps. She knew the older woman inside and out. And she would *not* repeat her mistakes.

HS-Gen17-A was the perfect soldier. And unlike Nina, she was going to complete her mission, and bring both of her sisters to safety.

ACKNOWLEDGMENTS

Hello from the past. As we're writing this in October of 2021, the world is in a moderately terrifying place. We're all wrung out from a pandemic whose destructiveness has been magnified by politics and selfishness. Tech headlines could be writing our plots for us. (I mean, Facebook nerfed their servers and locked themselves out of their offices while we were writing the end of this book. Conall thinks we made him work *way* too hard for this.)

Writing a tech and medical dystopia while living through one can be rough on the heart and the head. But throughout this book, we held on to the heart and spine of the story: that even when it looks bleak, you can reach out, grab hold of your people, and find a way to fight for a tomorrow that is a little bit better than your today.

A lot of people have held on and dragged us forward as we wrote this book. Our families and friends first and especially are always here to rage, vent, celebrate, and then delete all the group texts so no one can subpoena them.

Thank you to our discord, who are the most delightful and welcoming group an author can ever have hoped to cultivate. Even if you do occasionally start cults when we leave you unsupervised.

Thank you to our agent, Sarah Younger, who is our cheerleader, our coconspirator, our mama shark, and the reason we didn't quit writing to go live in the mountains with the goats.

Claire Eddy is the editor of our dreams, and always makes us better. She also didn't blink when we turned this book in with [cool action scene goes here!] in several spots, which is next-level understanding and incredibly gracious. Her editorial assistant, Sanaa Ali-Virani, remains the best at providing gentle executive function for two chaotic ADHD authors!

Our marketing and publicity team at Tor remains too precious for this world. Thank you to publicity royalty Caroline Perny and Laura Etzkorn, as well as marketing badasses Renata Sweeney and Rachel Taylor. You are the cinnamon rolls of our hearts.

As always, our gracious thanks to NaNá Stoelzle. Bree's chaotic and creative punctuation is a menace. She's sorry.

Lillie Applegarth remains the reigning queen of our series bible and timeline, as well as our cheerleader and a badass discord mod.

Thank you also to Quinn, resident server genius and moderator, who fixes the discord whenever Bree breaks it.

Sharon Muha has watched over the final proofreading pass on all of our books for a decade. Any mistakes that slip by them are our own. (And they worked for it!)

Finally, thank you to the readers, booksellers, and librarians who read, buy, recommend, hand sell, and share our books. We wouldn't exist without you. You're our community, our Southside, our neighborhood. Every time we've needed you, you've shown up with metaphorical shotguns in hand.

Let's make tomorrow a little bit better than today.

ABOUT THE AUTHORS

KIT ROCHA is the pseudonym for the *New York Times* and *USA Today* bestselling author duo Donna Herren (@totallydonna) and Bree Bridges (@mostlybree). They are best known for their gritty and sexy dystopian Beyond series, and were the first indie authors to receive a Romantic Times Reviewers' Choice Award. They currently live three miles apart in Alabama and spend their non-writing time caring for a menagerie of animals and crafting handmade jewelry, all of which is chronicled on their various social media accounts.

kitrocha.com
@KitRocha